# DAYS WITHOUT NUMBER

# DAYS WITHOUT NUMBER

## Robert Goddard

# BANTAM PRESS

LONDON · NEW YORK · TORONTO · SYDNEY · AUCKLAND

TRANSWORLD PUBLISHERS
61–63 Uxbridge Road, London W5 5SA,
a division of The Random House Group Ltd

RANDOM HOUSE AUSTRALIA (PTY) LTD
20 Alfred Street, Milsons Point, Sydney,
New South Wales 2061, Australia

RANDOM HOUSE NEW ZEALAND LTD
18 Poland Road, Glenfield, Auckland 10, New Zealand

RANDOM HOUSE SOUTH AFRICA (PTY) LTD
Endulini, 5a Jubilee Road, Parktown 2193, South Africa

Published 2003 by Bantam Press
a division of Transworld Publishers

A catalogue record for this book is available from the British Library.
ISBNs 0593 047591 (cased)
0593 047648 (tpb)

Typset in 11½/14pt Times by
Kestrel Data, Exeter, Devon

Printed in Great Britain by
Clays Ltd, St Ives, Suffolk

3 5 7 9 10 8 6 4

In memory of my father,
William James Goddard,
1903–1984

So teach us to number our days,
that we may apply our hearts unto wisdom.

Psalms 90:12

# PART ONE

# CHAPTER ONE

He did not regret agreeing to go. He had long learned to accept the consequences of every decision he took with a degree of equanimity. Regret, then, was hardly the word for it. But consequences hatch slowly and not always sweetly. The long drive west had reminded him of the point more forcefully with every mile. His past was a hostile country, his present a tranquil plain. By going home he was not only abandoning a refuge, but proclaiming that he no longer needed one – which, naturally, he would have said was self-evidently true. But saying and believing are very different things, as different as noise and silence. And what he heard most through the tinted glass and impact-proof steel of his sleek grey company car . . . was silence.

Heading west to reach home was also a contradiction in historical terms. However well he played the part of a coolly efficient middle-management Englishman, Nicholas Paleologus was, if his grandfather's genealogical researches were to be believed, something altogether more exotic: a descendant of the last Emperor of Byzantium. He had always displayed, and almost always felt, a keen disdain for his semi-legendary eastern roots. The attention they had attracted had been at best unwelcome, at worst . . . But he did not care to dwell on the worst he could remember. Since isolating himself from his family, he had been prepared to admit to Greek ancestry, but nothing more, denying any imperial connection to those pitiful few who recognized the name.

It scarcely seemed likely, after all, that the last of the Paleologi should have found their way to England. Yet so their patchy history insisted. The Paleologus dynasty had ruled Byzantium for the last and least glorious two hundred years of its existence, until Emperor Constantine XI of that ilk had fallen defending the walls of Constantinople in vain against the besieging Turks in 1453. The disaster had scattered those of the family it had not destroyed, to mix with humbler bearers of the name around the Mediterranean, until Constantine's great-great-great-great nephew, Theodore, fleeing an attempted murder charge in Italy, had set fugitive foot on English soil – and never left it. He had lived out his final years as a guest of the Lower family at their mansion, Clifton, on the Cornish bank of the Tamar, opposite Plymouth, in the parish of Landulph, where he had died in 1636.

It was Theodore Paleologus's memorial plaque in Landulph Church that had inspired Nick's grandfather, Godfrey Paleologus, to settle in the area and devote the numerous leisure hours a sizeable inheritance allowed him to proving his descent from the imperial line. He had bought a tumbledown farmhouse called Trennor halfway between the church and the village of Cargreen and slowly transformed it into a comfortable family home. A Plymothian by birth, he had never quite clinched his blood connection with the long-dead Theodore, but had at least achieved his ambition of being buried at Landulph, though not in the seventeenth-century Paleologus vault.

His son Michael had read archaeology at Oxford and gone on to teach it there. His five children, including Nick, had all been born in the city. But Michael had never sold Trennor, keeping it as a holiday home even after his parents' deaths and ultimately retiring there himself. Since his wife's death, he had lived alone, though four of his children were close by, tied to the area by choice or chance. Only Nick ploughed a distant furrow. And now he too was returning. Though not for long. And not, he suspected, for the very best of reasons.

It was Friday afternoon. A dank winter nightfall had outpaced him on the road. Maybe it was just as well, he thought, as the wayside mileage signs counted him down to his destination. Maybe the cover of darkness was what he needed. Cover of some sort, for sure. He always needed that.

Sunday would be his eldest brother's fiftieth birthday. Andrew farmed sheep on Bodmin Moor, cutting an ever more forlorn figure – according to their sister, Irene – thanks to divorce, estrangement from his only son and the dire state of British agriculture. A birthday party at Trennor – a gathering of the siblings – would do them all good, Andrew especially. It was a summons Nick could not very well ignore. But in luring him down, Irene had admitted that there was more to it than that. 'We need to talk about the future. I don't see how Dad can cope at Trennor on his own much longer. A possibility's cropped up and we'd like your input.' She had declined to be specific over the telephone, hoping, Nick inferred, to rouse his curiosity as well as his conscience. Which she had done, though not as conclusively as she must have hoped. Nick had agreed in the end because he had no reasonable excuse not to.

The rush-hour traffic was just beginning to thin as Nick reached Plymouth. He followed the A38 as it sliced through the city to the Tamar Bridge, where widening work slowed progress to a crawl over the broad, black expanse of the river. A train was crossing the railway bridge to his left, heading back the way he had come. He could not help wishing he was on it, could not help surrendering for an instant his well-practised equanimity.

But only for an instant. Then he was in control once more. On the other side of the bridge, he turned off into the centre of Saltash and doubled back through the oldest part of the town, descending the steep hill to the river, with the road and railway looming above him. As he turned right at the bottom of the hill, he saw at once ahead of him along the quayside the warmly lit windows of the Old Ferry Inn, where Irene Viner, née Paleologus, had presided as landlady for the past twelve years. The pub trade had been her husband's idea, following redundancy from Devonport Dockyard. But he had soon started drinking most of the takings, a problem Irene had solved only with the help of a divorce lawyer. She had freely admitted that running a pub had never been an ambition of hers, but had gone on to make a much better job of it than Nick would ever have predicted.

He pulled into the small yard behind the pub and edged his car into a narrow gap between Irene's Vauxhall and a large plastic bottle-bin, turned off the engine and climbed out. Only in that moment, he realized, had he really arrived, when he inhaled a first lungful of chill, moist riverside air. Almost vertically above him was the ancient span of the railway bridge, dark and silent now the eastbound train had passed. Ahead soared the modern road bridge, the workmen's cradles slung beneath it and the glare of the sodium lights confusing its shape. His sister had chosen a strange kind of home, one literally overshadowed by the structural necessities of travel and named in memory of one form of transport that was no longer to be found there. The Old Ferry was, however you viewed it, a dead end.

So it certainly seemed to Nick. But what of it? He was here for the weekend only. He had come, yes, but soon, very soon, he would go.

He fetched his bag from the boot of the car, walked round to the bar entrance at the front of the pub and dipped his head as he stepped in through the doorway. The nature of the building preserved the distinction between public and lounge, though Irene and her customers referred to the two rooms merely as front and back, served by a double-sided bar. The ceilings were low, the floors uneven, the walls as thick as a dungeon's. It did not wear its five hundred or so years lightly. But there was nothing museum-like about it either. Two fruit machines and a smattering of local youth ensured there was not a lot of fustiness to greet the newcomer.

Cigarette smoke was quite another matter. Nick, one of nature's non-smokers, coughed involuntarily as he strode through, drawing leery glances from the group by the fruit machine. The sight of a well-groomed, smartly suited stranger did not seem to please them, the family resemblance to mine hostess evidently escaping their notice.

The resemblance was, in truth, quite marked. They were of similar height and build; their sleek dark hair was touched with just about the same amount of grey; marginally too long in the face and aquiline in the nose to be described as conventionally good-looking, they were striking in appearance nonetheless, likely to draw the eye in any gathering. Irene was perched on a stool behind the bar, gazing vacantly into the empty back room, sustaining a murmured conversation over her shoulder with the bottle-blonde barmaid who was keeping the youths out front plied with drinks.

'Here he is,' Irene announced as Nick stepped into her line of sight. 'Hello, stranger.' She hopped off the stool and came out into the room to kiss him. 'You're looking well.'

'You too.'

'Like the ensemble?' She gave a half-pirouette to show off her hip-hugging skirt and high-heeled shoes. Lamplight shimmered across her scarlet blouse. 'Friday-night finery for the locals. There are quite a few that would defect up the road to the Boatman but for my ankles, let me tell you.'

'I can believe it.' So he could, though Irene's admirers seemed to be in short supply at present, a point her slowly fading smile seemed to acknowledge.

'They'll be in soon.'

'Glad to have beaten the rush.'

'Looks like you came straight from the office to do it.'

'I put in the morning there, yeah.'

'Fancy a drink?'

15

'Later, maybe. I'd like to freshen up.'

'Of course. I'm forgetting how far you've come. Go straight up. I've put you in Laura's room. There's a quiche and salad in the fridge if you're hungry.'

'OK. See you in a minute.'

Nick opened the door marked PRIVATE next to the ladies' and went through to the narrow staircase that led up to the living quarters. He climbed the stairs two at a time to a cramped landing giving on to a sitting room and bedroom at the front, kitchen, bathroom and another bedroom at the back. The rear bedroom belonged to his niece, currently away at boarding school. The bed had been made up for him. He dumped his bag beside it, puzzled briefly over the identity of the girl in the poster behind the door, then headed for the bathroom.

Forty minutes or so had passed by the time Nick went down again and a dozen or more of the fabled locals were now installed in the back bar, swapping jokes and gossip. Some of them he dimly recognized and they him. It soon became clear that Irene had briefed them about his visit and its ostensible reason: the party at Trennor. He was made to feel welcome and stood drinks like one of the crowd. He did more smiling and small-talking over the next few hours than he normally spread over a month, till his jaw ached and a knot of tension in his stomach tightened into a ball of pain. Nobody asked him an obvious question: why not stay at Trennor, big enough to boast several empty bedrooms, including the one he had shared for so many years with his brother Basil, rather than squeeze in amidst Laura's fluffy rabbits and girl-band CDs? Which was just as well, because he could not have supplied an adequate answer. Irene was still holding out on him. Perhaps, he idly wondered during the third pint of Guinness that he regretted accepting, the locals already knew. Perhaps he was the only one who did not know. Then again, he thought, catching his sister's wary, warning glance through a whorl of somebody's cigarillo smoke, perhaps not.

16

It was nearly midnight before the last of the customers had been steered out into the darkness and the barmaid sent home after some desultory clearing-up. Irene lit her first cigarette of the evening, poured Nick and herself double Glenmorangies and joined him at the table nearest to the flame-effect gas fire, the artfully wavering light from it flickering on a beaten copper surround and a token pair of flanking horse-brasses.

'They seem a good-hearted bunch,' he remarked of the departed carousers.

'Not too hard on you, then?' She gave him a sympathetic smile over the rim of her tumbler.

'No. They were all—'

'I mean the experience. You don't like crowds, do you? Especially when you're supposed to be one of them.'

'I get by.'

'Do you? I worry about you, all the way up there, alone and—'

'There's nothing to worry about.'

'There used to be.'

'But not any more.'

Seeming to take the hint, Irene changed the subject. 'Well, I'm glad you could make it.'

'Do you think Andrew will be?'

'Of course. Although . . .'

'He won't necessarily show it.'

'You know what he's like. And he's more like it than ever, let me tell you.'

'Is a surprise appearance by his kid brother such a good idea, then?'

'We *are* a family, Nick. It can't be a bad idea to get together. Besides . . .'

'You haven't dragged me down here just for the benefit of the birthday boy.'

'No.' She took a long draw on her cigarette. 'There's Dad too, of course.'

'Does *he* know I'm showing up on Sunday?'

'No. We thought we'd . . . surprise both of them.'

'*We*?'

'Anna and me.'

'What about Basil?'

'He knows what's going on.'

Since Basil had been living with their sister Anna for some time, that, Nick assumed, was more or less inevitable. 'Lucky him.'

Irene sighed. 'All right. Time to come clean. You haven't seen Dad in over a year. Well, he's gone down quite a lot lately. He's become . . . frail, I suppose you'd call it. I remember him as such a big man. Now he's . . . shrunken.'

'He *is* eighty-four years old.'

'And showing it. If Mum was still alive, it might be different. As it is, I don't see how he can stay at Trennor, rattling around that house on his own.'

'What about Pru?' Even as he mentioned his parents' long-serving cleaning lady, Nick calculated that she could hardly be far off eighty-four herself. 'Doesn't she keep an eye on him?'

'As far as her cataracts allow, yes. But she's not of much practical use any more. We have to face facts.'

'You mean Dad has to face them.'

'There's a place at Tavistock that Anna reckons would be ideal for him. Gorton Lodge.'

Anna being a nurse-cum-administrator at a residential home in Plymouth, she was, Nick supposed, qualified to judge in such matters. Still, there seemed to be an element of fence-rushing about it all. He winced at the unaccustomed sensation of sympathy for his father.

'She can tell you about it tomorrow night. She wants you to go over there for dinner. But Gorton Lodge *is* nice, believe me. The best money can buy round here.'

'That's something I—' Nick broke off. A thought had come to him, spirited up by mention of the word money. Who was going to pay Gorton Lodge's fees? His grandfather's inheritance had not survived to the next generation. And his father had always let it be known that an academic's salary –

not to mention five children – left him with little to provide for his old age. Nor were any of those children exactly coining it in. The only obvious source of funds was Trennor itself. But that was their inheritance. Why were Nick's brothers and sisters suddenly so eager to put it towards a comfortable dotage for their father? It was laudable, in a way, but it was also deeply uncharacteristic. 'The house would have to be sold, Irene.'

'Of course.'

'And if Dad lives another ten years or more, even five . . .'

'It won't make any difference.'

'No difference? That doesn't make sense. What's Trennor worth? Three hundred thousand? Three fifty at most.'

'On the open market, you're probably right.'

'What other market is there?'

'The closed kind. Someone's offered Dad half a million.'

Nick stared at his sister in astonishment. '*Half a million*?'

'That's right. Five hundred thousand pounds. Cash on the table.'

'But . . . Dad hasn't put it up for sale.'

'Hence the premium.'

'Some premium.'

'Currently lodged in a lawyer's suspense account to Baskcomb's satisfaction.'

Baskcomb was the family's solicitor, just as his father had been – and *his* father before him. The hopeful buyer was evidently serious. 'Who is this someone?'

'Name of Tantris. I know nothing about him. Sounds foreign. But then so do we. None of us has met him. He works through intermediaries.'

'Why does he want the place?'

'Does it matter?'

'It might. What does Dad say?'

'He says "no deal".'

'That's that, then.'

'Not if we talk him round. Show a united front.'

'So that's why I'm here.'

'Not really.' Irene looked reproachfully at him, as if disappointed by the suggestion that this was all there was to it. 'I thought you had a right to know. You stand to benefit along with the rest of us. Or lose, of course, if we throw Mr Tantris's money back at him.'

'It's Dad who'd be doing the throwing. And the benefit's questionable. It would just take Gorton Lodge that bit longer to work their way through the money. As far as I can—'

'Mr Tantris will pay the fees.'

For the second time that night, Nick stared at his sister in astonishment. '*What*?'

'Mr Tantris will pay. Some kind of trust fund. Legally watertight, according to Baskcomb.'

'Why would he be willing to do that?'

'To seal the deal.'

'But—'

'And to overcome our objections, of course. I imagine it's a ploy to get us on his side. I have no illusions about his motives.'

'But what *are* his motives? Why does he want Trennor so badly?'

Irene shrugged. 'Like I said, does it really matter?'

She was being evasive once too often. Nick leaned forward across the table towards her. 'Do you know, Irene?'

She devoted several seconds to stubbing out her cigarette, then said, 'Yes. We all do.'

'Except me.'

'Quite.'

'Well?' He did not bother to hide his irritation at having to prompt her.

'It's a little . . . unusual.'

'I'll bet.'

'Surprising, even.'

'Surprise me, then.'

'Actually . . .' She smiled appeasingly at him. 'I'm going to leave that to someone much better qualified than I am.'

'Oh yes. And who might that be?'

'Mr Tantris's assistant, Ms Hartley, wants to meet you and explain the situation. She'd much prefer it came from her first, and, frankly, so would I. She'll be able to answer all your questions.'

'*She'd* prefer it? She knows about me, does she?'

'She knows *of* you. I made it clear to her that your views would have to be taken into account. And she's anxious to ensure they are.'

'How very considerate of her.'

'Sarcasm.' Irene's smile broadened. 'That's a good sign, Nick.'

'What of?'

'Of rejoining the human race.' She looked at him with all her old sisterly fondness, which he felt unable either to match or to reject. 'It's where you belong.'

'When have you arranged for me to meet Ms Hartley?' he responded, clutching at practicalities.

'Tomorrow at noon.'

'Here?'

'No. St Neot. At the village church.'

'*St Neot?*'

'It's about halfway between Liskeard and Bodmin.'

'I know where it is, for God's sake. What I don't know is why I should have to go all the way over there to meet this woman.'

'No. But you will when you get there.'

'What's that supposed to mean?'

'It's supposed to mean that Ms Hartley will explain everything.' Irene drained her glass. 'Which is why I'm going to say goodnight.'

# CHAPTER TWO

Trying to persuade Irene to tell him something she was determined not to was a waste of energy, as Nick well knew from previous, indeed lifelong, experience. He derived some small satisfaction when he woke the next morning from not having made the attempt. He had at least avoided that mistake. But there was another mistake he had not avoided and was only now paying for. He had drunk more than he was used to, far more. And he regretted the second Glenmorangie, polished off after Irene had gone to bed, with every wincing movement of his head.

His customary Saturday morning run was thus more of a torment than a tonic. At least the weather was kind to him – grey, still and bracingly chill. He headed south, out past Saltash School and back along the path beside the railway line. He wound down afterwards on Town Quay, watching the swans and the seagulls and a graceful flight of geese across the Plymouth skyline. The headache was no better – worse, if anything. But at least he had atoned in some measure for inflicting it upon himself.

The aroma of frying bacon reached him as he approached the Old Ferry, an aroma which, to his surprise, he found distinctly alluring. Crispy bacon and scrambled eggs turned out to be Irene's patent hangover cure. Even more surprisingly, it worked. After topping up his cholesterol and caffeine levels and soaking in the bath, he felt more like the reasonably fit and relatively clear-thinking person he was supposed to be.

By eleven o'clock, he was on the road – an hour away from an explanation that was already overdue.

Nick could not remember whether he had ever visited St Neot before. It was one of several villages on the southern fringe of Bodmin Moor that family excursions from Trennor had probably taken him to in his childhood or adolescence. An ice-cream stop, perhaps? He could not say for sure. Nor were any specific memories jogged as he drove into it along a curving, wooded road up the Loveny valley. It looked a pretty place, though, smoke climbing lazily from the cottage chimneys beneath the gently sloping foothills of the Moor.

The church stood on the highest ground of the village, four-square yet elegant, a weathered granite testament to the skills of its centuries-dead builders. Nick pulled up beneath the churchyard wall at its western end, where parking was shared with the scarcely less venerable London Inn. The pub appeared to be open, but there was little sign of trade this early. The church clock showed the time as ten minutes short of noon. He was early.

But so was someone else. He had pulled in beside a small red Peugeot. As he climbed out of his car, so did the driver of the Peugeot.

She was a short, slim woman dressed in jeans, sweater and sheepskin coat, dark curly hair framing a pale, serious face. Nut-brown eyes regarded him solemnly through small, gold-framed glasses. 'Mr Paleologus?' she asked, with the barest hint of a Midlands accent.

'Yes. Ms Hartley?'

'The same.' They shook hands, Elspeth Hartley with a surprisingly strong grip. All in all, she was not living up to his expectations of PA – if that was what she was – to a million-aire – if that was what *he* was. 'Glad you could make it.'

'My sister didn't leave me much choice in the matter.'

She raised her eyebrows slightly at that. 'How much do you know?'

'I know your boss wants to buy Trennor. Virtually at any price, apparently. And I believe you're going to tell me why.'

'Actually, he's not my boss. More patron, really.'

'You're not his assistant?'

'I'm an art historian. Mr Tantris subsidizes my researches at Bristol University. But you're right in a sense. I do seem to have turned into his assistant. Kind of, anyway. The real one's too busy with high finance to come down here.'

'Down from where?'

'London. New York. Zurich.' She smiled, instantly persuading Nick that it was something she should do as often as possible. 'The location varies.'

'And Mr Tantris? What's his location?'

'Monaco, so I'm told. But I've never actually met him. I'm just grateful to him for funding my work. It's led me in some unexpected directions. I certainly never expected to come across descendants of the Byzantine emperors in the course of it, for instance.'

'Our lineage doesn't bear much scrutiny.'

'That's not what your father said. Shortly before he showed me the door.'

'Well, it's his door.'

'I know. But it's not as if Mr Tantris wants to pull Trennor down and build twelve executive houses on the site, is it?'

'Isn't it?'

'All right.' She smiled again. 'I'd better get to why we're here, hadn't I?'

'Seems a good idea.'

'Come into the church. Then you'll understand.'

Taking that on trust, Nick followed her in through the churchyard gate and round to the south door, near which were clustered amidst the gravestones the worn uprights of several Celtic crosses.

'Ancient precautions against the Devil,' said Elspeth Hartley, noticing him glance at them. 'A good deal older than

24

this church, which replaced a pre-Norman structure in the fifteenth century. Come on.'

She stepped into the porch, raised the latch on the door, pushed it open and led Nick into the body of the church.

He stopped and looked around. The nave and aisles were well enough proportioned, but what immediately took his eye were the stained-glass windows, glowing vibrantly yet delicately, somehow seeming to magnify the thin grey light he had left behind in the churchyard.

'I see you've noticed,' said Elspeth.

'Nice windows.'

'More than nice, I think. Magnificent. And historically precious. Pre-Reformation parish church glazing schemes are extremely rare. This is second only to Fairford in Gloucestershire for quality and completeness.'

'Why so rare?'

'Civil War iconoclasm's mostly to blame. Cromwellian troops were accompanied by the sound of smashing glass wherever they went.'

'Why did this survive? Too far off the beaten track?'

'Hardly. There was as much destruction of church windows and statuary in Cornwall as anywhere else. The Puritans were nothing if not thorough. No, no, St Neot's survived thanks to special pleading and elaborate planning. But we're getting ahead of ourselves. First of all, I want you to look at the glass, I mean, *really* look.'

She led Nick along the south aisle and through the gated rood-screen into a lady chapel filled with blue, red and gold light from the two corner windows on the southern and eastern sides.

'The Creation and Noah windows, substantially unrestored and dating from the fourteen nineties. Exquisite, I think you'll agree.'

'I do.' Nick was no expert, but he could recognize fine craftsmanship when he saw it. And he could also recognize the Creation story, set out in the brightly tinted panes, from God with his compasses planning the world to the treacherous green serpent coiled around the tree of the knowledge of good and evil. The last pane, clearly designed to lead on to the next window, showed God commanding Noah to build the Ark. And there, as he turned to look, *was* the Ark, golden-bowed and floating on a sea of light.

'It looks as if the original plan was to tell the whole Old Testament story window by window. But we can assume money ran short, because as we move back along the aisle what do we find but local dignitaries and their pet saints. Sponsorship, by any other name. But sponsorship of artistic excellence.'

The five windows between Noah and the south door were indeed a sequence of haloed saints and pious family groups, kneeling in prayer. Nick walked slowly along the row, Elspeth keeping pace beside him.

'And after the local dignitaries came the common parishioners. The windows in the north aisle were funded by subscriptions from particular groups: wives, young women, young men. The young men's window, depicting the life of St Neot, is particularly fine.'

Nick turned to admire these humbler but no less beautiful compositions, walking slowly back along the nave to the rood-screen, where he stopped and gazed up at the east window. 'The Last Supper?' he mumured, deciphering the scene.

'That's right.'

'But . . . different somehow from the others.'

'You're getting good at this. That's an eighteen-twenties window. There was a lot of cleaning and restoration done then, with quite a few tracery lights moved or replaced and several whole new windows installed. It takes some sorting out.'

'I'm sure it does.'

'But, however you look at it, there's one rather odd omission.'

'There is?'

'This is a church. These windows are not just *objets d'art*.

They're lessons in glass. The Creation. The Fall. The Flood. In the ordinary way of things, you'd expect at least some reference to the Day of Judgement.'

'Isn't there any?'

'Not as it stands. And there should be. Take it from me, a Doom Window was *de rigueur*.'

'So, why isn't there one?'

'Oh, there was. We have that from a churchwarden of the period. And talking of churchwardens, one of the present incumbents has lent me the key to the tower. This way.'

She walked back down the nave and unlocked the door leading to the ground floor of the tower. Nick followed her into the bellringing chamber. The ropes were tied back against the walls to either side, allowing a clear view of the west window, hidden from the rest of the church. But all Nick could see were illuminated saints. The Day of Judgement did not seem to have dawned in the glass.

'We think this is where the Doom Window was. Well, *I* think so. There were two major periods of iconoclasm: one in the mid sixteen forties, another in the early sixteen fifties. St Neot came under most serious threat during the second period, specifically in the spring of sixteen fifty-one. There were lots of raids on neighbouring churches around then. But not here.'

'Why was St Neot spared?'

'It was down to the churchwardens. The vicar had been expelled from his living by then. They enlisted the help of the Rous family, who lived at Halton Barton, beside the Tamar, just a few miles north of Landulph. A member of the family, Anthony Rous, was a Parliamentary colonel and county commissioner. But other members seem to have had High Church sympathies. And some cousins of theirs, the Nicholls, sponsored one of the windows here. So, strings were pulled. The windows were whitewashed, to avoid causing offence, but preserved for posterity.'

'Where's all this leading, Ms Hartley? You just mentioned Landulph.'

'So I did. What is it from here? Twenty miles? A long but feasible day's return ride in sixteen forty-six.'

'Sixteen forty-six? I thought you—'

'A letter from one of the churchwardens at the time, Richard Bawden, has recently come to light. He refers to precautions taken prior to the 'fifty-one crisis. "Our finest window", he writes, "was removed six years prior thereto. We could not suffer it to stand at risk with Cornwall in the Parliament's hands. It was immured safe in the keeping of our staunch friend, Mr Mandrell, and is safe there still, I warrant." The letter dates from sixteen sixty-two, two years *after* the Restoration. "Safe there still". Interesting, wouldn't you say?'

'Why wasn't it brought back and re-installed?'

'Good question. To which I think I have the answer. The Rous connection led me to look for Mandrell in the Halton Barton area. The Lowers of nearby Clifton were Royalist sympathizers and definitely High Church. Their friendship with your own forebear suggests deep antipathy to Puritanism. A son of Theodore Paleologus died fighting for the King at Naseby, as you probably know. Well, a parochial neighbour of the Lowers turns out to be one Thomas Mandrell, who was married to a Rous. I think the window was hidden with him. But he died in sixteen fifty-seven and his property was made over to the Parliamentarian holder of the manor of Landulph, Sir Gregory Norton. A member of the Norton family continued to live in Mandrell's house after the Restoration. And Bawden says the window was "immured there", by which I think he means walled up in some way. If the new occupant remained at heart a Parliamentarian, then it was probably best not to draw his attention to the Royalist treasure lying unsuspected ... within his walls.'

'And where were these walls?'

'Can't you guess?'

Nick smiled in grudging recognition of the obvious. 'Trennor?'

She nodded. 'In one.'

                              *      *      *

They left the church and went into the pub, where Elspeth
surprised Nick by ordering a pint of beer and a round of
sandwiches. Irene's fry-up had left him in little need of lunch,
so he contented himself with mineral water. With those pre-
liminaries out of the way and a fireside table commandeered,
they returned to the subject of the long-lost and perhaps soon
to be found Doom Window of St Neot.

'You're seriously telling me this is all about antique stained
glass?'

'Yes, Nick, I am.' (First-name terms had been adopted
somewhere between church and pub.) 'It's Mr Tantris's con-
suming passion, so I'm told.'

'Has he been down here?'

'Apparently. But he's something of a recluse. It'll have
been a discreet visit – not to mention a flying one.'

'And he wants to buy Trennor on the off-chance of finding
the missing window there – in a wall, under a floor?'

'It's a rather good chance, actually. The Bawden letter
doesn't leave much room for doubt.'

'Except that Trennor's a fair-sized house. And the people
who know where the window was concealed have been dead
for more than three hundred years.'

'Exactly. Which is why vacant possession is essential. We
might have to pull several walls apart to find what we're
looking for. Remember, the window will have been dismantled before it was transported to Landulph. That means
thirty or more separate panes of glass, wrapped and stored in
a large wooden trunk for the journey, then . . . immured. I
understand your grandfather extended the original dwelling,
so we're probably talking about walls that are now internal.
They all looked plenty thick enough for the job to me. As far
as I could judge, anyway. I wasn't exactly given the run of the
place.'

'Dad a bit curt, was he?'

'No more than he had a right to be, I suppose, given what
I'm proposing to do to his home.'

'Glad you appreciate that.'

'It's why Mr Tantris is prepared to be so generous.'

'But he can afford to be.'

'Yes. A rich man indulging his whims. You can resent him if you like. But remember Bawden said it was their finest window. Finer, then, than the Creation or the Noah. And I think you'll agree they're fine enough. Quite possibly the oldest window as well, since the tower is older than the rest of the church. It could predate the others by up to a hundred years. Maybe more, if it was part of the earlier structure. It would be an extraordinary find – both historically and artistically.'

'Quite a career boost for you, I imagine.'

'Absolutely. I don't deny it. It's a wonderful opportunity for me. And not such a bad one for you and your family.'

'Because of the money?'

'Well, yes.' She grinned. 'We all need it, don't we? To lesser or greater degrees. And from what your sister told me, it doesn't seem likely that any of you would want to hold on to Trennor after your father's death.'

'Probably not, no.'

'So, it makes sense to accept Mr Tantris's offer.'

'Maybe it does. But my father doesn't seem to agree. And he's the one who counts.'

'Please do your best to change his mind, Nick.' Her expression somehow implied that he would be doing her an enormous favour – as well as himself. 'That is, assuming you think he *should* change his mind. Do you?'

'Yes.' He nodded slowly in final acceptance of her argument, swayed in the end as much as anything by her sheer enthusiasm for the Doom Window project. As she had put it, there really seemed no sane alternative to going ahead. 'I rather think I do.'

Elspeth would be in Cornwall for another week, she told Nick, fine-tuning her researches. Irene had her mobile number and Elspeth was hoping to hear good news before she

30

went back to Bristol. By good news she meant his father's conversion by force of filial argument to the line of least resistance.

To someone unfamiliar with the character of Michael Paleologus, this no doubt seemed a probable outcome. Nick took a less optimistic view. His father was a stubborn man and susceptibility to reason had never been his strong suit, especially when one of his children was presenting the reason. In this case, of course, they would also be presenting a united front, which was unusual, if not unprecedented. And even the old man could not deny that he *was* old. And alone. And short of money. And frail, according to Irene.

But the last he could be relied upon to deny. He would say they only thought him in need of residential care because it was suddenly worth their while. Cooped up at Gorton Lodge, he would cost them nothing, while Tantris's money sat in the bank, earning interest until the day they inherited it. Yes, Nick could well imagine that was *exactly* what he would say.

From St Neot Nick drove up onto the Moor. He parked near the dam at the southern end of Colliford Reservoir and walked out along the shore, turning the situation over in his mind. The silence was almost audible.

The oddest feature of his father's response to Tantris's offer, Nick reflected, was that in normal circumstances he would urge on the search for the window. He was an archaeologist. He believed in excavating the past. As Elspeth had said, this was exciting stuff. And it was the stuff of Michael Paleologus's professional life. If he co-operated, he could probably find himself taken on as some kind of adviser. There could be a book in it. A documentary film. Did he not see that? Did he not appreciate the potential?

Of course he did. Frail or not, he was no fool. If he had come up with the idea, there would have been no holding him. His intransigence was founded on resentment. He needed to have his ego massaged as well as his bank balance boosted.

31

Irene was trying to push him. And he did not like to be pushed.

Nor did Nick, come to that. Irene had called him down to dance to her tune and that was precisely what he was doing. He would feel better about all of it if he could rewrite at least part of that tune.

As he gazed out across the reservoir, a way of doing so came suddenly to his mind. He smiled and started back towards the car.

It was only a couple of miles across the Moor to Carwether Farm, a huddle of grey, slate-roofed, granite-walled buildings in a curl of the Bedalder Valley south of the village of Temple. Nick would have hesitated about driving there, though, even if Irene had not wanted to spring his presence on their brother as a birthday surprise. Nick's relationship with Andrew had always been an edgy one. Their personalities were more similar than either would have been prepared to admit, though they had found very different expression. Andrew had an affinity with land and stone and dumb animals, while for Nick a problem was something you thought, not laboured, your way out of. In common they had a certain social maladroitness, but as bonds went it was hardly a strong one.

In visiting Carwether, moreover, Nick was offsetting the advantage of surprise with a greater disadvantage. They would be meeting where Andrew felt at home. And where he felt like the interloper.

The dog was first to detect his approach. It emerged, ears pricked, from the shadow of a barn as he drove slowly down the potholed track and it started barking as he passed the open gate. Nick pulled up and glanced hopefully towards the house as he turned off the engine. It would have been a relief to see Andrew emerging to call off the brute before he had to climb out and discover whether its bite was worse than its bark. He tried a blast on the horn, but that only seemed to annoy the dog, something Nick had absolutely no wish to do.

Then to his considerable relief, he heard his brother's voice. 'Quiet, Skip.' Skip instantly was. Nick looked away from the house towards a corrugated-iron-roofed shed, where the call had come from. And there was Andrew, dressed in a grease- and mud-smeared boiler-suit, stepping out round the rusting rear of a Land Rover, wiping his hands on a rag.

His hair was a good deal greyer than when they had last met, his face gaunter. And there was a hint of a stoop where once he had been square-shouldered. Andrew Paleologus was one day short of fifty, but could have been taken for several years past it. The greyness went further than his hair, probably deeper too. He looked like a man who had been struggling for a long time to achieve something he now knew was ultimately beyond him.

Nick got out of the car. Skip growled, but made no move. The two brothers regarded each other solemnly across the yard. 'Hello, Nick,' said Andrew, just when it had begun to seem he might say nothing at all.

'Hello, Andrew.'

'No need to ask what brings you here.'

'I thought you'd be surprised to see me.'

'Hardly.'

'Irene's got me down for your birthday.'

'Glad I could provide her with an excuse.'

'It's only partly that.'

'But the biggest part, I'd say.' He moved closer. 'Want some tea?'

'Coffee would be nice.'

'Got none.'

'Tea, then. Fine.'

'Come on in. You'll have to take me as you find me.'

Nick found him as he would have expected rather than hoped. Carwether was a middle-sized, solidly built moorland family farmhouse. It needed roaring fires and gambolling children to

33

make it feel like a home. Instead it was cold and silent as a grave, sparsely furnished and echoing to their footfalls. They went into the kitchen, where a range gave off a meagre hint of warmth. Andrew set the tea going while Nick glanced up at a feed merchant's wall calendar hanging near the door. Every day was blank.

'As soon as Irene told me she'd cook me a Sunday lunch at Trennor for my birthday, I knew it was cover for a family conference,' Andrew said over his shoulder as he filled the teapot. 'So, it stood to reason you'd be in on it. She was bound to want you down. The only question was whether you'd come.'

'Well, here I am.' Nick sat down at the table. The *Western Morning News* was folded open in front of him. He closed it and saw, lying beneath, a large-scale Ordnance Survey map of Bodmin Moor. It too was folded open. Someone – Andrew, presumably – had marked apparently random locations on it with bright red crosses. Half a dozen or more were clustered around Blisland, on the western fringe of the Moor. The rest were scattered more widely. 'Plotting something, are you?'

'What do you mean by that?' There was aggression in Andrew's voice as he turned from the sink.

'These crosses.' Nick smiled to defuse the moment. 'On the map.'

'Oh, those.' Andrew sniffed, fetched a couple of mugs from the cupboard and plonked them down next to the map. 'Yeah. You could say I am. They're a year's worth of recorded sightings.'

'Sightings of what?'

'Big cats.'

'You buy into that?'

'They're out there. If you'd seen what was done to one of my ewes last back end, you'd not doubt it.'

'I thought it was just . . . rural myth.' And that was what he would have expected Andrew – an unvarnished rationalist, if ever there was one – to think as well.

'What I've seen I've seen.'

'You've seen one?'

'More than one. Or the same one twice. Most recently, there.' He pointed to one of the crosses closest to Carwether. 'A panther of some kind. Large, loose-limbed and black as pitch, a field away from me. Dusk, it was. They're nocturnal, of course. Creatures of the night.'

'Dusk can be a confusing time, visually.'

'You don't have to believe me, Nick.' Andrew gave him a half-smile that was almost contemptuous. 'It really doesn't matter. I'll prove it in the end. To everyone.'

'How will you do that?'

'Infra-red photography. I've been going out after dark with a special image-intensifying video camera and nightscope. I'll get one on tape sooner or later.'

'But you haven't yet.'

'No. Not yet.' Andrew poured the tea, then sat down at the other end of the table. 'Anyway, you're not here to discuss big cats. Fat ones, now, that's a different matter. We seem to have one by the tail.'

'You mean Tantris?'

'You know all about it?'

'I've just come from St Neot. I met Elspeth Hartley there. She filled me in.'

'Persuasive woman.'

'Not as far as Dad's concerned, apparently.'

'He's bound to see it differently.'

'I'd have thought he'd want to be involved in the project. It's right up his street. Buried treasure. Historical mystery. Irresistible, surely, to someone who's made a career out of digging up all our yesterdays.'

'You should tell him that, Nick. It might shame him into agreeing.'

'Maybe I will.'

'Don't mind me. I don't want a fuss to be made about my birthday. A handy way to avoid that is for you to make a fuss about something else.'

35

'You are in favour of this, aren't you, Andrew? I mean, Irene said you were, but . . .'

'No harm in checking, is there? Of course I'm in favour.' He leaned back in his chair and gazed through the window into the yard. 'Why wouldn't I be? This farm makes less and less money every year. What's the point of struggling on with nothing to show for it and no-one to pass the place on to?'

'Tom not interested?' Andrew's son had never displayed any enthusiasm for farming that Nick knew of, but still he felt obliged to ask.

'I wouldn't know what he's interested in. Haven't heard from him since Christmas. And that was just a card with his name on it. No message.'

'Is he still in Edinburgh?'

'According to the postmark, yeah. His course finished last summer. I didn't even get invited to the degree ceremony. I'm sure Kate went, though. And that Mawson slob.' The references to his ex-wife and her second husband did not suggest any lessening of hostility with the passage of time. But Andrew did not seem to want to dwell on the point. He had probably dwelt on it too long already. 'Look, Nick, the way I see it we could net at least half as much again as Tantris is currently offering by playing hard to get. He'll pay whatever he has to. It'd be crazy to turn our backs on a deal like this. Naturally, we're agreed. Irene doesn't want to be a pub landlady for the rest of her life any more than Anna wants to go on emptying bedpans. I need the money, God knows. So does Basil. And you're obviously not going to refuse your share. Dad just has to be made to appreciate how much we stand to gain.'

'But what does he stand to gain?'

'The comfort of knowing that he doesn't have to worry about us any more.' Andrew raised a smile. 'Wouldn't you think that'd be enough?'

It was agreed when Nick left that they would say nothing about his visit when they met at Trennor the next day. In truth, Nick found himself wishing he really had not gone to Carwether at all. Absence – of Kate, of Tom, of hope – had been stronger there than Andrew's own presence. Farming had been his vocation since boyhood. He had wanted to do only that and nothing else. But now his vocation was exhausted. Maybe Tantris's offer had forced him to acknowledge that painful truth. If so, what might follow upon rejection of the offer did not bear thinking about.

Nick took the A30 east across Bodmin Moor, then headed south through Callington towards Saltash. He chose the route despite, or perhaps because of, the diversion he would be tempted to take. And sure enough he did not resist the temptation.

At Paynter's Cross he turned off along the well-remembered lane between the high hedges and the anciently bounded fields that sloped down towards the long, lazy meander of the Tamar as it broadened into the estuary. Not far off now, across those silent pastures, his father was living and breathing and whiling away his day. But Nick was not going to see him. Not if his luck held, anyway. He was not going home – if that was what Trennor really was. He was merely visiting his roots.

Landulph as a settlement barely existed. The parish was centred on Cargreen, a mile away. There were a few cottages near Landulph Church, at the far southern end of the lane Nick had followed from the main road, and a couple of farms within sight. That was it. Trennor lay half a mile off to the west, concealed by a fold of the land. A track led down from the church to the mud-flats bordering the Tamar, winding as it did so between the grounds of the old rectory and an area of marshland converted to meadow in the early nineteenth century and protected from flooding by a dyke.

Nick knew the area with an exactness only lengthy childhood explorations could confer. Every field, every farm, every step of the path round the foreshore to Cargreen and beyond.

He did not need to walk down the track and stand on the dyke to look across at Warleigh Wood and the delicate span of the railway bridge over the Tavy. He could see them clearly enough in his mind's eye.

The church dated from the same period as St Neot's, but was a plainer, less ambitious structure. It was not noted for its stained glass, nor famed for much beyond some artfully carved bench ends and the historical curiosity of Theodore Paleologus's memorial plaque. Nick found the church door locked, as he had expected, so he could not view the plaque. But its wording was lodged in his mind beyond forgetting. *Here lyeth the body of Theodore Paleologus of Pesaro in Italye descended from ye imperyall lyne of ye last Christian Emperors of Greece . . .* Above it, engraved in the brass, was the double-headed Byzantine eagle, symbolizing the unattainable union of western and eastern Christendom.

But the double-headed eagle was not confined to brass at Landulph. Nick walked through the churchyard to the area of twentieth-century burials and round to his grandparents' grave. GODFREY ARTHUR PALEOLOGUS, DIED 4TH MARCH 1968, AGED 81. ALSO HIS LOVING WIFE, HILDA, DIED 26TH SEPTEMBER 1979, AGED 87. REUNITED AND SADLY MISSED. There also, carved in the stone above the inscription, was the double-headed eagle of Byzantium.

Nick's mother had been cremated at her own wish. He suspected that his father would prefer burial and that another Paleologus would eventually rest in this quiet, yew-fringed field of graves. But that would be the end. Whether they took Tantris's money or not, he and his siblings were gone from here. Not far, perhaps, but far enough. The eagle had stayed, but they had flown.

# CHAPTER THREE

Irene was naturally pleased that Elspeth Hartley had been able to secure Nick's support for Tantris's scheme. For her, it was the sealing of an alliance which their father could surely not resist. And she greeted with enthusiasm Nick's contention that the old man would have to go along with it eventually unless he was willing to sacrifice his scholarly integrity, which they agreed he prized above all things. Viewed in that light, it was an argument they could not lose.

Whether it was an argument they would actually win at Trennor next day was a different matter. That depended on how subtly they presented it. Emphasizing their father's alleged inability to cope on his own struck Nick as a poor tactic. But it was the tactic Irene had adopted and she was reluctant to abandon it. She always had enjoyed telling her nearest and dearest what was good for them, even when she knew they would not listen. It was clear to Nick that the occasion was not going to be without its flashpoints.

He set off for dinner with Anna and Basil, wondering what view they took of the matter. He knew what Irene had told him: that they were right behind her. But he also knew he would be more confident about that when he heard it from their own lips.

Rain had set in by the time he crossed the bridge into Plymouth. Rear lights blurred by spray trailed him into the city centre. He parked in Citadel Road, a little way short of Anna's flat, and walked up on to the Hoe, relishing the dark wind and cold rain buffeting in from the Sound. He was nearly half an hour early, which was par for the course. It was a tendency that annoyed him, but which he was helpless to shake off. He turned east, towards Drake and the Barbican, the rain sheeting past him, halyards slapping against the flag-poles ahead.

There was only one other person on the Hoe, which was one more than he might have expected. A hunched figure in a hooded anorak was bearing down on him from the other end of the promenade. As the figure drew closer, some quality of posture and bearing suddenly struck Nick as familiar. Or maybe it was pure instinct that told him who it was.

'Basil?'

'Nick?' It *was* Basil, his narrow, bony face peering at him from beneath the brim of the hood. 'Trust you to be the only other poor fool game for a stroll on the Hoe in this weather.'

'I got here a touch early.'

'Not a much better excuse than mine.'

'Which is?'

'Cooking for a guest makes Anna nervous. And a nervous Anna is a short-tempered Anna.'

'I'm hardly a guest. And since when did Anna ever get nervous about anything?'

'Since I moved in. She tells me I'm enough to try the patience of a saint. Which is obviously true, as I invariably rejoin. I tried the patience of several and am in a position to know that their funds of it weren't inexhaustible.'

'Shall we go and see how she's getting on?'

'There's another twenty minutes yet before you're due. I think we should wait until then.'

'We'll be soaked to the skin by that time.'

'True. But I wasn't thinking of waiting here.'

40

*　　*　　*

The nearest pub was Basil's recommended loitering spot. This was the Yard Arm, nestled in the lee of the towering Moat House Hotel just off the Hoe. Basil ordered a tonic water and, thinking of the drive back to Saltash, Nick did the same. The bar was half-full, gearing up slowly for Saturday night. They found a table just inside the door.

Only when they sat down did Nick take a serious look at his by now unhooded brother. He was certainly not getting fat on a diet of idleness and whatever Anna served up in the way of meals. Like Andrew, he had grown gaunt with age, but unlike Andrew there was no greyness to his features; rather, a strange, animated flush. He had shaved his head, which made his eyes look disproportionately huge. Since he had always possessed a faintly bolt-eyed gaze, the effect on strangers, Nick suspected, would be disquieting.

This was not altogether inappropriate, since Basil had led a generally disquieting life. More preoccupied with their Greek roots than his brothers and sisters, he had embarked on a classics degree at Oxford, living at home rather than in college, but had failed to complete the course. Visiting Greece during the second summer of his studies, he had persuaded an Orthodox monastery near Corinth to take him on as a trainee monk. The training had stretched to more than twenty years, following which he had suddenly reappeared in his relatives' lives, beardless, unhabited and apparently bereft of his monastic vocation. He had lived at Trennor for a while, then vanished to the Scilly Islands, then returned and been taken in by Anna.

'I often come in here, you know,' he said, just as Nick took his first sip of tonic water and realized that it really would have been much better with gin. 'I look at the other customers – the groups of lads, the pairs of boyfriends and girlfriends, the solitaries like me. I think I'm beginning to understand society. But as for joining it, well, I'm forced to conclude that I've left it too late.'

'Do you miss Greece?'

41

'Of course. Especially the light. But I had to leave, Nick. I was fooling myself there. And others. Here I amount to very little. But that very little *is* me.'

'See much of Dad?'

'Only under escort. To say I'm a disappointment to him would be a gross understatement.'

'I don't think he's overly impressed with any of us.'

'The record of our achievements is a thin one, it's true. But mine is so thin as to have disintegrated. Hence I shall take a back seat when you all explain to him tomorrow why he absolutely must accept Mr Tantris's offer.'

'You don't sound convinced that he should.'

'Oh, I'm not disputing the logic of acceptance. It's unarguable. Though I suspect Dad *will* argue.'

'So do I.'

'The question is: why? If this Doom Window really is hidden at Trennor, our father the celebrated archaeologist should be straining at the leash to start looking for it. But not so.'

'I expect he thinks we're trying to steamroller him.'

'Which we are, of course.'

'For the best of reasons.'

'Really?' Basil cocked a sceptical eyebrow. 'Pardon me, Nick, but the overriding reason is greed, isn't it? Andrew, Irene and Anna want the money. So do you, I presume. It's as simple as that.'

'You seem to have left yourself off the list.'

'Ah well, I *don't* want it, you see. Wealth – even to the limited degree that appears to be on offer – wouldn't agree with me. I've decided to forgo my share. You can split it between you.'

'You're not serious.'

'Anna doubted I was when I informed her of my decision. It seems you doubt me too. Never mind. I know I'm in earnest. It's quite a relief, actually, quite pleasant being . . . disinterested. I don't want you to worry that I'm going to be holier-than-thou about this. You can all put the proceeds to

42

good use. And Dad will be royally pampered at Gorton Lodge. I don't disapprove of the arrangement.'

'You just don't want to profit from it.'

'It's not that. It's something more . . . well, something quite pitiful, actually.'

'What?'

'Having nothing is the only knack I've perfected.' Basil shaped a grin. 'I think I'd better hang on to it.'

Anna's basement flat was full of cheese and garlic fumes when Nick and Basil entered. She emerged from the kitchen, her face as shiny as her PVC Dennis the Menace apron, greeted without comment their claim to have met in the street and gave Nick a hug and a kiss before hurrying back to the stove with a parting instruction for them to open some wine.

Anna had always been the loudest and most physically demonstrative of the siblings. She was now also, beyond dispute, the largest, her curvaceous figure having expanded well beyond buxomness. She and the rifle pull-through Basil made an odd pairing. But Anna was also the most generous member of the family, which explained why she had been willing to take in an unemployed and unemployable lapsed monk possessed of a discombobulating stare.

Not that sharing a home with her brother involved surrendering territory to him. The lounge-diner bore no trace of his presence, dominated as it was by Anna's exuberant taste in wall-hung rugs and zigzag-patterned armchairs. Stacks of leaflets and newsletters dedicated to her pet campaign against nuclear-submarine repairs at Devonport Dockyard were piled on the floor next to the table, as if they had just been cleared from it, making way for cutlery, glasses and a bottle of Chianti.

Nick found the corkscrew on the mantelpiece, next to a propped-up postcard of the Sydney Opera House. He turned the card round and read the message. *Hi, Anna. It's hotter than your curry here, but I'm cool. Making out good. I'll email soon. Love, Z.* Z, as Nick knew but no stranger was likely to deduce from the wording, was Anna's eighteen-year-old son, Zack, currently occupied in gap-year globetrotting and the same age now as Anna had been when he was born. Nick's nephews and niece were widely scattered, no question: Zack bumming around Australia, Tom doing whatever his thing was in Edinburgh and Laura learning to play lacrosse and walk with her knees brushing together at some academy for the daughters of gentlefolk in Harrogate.

'No message for his uncle, you'll notice,' said Basil, peering over Nick's shoulder.

'I wouldn't have expected one.'

'I meant for *me*. I do live here, you know.'

'And I'm sure Zack's glad of that. Must be comforting for the lad to know there's someone here to look after his mother.'

'Open the wine,' said Basil, mock-tetchily. 'It's obvious you need a drink.'

Basil was spot-on with his last observation. Nick had neither welcomed nor been able to refute his brother's diagnosis of greed at work in the family. He did not feel greedy. He did not believe he *was* greedy. Yet he could not imagine out of existence the pound signs attached to Tantris's offer. They made a difference, as no doubt they always did in Tantris's high-rolling experience. They made the man impossible to ignore.

For as long as it took them to work their way through Anna's generously portioned moussaka there was no direct discussion of the sale of Trennor and their father's future. It was only when Basil had been dispatched to the kitchen to load the dishwasher and a second bottle of Chianti had been opened that Anna decided the time had come to make her position clear.

'Irene phoned me after you left this evening and said you saw things our way, Nick. Thank God we don't have to argue about it.'

'Except with Dad.'

'He'll see reason in the end. He has to. He can't stay there much longer on his own, he really can't. Pru found him on the drawing-room floor when she arrived to clean one day a few weeks back. He'd fallen over and couldn't get up. What would have happened if she hadn't turned up? He drinks too much, you know. It's got steadily worse since Mum died. I don't blame him, but, well, this *is* a golden opportunity to do something about a problem we'd otherwise have to face up to sooner or later.'

'I think we should appeal to his professionalism. Stress the historical importance of Elspeth's project.'

'Elspeth already, is it?'

'If you let Irene emphasize Dad's supposed inability to look after himself,' Nick hurried on, 'he'll just dig his heels in.'

'OK. I'll restrain her as best I can.'

'Basil tells me he doesn't want his share.'

'That's his vow of poverty, chastity and obedience for you. He manages the first two like a dream. Anyway, he can't hold himself totally aloof. If I get the money together to buy a little house, he'll move with me. He'll benefit even if he doesn't profit.'

'It's cramped here for the two of you, I can see that.'

'It was a sight worse when Zack was still at home. Not that he did much more than sleep here a few nights a week.'

'It was good of you to take Basil in.'

'No choice, really. He *is* my brother.'

'And counsellor on the larger mysteries of the world,' said Basil, padding in from the kitchen. 'Of which our potential benefactor is a prime example.'

Nick looked up at him. 'How do you mean?'

'Well, who is Mr Tantris exactly?'

'A rich man with a weakness for antique stained glass,' said Anna.

'And that satisfies you as a comprehensive study of his character and career?'

45

'I don't need satisfying.' Anna chuckled. 'Not where friend Tantris is concerned, anyway.'

'We know absolutely nothing about him.'

'He wants to buy Trennor for more than it's worth, Basil. What more do we need to know?'

'Aren't you even curious about him?'

'I'm curious about what I'll find to do with his money.'

'It'll be Dad's money, actually.'

'I can see why you were thrown out of that monastery, you know. You're so picky.'

'I wasn't thrown out. I left of my own accord.'

'Sounds to me like getting your resignation in before you were sacked.'

'Is it always as bad as this here?' put in Nick.

'Usually worse,' Basil replied with a cosmetically beatific smile. 'Anna's on her best behaviour for your sake.'

'Shut up.' Anna's snappishness was still good-humoured, but it was apparent to Nick that it would not be so indefinitely.

'Can't I ask a couple of simple questions?'

'No.'

'But—'

'*No.*'

'That's a pity.'

'Or a mercy.'

'Only . . .'

Anna sighed heavily. '*What?*'

'They were rather pertinent questions, actually.' Basil looked at each of them in turn. 'But I suppose they can wait.'

And wait they did. Which was just as well, Nick reflected, as he drove back to Saltash that night. Because some of the answers might have made the prospect of their family gathering at Trennor the next day seem less appealing – and less straightforward – than they all wanted to believe. The way ahead was clear and logical and mutually beneficial. And it was about more than money. A small piece of history would be served in the process. The Doom Window project was not just a pretext to winkle their father out of Trennor and liberate some capital. It was an opportunity that grew more golden the longer you studied it. All that remained was to convince one old man of the obvious.

# CHAPTER FOUR

Godfrey Paleologus had extended Trennor to either side, so that it was noticeably wider than it was deep, with several rooms having windows to both front and back. With the stonework obscured by whitewash, the only clues to its original size were the plainer casements of the central block and the ancient granite porch over the front door. A barn behind the house was also original, and looked it, despite re-roofing. It shared what had once been the farmyard with a large and unattractive garage. There was a flower garden at the front, divided by a path that led straight to the door from a pedestrian gate on to the lane. Once it had passed Trennor, this lane dwindled into a track – a muddy one at that, thanks to the proximity of a stream that trickled down from the hill above into a creek several fields to the south.

Before reaching the house, the lane ran past the long, Cornish-hedged lawn that old Godfrey had fashioned out of a weed-choked paddock. From an approaching car this was the first part of the property that came into sight round a kink in the lane to the west. It led, like a broad green carpet, towards the house itself.

Many years' worth of memories were compressed into the moment when Irene steered out of the bend late on Sunday morning and Nick saw the lawn, and then the house, ahead of them. Every arrival of his childhood – Easter, summer and Christmas – was simultaneously conjured in his mind. In early years, his mother had driven Irene, Anna and him down in the Mini, while his father had taken Andrew and Basil in the Rover. Later, about the age of eleven, Nick had been elevated to the boys' car. He smiled at the recollection of how proud that had made him, seeming to smell again as he did so the exact scents of the worn leather seats and his father's pipe-smoke.

'I'm glad you're in a good mood,' said Irene, glancing round at him. 'Let's hope it lasts.'

Irene's apprehensiveness had been apparent all morning. She had blamed it on worries about whether Moira and Robbie, her bar assistants, would be able to cope with the Sunday lunchtime trade at the Old Ferry. Nick had not even tried to reassure her on the point. He knew her state of mind had nothing to do with Moira and Robbie. And he strongly suspected that she knew he knew. 'What do you think Mum would say about all this?' he asked as Irene slowed for the turn into the yard.

'She'd see it as a heaven-sent opportunity to move somewhere smaller and more manageable.'

Yes, Nick silently agreed, she probably would, being even less sentimental than their father. And she would know how to manipulate the old man into agreeing with her. It remained to be seen whether her children would prove equal to the task.

'Good. The others are already here.'

Since Nick was supposed to be the surprise package of the day, it had been agreed that they should arrive last. Andrew's Land Rover and Anna's Micra were standing next to each other in the lee of the barn. Irene pulled in behind them and stopped.

'Here we go, then.' She lowered the sun-visor and squinted into the mirror, primping her hair and checking her make-up. 'Over the bloody top.'

'We're not going into battle, Irene.'

'Go on thinking that and you could end up as the first casualty.'

'There don't need to be *any* casualties.'

'OK.' Irene took a deep breath. 'I'll be calm and positive. And the soul of diplomacy. Will that do?'

'If you can keep it up.'

'Think I can't?'

'I'm not saying that. I just—'

'Come on,' she cut him short, opening the door and turning to climb out. 'Let's get on with it.'

Michael Paleologus at home among his children was as rare a spectacle as it was deceptive. He looked every inch the fond and doting parent, smiling and joking as they gathered round. He appeared both surprised and pleased when Nick came in with Irene and emphasized how it did his heart good to see them all together.

Only the addition of the words 'here at Trennor', accompanied by a knowing twitch of his smile, hinted at the argument they had come to present.

Nick's first impression was that Irene and Anna had exaggerated their father's frailty. True, he was rounder-shouldered and thinner than ever, but no more so than the general ageing process could account for. This was a man, after all, born in the summer the Battle of the Somme had been waged, whose first memory of world events was, appropriately enough, Howard Carter's discovery of the tomb of King Tutankhamun in 1922. He still dressed much as he had sixty years ago – in baggy tweed and corduroy and a cardigan whose pockets sagged under the weight of pipe, matches and tobacco-pouch. Smoking, combined with the effects of sundry archaeological expeditions over the years to North African wadis and West Asian plains, had left his face creviced like a dried river-bed. His hair – of which he still had a fine head – was yellowy grey, his eyes blue-green and magnified by the lenses of his glasses, on which Nick noticed a blurring galaxy of fingerprints and grease smears.

Only when the old man walked any distance – such as from the drawing room to the dining room – did his unsteadiness and shortness of breath reveal themselves. He clutched at chair-backs and door frames on the way, looking in such moments bewildered by his own feebleness. Then Trennor suddenly ceased to seem a place where he could be safely left to live out his days. The rambling layout and inadequate heating were bad enough. But there were also rugs curling at the edges and worn stair-carpet to be taken into consideration, not to mention the treacherously steep steps down to the cellar. Nick saw decrepitude wherever he glanced, in the sagging furniture and fraying curtains, in the dust-laden display cases of Roman coins and pre-Roman skull fragments, in the faded photographs and oriental urns, in all the accumulated detritus of his family's past. Their very surroundings spoke of the need for change.

For some time, however, that need was to go unmentioned. They had assembled, after all, to celebrate Andrew's fiftieth birthday. Pru had baked a cake, laid the dining table, prepared some vegetables and put a joint in the oven. All the family had to do was eat, drink and be as merry as they could contrive. The birthday boy himself had done little in the way of smartening up. Nor, come to that, had Basil. But their sisters had put on their contrasting party clothes – Irene one of her more elegant pairings of skirt and blouse, Anna alarmingly tight white trousers and a poppy-red off-the-shoulder sweater, with one or other bra strap constantly on view.

Conviviality prevailed before and during lunch, albeit conviviality of a brittle kind. Andrew put up a decent show of surprise at Nick's presence, pleasure at the presents he was given and general appreciation of the efforts being made to mark his mid-life milestone. Anna talked and laughed too much, Basil too little. Irene steered the conversation between rocks and shallows with considerable finesse. And Nick kept subtle watch on their father, who, it seemed to him, was keeping still more sutble watch on all of them.

51

But Michael Paleologus was also drinking at a pace somewhere between steady and stiff. Whisky had been taken before the birthday champagne. He had not stinted himself on the wine with lunch. And, as the meal drew to a close, he broke out the port. By then his subtlety had faded. And his reticence had begun to loosen.

'We drank a toast to Andrew before lunch,' he announced. 'Now I'd like to propose another. Your mother was a good wife to me. I loved her dearly and miss her sorely.'

'So do we, Dad,' said Anna.

'I know, my girl, I know. It's to her memory I'd like to drink. She'd be pleased by this . . . gathering. Pleased that the family's still drawn together from time to time, back here at Trennor.' If the last four words had been written down, Nick felt, they would undoubtedly have been italicized. 'To your mother.'

Glasses were clinked and port swallowed. Then Irene chimed in adroitly with a well-worn anecdote from her childhood. Andrew had taken her for a nerve-jangling spin on his motorbike one weekend, much to their father's horror. 'Good God, boy, what could you have been thinking of?' he was recorded as spluttering. Their mother had falsely insisted that she had given them permission, thus defusing the situation, though later she had taken them both severely to task. It was a familiar story, expertly told. But the events had occurred in Oxford, Nick reflected. Irene had chosen her tale carefully, pointing up as it did their mother's delicate management of the family and Andrew's lovable irresponsibility, as well as reminding them of their other home in Oxford, which they had abandoned readily and willingly when the time had come.

The moment passed, though not all of the tension. Irene had warned Nick that she meant to raise the subject of the Doom Window project over tea, when, according to her, everyone, especially their father, would be relaxed. But the old man was just as likely to be liverish and tetchy following an afternoon doze. Nick was not sure they should wait so long. Nor, however, did he wish to take the initiative himself. The next few hours promised to be anxious ones.

Lunch ended. Their father retired to the drawing room for a snooze by the fire. Irene and Anna set to in the kitchen, assisted by Basil. Nick accompanied Andrew on a stroll down the lane. The weather was grey and smokily chill: a January afternoon of thin light on bare trees, a moist breeze blowing in fitfully from the east, bearing the tang of river mud and the desultory shriek of gulls.

'Before you turned up,' said Andrew, 'Dad asked me if his grandson was likely to put in an appearance. Being my birthday and all.'

'Everyone would have been pleased to see him.'

'Yeah. I'm sure they would. Me especially. No such luck, though. Dad didn't say it in so many words, but he blamed me for Tom's absence. I could tell. Something in his eyes. It's always been there . . . for me. Contempt, that's what it is.'

'Come on, Andrew. That's not true.'

'Isn't it?'

'None of his grandchildren are here.'

'No. But Laura's a girl, and Zack's illegitimate. They don't count in Dad's scheme of things. Tom, now, he's different. Only son of his eldest son. Dad sees him as the torch-bearer. Except that he *doesn't* see him. Any more than I do. It might be different if you or Basil had . . .' Andrew shrugged. 'Well, you know.'

'Married and had children?'

'Yeah. Especially sons. To carry on the name.'

'I expect Tom will manage that.'

'But will I know about it?'

'Of course. He's just . . . growing up. I wasn't exactly a model citizen at his age.'

'That's a fact.' Andrew cast him a knowing look.

'I don't suppose Dad was either,' Nick said levelly.

'Maybe not. But he's unlikely to volunteer any details. And

53

it's not his past we have to worry about, is it? It's his future. And ours.' Andrew glanced back at the house. 'I could do with this going well. I really could.'

Michael Paleologus's study looked out over the lawn from the side of the house. There was also a door by which he could step straight out on to the grass without going round by the front. As Nick and Andrew wandered back past the hedge flanking the lawn, Nick caught some movement out of the corner of his eye that he thought might be the study door opening or closing. It was a double surprise, since not only had he assumed their father was still asleep but also the exit was never used in winter, when it was as likely as not to be blocked by a pile of books.

He could see no sign of anyone in the study, no stooped figure watching from the window. His father would surely need the light on if he was in there. His seated silhouette against the glare of the anglepoise desk lamp was a familiar sight from that side of the garden. But he was not at his desk, poring over an archaeological journal. He was not there at all, as far as Nick could tell.

They went in by the front door, to be met by Basil emerging from the kitchen.

'Ah, there you are,' he intoned. 'I've been sent to wake Dad. Irene seems to think he'll be in need of coffee.'

'We'll do that,' said Andrew. 'I'd prefer tea, by the way.'

'Coffee for me,' said Nick.

'I'll report back.' Basil grinned and beat a retreat with some alacrity.

They pressed on into the drawing room. Michael was sitting where they had left him by the fire, but he was not asleep and Nick noticed his chest was heaving, like someone out of breath doing his poor best to disguise the fact.

'Are you all right, Dad?'

'As all right . . . as I'll ever be . . . Where is everybody?'

'They're just finishing up in the kitchen.'

'Good.' He coughed, taking a moment to recover himself. 'Why don't you two sit down.'

They obeyed, perching together on one of the sofas. Half a minute or so passed, during which neither found anything to say. Michael took out his pipe and laboriously filled and lit it, studying them through the first puffs of smoke and seeming to smile faintly – unless it was merely the curl of his lips round the pipe stem.

'Caught that big cat yet, Andrew?'

'No, Dad.'

'Think you ever will?'

'On videotape, yes. Eventually.'

'And that'll be the proof you're looking for?'

'It'll be the proof everyone's looking for.'

'I doubt it. A skeleton's what you need. Tangible remains. Strange none have ever turned up. These creatures have to die . . . if they live.'

'They live.'

'What do you think, Nicholas?'

'Me?' Nick had been hoping not to be asked for his opinion. He wondered if his father had realized that. 'Oh, I've got a pretty open mind on the subject.'

'An open mind? Well, that's an excellent thing to have in its way. Pity you've not put it to better use, but . . . there's still time, I suppose.'

'Tell us what *you* think, Dad,' said Andrew, so abruptly that Nick suspected he had intervened for his sake. 'About big cats.'

'What I think, my boy, is that people want to believe in them. Perhaps they need to believe in them. Myth can be as powerful as reality. That was one of the first lessons I learned as an archaeologist. Your grandfather and I assisted Ralegh Radford with his excavations at Tintagel in the nineteen thirties.' Nick and Andrew nodded in unison. This was, after all, a tale they had heard before. The first serious archaeological investigation of Tintagel, north Cornwall's famous clifftop version of Camelot, had begun in 1933, under

55

the supervision of the subsequently celebrated director of the British School at Rome, C. A. Ralegh Radford. Godfrey Paleologus and his teenage son Michael had been among his amateur helpers. There was a photograph in the study of the pair of them on site with Radford in the summer of 1935. 'Those excavations revealed that the castle was constructed, probably in the twelve thirties, at the behest of Richard, Earl of Cornwall, brother of King Henry the Third. There wasn't a trace of King Arthur. Not a splinter of the Round Table, nor a single shard of knightly lance. But do you think that stopped the Arthurian connection being peddled? Do you think that stopped people believing they beheld the ruins of Camelot? Of course not. They saw what they wanted to see. Well, much the same applies to your elusive big cats, I'm afraid. They—'

'Beverages ahoy,' announced Basil, propelling the door open with his foot and steering the tea trolley smartly through. 'Plus birthday cake, of course. We're all sybarites today.'

Basil was hardly to know it from the response he received, but Nick for one was grateful for his arrival. Their father's lecturing mode could easily segue into a rant, which would make even-tempered discussion of a delicate issue all but impossible.

Oddly enough, however, Michael did not seem to mind breaking off from his disquisition. He puffed at his pipe and spectated placidly as seats were taken, cups of tea or coffee distributed, slices of cake handed round. He even mumbled an endorsement of the tribute Irene paid to the absent Pru. He laid his pipe aside, nibbled at his cake and drank his tea, then asked for a second cup.

And then, after Andrew had given a vaguer answer to a vague question from Anna about how it felt to be fifty, he suddenly made his move.

'Which of you has been nominated to tell me I've got to go, then?' All eyes were suddenly upon him. He smiled, relishing the intentness of his audience. 'Have you perhaps been brought down specially to do the deed, Nicholas?'

Nick did not know how to respond. He felt his stomach

tighten. 'It's not a question of . . .' He looked round helplessly at his siblings. 'I mean . . .'

'I was going to raise the subject of Mr Tantris's offer, Dad,' said Irene. She set down her cup. 'We didn't draw straws to decide. It's something we all agree has to be discussed.'

'So, let's discuss it.' Michael finished his tea and beamed at them. 'Tantris has offered me half a million pounds plus my fees at some de luxe old fogeys' home in Tavistock to get his hands on Trennor. Correct?'

'Well, it's not—'

'The full story? No, it isn't, is it? About Tantris we know nothing, except that he has money and an interest in antique stained glass. Miss Hartley the ecclesiastical art historian theorizes that the Doom Window of St Neot lies hidden somewhere in this house. Tantris wants me out so that his minions can tap and scan and probe every square inch of wall and floor and ceiling in search of something that will tell them where to start in with the drills and pickaxes. To get me out, he proposes to pay me about fifty per cent more than the house is worth and to bribe you five with the cost of putting me up in conscience-salving comfort at Gorton Lodge. Since I won't get the chance to spend my savings because I'll die of sheer bloody boredom within a twelvemonth, that'll leave you to share the loot between you, which I expect you've already calculated could be substantially more than half a million pounds if you negotiate hard enough with the fabled Tantris of the bottomless pockets.'

'You're painting this in the worst possible light, Dad,' Irene protested.

'I'm being accurate, my girl, that's all. The time has come to be, I rather think.'

'We're genuinely concerned about you.'

'You had a fall recently,' put in Anna.

'How considerate of me.'

'What if Pru hadn't found you?'

'It had just happened when she arrived, for God's sake. I'd have got back up without her help perfectly easily.'

'That's not what she said.'

'She's nearly as old as I am and about one twentieth as intelligent. You can't seriously give her version of events any credence.'

'You're not getting any younger, Dad,' said Andrew. 'Sooner or later you'll have to think about moving to more practical accommodation.'

'Perhaps I'd prefer that to be later.'

'So might we,' said Irene, 'if this offer hadn't been made. But it has been. We can't ignore it.'

'I'd like to know why not.'

'There's surely a compelling reason that has nothing to do with money,' said Nick, sensing his chance had come.

'And what might that be?' His father's gaze focused on him narrowly.

'The glass. The Doom Window. You said myth can be as powerful as reality. But this is both, isn't it? A historical mystery. An artistic treasure. An archaeological quest. This should be meat and drink to you, Dad. You should be eager to lead the search, not trying to obstruct it. I don't understand. I can't believe sentiment is clouding your academic judgement. You'd condemn that in anyone else, wouldn't you?'

Michael stuck out his lower lip and glowered at Nick for half a minute of suspended silence, then growled, 'Not in these circumstances.'

'What makes them so different?'

'Judgement is the key to it, boy. I don't happen to think tearing this house apart – the house your mother died in – on the say-so of a dubiously qualified chit of a girl—'

'Oh God, Dad,' Anna interrupted. 'This isn't about being upstaged by a woman, is it?'

'Is there something amiss with Ms Hartley's qualifications?' Basil mildly enquired.

'They're not on a par with mine, since you ask. Not remotely.'

'The Bawden letter is the link between Trennor and the St Neot glass,' said Nick. 'Ms Hartley explained that quite clearly. Are you questioning her interpretation of the evidence?'

'You've seen the evidence, have you, boy?'

'Well, no, but—'

'Exactly. You've accepted her word for it. You all have, because it suited you to do so. Trust nothing except primary sources in this game. And not always those. That's my motto.'

'I'm sure Ms Hartley would be delighted to show you the letter.'

'Maybe so. But why hasn't it come to light before? That's what I'd like to know.'

'Ask her.'

'I have. Unnoticed until she cast her eye over the archive it was part of. That was her answer.'

'But you don't believe her.'

Michael looked down, his confidence ebbing marginally. 'I'm not saying that.'

Irene sighed. 'Then what *are* you saying, Dad?'

The question seemed to give the old man pause for considerable thought. He picked up his pipe, then put it down again, then said, 'I'm saying I'm the only unbiased judge of what's best to do.'

'We're biased,' said Anna, 'but you're not?'

'I can put my bias to one side, Anna.'

'And we can't?'

'Apparently not.'

'That's . . . ridiculous. And arrogant to boot.'

'Arrogant? Depends on your point of view. And if you want to think me ridiculous, fine. I've reached an age where that's more or less taken as read anyway.'

'*What*?' Anna sunk her head in her hands.

'I won't be selling Trennor to a faceless millionaire to facilitate a wild glass chase *or* to rescue any of you from the financial consequences of your own fecklessness and there's an end to it.'

They were words uttered in anger. His children knew that. He probably knew so himself. But since he had always maintained that a man should stand by his words as well as his principles, he was unlikely to withdraw the remarks. They were on the record. And they told a truth that comforted no-one. He believed they had mismanaged their lives and thereby forfeited the right to prevent him mismanaging his own.

A silence had fallen. Basil's clearance of his throat broke it, but Andrew was first to speak. 'An end of it? Yeah, Dad, it certainly sounds like it to me.' He stood up. 'Reckon I'll be on my way. Before I say something I might regret.'

'If you think I'll regret a single—'

'No, Dad, I don't. Regrets, you haven't had a few, right? In fact, not one. *Vous ne regrettez rien*. That's wonderful. That's a real achievement.'

'Andrew,' said Irene, 'don't go like—'

But he was already making for the door. 'Let him go if he wants to,' said Michael, shaking his head in apparent denial of responsibility for his son's reaction.

'It's his birthday, Dad,' said Anna. 'Can't you lighten up just a little?'

'I remember his real birthday, my girl. The day he was born. Fifty years ago almost to the hour. I remember the hopes I had for him. And for the brothers and sisters we planned he would have. Those hopes haven't been fulfilled, let me tell you, not nearly. So, don't ask me to . . . "lighten up".'

Andrew was in the kitchen by now. So was Irene. The others could hear her trying to dissuade him from leaving. Nick knew she was wasting her time. Andrew was almost as stubborn as their father. Irene had never quite grasped that simple truth. He could remember her pleading with Andrew to come out of his bedroom and rejoin the family in the living room at their house in Oxford after some row with the old man. The memory was a collation of innumerable similar incidents, in which Irene was always the mediator – and always in vain. Nothing had changed. And nothing, he realized now, was going to.

Basil caught his eye and gave a despairing grimace, sowing

the suspicion in Nick's mind that Basil for one had anticipated this turn of events in every grisly detail. Including Anna's loss of temper, which was gathering momentum at that moment.

'*Your* hopes, Dad. Yes, we've heard a lot about them and how far short of them we've fallen. Do you ever wonder why we've disappointed you? Do you ever consider that it could have something to do with your own narrow-minded, mean-spirited approach to life?'

'Don't be absurd.'

'Have you any idea how hard it's been for Andrew recently, scraping by at Carwether?'

'Farming was his choice, not mine.'

'So what? I'm not asking you to give him careers advice. I'm asking you to sympathize with him. To *understand*. But you can't, can you? Or won't. You refuse to understand any of us.'

'I understand you only too well.'

'Yeah? Well, that works both ways. Don't think I haven't rumbled you.'

'As a matter of fact, my girl, I—'

The back door slammed so hard that the china in the cabinet next to the fireplace tinkled like a wind chime. Then Irene came back into the room. 'He's gone,' she said with a sigh. 'There was no talking him out of it.'

'There was no talking him out of any of the many follies he's embarked on in his time,' said Michael, quite neutrally, almost analytically. 'It's not in his nature to take advice.'

'Any more than it's in yours,' snapped Anna.

'On the contrary. I heed the advice of those qualified to give it. I always have. It's how I made my way in the world. It's how I made a success of my life. Whereas . . .' He smiled at them. 'Well, we demonstrate our own cases.'

'This is hopeless,' said Irene, her expression underlining the point. She looked like someone who had carefully and lengthily planned a course of action, only to see her plan disintegrate as soon as she embarked upon it. Which was, of course, exactly what had happened. 'I think I'd like to go home. Nick?'

He shrugged. 'Fine by me.'

'Withdraw and regroup,' said Michael. 'Yes. Quite the best tactic, in the circumstances. Retreat to a place of safety and prepare an alternative approach. It won't work, of course.' His smile broadened into a beam of contentment at what he clearly regarded as their rout. 'But don't let me stop you trying.'

'Why did we think it would be any different?' Irene asked rhetorically an hour later, in the back bar of the Old Ferry Inn. There were no customers to hear her words, evening opening time still being some way off. Her audience comprised Nick, Anna and Basil. They had left Trennor more or less simultaneously and proceeded in convoy to Saltash. Now they sat around the fire, staring glumly at each other and wondering where any of them went from here. 'I mean, how could we be so naïve as to believe he'd see reason when he's never seen it in my experience so much as once in his life? How *could* we?'

'It is difficult not to think of one's father as one would wish him to be rather than as he truly is,' Basil mused.

'I don't like him,' said Anna, sounding surprised by the realization. 'I love him, of course. But I don't actually like him. I mean, not at all.'

'I think I'll phone Andrew,' said Irene, jumping up. 'See how he is.'

She went to the wall-mounted phone behind the bar to make the call. They watched her dial and stand with the receiver in her hand, listening to the ringing tone on the line. A minute slowly passed. Then she put the phone down.

'I wish he'd get an answering machine,' she murmured.

Perhaps he was already out searching for big cats with his nightscope and video camera, Nick thought. He would find them easier to catch than their father, that was for sure. 'We should take Dad's advice,' he said softly.

'*What*?' Anna gaped at him.

'Reasoning with him won't work. He's made his mind up and there's nothing – absolutely nothing – we can do to change it. It's as simple as that. Forget Tantris's offer. Forget Gorton Lodge. And tell Elspeth Hartley it's no go. Anything else is a waste of effort.'

'That's pure defeatism,' Irene protested.

'If you like.'

'Well, I don't like.'

'We could change *our* minds,' said Basil. 'Urge Dad to reject the offer.'

Anna made a face. 'You mean on the basis that he'd accept it just to be contrary?'

'Quite so.'

'You are joking, aren't you?'

Basil grinned at her. 'In the circumstances, what else can one do?'

After Anna and Basil had left and Irene had opened up for the evening, Nick went for a walk round the town. Saltash on a Sunday night in January was about as lively as a graveyard. He was surrounded by thousands of people of whom he saw barely a dozen. Not that he was in search of company. He could have had that by remaining at the Old Ferry. Solitude was what he most needed after the débâcle that the day had been. He had had his fill of talking. And of thinking.

But thoughts nevertheless swirled in his head. Why was his father so implacably opposed to the Doom Window project? Had he deliberately antagonized them in order to avoid answering that question? And what had he been getting at when he asked why the Bawden letter had been overlooked for so long? His behaviour made no obvious sense. He had always been obstinate, but that afternoon he had gone beyond obstinacy, fomenting an exchange of insults that would sour relations with several of his children for months to come. Andrew and Anna would probably refuse to speak to him for

63

the foreseeable future, and Irene would certainly keep her distance. He must have known . . .

That was it, of course. He *had* known. Nick could not help smiling at the old man's audacity. A family rift was just what he needed to nix the Tantris deal without having to explain his opposition to it, which he knew he would not be able to do. He had found himself in an impossible postion. And then he had found a way out of it. With a little help from his children.

# CHAPTER FIVE

Nick's departure next morning went unmarked by much in the way of a send-off. Irene was depressed and distracted by the events of the previous afternoon. She had still not spoken to Andrew and could hardly imagine when she might bring herself to speak to their father. She would bounce back, of course – Nick knew her well enough to be sure of that – but it would take a few days at least. Accordingly, he did not ask what she would tell Elspeth Hartley. She would think of something – in due course.

The morning was grey and mizzly, the Hamoaze draped in a veil of murk, orange-clad workers swarming over the damp girders of the Tamar Bridge. Nick followed the nose-to-tail commuter traffic over to the Devon shore, paid his toll, then put his foot down as soon as he hit the dual carriageway. It was time to leave. And in so many ways, he was glad of it.

Two and a half hours later he pulled into Delamere Services on the M4 to grab a coffee and stretch his legs. Before getting out of the car he checked his mobile, which he had switched off for the drive. There was a message waiting for him – from Irene.

'Something terrible's happened, Nick. Call me as soon as you can.'

He pushed the car door open and puzzled over her words as he breathed the chill air and listened to the rush of vehicles on the motorway. Then he phoned the Old Ferry, already anticipating, even before Irene answered, what 'something terrible' might mean. He thought of Andrew and the state of mind in which he had left Trennor. He thought . . . and he wondered. Then the phone was picked up.

'Old Ferry Inn.'

'Irene? It's me.'

'Nick. Thank God. Where are you?'

'Never mind. What's happened?'

'Are you at the wheel?'

'No. I'm parked. What—'

'Dad's dead.'

'Sorry?' He had heard, of course. But he could not trust himself to have heard correctly.

'Dad's dead.' Irene sobbed, then swallowed hard. 'Pru found him this morning at Trennor.'

'I can't . . . What . . .'

'I know. It's hard to come to terms with. He was so very much alive yesterday. All his wits about him – too much about him, for our liking.' She sniffed. 'Sorry. It's a shock, I know. Sorry to have to inflict it on you.'

'What happened? Was it . . . his heart?'

'No. A fall of some kind. Down the cellar steps, apparently. The policeman said he seemed to have hit his head, probably on the handrail.'

Nick closed his eyes. There had been many times in his life when he had silently wished his father dead. He could admit that to himself, though he never would to anyone else. Those times were behind him now, buried by the overdue realization that the mistakes he had made were not his father's fault, even though he had displayed such outspoken intolerance of them that it was tempting to lay them at his door. Michael Paleologus had been no-one's idea of a perfect

66

parent, treating his family much as he had his students, with a kind of baffled disbelief at their capacity to misunderstand how and what to think. The older he had become, the more Nick had grudgingly admired his refusal to compromise. He had died as he had lived – believing he knew best.

'Nick?'

'Yes. Sorry. A fall, you say?'

'So it seems.'

'He was unsteady on his feet. You were right.'

'I know. But . . .'

'What?'

'Do you think we upset him yesterday, badgering him about selling up? Do you think that might have . . . led to this?'

Nick recalled the expression on the old man's face as he had laid into them the previous afternoon. He had not been angry. He had not even been hurt. He had merely been as self-righteous as ever – and as he would probably want to be remembered. 'No, Irene. I don't think so for a moment.'

Michael Paleologus's innate sense of timing had not deserted him in death. Nick had been absolutely certain he was returning that day to the known quantity of the life he led away and apart from his family. Instead, five hours after driving out of Plymouth, he was driving back into it. His father had posthumously decreed that he was not to escape so lightly.

His destination was not the Old Ferry, nor yet Trennor, but 254 Citadel Road. Irene had phoned him when he was half-way back along the M5 to say that she had contacted Andrew, who was coming into Plymouth to assist with the 'arrange-ments', by which Nick took it she meant consulting an undertaker. It was more convenient for them all to meet afterwards at Anna's flat.

They made a sorrowful gathering in the cramped basement lounge. Basil doled out tea, coffee and biscuits as soon as Nick arrived and Irene gave him a tearful hug.

'The police wanted a formal identification,' she said. 'Andrew and I went.'

'Sod of a place, that mortuary,' put in Andrew, shaking his head. 'Dad lying there, looking as if he might sit up any minute and tell us not to be so stupid.'

'He'll be transferred to the chapel of rest tomorrow,' Irene went on. 'After the post-mortem.'

'Post-mortem? I thought you said he'd hit his head.'

'So it seems. But they need to check, I suppose. There'll have to be an inquest.'

'Did you . . . see the wound?'

'No. It was at the back of his head, they said. We didn't ask to see it.'

'Nor would you have,' murmured Andrew. 'Believe me.'

'Have you talked about a date for the funeral?'

'It'll probably be next Monday,' Irene replied. 'You can stay down until then, can't you?'

'Of course.'

'We've made an appointment to see Baskcomb tomorrow.'

'Right.'

'We'll need to think about hymns as well. And flowers. And announcements. And—' She broke off, sighing and sat down, pressing a hand to her forehead. 'I thought he'd live for years, I really did. Years and years.'

'You won't have to do all the sorting out, Irene,' said Anna, putting her arm round her sister. 'It'll be a team effort.'

'How's Pru?' asked Nick.

'Pretty upset when I saw her,' Anna replied. 'Not exactly coherent. The police had fazed her with all their questions. They won't let us into Trennor, you know.'

'What?'

'Just routine,' answered Irene. 'It won't be for long.'

Nick frowned down at his sister, puzzling over exactly what was being left unsaid. 'Routine?'

'In case it was not an accident.' Basil's voice sliced softly through the silence left trailing by Nick's query. 'They are paid to think of such things.'

*   *   *

The ramifications of Basil's tartly accurate observation coursed through Nick's thoughts, much as they no doubt did through his brothers' and sisters'. But they were not discussed, nor even referred to, until later in the evening. Andrew had asked if anyone wanted to join him for a drink at the Yard Arm before he headed back to Carwether. Sensing there were going to be no other takers, Nick volunteered.

It was a quiet night at the pub. They settled themselves at a table set in its own discreet corner and toasted their father's memory in Courage Best Bitter.

'A real shock, eh, Nick? Who'd have thought it, after that vintage performance he put on yesterday?'

'Perhaps it took too much out of him.'

'Less than it took out of me, I'll bet. I'd have made sure we parted on better terms if I'd . . .' He shrugged. 'Well, you know.'

'Yes. I know.'

'It'll take some getting used to. Him not being around, I mean.'

'It certainly will.'

'Some getting used to, yeah.' Andrew took a deep swallow of beer. 'I'll say.'

'When I got Irene's message, that something terrible had happened, I thought for a moment . . .' Nick hesitated.

'What did you think?'

'That it was you.'

'*Me*?'

'Well, after the way you stormed out of Trennor . . .'

'You thought I might have gone home and strung myself up from a beam in the barn?'

'Not exactly. I just—'

'I was pretty upset, Nick, I don't mind admitting. But what's new? Dad's needled me for years.' Andrew looked away, apparently lost momentarily in recollection of such times.

'What's new is that he won't be needling you any more.'

69

'No. He won't.' Andrew chuckled wryly. 'And you know what? I'll miss it.'

'Me too.'

'Yeah.' Andrew looked back at his brother. 'Be hard to explain that to anyone, though, wouldn't it?'

'It would.'

'Which is why we ought to keep quiet about yesterday's bust-up, in the unlikely event that the police start sniffing around. Mention a family row – or Tantris's money – and that lot could begin to wonder whether, well . . .' He lowered his voice, unnecessarily, since there was no-one within earshot. 'Did he fall or was he pushed?'

'Nobody's going to wonder that, Andrew.' Even as he said it, Nick felt uncertain on the point. To an outsider, apprised of the circumstances, it could seem a possibility. 'Oh God. You don't think they might, do you?'

'Not if we don't give them any reason to. Look, obviously we'll accept Tantris's offer, but there's bound to be a delay. Dad's will will have to be probated and the rest of it. Then there's the inquest. We don't need to rush into anything.'

'From what you're saying, we can't.'

'Exactly. Tantris isn't going to go away. We just have to bide our time.' Andrew stared thoughtfully into his beer. 'Dad was right. He'd have hated being in an old folk's home, however well appointed. It was a quick exit and maybe a merciful one. We could look back on this one day and think it was, well, the best way for it to be.' He glanced up at Nick. 'Don't you reckon?'

Andrew had parked his car in one of the streets that led up from Citadel Road towards the Hoe. Nick walked to it with him after they left the Yard Arm. A cold wind was getting up, clearing the drizzle and revealing a window of stars in the inky cloudbank out over the Sound.

'I'm hoping Tom will come down for the funeral,' said Andrew as they neared the Land Rover.

'He's bound to, surely.'

70

'Only if I succeed in contacting him. All I've reached so far is his answerphone. I could ask Kate if she's got a mobile number for him, but . . . I'd rather not.'

'Won't you tell her about Dad? They used to get on well together.'

'Suppose I'll have to. Christ, you don't think she'll want to attend, do you?'

'I don't know.'

'Can't stop her, I suppose. As long as she doesn't bring that smug bastard Mawson with her. Wives and children and ex-wives' new husbands. You're well out of all that, Nick, take my word for it.'

'Glad to.'

'Yeah. I'll bet.' They came abreast of the car. Andrew unlocked the door, climbed in, wound down the window and started up, the engine spluttering in the cold air and sending up a plume of exhaust. 'See you soon, then. I'll—' Something caught his eye. He gestured through the windscreen at a piece of paper wedged under the wiper. 'Bloody fly posters. Shift that, would you, Nick?'

Nick slid the offending item out from beneath the wiper blade. Before he had a chance to examine it, however, Andrew had clunked the Land Rover into gear and pulled away, shouting a goodnight as he went. Nick gave a half-hearted wave and watched him turn out of sight at the end of the street.

Only then did he walk into the pool of amber light beneath the nearest streetlamp and look at what he held in his hand: a sealed blank white envelope, dampened by the drizzle. He tore it open, pulled out the contents, and found himself looking at a condolences card. There was an artist's impression of a candle, beside the Gothically scripted words *In Sympathy*. He opened the card, where more words were printed. *Thinking of you at this sad time*. But there was no signature. No name. No message. The condolences were strictly anonymous.

\*　　\*　　\*

71

The incident grew more worrying the longer Nick thought about it. He could not help turning it over in his mind as he drove back to the Old Ferry later that evening, secretly glad that he and Irene were making the journey in separate cars. He did not want to tell her about the card for the simple yet disturbing reason that it made no sense. No-one in the Citadel Road area knew Andrew, let alone his Land Rover. If the card had been dropped through the letterbox at Anna's flat, it would have been puzzling enough. As it was, the message seemed intended for Andrew alone – for reasons which Nick could not even guess at.

Irene had closed the pub for the evening. A sign apologizing for the fact and citing a family bereavement as the reason hung on the door, palely lit by the headlamps of Nick's car as he slowed for the turn into the yard.

He entered by the back door, which had been left unlocked for him, cut through the darkened bar and carried his bag up the stairs. As he reached the top, the television news cut out in the sitting room and Irene called to him through the open doorway. 'Nick?'

'Who else?'

'Join me for a nightcap?'

'OK.'

Irene had left Anna's flat half an hour or so ahead of Nick. It looked to him as if she had hit the whisky since then. The heat from the gas fire had filled the room with the smell of it. He poured himself a finger and sat down opposite her, noticing as he did so the tears welling in her eyes.

'Bad times, eh, sis? Bad, sad times.'

'I think it was worse when Mum died.' Irene thumbed away the tears and sniffed. 'This is mostly shock.'

'Well, we had plenty of warning with Mum, didn't we?'

'Too much.'

'Is none at all better?'

'Not sure. Maybe.'

'Did they tell you . . . exactly when they think he died?'

72

'Ten hours or so before Pru found him, apparently. So, late last night.'

'And he was at the bottom of the cellar steps?'

'Yes.' She smiled. 'Maybe he'd gone to fetch a vintage claret to celebrate the defeat of his children.' More tears came then, which she mopped with a tissue.

'Did he have a bottle with him?'

'Sorry?'

'Was he carrying a bottle when he fell? I mean, why else would he have gone down there?'

Irene frowned. 'I don't know. Nobody's mentioned it. Maybe he hadn't got that far.'

'But he must have, if he fell as he was leaving. Why would he be leaving empty-handed?'

'How do you know he fell as he was leaving?'

'Because the injury was to the back of his head. That's what you told me.'

'Yes, but . . .' Irene's blurred gaze snapped into focus. 'What are you getting at?'

'Nothing. Just . . . trying to understand what happened.'

'What happened was that he slipped or tripped . . . and fell. What possible difference can it make whether he was coming or going at the time?'

'None, I suppose. Except . . .' Nick took a sip of whisky. 'Andrew reckons we should be careful not to mention Tantris's offer to the police.'

'It's none of their business.'

'No. Precisely. But if they got wind of it, well, they might put two and two together and make five. Like Basil said, they're paid to be suspicious.'

'Rubbish. They're far too busy trying to solve real crimes to waste time looking for imaginary ones.'

'Let's hope you're right.'

'Of course I'm right.'

'OK, OK.' Nick sipped some more whisky and smiled appeasingly. 'The shock's probably got to me too.'

'Probably.' Irene looked fondly at him, her anger fading as

quickly as it had flared. She leaned forward and patted his hand where it was resting on his knee. 'I didn't mean to be tetchy. We need to help each other through this, not bicker.'

'You're right. Sorry.'

'Me too.'

'Have you spoken to Laura?'

'Yes. She's coming down at the weekend. The school were happy for her to leave earlier, but I couldn't see the point. It'll be nice to have all the formalities out of the way when she arrives.'

'She'll be needing her room. I'll move out.'

'Where to?'

'A hotel, I suppose.'

'Wouldn't it make more sense to stay at Trennor?'

It would, of course. Nick could not deny it, intimidated though he was by the prospect, for reasons he preferred not to analyse.

'It'd be good to have one of us in residence, however briefly. So that the place doesn't feel completely abandoned.'

Nick decided against challenging his sister's ascription of feelings to a pile of granite and mortar. 'That's settled, then,' he said, before finishing his whisky.

Nick did not sleep well that night. He was glad he had pulled back when he had in his conversation with Irene. There was no knowing how she would have reacted had he pursued the logic of his argument. Their father had died as the result of a fall, attributed by Irene to a trip or a slip, which he was undoubtedly prone to. He could equally well, of course, have been pushed. In theory, at least. But if so – theoretically – then who might have pushed him? And why? What kept Nick awake was not the difficulty of finding answers to those questions. It was the effort needed to avoid finding them.

Next morning, on his jogging route round Saltash, he dropped the torn quarters of the condolences card into a litter bin he passed.

# CHAPTER SIX

Their appointment with Baskcomb was at four o'clock, timed so as not to interfere with opening hours at the Old Ferry or Anna's shift at the nursing home. Nick was glad of the delay in one sense, since it gave him an opportunity to learn what he could from the only person with any first-hand knowledge of the circumstances of his father's death.

After Irene had opened up for the day, he slipped out and drove north towards Landulph. Trennor was embargoed, he knew. But Pru Curnow's cottage was not. And the old lady was scarcely noted for her reticence.

Rain was falling and had been since dawn. Either side of the main street sloping down through Cargreen towards the river had become a watercourse. Drains were spouting and gutters overflowing. There was no-one about and Nick was hardly surprised. He was actually quite pleased by the weather, since it reduced the chances of Pru being anywhere but in her own home.

He parked as close as he could to the door of Chough Cottage, but that was not close enough to spare him a drenching dash through the rain. Nor did the cottage boast much in the way of a porch. Fortunately, though, Pru responded promptly to his yanks at the bell-pull.

'Nicholas,' she announced, peering up at him through glasses that made her eyes look like those of some giant deep-sea fish. 'This is a nice surprise. You best ways come in before you drown.'

The front door led straight into the sitting room, which was crammed with a car-boot sale's worth of bric-à-brac. Nick had forgotten just how small the house was. The same applied to its owner. Pru Curnow bustled ahead of him, a tiny figure in a floral housecoat, her white hair recently permed and blue-tinted. A West Highland terrier yapped excitedly from its station by the television and cocked a snowy-fringed eye at Nick.

'I'm that sorry about your father, Nicholas. 'Twas a fearful shock, I don't mind telling you.'

'It must have been.'

'Will you have some tea? Or sherry? I sometimes have a glass around this time. I had to have several yesterday.'

'All right. Sherry. Thanks.'

Pru opened a corner cabinet, setting its contents rattling and tinkling, which drew another volley of yaps from the dog. 'Be quiet, Finlay, do.' The plea had a measure of success. Finlay slowly lapsed into silence as Pru poured the Bristol Cream. 'Here's to your father,' she said, taking a generous sip. 'May he rest in peace.'

They sat down either side of the electric fire, whose glowing bars were emitting a fearsome though narrowly focused beam of heat. Finlay pattered between their feet before settling on the rug.

'We're grateful for everything you did, Pru,' said Nick. 'Not just yesterday, I mean. Looking after Dad can't always have been easy.'

'No more it was. When your mother passed away, 'twas in my mind to leave him to it, being as he didn't have what you'd call an accommodating nature. But as it turned out . . . we rubbed along.' She took another sip of sherry. 'I'll miss him, temper and all.'

'We all will.'

'Have you settled on a date for the funeral?'

'It'll probably be next Monday. We'll let you know when it's confirmed. There are . . . one or two complications. A post-mortem, things like that.'

'There'd have to be one, of course. I perfectly understand that. Though why I'm not allowed into Trennor to clear things up in the meantime is a mystery to me.'

'It won't be for long, Pru. We're seeing Mr Baskcomb later. He'll sort it out.'

'I do hope so. There'll be a goodly amount of bottoming to do after your party on Sunday.'

'There's no need for you to worry about that.'

'Who else is there to worry about it? I should hope you'll still want me to look to such things. For as long as you keep the house, any rate.'

'Of course, of course. If you're happy to.'

'Least I can do, Nicholas. Your mother was very kind to me. She'd want me to keep an eye on the place.'

'You don't mind going back, then? After what happened yesterday morning?'

'Lord bless you, no. I'm that close to the grave myself that death holds few terrors for me. If your father came back as a ghost, it'd give me the chance to give him a piece of my mind without fearing for my job.' She laughed and Nick joined in. Then she stopped. ''Twas no sight for the squeamish, though, and that's a fact.'

'How did you . . . I mean . . .'

'How did I come upon him? Well, I let myself in as usual, around ten o'clock, and there was neither sight nor sound of him. I thought he must have gone out for a walk or somesuch, though the weather was scarcely fit for strolling and his car was in the garage. Then I noticed the cellar door standing open, with the light on inside. I popped my head round the door and looked down the steps. And there he was, sprawled on his back at the bottom. I knew he was dead at once, just by the way he was lying. I thought he'd broken his neck, though that young constable who spoke to me yesterday reckoned a crack on the back of his head was what did for him. Well, I didn't see that, of course.'

'Poor old Dad.'

'I should say. It only takes one slip at our age, his *and* mine, and slips are what you grow liable to, take my word for it. He had that fall a few weeks back. It should have been a warning to him.'

'Dad wasn't one to heed warnings.'

'No more he was.' Pru set down her glass and stared thoughtfully at it. 'He'd got a little too fond of the liquor these last few years, which can't have helped.'

'So I gather.'

'That'll be what took him down to the cellar, I dare say. One of those fine wines of his.'

'Did he have a bottle with him?'

'Pardon?' Pru frowned.

'Well, if he went down to fetch a bottle of wine, he'd have had it with him when he left, wouldn't he? It would probably have smashed as he fell.'

'There was no smashed bottle.'

'No?'

'No.'

'You're sure.'

'Definitely. Is it important?'

'Shouldn't think so,' Nick lied, feeling certain in his own mind that it almost certainly *did* matter.

'Course, if you don't mind me saying, Nicholas, as far as the liquor went . . .'

'Go on.'

'It's not my place to comment on such things, really.'

'I'd be grateful if you did.'

'Well, he'd been drinking even more just lately, not a doubt of it. A lot more.'

'Really?'

'Oh yes. I'd know, wouldn't I? He wasn't one to chuck out his own empties.'

Nick grinned. 'I suppose not.'

'I put it down to all the argufying about selling the house.'

'Ah. You know about that, do you?'

'Couldn't help knowing. Matter of fact, I was at Trennor the day Miss Hartley called round, which was the start of it all, seemingly. I didn't know what they were talking about at the time, of course. I had my work to attend to. But your father told me about the offer later. Came right out with it, he did. Said I had a right to know, seeing as I'd be out of a job if the sale went through.'

'Look, Pru, we'd have—'

'Oh, don't worry about me, Nicholas. If someone's offering you a fair price for the place – and this is more than fair, so your sister tells me – then you should take it. Time I retired, anyhow. Why your father set his face against it I wouldn't know. I don't think he quite trusted Miss Hartley, though. I can say that. And I can see why. There was something, well, strange about her.'

'Was there?'

'Like her mentioning you, for one thing.'

'Mentioning me?'

'When she called at Trennor.'

'She mentioned *me* – specifically?'

'As she was leaving. I heard them talking at the door from the kitchen. Miss Hartley said, "Are you the father of Nicholas Paleologus?" Like she knew you.'

'But she didn't.'

'No. That's right. 'Cos when your father said yes and asked her if she knew you, she said, "No, but I've heard of him." Peculiar, I thought. Very peculiar.'

'What did Dad think?'

'Well, your father asked her what she meant by it, but she only said, "It doesn't matter," then took herself off smartish. I suppose it doesn't matter really, when you come down to it.'

'Probably not.' But that was Nick's second lie of the morning. It mattered. Oh yes, it mattered all right.

\*　　\*　　\*

79

Nick found himself with plenty to think about over a solitary lunch at the Spaniards, Cargreen's riverside pub. The foul weather had deterred most potential customers and he had the bar more or less to himself. He sat by the fire, listening to the rain beating against the windows, wondering what exactly was going on. How had Elspeth Hartley heard of him? He had certainly never heard of her. The only answer that came to mind was one he very much wanted to disbelieve. And the only way to find out if he could disbelieve it—

Nick's mobile trilled, causing him to jump with surprise. But a bigger surprise followed when he pulled the phone out of his pocket and pressed the button.

'Hello.'

'Nick? Elspeth Hartley here.'

'Elspeth.' His heart missed a beat. 'Hi.'

'I've just been speaking to Irene. I was really sorry to hear about your father. It must have been quite a shock.'

'It certainly was.'

'Please accept my condolences.'

The sentiment was faintly old-fashioned, sowing the fleeting suspicion in Nick's mind that she might already have tendered her condolences – anonymously. 'Thanks.'

'Is this a bad time to talk?'

'No.'

'OK. Good. I phoned Irene to ask if you'd been able to persuade your father to change his mind over the weekend. I never expected— Well, it's just terrible, what happened.'

'Yeah.'

'Irene couldn't say much. There were a lot of customers in. She suggested I call you and ask . . . well, where we go from here, I suppose.'

'*We* go to see our solicitor. Then we go to our father's funeral.'

'Sorry. Of course. Look, I—'

'Tell you what. Why don't we meet, later today, after the solicitor's said his piece? I should be able to answer your questions then.'

'Oh. All right. Great.' She sounded relieved at his change of tone. 'In Plymouth?'

'If that's where you are.'

'It is, yeah. What time would suit you?'

'Six o'clock.'

'That's fine with me. Where do you want to meet?'

'You choose.'

'OK. Do you know the Compton? It's a pub in Mannamead.'

'Can't say I do. But, don't worry, I'll find it.'

'Until six, then.'

'Yeah. Until six.'

Baskcomb and Co. shared a Georgian terrace house with a dental surgery in The Crescent, on the western fringe of the city centre. Maurice Baskcomb, Michael Paleologus's solicitor, was the grandson of the founder of the business. He was in his sixties now, Nick calculated, though he looked about fifty-five, just as he had in his forties, a ruddy-cheeked, bald-pated, plain-mannered man of the law who valued efficiency and economy and attracted clients of like mind.

Elegant accommodation and stylish attire did not figure in Baskcomb's mental landscape. He received the Paleologus siblings in his skew-ceilinged junk-room of an office, dressed in a suit that had seen better days but so long ago that they had passed from memory. The gathering of sufficient chairs seemed to strain the firm's resources of furniture close to breaking point. And Baskcomb's offer of sympathy verged on the perfunctory. But that, Nick bore in mind, was the nature of the man. Michael Paleologus would probably have approved mightily. Maurice Baskcomb was no more an ambulance-chaser than he was a skirt-chaser.

'I've been in touch with the police and coroner as you requested, Mrs Viner,' he announced, with a nod to Irene. 'You'll be pleased to know that your father's death is not being treated as suspicious. The post-mortem raised no cause for concern and your father's body has now been transferred to the care of the undertaker. The coroner will grant a disposal certificate tomorrow, so you may proceed with funerary arrangements as soon as you wish.'

'But there'll still have to be an inquest?' asked Andrew.

'In due course, Mr Paleologus, yes. A mere formality, though. Its only real significance is that it will delay the final settlement of your father's estate.'

'By how long?'

'That depends on the coroner's schedule.'

'What my brother is concerned about,' Irene began, 'as I think you're aware . . .'

'Is the offer for Trennor.' Baskcomb grinned at them in that way he had of conferring his blessing on his clients' pecuniary preoccupations. 'I quite understand, Mrs Viner. But the law is hard to hurry. Believe me, I speak from experience. Your father's will is a straightforward document, sharing his estate equally between the five of you and appointing his sons as joint executors along with me, as I believe you know. I gather his financial affairs were uncomplicated. The estate amounts in essence to Trennor, on which there is no mortgage or secured loan, plus a modest amount of savings. I foresee no difficulties. Even so, it will be several months before probate is granted. And that assumes the coroner proceeds expeditiously, which . . .' His grin became a wry smile. 'Which is not invariably the case.'

'Well,' said Irene. 'I suppose it can't be helped.'

'Does that mean we have to wait several months – at least – before selling the house?' asked Anna in her no-nonsense fashion.

'Technically, Miss Paleologus, yes,' Baskcomb replied. 'But there would be nothing to prevent you entering into a provisional agreement to sell, which is something I could discuss with the vendee's solicitor if you so instructed me. The agreement would come into effect as soon as you obtained title. Of course, you would all need to be party to such an arrangement. I'm sure you can appreciate that.'

'Yes,' said Irene. 'Naturally.'

'Well, you'll want to discuss that amongst yourselves before coming to any decision. Just let me know.'

'We will.'

'Good. Now, the only other thing I should mention is that I require sight of any and all financial documentation kept by your father. Bank statements, chequebooks, shares and savings certificates, tax demands and so forth. The sooner I have all the details to hand, the sooner I can finalize matters. To which end . . .' Baskcomb ferreted in the drawer of his desk. 'The police have asked me to pass these on to you.' He laid a bunch of keys on the blotter in front of him.

They were the keys to Trennor. Nick recognized them at once by the brass whistle threaded onto the ring, which his grandfather had carried in his pocket as a junior officer in the First World War. One of them, Andrew probably, would take it and in due course thread it onto his key-ring. Then, one day, Tom would inherit it and probably do the same. The keys – and the doors they opened – would change. But the whistle would remain. Nick found the thought comforting. Yes, the whistle would in all likelihood survive. Something always did.

They adjourned to Anna's flat when the meeting had ended. Their talk was dominated by practical matters: the funeral, the house, the documents Baskcomb had asked for. It was agreed that Nick, Irene and Basil would visit Trennor next morning and go through their father's papers. As for Tantris's offer, there was apparent unanimity. As soon as the funeral was out of the way, they would ask Baskcomb to open discussions with Tantris's solicitor about a provisional agreement to sell.

Nick detected a latent difference of opinion, however, though he did not draw attention to it. Andrew reckoned more money could be squeezed out of the situation. And Anna might be persuaded to reckon the same. Irene was too scrupulous to go back on what they had in effect already agreed. And Basil would condemn the idea as unethical, if not immoral. That would leave Nick to take one side or the other and already he dreaded being called upon to choose.

Fortunately, that moment was still some way off. Far closer was his meeting with Elspeth, to which his thoughts increasingly turned. He knew he ought to tell the others about it, but felt strangely reluctant to do so. In the end, his hand was forced.

'We need to tell Miss Hartley something,' Irene pointed out.

'Something, but not too much,' stressed Andrew.

'Did she speak to you after phoning me, Nick?' Irene asked.

'Er, yes. Actually . . . I'm seeing her, er, well . . .' Nick glanced at his watch. 'In about half an hour.'

'You might have mentioned it,' said Andrew darkly.

'Yeah,' Anna joined in. 'You might.'

'I was going to. I was just, well . . .' Nick smiled. 'Waiting for a consensus to emerge about what I should say to her.'

'And has one emerged?' Basil enquired innocently.

'Say as little as possible, right?' Nick glanced around and received consenting nods of varying emphasis. 'Well, that's what I'll do. In fact, I'll let her do all the talking.'

It was still raining when Nick reached the Compton. And the rain was Plymouth's specially wet variety, driven in by wind and night. Early drinkers had not turned out in abundance. But for Nick and Elspeth, who was waiting for him when he arrived, there would in fact have been none.

She could not have been there long, though she was already a third of a way through her pint of beer. Nick bought himself a half and joined her at a window table. She repeated the condolences she had proffered earlier over the telephone.

'A fall, Irene said. Is that right? Your father fell down the stairs?'

'The cellar steps, actually.'

'And, what, hit his head?'

'Seems so.'

84

'Terrible.'

'Yeah. But on the cards, given how unsteady on his feet he'd become. At least it was quick.'

'Very quick.'

Some intonation in Elspeth's voice struck Nick – almost retrospectively – as odd. He frowned at her. 'Sorry?'

'Very quick. Like you said.'

'It was certainly a shock. He was full of life on Sunday.'

'How did the party go?'

'Not very well. Dad didn't . . . see eye to eye with us.'

'I was afraid he wouldn't.'

'Not that it matters now.'

'No. But, Nick, you must realize I for one would much rather your father was alive and well and you'd been able to talk him round. Nobody – including Mr Tantris – is going to take any pleasure from this turn of events.'

'I thought you'd never met Tantris.'

'I haven't. But as far as I know—'

'How far's that?'

Elspeth looked at him in silence for a moment, then said, 'I *am* sorry about your father.'

'Thanks.'

'Is something wrong?'

'Not sure.'

'What did Mr Baskcomb say?'

'Oh, that everything's straightforward. The five of us inherit the house jointly. Once the funeral's come and gone, we'll put Baskcomb in touch with Tantris's solicitor.'

'Good.' She drank some beer, watching him over the rim of the glass. 'So, what aren't you sure about?'

Nick smiled hesitantly. 'You.'

'Me?'

'That's right.'

She set the glass down and stared at him. 'What do you mean?'

'Had we met before Saturday?'

'No. Of course not. You know we hadn't.'

'Yeah, I do. But in that case why did you ask my father about me? I mean, specifically *me*.'

'Ah. He mentioned that, did he?' Elspeth's gaze shifted evasively to the middle ground. 'Somehow, I thought he wouldn't.'

'You thought right. Pru, his housekeeper, overheard your conversation. She told me.'

'I should never have asked him.' She ran a hand through her hair. 'It was a spur-of-the-moment thing.'

'And what was the spur?'

'No getting round it, is there?'

'I don't think so.'

'Well, you must know the answer anyway.'

'No.'

'I was there, Nick. Cambridge, graduation day nineteen seventy-nine.' She smiled. 'I wouldn't have recognized you. But your name stuck in my mind.'

'You were there?'

'Went with my mother to see my brother pick up his BA. He's a few years older than you, of course.'

'You were there?' Nick repeated numbly.

''Fraid so.'

'Oh God.'

'It's not so bad.'

'Yes, it is. I've tried very hard to forget about it, you see. Very hard. For a very long time.'

'Sorry to remind you.'

'Thanks. I'm sorry to *be* reminded.'

That was about as big as understatements come. Nick, formerly with the help of others and more recently with the aid of his own carefully husbanded resources, had fortified himself against his previous existence as *wunderkind* Nicholas Paleologus, the academic prodigy who had gone up to Cambridge at the age of sixteen laden with early attainment and infinite promise, only to emulate his brother Basil by failing to stay the course. Technically, he *had* graduated, thanks to the award of an aegrotat in recognition of his illness.

But the university authorities might have thought twice about that had they realized he would present himself at the Senate House on graduation day, force his way in and strip in the midst of the ceremony. Mercifully, Nick had no recollection of his actions that day, nor many days before and after. Jumping out of a punt somewhere near Grantchester, wading to the bank and walking aimlessly across fields towards the setting sun was as close as conscious memory took him to the long months of his separation from reality and the still longer years of his slow reacquaintance with it. Not that he *had* completely recovered. Like a reformed alcoholic, he carried the affliction with him, no matter how long it had been since he had succumbed to it. And that, he supposed, was what hurt him most to be reminded of.

'What did your brother read?' Nick asked irrelevantly, unsure how far the silence had stretched.

'Land Economy.'

'Really?'

'Yeah, really. At the time when it happened – your graduation-day stunt, I mean – I laughed. It made the day for me. It had been pretty boring up until then – all that ermine-hooded processional. Later, when I read a piece about you in one of the papers—'

'*Cracking up at Cambridge*?'

'I don't remember the headline.'

'Good. But that's what it was.'

'OK. Well, I thought it was sad.'

'Sad *and* laughable. That's about spot-on.'

'What went wrong, Nick?'

'Didn't the papers tell you?'

' "Too young to handle the pressure" is more or less what they said.'

'And it's more or less true. Complicated by underlying sociopathy, according to one of several psychiatrists I was treated by.'

'What does that mean?'

'It means I don't function well socially. It means my

87

intellectual overdevelopment was a camouflage for my emotional *under*development – apparently.' Nick smiled, failing to relax the all too familiar tension gripping him. 'Alternatively, you could take my father's line: I funked it.'

'What happened to you . . . afterwards?'

'Mental hospital. Care in the community was only a gleam in Thatcher's eye back then. Just as well for us repressed sociopaths. To tell you the truth, I'm not the right person to ask what really happened to me. "Out of your mind" can mean literally that.'

'But you came through it.'

'So it seems.'

'What do you do now? Irene said you work for some kind of quango.'

'English Partnerships. You know, urban regeneration and all that.'

'Where do they hang out?'

'Milton Keynes. Excited yet?'

'Do you enjoy your work?'

'Too soon to say.'

'How long have you been there?'

'Eight years.'

Elspeth laughed. 'Sociopathy obviously isn't incompatible with humour.'

'Who said I was joking?'

'OK.' She gave him a knowing look. 'Change of subject. How well do you know Istanbul?'

'Never been there.'

'You're a Paleologus. And you've never been to Istanbul?'

'Paleologus is my name, nothing more.'

'You're not affected by its history?'

'I try not to be.'

'A vain effort, I should have thought. History's part of us, like it or not. Look at what brought me down here and prompted Tantris to make his offer for Trennor. History is why we're sitting here talking to each other.'

'History is your profession, Elspeth. Naturally it affects you.

And your attitude to my father's death. It's nice of you to have expressed your regret, but I do understand that you must be looking forward to the search for the Doom Window. Well, this has probably brought that search a good deal closer.'

'Not for me. I've decided to bale out.'

'What?'

'I won't be doing any searching at Trennor. Tantris will have to find someone else to do it.'

'I don't understand.'

'I did the research. I'll opt out of the hands-on part. That's all.'

'Why?'

'Because research is my forte and there's plenty more waiting for me elsewhere. My task was to dig out the facts and try to win your father over. The first I've done. The second . . . is sadly no longer relevant. Your solicitor can talk to Tantris's solicitor and take it from there. I'm heading back to Bristol. Good news for Tilda. I think she's been having second thoughts about inviting me to—'

'Who's Tilda?'

'A friend of mine from student days. She's a curator at the Museum here in Plymouth. I've been staying with her. It was supposed to be until the end of this week. But in the circumstances . . . I've decided to bring my departure forward.'

'To when?'

'Tomorrow.' She grinned at him lopsidedly. 'So, this is a farewell drink. Fancy another?'

# CHAPTER SEVEN

Nick was unsure which had been the greater shock: Elspeth's knowledge of his breakdown at Cambridge or her abrupt detachment from his family's dealings with Tantris. He should have questioned her more closely about both. Had he known her brother? He could remember no Hartleys among his fellow students, but his memory of that time was too fragmentary to rely on. And why was Elspeth passing up the chance of all that academic kudos the Doom Window's discovery would confer on the discoverer? No-one would be interested in who had carried out the preliminary research. Purely in career terms, her decision made no sense.

The truth was that the primal instinct of self-preservation had held him back. The less said about his past the better he was able to cope with his present. Nor did he wish to confront the possibility that Elspeth was pulling out for reasons connected with his father's death. The fear of knowing too much balanced the fear of knowing too little. But the balance was a fine one.

Only after Basil had arrived by bus from Plymouth to join Irene and him in their document hunt at Trennor did Nick mention Elspeth's departure from their lives. Irene, though puzzled, made little of it. 'I imagine it'll be her loss in the long

90

run, but it's really not our concern, is it?' Basil, on the other hand, was inclined to think it could well be. 'Do you believe that?' he asked, after Nick had reported her explanation. To which Nick could only say, 'Why should she lie?'

Why indeed? Basil gave him an elder-brotherly look, then quietly observed, 'One object of a lie is to conceal the purpose of its telling.'

With which Nick – though he had no intention of saying so – could only concur.

The rain of the previous day had given way to clearing skies and sporadic showers. Springlike mildness prevailed in Landulph, birds singing in the bare-branched trees above the gurgle and trickle of water in ditches and drains.

Despite the mildness, it felt clammily cold at Trennor. The house had been unheated for a couple of days, though not unvisited, as the muddy footprints of policemen and morticians confirmed.

Nick, Basil and Irene stood at the top of the cellar steps, looking down at the place where their father had died. There was nothing to mark or draw their eye to the exact spot. Dusty sixty-watt light fell on the concrete treads and wooden handrail, shone back dully from the grey-painted floor and gleamed dimly on the racked necks of hard-bargained-for clarets.

'What's the name of the policeman you spoke to, Irene?' Nick asked.

'DC Wise. He's based at Crownhill.'

'Maybe I should ask him about the bottle.'

'What bottle might that be?' asked Basil.

'The one Nick thinks Dad should have dropped when he fell,' said Irene with a sigh. 'He's like a dog with a bone about it.'

'Pru says there was no bottle.'

'And DC Wise never mentioned one,' Irene responded. 'So, why go on about it?'

'Because Dad came down here to fetch a bottle of wine.

That's obvious. What's not obvious is why he should leave without one.'

'Perhaps he changed his mind,' said Basil. 'Perhaps the telephone rang. Perhaps he remembered something.'

'Exactly,' said Irene. 'There's absolutely no reason for you to speak to DC Wise, Nick. He'll only be confused by you querying the circumstances.'

'And confusion is not a condition we should wish upon the constabulary,' murmured Basil. 'It can so often be transmuted into suspicion.'

Irene flashed a glare at both of them, then said, 'Why don't you two start looking for the papers Baskcomb wants while I turn on the heating and vacuum up the worst of the dirt that's been tramped into the house? We have work to do. Remember?'

Nick and Basil set to, though with little enthusiasm. The study was their father's sanctum, a place of refuge as well as cogitation. In life, he would have been apoplectic to find them rifling through the drawers of his desk and filing cabinet. And if it was possible to be apoplectic in death, Nick felt sure he would be that as well.

They were thwarted at the outset on discovering that one of the desk drawers was locked. The unlocked drawers contained only stationery, so it was clearly important to find the key. Basil began a hunt for it, while Nick worked his way through the filing cabinet. He soon came upon bundles of bank statements and receipted bills. These he took out and put to one side. As far as he could see, most of the remaining space was devoted to academic correspondence – letters to and from assorted archaeological journals and institutions concerning articles, surveys and expeditions the old man had written or undertaken. Most of it was many years out of date, of course. But Michael Paleologus had devoted too much of his life to retrieving the past to discard the records of his own.

That was one reason why Nick persisted in the search. He

was looking for something more than financial records and reckoned he would find it. Properly speaking, he should have moved on to the computer and checked through its files, but what he sought lay much further back in time than his father's relatively recent conversion to modern technology. Besides, Basil's hunt for the desk key had now taken him out of the study, so for the moment Nick had the room to himself. Doing his best to avoid the flinty gaze of its former occupant from one of several framed photographs around the walls, Nick pressed on.

In the bottom drawer of the cabinet, he found it: a bulging manilla file with his name written in faded black felt-tip on the leading edge of the folder. He heaved the folder out on to the desk and leafed apprehensively through the contents. As he had feared, it was all there: letters to and from his college and the hospital he had been sent to, tracking his breakdown and subsequent treatment over a five-year period. There were bills too, substantial ones, from his psychiatrist.

But they were one tranche of financial documentation Baskcomb had no need to see. Nick closed the folder and leaned forward, his hands pressing down on the cover as he shut his eyes and winced at the sudden rush of memories. Then they were past and behind him. It was a sensation he had at one time experienced frequently and now realized he had almost succeeded in forgetting altogether. It was foolish to have supposed it would never recur. In the wake of his father's death, it was bound to, even without Elspeth's unintentional prompting. He opened his eyes and pulled open one of the unlocked desk drawers in search of an envelope large enough to hold the contents of the folder. They would be leaving with him and reaching no other hands.

In his haste, he yanked the drawer out as far as it would come. A slew of paperclips, rubber bands, pencils, stray strands of tobacco and assorted envelopes slid forward with the momentum, leaving the rear of the drawer empty. Except, Nick noticed, for a short strip of black insulating tape, stuck to the base. There was an object held beneath it. He stretched out his hand and ran his fingers over the small bulge. It felt like what it undoubtedly was: a key.

Nick prised the tape loose with his thumbnail, picked up the key and slid it into the keyhole of the locked drawer. The lock released at the first turn. He sat slowly down in his father's worn old leather swivel-chair and pulled the drawer open.

Inside there was just one object: a large white envelope, bearing the words, written in his father's hand, *Last Will and Testament*. Nick lifted the envelope out. The flap was folded in, but not sealed. He raised the flap and slid the contents out. There was a single sheet of paper. It was certainly his father's will. But it was not the one lodged with Baskcomb. And the date on it was much more recent.

The document was handwritten, succinct but legalistically worded, and utterly shocking.

This is the last will and testament of me Michael Godfrey Paleologus of Trennor Landulph Cornwall which I make this fifteenth day of January 2001 and whereby I revoke all previous wills and testamentary dispositions.

I hereby appoint my cousin Demetrius Andronicus Paleologus of Palazzo Falcetto San Polo 3150 Venezia Italy to be the sole executor of this my will.

I give my house the aforementioned Trennor Landulph Cornwall and all its contents to my cousin the afore-mentioned Demetrius Andronicus Paleologus absolutely.

I give the remainder of my property real and personal in equal shares to my children.

Nick stared at the words, transfixed. His father had written them. There was no doubt about it. And he had signed his name beneath them. Two witnesses had also signed.

Signed by the testator in the presence of us both present at the same time who at his request in his presence and in the presence of each other have hereunto set our names as witnesses.

Frederick Davey of 3 Butcher's Row Tintagel Cornwall retired quarryman.

Margaret Davey of 3 Butcher's Row Tintagel Cornwall housewife.

Nick had never heard of a cousin Demetrius, nor of retired quarryman Fred Davey and his wife. They were strangers to him. But one of those strangers, if this will was valid and genuine, as it certainly appeared to be, was now the rightful owner of Trennor.

'Keyless in Trennor isn't a lot better than eyeless in Gaza,' said Basil, re-entering the study. 'But such is our—' He stopped, the stillness of Nick's posture behind the desk seizing his attention. 'Is something wrong?'

'I found the key,' said Nick.

'Splendid.'

'You won't think so when you read this.' He held up the will.

Basil walked across to the desk and took the sheet of paper from his brother's hand. As he read it, the sunlight beyond the window vanished behind a cloud and the room seemed to fill with darkness.

'My, my,' said Basil when he had finished.

'What do we do?' Nick asked.

'What do we do?' Basil smiled. 'We ask Irene, of course.' The vacuum cleaner was roaring somewhere in the house. 'I'll fetch her.'

Basil dropped the document on the blotter and hurried from the room. Nick sat where he was, studying the copper-plate loops and uprights of his father's handwriting. Then, suddenly, he noticed the dog-eared folder with his name on it lying on the desktop just to his left. For a moment, he did not know what to do with it. He knew only that there was little time to do anything. He jumped up, carried the folder to the cabinet he had taken it from and dumped it back in its pocket. Then he noticed the silence. The vacuum cleaner had stopped.

A moment later, Irene bustled into the room, Basil lagging a few yards behind. 'What's this about a will?' she demanded.

'See for yourself.' Nick passed her the sheet of paper.

It took no more than two or three seconds for Irene to grasp the significance of what she held in her hand. In those seconds Nick saw her expression move from irritation to something midway between fear and anger.

'The will Baskcomb has dates from a few months after Mum died. This is . . . far more recent. It's dated . . . just last week.'

'Quite,' said Basil.

'Is it valid?'

'Signatures of the testator and two witnesses are all that's required, I believe. And there they are. It's clearly not a forgery. So, the answer to your question must be yes.'

'But it's not been drawn up by a solicitor.'

'It doesn't have to be.'

'I've never heard of a cousin Demetrius.'

'Nor have I,' Nick joined in.

'Which makes three of us,' said Basil. 'Three of us who *had* not heard of him. Until now.'

'Who are these people?' Irene continued. 'I've never heard of the Daveys either.'

'No doubt we shall find out in due course.'

' "The remainder of my property real and personal". What will that amount to?'

'Without Trennor, very little.'

'I don't believe it.' But what Irene really meant was that she did not want to believe it. 'Why would Dad do this to us?'

'To prevent us selling the house to Tantris,' said Nick.

'And to punish us for trying to force him to,' concluded Basil. 'It seems the only thing we talked him into doing . . . was disinheriting us.'

'You think so?' Irene glared down at the will, as if she could somehow wish its contents out of existence. 'Well, we'll see about that.'

'What do you have in mind?' asked Nick.

'It's handwritten. So, there's no copy. And no solicitor's involved. The only living people who know of the will's existence are we three plus the Daveys. And the Daveys may not even know what's in it.'

'Are you suggesting what I think you're suggesting?' enquired Basil.

'What do you *think* I'm suggesting?'

'Something deeply criminal. Besides, how can you be sure no-one else knows? Dad may well have advised cousin Demetrius of his intentions.'

'But cousin Demetrius isn't here. We are. As is the will.'

'Even so—'

'Call Andrew and Anna.' Irene was much calmer now, Nick noticed. She had absorbed the blow and already was preparing to strike back. 'I think a family conference is in order.' She dropped the will back on to the desk in front of him. 'There's a great deal to discuss . . . before we do anything.'

Anna's shift did not end until mid-afternoon and Andrew was likely to be out and about on the farm until dusk, so the conference Irene had decided to convene could not feasibly take place before early evening. She went back to Saltash to open up for lunchtime at the Old Ferry, confident that she would be able to arrange for Moira and Robbie to cover for her later. Nick engineered a solitary moment in which to stuff the contents of the file about his breakdown into an envelope and take it out to his car. Then he accompanied Basil into Cargreen on foot. They were to call on Pru and tell her she could resume cleaning duties at Trennor whenever she wished.

There was an ulterior motive for their visit, of course. That was to tap the old lady for information about their father's activities on 15 January, the date he had recorded on the will. The fifteenth was Monday of the previous week, recent enough for Pru to remember the Daveys of Tintagel calling round.

But they had not called round. Persuaded to review her

employer's activities for the week on the grounds that they might yield signs he had been doing too much, Pru was adamant that he had had no visitors from outside the family circle and had gone out only on Monday . . . the fifteenth.

'He left not long after I got there and hadn't got back by the time I left. He didn't say where he was going, but there was nothing out of the ordinary about that. 'Twas no concern of mine, when all's said and done.'

'Which means,' Basil soundly reasoned after they had adjourned to the Spaniards, 'that he took the will up to Tintagel for the Daveys to witness. Irene's idea that they might be unaware of the contents strikes me as even less plausible now.'

'But who are the Daveys, Basil?'

'I don't know. Dad used to take us to Tintagel quite often during the holidays, didn't he?'

'Yes. We'd get long lectures on archaeology when all we wanted to do was scramble around the ruins.'

'Quite. But I don't remember those lectures ever including mention of a quarryman called Fred Davey. Could he have been employed on the dig, do you suppose? Quarrying's a similar line of work.'

'In the 'thirties, you mean? If so, he must be at least as old as Dad, possibly older.'

'Yes.' Basil stared thoughtfully into his cider. 'The same generation. Like cousin Demetrius.'

'Grandad was obsessed with genealogy. Why didn't he know about Demetrius? He must have been his cousin too, right?'

'Or nephew. Except that Grandad was an only child, so he didn't have any nephews. He had uncles, though. One of them could be Demetrius's grandfather. Or he could be a more distant cousin. Who knows?'

'Dad did, apparently. Why did he never tell us about him?'

'Perhaps he only found out about him recently.'

'And was so bowled over by the experience that he decided to leave him the house? It doesn't make sense.'

'But it did make sense, Nick. Oh my word, yes. It made very good sense to Dad. The question is: why?'

But there was a more urgent question still, which Basil raised on their way back along the lane to Trennor through the thin sunlight of early afternoon.

'What are we going to do about the will? You do realize what's in Irene's mind, don't you, Nick?'

'I think so.'

'Andrew and Anna will agree with anything she proposes that spares us having to hand over the house – and hence as much money as Tantris can be persuaded to pay for it – to our mysterious Venetian cousin.'

'Pretending we never found it is the only way to do that.'

'Precisely. And destroying the evidence is the only way to sustain that pretence.'

'Is that what you meant by "deeply criminal"?'

'How else would you describe it? Merely unethical, perhaps? Or not even that?'

Nick sighed and glanced away across the field beyond the hedge towards a patch of woodland, where rough-throated rooks were cawing and flapping among the leafless branches of the trees. 'I don't know, Basil. That's the honest, useless truth. I have absolutely no idea what we should do. Or what we will do. Which mightn't be so bad, but for the fact that I know we'll—'

A car horn blared behind them and they turned to see Andrew's Land Rover trundling down the lane towards them. 'Well, well,' said Basil. 'It seems I'm to be granted an earlier opportunity than I expected to gauge the accuracy of my prediction.'

Andrew waved at them through the windscreen as he approached and smiled broadly. 'He looks in a good mood,' said Nick.

'It won't last.'

'No. I don't suppose it will.'

\*　　\*　　\*

99

Andrew drove them the rest of the way to Trennor. He had not heard from Irene and had travelled over from Carwether merely to see how their document hunt was progressing. He *had* heard from Tom, however, who would be coming down at the weekend. He was clearly relieved about that.

But his relief gave way to seething disbelief when they told him about the will. Actual sight of it seemed to make him even less capable of understanding how their father could have done such a thing. And as for forgiving him . . .

'The devious, scheming, treacherous old bastard. He sat here on Sunday making all those acid-drop remarks about how we'd sell up as soon as we had the chance knowing that he'd done his best to make sure we'd never *get* the chance. Who in God's name is this cousin Demetrius?'

'We don't know,' said Nick.

'And these witnesses – the Daveys.'

'We don't know them either.'

'How could he do it? *Why* would he do it?'

'I fear that's all too obvious,' said Basil.

'Yeah. I suppose it is. Well, he isn't going to get away with it.'

'Isn't he?'

'Of course he bloody isn't. You're not seriously suggesting we let this scrap of paper stand in our way?'

'It's rather more than a scrap of paper.'

'To you, Basil, maybe. The way I see it, Dad missed a trick. He should have stuck this in a safe-deposit box at the bank or had Baskcomb put it in his office safe. But he didn't. He left it here for us to find. And now we have. So, what happens to it is up to us and no-one else.'

'You have a suggestion?'

'Damn right I do. And I reckon you must know what it is.'

'I have a shrewd idea.'

'Don't get moralistic with me about this, Basil. Just don't.'

'Irene will be back later,' Nick temporized. 'We'll phone Anna as soon as she gets off work. Then we can all sit down together and discuss the situation.'

'Fine,' said Andrew. 'Let's discuss it. I don't mind. But you two may as well know right now that there's no way – no way in this world – that I'm knuckling under to this.' He turned the sheet of paper round in his hands and held it lightly in his forefingers and thumbs, as if about to tear it in half. His gaze flashed from Basil to Nick and back again. He seemed to be daring them to protest. Neither said a word. Then he let the sheet of paper fall on to the desk. 'We'll hear what everyone has to say. Then we'll burn the bloody thing. And to hell with cousin Demetrius. OK?'

'I know we'll regret whatever we do.' That was what Nick had been about to say to Basil in the lane when Andrew had sounded his car horn at them. The conviction set dully within him as the afternoon progressed. Obey the letter of their father's most recent will and they would wonder for the rest of their lives why they had been so compliant to his whim. Destroy it and they might reap other, bitter consequences of his devising. Nick could not rid himself of the suspicion that the old man had deliberately bequeathed them this dilemma; that he had given them a stark but by no means simple choice; and that he had been certain of what they would choose.

When the time came, it was Anna, given less warning of the issue than any of the others, who nonetheless presented the clearest case.

'If we take this to Baskcomb, he'll have no choice but to abide by it. Maybe we can contest it, maybe not. Even if we did, we might lose in the end and have nothing but a fat legal bill to show for it. This is our house, our *home*. Dad inherited it from Grandad and we should inherit it in turn. I don't think Dad had the right – morally, I mean – to leave it to some long-lost cousin we've never even met. We should stand by the earlier will. We should destroy this one. Even if the Daveys – or cousin Demetrius – know what's in it, they can't know for certain that Dad didn't destroy it himself some time after writing it. The fact that he left it here suggests he might

101

have had second thoughts. So, let's give ourselves the benefit of the doubt.'

Doubt there certainly was in Nick's mind as he listened to Anna and studied the expressions on his siblings' faces. Irene looked perfectly calm, but he knew that meant nothing. The deep furrows on Andrew's forehead and the set of his jaw told a more accurate story. As for Basil, leaning back far enough in his chair to bury his eyes in shadow, he was already halfway to dissociating himself from the decision they were manoeuvring their way towards. In this room of flickering firelight and thick-shaded lamps, the memories were ranked close about them. Only three days before, their father had sat there too, deriding their arguments and scorning their achievements. Anna was right. The old man had gone too far. But what worried Nick was the thought that they were about to do the same.

'I agree with Anna,' said Irene. 'Besides, I don't think Dad actually meant to go through with it. I suspect he intended merely to threaten us with disinheritance and use this document to persuade us he meant it.'

It was a neat line of reasoning, Nick had to admit. But he did not believe it. Nor did he believe that Irene believed it. Their father had never bluffed. What he had threatened he had always delivered.

'I don't care whether he meant it or not,' growled Andrew. 'Anna's put her finger on it. He had no right to try to do this. Once the will's gone, no-one can prove anything. It's obvious what we should do. I don't know what we're waiting for.'

For everyone to have their say. That, of course, was what they were waiting for. Nick cleared his throat uneasily, struggling to find the words to replace the only ones that came into his head. '*We want the money. And we mean to take it.*' No, that would not do. That was not what any of them wanted to hear. Instead, all he could say – and all he needed to say – was, 'I agree.'

'That we should destroy the will?' Irene's tone was mild but insistent.

'Yes.'

'Basil?'

'Ah.' Basil leaned forward. 'My turn, is it?'

'Here we go,' muttered Andrew.

'Fear not,' said Basil, with a sidelong glance at his brother. 'I shall not attempt to dissuade you. I have already made it clear that I will decline my share of the proceeds from the sale of this house.'

'Yeah. You're the man with the clean hands all right.'

'Please, Andrew,' said Irene. 'Let him speak.'

'OK, OK.' Andrew raised his hand in mock surrender.

'I believe,' Basil continued, 'that when President Nixon's advisers came to him to report some damaging leak to the press, he was wont to ask, not whether the particular allegation against his administration was true or false, but whether it was deniable. Well, to apply the Nixon test, is destroying the will deniable? The answer, obviously, is yes.'

'Does that mean you agree?' asked Anna.

'It means I regard its destruction, given the circumstances of its discovery, as inevitable.'

'We should be clear,' said Irene. 'Once we've done this, there's no turning back. We must behave as if we've never heard of a cousin Demetrius or a Mr and Mrs Davey. We must forget the will ever existed. I shall say nothing to Laura about it and you must say nothing to Tom, Andrew, nor you to Zack, Anna. Now . . . or ever.'

'Agreed.'

'In fact, none of us must breathe a word to anyone.' There were nods of assent, even, albeit tardily, from Basil. 'We draw a line under the whole business. All right?' There was another round of nods. 'That's settled, then.'

'Good,' said Andrew, jumping up and plucking the will, now restored to its envelope, from the coffee-table. 'As the eldest, I think this is my prerogative.'

He tore the envelope and its contents into four, took two strides to the fireplace and tossed the fragments in amongst the blazing logs, stooping to hurry their extinction along with

103

a few prods of the poker. The paper curled and blackened and flamed . . . and was gone.

'Feel better now?' asked Basil as his brother turned away from the fire.

Andrew smiled grimly. 'Much.'

# CHAPTER EIGHT

Irene had drawn a line for them all to toe. Over the next couple of days arrangements were finalized for the funeral and a headstone was ordered. Baskcomb took delivery of the financial documentation they had assembled and set about the protracted business of probating what he believed was his late client's only will. Nick telephoned an assortment of his father's friends and former colleagues to determine who would and who would not be attending the funeral. He was kept busy with the administrative minutiae of death, though not so busy that he could not have found time to visit the chapel of rest to take a private farewell of the deceased – had he wished.

But he did not wish. And he did not go. His father continued to intimidate him from that halfway ground where he dwelt between death and burial. They had posthumously defied him. But had he found a way, also posthumously, to defeat them? Or was the will he had left in the desk drawer just a macabre joke, a way of guaranteeing himself the last laugh? Nick could not stop thinking about it, partly because he was forbidden to talk about it.

Yet his nerve held. Until the funeral, he was bound to play his part, with gritted teeth. After that, he would be free. The dull normality of his other life beckoned comfortingly. It would not be long now before he could return to it.

Meanwhile, he had to move out of the Old Ferry to make way for Laura and live for several days at Trennor. He did not relish the prospect and secretly planned to spend as little time as possible there. On Friday, he drove up from Saltash with his few belongings.

Pru had made up a bed for him in his old room and was still on the premises when he arrived. He kept her chatting over a pot of tea for as long as he reasonably could, but by mid-afternoon she was gone.

Shortly afterwards, Nick was also gone, almost on a whim, driving west through the rain-washed back roads to Liskeard, where he bought a serviceable black tie for the funeral, then on west along the lanes to St Neot.

The church was open but he was the only visitor. The cloud-filled winter light seemed warmed and gilded by the stained glass. He sat in a pew in the south aisle, gazing at the Creation Window beyond the rood-screen ahead of him. This and the other windows, maybe the Doom Window too, had endured for five centuries. Generations of parishioners, poor as well as rich, had preserved the glass, sometimes at considerable personal risk. None of them had done so for profit or gain. They had acted out of a combination of religious faith and artistic sensibility, motives that made his family's involvement in the strange history of the St Neot glass seem venal and ignoble. They *would* profit from it. They had destroyed a solemnly executed last will and testament to make sure of that. And they would have their reward, Nick along with them, whether he wanted it or not.

A churchwarden eager to lock up with dusk coming on soon obliged Nick to take his leave. He drove slowly back to Landulph through thickening, wind-slanted rain. When he reached Trennor, the house's dark and empty present seemed to him a feeble reality to set against its teeming past. He entered through a thicket of memories, switched on lights in every room and turned one of his mother's Maria Callas CDs up loud on the hi-fi.

Pru had left him a casserole to put in the oven, apparently

convinced that he was unable to cook for himself. He set it to warm, then lit the fire in the drawing room, listening to the wind keening in the chimney and remembering, almost against his will, giving cack-handed assistance to his father during the fitting of an H-pot to the chimney a quarter of a century or so before. Yet the event felt as close as yesterday in that instant – his father barking instructions at him as they perched vertiginously on the roof, his mother watching anxiously from the garden below.

With the fire going, Nick hunted around the kitchen and scullery for a bottle of wine, but drew a blank. He was, in one sense, unsurprised by this, supporting as it did his theory that his father had gone down to the cellar specifically to fetch some wine. Nick had not been down there since the old man's death. It was time, he decided, to cross that line.

The cellar was still and silent, the walls and floor coated with grey masonry paint that made it resemble the hull of a ship. Most of the storage space was taken up with the racks in which Michael Paleologus had kept his stock of chosen vintages. The stock was thinner than had once been the case, Nick noticed. The old man had been running it down, factoring the approach of death into his ordering. Nick smiled at the thought, typifying as it did his father's cast of mind. He would not have wanted to spend money on wine he would not live to drink, even though he was unlikely to spend the money on anything else.

Not that Nick or any of the others had ever shown signs of connoisseurship for him to encourage. Nick and Basil had even succeeded in being banned from the cellar during their childhood following an incident when a bottle had been dis-lodged from one of the racks and broken. 'A 'sixty-one St Emilion sacrificed to the stupidity of two small boys,' as their father had raged at the time, subsequently became an oft-swapped catch-phrase between them.

At this recollection too, Nick smiled. The breakage had happened because of his attempt to conceal himself in the narrow gap between the far wall and the last rack, which was single-sided, during a game of hide-and-seek. He walked along to the rack to remind himself just how narrow the gap really was.

But it was not there. The rack was hard against the wall. Nothing larger than a mouse could squeeze between them. Nick was puzzled. Even his father was not normally that cautious. Then he noticed several white patches near the base of the rack. Glancing down, he saw that some of the paint had been scraped from the floor. There were curved grooves in the surface, as if the rack had been pulled away from the wall at one end.

Nick crouched down for a closer look. Yes, that was indeed the only possible explanation. It had been done recently, too. Flakes of the dislodged paint were still lying around. But who had moved the rack? Surely it could only be his father. Was that why he had come down there on the night of his death? It would at least explain why he had left without a bottle. Yet it would leave much else unexplained.

'Nick?'

Nick started violently at the sound of Andrew's voice behind and above him. He stood and turned to see his brother descending the steps, a frown mingling with a smile on his face.

'Not planning to drink our inheritance, are you?'

'God, you nearly gave me a heart attack,' Nick complained, aware of the thumping in his chest. 'Couldn't you have rung the doorbell?'

'I did, but I got no answer, so I let myself in. You can't hear the bell down here.'

'Obviously not.'

'I thought I'd see if you were all right. First night alone in the old place and all that. Something in the kitchen smells good.'

'One of Pru's casseroles.'

'Which you're planning to wash down with a Château Lafite before we can auction the lot off and share the proceeds?'

'That's right. You've caught me in the act.'

'Never mind. Break out one for me and we'll say no more about it.' Andrew walked up to where Nick was standing. 'Actually, though, I think it's all whites down this end.'

'What do you make of this?' Nick pointed to the marks on the floor.

Andrew looked down, then back up at Nick. 'What do *you* make of it?'

'Somebody's moved the rack.'

'Yeah. I reckon they have.'

'Dad?'

'Who else?'

'Alone?'

'Two people could have lifted it without scratching the floor.'

'Why would Dad want to move it at all?'

'Search me.'

'It didn't use to be hard up against the wall.'

'No?'

'Definitely not.'

'Double mystery, then.' Andrew glanced around, turning the matter over in his mind. 'Shall we just forget about it?'

'I don't think I can.'

Andrew smiled. 'Me neither.'

They transferred the bottles to spare slots, of which there were plenty, in the next rack. The empty rack was no great weight, though cumbersome. They lifted it clear of the wall without much difficulty. Nothing sinister revealed itself amidst the dust and cobwebs in the corner of the cellar, as far as they could make out in the shadow cast by the rack. Andrew fetched the torch from the scullery to check if the shadow was concealing anything significant. The answer appeared at first glance to be no.

Then Nick noticed something: an unevenness in the otherwise smooth surface of the floor. Peering closer, he saw two lines of roughness, like flattened ridges, leading out at right angles from the wall, and a third linking them, running along close to the foot of the wall. Neither he nor Andrew could be sure if they had always been there. They suspected not, although their suspicion did not amount to much. They moved the rack as far across as they could for a clearer view.

This revealed a fourth line, further out and parallel to the wall, completing a rectangle about six feet by three. The suspicion strengthened. Nick stepped into the gap they had opened up between rack and wall and walked along to the rectangular patch of floor. Something felt different as he trod on it. He could not have said what it was. But it was certainly different.

'Is there a hammer over there?' Nick pointed to the shelf running most of the length of the wall behind Andrew. Various tools were stored on it, along with empty bottles, spare light bulbs and forgotten boxes of who knew what.

'Yeah.' Andrew held up a wooden-handled ball-pein of indeterminate age.

'Pass it to me, would you?' Andrew handed it over. Nick crouched down and gave the floor several taps either side of the line around the suspicious patch. 'This part of the floor sounds . . . less solid.'

'Less solid? You mean hollow?'

'Maybe.'

'It can't be. There's never been anything below here.'

'Well, it sounds like there is now. And this line round here? What's that about?'

'You tell me.'

'Well, at a guess, I'd say somebody's dug a hole, laid a slab across it, cemented it in and painted it over.'

'Then pushed the rack over the top to hide it.'

'Certainly looks that way.'

Andrew tried hammering for himself. He nodded. 'You could be right.'

'It has to be Dad who did this.'

'Suppose so. When, do you think?'

'When was the rack moved?'

'I don't know. It's not the sort of thing you keep tabs on, is it? Could be any time in the last twenty years.'

'You don't remember Dad doing any . . . digging?'

'Nope.'

'But he must have done. Or got someone in to do it.'

'The answer's the same, Nick. I don't remember. Anyway, why would Dad want to dig a hole down here?'

'To . . . hide something.'

'Yeah. Exactly. To hide something.'

But what? That was the question they had no hope of reasoning out an answer to. They went back upstairs and helped themselves to some of the old man's Scotch. Nick turned off the oven, his appetite suddenly gone. Then he and Andrew sat down by the fire.

'Bloody odd,' said Andrew, after they had brooded in silence for a while. 'I don't know what to make of it.'

'Perhaps one of the others knows what it's all about.'

'Doubt it. Painted over and covered with the rack? Dad didn't want *anyone* to know.'

'Can we be certain he knew himself?'

'Of course we can. It hasn't always been there. He dug it – or got someone else to dig it. Christ knows why, though. What's down there?'

'More than just a hole, I suspect.'

'You bet.' Andrew laughed. 'Maybe it's a tunnel. An emergency exit.'

'It's strange. Elspeth Hartley reckons something is hidden in this house. Now we find a hiding-place. Coincidence?'

'Has to be. I'm not even sure the cellar's original. Either way, nobody was stashing anything down there in the seventeenth century.'

'But there's something stashed there now.'

Andrew's eyes narrowed as he reflected on their father's famously devious thought processes. 'It couldn't be the window, could it, Nick? Dad couldn't have found it and hidden it down there?'

'Why would he do that?'

'To spite us, maybe.'

'That hole wasn't dug last week. And it must be years since Dad was physically capable of the work involved.'

'He could have hired somebody to do it.'

Nick sighed. 'We're going in circles.'

'Not indefinitely we aren't. When Tantris gets his hands on this house, that hole will be opened up.'

'True enough. But I doubt he'll find the Doom Window of St Neot down there.'

'Me too.' Andrew smiled mischievously. 'But why wait to find out for certain?'

Andrew fetched from the barn the tools he reckoned he would need for the job: sledgehammer, chisel, crowbar, shovel. There was no stopping him at this stage, much as Nick would have liked to. Instinct told him they should think long and hard before doing anything. But Andrew was past thinking. Nor, Nick realized, was he taking this action purely to solve a riddle left behind by their father. It was about more than that. It was about several decades' worth of resentment and deception. Now, with the old man gone, Andrew was free to have done with both.

'He screwed us up good and proper, didn't he?' Andrew voiced his thoughts almost on cue as he and Nick lugged the tools down into the cellar. 'Well, maybe not Irene and Anna. But you, me and Basil? He had a way with his sons all right.'

'I stopped blaming Dad for my problems a long time ago,' said Nick.

'Good for you. But that doesn't mean he *wasn't* to blame for them.'

'Maybe not. I just don't see how it helps to load it all on him.'

'It feels as if it helps.' Andrew peeled off his sweater and rolled up his shirtsleeves. 'And this may help some more.' He crouched over the slab and tapped it with the chisel, flaking off some of the paint to reveal the surface of the stone beneath. 'Looks like elvan. One good blow should do it.' With that he stood up, grasped the sledgehammer and let fly.

One good blow was not, in the event, enough. Debris sprayed up from the slab, pinging against the metalwork of the empty rack and bouncing away past Nick across the room. Only at the third blow was there a loud, cracking sound. Andrew stopped and, stepping closer with the torch, Nick saw a jagged line across the centre of the slab.

'That's got it,' said Andrew. He moved back and aimed at the crack.

This time the slab broke, a chunk falling into the space below, leaving another chunk sagging. Andrew pulled it up with one end of the sledgehammer. As it fell clear, a jagged hole about a foot across was revealed.

'Give me that torch.'

But, as Andrew turned to take it, Nick recoiled, amazed to see a swarm of tiny flies rising from the hole in the slab. A strong smell hit him in the same instant, not just of stale air, but of something much fouler.

'Bloody hell.' Andrew saw the flies as well and coughed at the smell. 'What in God's name . . .'

Nick moved reluctantly forward, batting his way through the flies as he might through a cloud of midges on a summer evening. He trained the torch on the hole in the slab and saw . . . the ribcage of a skeleton.

'Christ almighty,' murmured Andrew. 'Is that what it looks like?'

'I hope not.'

'Get out of the way.' Andrew cast the sledgehammer aside and fetched the crowbar. 'Let's see for sure what's there.'

He wedged the crowbar under the slab on the far side of the hole and levered it up. Cement cracked off at the margins as the slab rose. Nick craned round him and shone the torch into the space below.

And there, beyond the ribcage, was the skull, unquestionably human, staring back at them through empty eye-sockets, with flies crawling and hopping across the bone and the suety remnants of flesh.

But the flies were not what caused Nick to mutter 'My God!' under his breath. An inch or so above the left eye-socket there was a large, splintered hole in the bone. There was no doubt in Nick's mind: they were not looking at the remains of someone who had met a natural death.

# CHAPTER NINE

The body had been buried carefully, almost respectfully. That was clear from the planking lining the trench in which it had been laid. Digging a crude hole in the earth would have been quicker and easier. But there was something meticulous about this covert interment that made it more mysterious still.

Nick and Andrew covered the broken slab with the tarpaulin their father had long kept in the garage and stood the empty rack back across it. Then they left the cellar, locking the door behind them.

'Dad only fitted that lock to the door to stop Basil and me going down there and wreaking havoc,' said Nick, breaking a long silence during which they had done what needed to be done through a fog of bewilderment. 'There was nothing to hide then.'

Andrew did not at first respond. He led the way back into the drawing room, flung another log on the fire and poured large Scotches for both of them. He sipped his while leaning against the mantelpiece, on which a gilt-framed photograph of their parents on their ruby-wedding anniversary in 1989 projected an entirely conventional image of a contented old couple posing proudly in the entrance porch of their charmingly rustic family home. 'Think that was down there then?'

he asked, tapping the rim of his tumbler against the frame. 'Think Mum knew about it?'

'I doubt it.'

'Bloody difficult to overlook, though. Burying a corpse in the cellar. Not to mention turning some poor sod into a corpse in the first place.'

'We don't know what happened.'

'We know what killed him, though. A hole in the head. And I don't reckon he got it accidentally.'

'I'm no pathologist, Andrew. Nor are you. We can't even be sure it's a man.'

'Where did those flies come from? How did they get down there?'

'We're not entomologists either. There are human remains under the cellar. That's all we can be sure of.'

'Not quite. We can also be sure we're supposed to report a discovery like this to the police. Then they can call in the experts. Establish sex, age, cause of death, date of death – all that stuff.'

'You're right.'

'Is that what you think we should do, then?'

'I suppose so.'

'Really?' Andrew pushed himself away from the mantel-piece and flopped down into an armchair opposite Nick. 'Just let's talk it through. It won't only be this house the police start swarming all over, you know. It'll be Dad's past – our family's past. Whoever Joe Skeleton is, somebody did him in. Who are the police going to finger for that? I can't see any way round it. Dad's got to be the prime suspect. And the police will give *us* the third degree in his absence. They may even pencil us in as possible accessories.'

'That's nonsense. We'd hardly dig up the body and report it if we knew it was there.'

'Wouldn't we? With Tantris's big fat offer sitting invitingly on the table? Be serious, Nick. They'd look at every angle, every single dark and dirty theory they could come up with. And then there'd be the media. Journalists hanging on

116

my gate, ringing your doorbell. Before you could say "No comment" they'd haul your five minutes of fame in Cambridge out of the archives.'

'Surely not.' But, even as he said it, Nick sensed that Andrew was right. They were at the beginning of something that might have no end. 'Well, OK. Maybe it would pan out like that. But—'

'And what about Tantris? A wealthy recluse like him might be scared off by tabloid headlines with the word murder in them. A police investigation would sure as hell hold up the sale. It might scupper it altogether.'

'Yeah. It might. But what alternative is there, Andrew? Tell me that.'

'We could . . .' Andrew leaned forward and lowered his voice, though who exactly he was worried about being over-heard by was unclear. 'We could cover it over again. Pretend we knew nothing about it.'

'And leave Tantris's people to find it?'

'Yeah.'

'Then they'd call in the police.'

'But we'd already have the money for the house.'

'Which could make it look worse for us if the police noticed the slab had been recently replaced as I suspect they would.'

'All right.' Andrew thumped the arm of the chair in irrita-tion. 'There's no easy answer. I admit it. Our father is likely to be branded a murderer. It looks as if he almost certainly *was* a murderer, though who he murdered – and why – we haven't a clue.'

'You don't know it was murder. It could have been self-defence.'

'Yeah. It could. I'm happy to believe it was. But will the law be? I doubt it. More dirty laundry than we knew existed is going to be washed in a glare of publicity. And it'll drag on for months, maybe years. They may never get to the bottom of it. Just how much evidence is there in a bundle of bones? This could be an unsolved mystery hanging round our necks for the rest of our lives. Dad may have failed to cheat us out of

Trennor, only to succeed in—' Andrew stopped abruptly. A slow frown of realization crossed his face. 'Hold on. Is this why he changed his will?'

'Maybe.' But another thought had already occurred to Nick. 'It certainly explains his refusal to sell the house.'

'Yeah. He couldn't, could he? Not at any price. Especially not to someone who wanted to start checking it over for hidey-holes. All that crap about knowing better than us was just to save his own skin.'

'Tantris's offer must have come as a nasty shock to him.'

'Not as nasty a shock as the one we've just had. He knew the body was there. He put it there. And he thought he could leave it there. Then he realized he wasn't going to be allowed to. He knew we'd sell the house to Tantris, which meant it was bound to be discovered. He didn't want to be remembered as a murderer. His reputation was always important to him.'

'Maybe he was thinking of us.'

'By disinheriting us? Nice try, Nick. But it won't work. This was all about him.'

'If you're right—'

'Oh, I'm right.'

'Well, if so, that means he was confident cousin Demetrius wouldn't sell. The risk of discovery would be just as great otherwise.'

'Christ, that's true. Demetrius wouldn't sell. Why not?'

'Only one answer springs to mind. Demetrius knows about the body . . .'

'Bloody hell.'

'He may even have helped put it there.'

'Jesus.' Andrew sat slowly back in his chair 'Who *is* this Demetrius?'

Nick shook his head. 'No idea.'

'What do we do about him?'

'There's nothing we *can* do. We can't even mention him to the police without admitting we destroyed the will.' Nick sighed. 'A will that could have been a valuable piece of evidence in a murder inquiry.'

'Which we put on the fire.'

'Yeah.'

'Well, *I* did.'

'We all agreed.'

'Nice of you to say that, Nick.'

'It's true.' And it *was* true, much as Nick would have liked it not to be. To every action there was a consequence, though not necessarily the one foreseen. 'We thought we could get away with it.'

'And we still can.' Andrew sat forward again, his eyes suddenly wide. 'Don't you see, Nick? It makes no difference whether we go to the police or leave it to Tantris. We're buggered either way.'

'No, no. Going to them now has to be less risky.'

'Except for the money. If Tantris took fright, where would we find another bidder for this place? Murder sells papers, not houses. I need my share, Nick. Maybe you don't. And maybe Basil thinks he doesn't. But I do. And I'm not about to give it up without a struggle. As far as I'm concerned, going to the police is a risk I can't afford to take.'

'We can't ignore what's down in that cellar, Andrew.'

'I'm not suggesting we should.'

'Then what *are* you suggesting?'

'We could take the body out. Lose it somewhere.'

'Lose it?'

'Cornwall's not short of old mine shafts.'

'You're not serious.'

'Why not? I reckon it's an easy two-man job. The body's rotted down to the bone, so it's no great weight. These mine shafts are dangerous places. One collapsed under the car park on Kit Hill a couple of years ago. Nobody pokes around in them.'

'Sure of that, are you?'

'Pretty sure, yeah. But what would it matter if a skeleton was found down one a year or so from now anyway? There'd be nothing to connect it with us.'

'Assuming we weren't spotted dumping it in the first place.'

'We wouldn't be. For God's sake, Nick. Out on the Moor after dark? The chances of being seen are thousands to one. Look at how long and hard I've been on the big cat trail with bugger all to show for it.'

Involuntarily, and much to his own surprise, Nick let out a snorting laugh.

'What's so funny?'

'Sorry. It's just . . . Remember what Dad said about big cats? "A skeleton's what you need. Tangible remains." Well, that's exactly what we've got. Remains that are all too tangible.'

'Probably his idea of a joke.'

'If so, the joke's on us.'

'Only if we play along by going to the police. Ditching the body's the answer, I'm sure of it.'

'But I'm not.'

'You seriously want all the publicity, the attention, the rumour-mongering, the finger-pointing? We'll never be rid of it, you know.'

'Of course I don't want it.'

'Then take your big brother's advice.'

'You're really willing to go through with this, aren't you?'

'You bet.'

'What about Basil and the girls?'

'Spare them the angst.'

'You mean not tell them?'

'We don't have long. Laura's due to arrive tomorrow, Tom the day after. We have a chance to settle this the quick and easy way. Let's not blow it. We don't need another family conference. What the others don't know about they won't worry about. You and I can solve the problem. Together.'

'Yeah, but—'

'Don't turn me down, Nick.' There was a gleam of sheer desperation in Andrew's gaze as he stared at his brother through the firelight. 'I've never asked much of you. And I've never begged for anything. But I'm begging now. I need your help.'

Andrew spent the night at Trennor. Even if his whisky con-
sumption had not rendered that essential, Nick still reckoned
he would have stayed. Andrew was determined to reach some
sort of decision about their discovery in the cellar and hold his
brother to it. Nick, for his part, feared that every decision was
in one way or another the wrong one. There was just too
much they did not know. And too little time for them to learn
any of it.

When he eventually went to bed in the small hours he could
not sleep, his mind racing and whirling in pursuit of an
unattainable truth. Without it, every course of action was at
best a fifty–fifty guess. And Nick strongly suspected that the
odds were not really even that good. Ever since arriving in
Saltash one short week before, what he had most wanted was
to leave again, free of family cares, unfettered by sibling
woes. Now that happy state seemed like an impossible dream.
Unless . . .

'I'll do it.'

Nick held Andrew's gaze across the kitchen, greyly filling
with dawn twilight. He had entered to find his brother sipping
from a mug of tea, staring out through the streaks of rain
on the window into the vagueness of early morning. Then,
hearing his tread, Andrew had turned to face him and slowly
set down the mug on the draining-board.

'I'll help you dump the body.'

'You will?'

'Yeah.'

'I was . . . kind of expecting you to turn me down.'

'I was expecting to myself.'

'What changed your mind?'

'I just can't face the prospect of this taking over my life.
Honestly, Andrew, I can't. If I thought the police would take
it all off our shoulders and leave us in peace, I'd happily let
them. But it wouldn't be like that, would it? It wouldn't be
anything like that simple.'

'Not a chance.'

'Whereas . . .'

'My way, it's done and dusted within twenty-four hours.'

'Let's hope so.'

'Can't fail. Look, I don't know about you, but I didn't get much sleep last night. Which gave me plenty of time to think about . . . good sites for this sort of thing.'

'Come up with many?'

'We only really need one. And I reckon I've got it. Why don't we drive over there and take a look? If it seems OK, we can go back tonight and get the job done.'

'And if it doesn't seem OK?'

'We find somewhere else.'

They set off in separate cars, so that Andrew could carry on to Carwether afterwards. Their destination was Minions, a village of two pubs and a post office on the south-eastern edge of Bodmin Moor. Nick knew the area reasonably well from family outings in times gone by. Industrial archaeology had been no competitor in Michael Paleologus's estimation with the real and ancient thing, but it was better than no archaeology at all, so the ruins of the Phoenix Mines near Minions had been deemed by him worthy of occasional exploration, especially since they were spiced up by proximity to some Bronze Age stone circles.

The car park at Minions commanded a wide-ranging view of Dartmoor to the east and the sea to the south, with Caradon Hill and its giant television transmitter bulking large in the foreground. It was an exposed spot, with a biting wind speeding the clouds overhead. There was a dusting of snow on the distant heights of Dartmoor, but only drifts of hail to whiten the track of the long-vanished railway that had once served the scattered tin and copper mines of the district. There were a few brave dog-walkers out and about, but they were hardly likely to see anything odd in two men without a dog setting off north along the track as it described a gently inclined curve round the flank of Stowe's Hill.

'Most of the shafts round here have been capped,' said Andrew as they strode along. 'The safety lobby have a lot to answer for.'

'Where does that leave us?'

'Hoping they haven't got round to all of them. We'll see soon enough.'

Ten minutes' brisk walking took them to the highest stretch of the line, on a shelf of land looking down across a hummocked stretch of old workings towards the surviving engine house of the Prince of Wales Mine on the other side of the valley. A lane wound up the valley from Minions in the direction of various farms and hamlets to the north.

'See that clump of trees down by the lane?'

'Yeah.'

'There's a shaft in there. I can remember heaving a rock down it when we were boys to see how deep it was.'

'And how deep was it?'

'Deep enough.'

'Close to a road, I see.'

'Just what I was thinking. Let's go and check it out.'

They made their way down the uneven slope through gorse and bracken and tussocky grass, crossed a fast-flowing stream and reached the clump of trees, startling an unsuspecting sheep in the process. The trees turned out on closer inspection to be hawthorn bushes and cotoneaster run wild. A barbed-wire fence about five feet high, reinforced in several places, enclosed them and the overgrown ruin of an engine house.

Andrew prowled around the perimeter until he found what he was looking for: a clear view of the shaft. Nick joined him and peered through the undergrowth. The mouth of the shaft was only a few feet beyond the fence. And it was open.

'Looks like we're in luck.'

'We need to be sure.' Andrew prised a large stone from the nearby turf and tossed it over the fence. They listened and counted the seconds as it vanished into the shaft. Nick had made it to six by the time it clanged against something metallic far below and came to rest.

'Like you said: deep enough.'

'This barbed wire is the only problem.' Andrew turned and looked around. There was no-one within sight. He reached into his pocket, took out a pair of pliers and stooped by the nearest fence post. 'I'll pull out a few of the staples. That'll make the wire easier to bend.' A few minutes later he stood up. 'That should do it.'

They walked clear of the fence and looked down the slope to the lane. It was no more than twenty feet to the verge. 'You'll pull in there?'

'Yeah. It'll go like clockwork, Nick. I promise.'

'When do you want to do this?'

'Tonight. I'll come to Trennor around eleven.'

'There's something you ought to know before then.'

'Tell me what it is on the way back to the car park. No sense our hanging around here.'

The condolences card left under the Land Rover's windscreen wiper in Plymouth on Monday night was the thing Nick now reckoned Andrew needed to be told about. It might not be important. But Nick would not have bet on it. The card, the will, the body in the cellar: they all pointed to events in the past and people in the present that he and Andrew had no knowledge of. And ignorance was a poor basis for any plan.

'You see what I'm saying?'

'That there's more going on than we have any idea of?'

'A lot more would be my guess.'

'You're probably right.'

'Doesn't that worry you?'

'No.'

'Don't you think it should?'

'No. Because one of the few pieces of good advice Dad ever gave me was "Don't worry about what you can't control". This' – he gestured with his thumb back towards the shaft – 'I *can* control.'

'And the rest?'

'Won't be any concern of mine or yours once we've

124

emptied that hole under the cellar.' Andrew grinned. 'And banked Tantris's cheque.'

Nick went back to Trennor anticipating that Pru would have turned up in his absence. But she would see nothing odd in Andrew having stayed at the house overnight and he reckoned the chances of her having tried to open the cellar door were negligible. Even if she had, he could cobble together a cover story.

As it transpired, however, there had been plenty to occupy Pru's mind in his absence. A strange car parked in the yard was the first warning Nick had of this. As Pru shortly afterwards explained, in a whispered conversation in the kitchen, they had a visitor. Or rather, strictly speaking, Michael Paleologus had a visitor.

'I've put him in the drawing room, Nicholas. He was real shook up when I told him your father had passed away. He was expecting to see him today.'

'Who is he?'

'Says his name's David Anderson.'

'Never heard of him.'

'A former student of your father's, apparently.'

'Did he say what he wants?'

'I didn't ask. Well, it's none of my business, is it?'

'It may be none of mine either, Pru. I'll go and find out.'

David Anderson looked to be in his late thirties or early forties, a bulky, stooping figure with a mane of greying curly hair, aviator glasses and a ready smile. His corduroy jacket, sweat-shirt and jeans were all threadbare enough to date from his student days. In fact, it was not entirely clear that those days had ended. There was more than a touch of academic shabbiness about him.

'Mr Paleologus. Good to meet you. You're, er, Michael's son?'

'One of his sons, yes.'

'I'm sorry to hear what's happened. Can't say how sorry.'

'We all are.'

'A fall, your housekeeper said. Is that right?'

'Yes. Last Sunday.' Nick decided against specificity about the circumstances. A request from Anderson to see the offending cellar steps was unlikely, but had to be avoided at all costs. 'He'd been increasingly frail for quite a while. An accident was always on the cards, I'm afraid.'

'He sounded as sharp as ever when I spoke to him.'

'There was nothing wrong with him mentally. Like you say, as sharp as a razor. When did you . . . speak to him?'

'He got in touch with me about ten days ago.'

'Uh-huh. You'd stayed in contact since Oxford, had you?'

'Off and on. I teach history at Sherborne. Michael helped me get the job. So, I'd always have been happy to do him a favour. This is the first time he's actually asked. I'm only sorry it's too late now to give him the results.'

'What did he want you to do?'

'Oh, just a spot of research. Straightforward, really, though fitting it in round my teaching was a bit of a bugger. These places are never open when you want them to be, that's the trouble.'

'What places?'

'Well, in this case, Exeter Cathedral Library. But I managed to get down there on Wednesday afternoon and take a look at the stuff Michael was interested in. Sadly, it seems I was too late.'

'I'm afraid so. But, er, what was this . . . stuff?'

'Pretty esoteric. You don't want me to bore you with it, I'm sure.'

'I'd happily take the risk.'

'Really?'

'It seems a pity for you to do all that work and not get to tell anyone about it. He *was* my father. I've always been interested in his . . . enthusiasms.'

'That's nice.'

'There's something I don't understand, though. Why couldn't he go himself? I don't mean to be rude, but—'

'It's the nature of the material, Mr Paleologus. Reading seventeenth-century script isn't a simple matter. Michael knew I'd had more experience than he had in the field. He was first and foremost an archaeologist, after all.'

'Seventeenth-century script?'

'Yes. To be precise, a haphazardly bound volume of correspondence from successive vicars and churchwardens of the parish of—'

'St Neot.'

Anderson looked at Nick in surprise. 'You already know.'

'Only that Dad was interested in the history of St Neot Church.'

'He certainly was. I mean, this is pretty obscure material.'

'What's it doing in Exeter?'

'Oh, there was no diocese of Truro in the seventeenth century. All Cornish parishes answered to the Bishop of Exeter. Though I doubt many of them produced such voluminous correspondence as St Neot. The collection goes back to the fifteenth century, as a matter of fact, and there's a lot of it. But it was the mid-seventeenth century that Michael wanted me to concentrate on. He'd heard about a letter written by one of the churchwardens, Richard Bawden, in sixteen sixty two, concerning precautions that had been taken during the Civil War to protect the church's evidently rather fine stained glass. He wanted me to confirm the contents of the letter. It was his understanding that Bawden stated in the letter that one of the windows had been removed in sixteen forty-six and entrusted to a gentleman called Mandrell.'

'And did you confirm that?'

'Well, it's a little complicated. I tried to telephone Michael to explain the situation, but, of course, I wasn't able to speak to him. We'd already settled on this morning to meet, so—'

'You could have left a message.'

'Michael specifically asked me not to.'

'He did?'

'Yes. I can't imagine why, but he was most insistent. And

I'm sure you don't need me to tell you how insistent he could be.'

'No.' Nick smiled. 'I suppose I don't.' What he really needed, of course, was an explanation of why his father should so particularly wish to prevent a message being left on his answerphone. The only reason Nick could think of was because such a message would have been evidence of Michael Paleologus's reluctance to accept the case Elspeth had made to him. But he could have justified that on the grounds of academic thoroughness. Secrecy on the point seemed oddly excessive. 'So, what was this . . . complication?'

'Are you really sure you want me to go into it?'

'Absolutely.'

'OK. Well, let me show you this.' Anderson burrowed in a briefcase beside him and pulled out a folder. 'It's a photocopy of the Bawden letter.' He laid the folder on the coffee-table and opened it.

Nick peered down at the sheet of paper on which the letter was copied. At once Anderson's comment about seventeenth-century script made sense. The sloping scrawl was clearly a letter, but, as to what it said, Nick saw only a jumble of curled and tangled pen-strokes. 'Good God. You can read this?'

'With practice, yes. Bawden was writing in answer to a letter from the Bishop's secretary of which there's no copy, at least not in this collection. He says here' – Anderson pointed to a passage that was indistinguishable from the rest as far as Nick was concerned – ' "Mr Philpe has asked me to state my best intelligence of the precautions we took to preserve the great and particular treasure of the parish and how it so came to be spared the attentions of the Parliament's soldiery in those dark days nine years since." That takes us back to sixteen fifty-one, since the letter's dated' – Anderson's finger moved up the page – 'the twenty-first of May, sixteen sixty-two. Right. Now, Bawden goes on to say' – the finger moved back – ' "It was removed five years prior thereto." That means sixteen forty-six. "We could not suffer it to stand at risk with Cornwall in the Parliament's hands. It was immured

128

safe in the keeping of our staunch friend Mr Mandrell, and is safe there still, I warrant." The rest is just respectful gush. Those sentences are the essence of what Bawden communicated.'

'Where does he actually mention the window, then?'

'That's the complication. He doesn't.'

'What?'

' "The great and particular treasure of the parish" is the phrase he uses. He doesn't define what that treasure was. Probably he didn't need to. His correspondent would already have known. It's a good guess that the stained glass is what he's referring to, if it's as fine as I'm told. But that's all it can be: a guess.'

*'The great and particular treasure of the parish'*. Nick studied the phrase, legible now it had been spelt out for him, at some length after Anderson had gone. Elspeth had quoted Bawden as referring to 'our finest window'. Nick was certain about that. Yet here, in Bawden's own hand, was something altogether more ambiguous. It could mean the window, of course. It might well do. But it was not explicitly stated. It was not in black and white. There was an element of doubt, which his father would undoubtedly have seized on. 'Trust nothing except primary sources in this game' was one of the last things the old man had said. And here was the primary source. But what was the game?

Elspeth's misrepresentation was understandable in a way. She had been asked to find the Doom Window and this was as close as she had got. After all, what could the treasure be *but* the window? To call it a guess, as Anderson had done, was to undersell it. Elspeth had merely oversold it to a similar degree.

But was that all she had oversold? 'Michael said there was a "further ramification" of this he might want me to look into,' Anderson had revealed on his way out. 'What do you suppose that was?'

'No idea, I'm afraid,' Nick had replied.

That had not been quite true. Nick felt sure his father would have proceeded next to the question of Mandrell's connection with Trennor. Would that stand up to scrutiny any better than the Bawden letter? It was suddenly a pressing question.

But it was not a question Nick could risk asking Anderson to ponder. More than ever, he had to keep his doubts to himself. There was one person he could ask, however, quite legitimately. He rang Elspeth's mobile number.

The phone was switched off. 'Please try later' was advice Nick did not welcome. Irritatingly, he had failed to ask Elspeth for her home number and, on a Saturday, he was never going to be able to contact her via the Bristol University switchboard. There was her friend at the museum, of course, but there again Nick was out of luck. Tilda Hewitt, a member of the curatorial staff, would not be in again until Monday and her home number was not about to be volunteered, perhaps because, he shortly afterwards established, she was ex-directory.

The remorseless rules of a weekend were borne in on Nick. He could make no progress until Monday. But the drastic action he had agreed to participate in would not wait so long. Andrew was intent on disposing of the body that night. He would brook no delay. But what if, later, the chain of evidence linking the Doom Window to Trennor fell apart in their hands? What would they have achieved then by bundling a corpse down a mine shaft – other than their own incrimination?

Nick kept trying Elspeth's mobile number through the afternoon and evening. Without success.

'I've brought a couple of rubble bags, a roll of duck tape and a length of rope.' Andrew's announcement on arrival at Trennor late that night was severely practical. 'Two bags should be enough. Then we truss it up inside the tarpaulin and go. We can cover the slab with the rack and play dumb if anyone ever finds the hole. OK?'

'As far as it goes, yes.'

'Not getting cold feet, are you, Nick?'

'There's something I have to tell you.'

'Not again.'

'It's important. It concerns . . . well, look at this.' Nick showed him the photocopy of the Bawden letter and tried to explain its potential significance. But, even as he did so, he could see that Andrew was having none of it. He had made up his mind what to do and the phraseological nuances of a barely legible seventeenth-century letter were not going to change it. 'Elspeth Hartley hasn't quite played fair with us. We should check this out before—'

'Bloody hell, Nick. You can't seriously be trying to make something out of . . . out of *that*.' Andrew stabbed derisively at the sheet of paper. 'I can't even read it. Elspeth Hartley's the historian, not you. If it's good enough for her, it's good enough for Tantris. And that means it's good enough for us.'

'Anderson's a historian. And he thinks—'

'I don't care what he thinks. Yeah, Dad probably would have tried to quibble about it. But it doesn't sound to me like anything more than the tiniest of exaggerations.'

'Even so, I think we should ask Elspeth to explain herself.'

'Well, I don't. Are you *trying* to unravel this deal?'

'Of course not.'

'Good. Then let's concentrate on the matter in hand.'

'But that's the point. If there's really no substantial evidence that the Doom Window—'

'I'll tell you what the bloody point is.' Andrew grasped Nick by the shoulder and stared at him. 'Those bones down in the cellar are leaving. Tonight. I'll do it alone if I have to. It won't be easy, but I'll do it. I'd rather you helped me, though. I was counting on it, in fact. You promised you would. The only question that matters to me is: are you going to?'

# CHAPTER TEN

In the end, Nick did help his brother. Short of telephoning the police, he could not in fact have stopped Andrew going ahead. After watching him for several minutes struggling to pull all that remained of whoever their father had buried out from beneath the slab, Nick lost patience with his own doubts and stepped forward to lend a hand. Andrew acknowledged his assistance with the faintest of smiles, as if he had known it would be forthcoming sooner or later.

It was a struggle even for two, a mutual revulsion at having to handle the slimy bone and rotted flesh of a dead human complicating the task. Eventually, with a rubble bag taped round the head and torso and another round the pelvis and legs, it became easier. The visual and tactile reality of the thing they were dealing with was suddenly shielded from them. They tied the tarpaulin tightly round the bundle until it resembled nothing more sinister than a roll of carpet and hauled it out to the Land Rover. Then they cleared up behind them in the cellar and set off.

As Andrew had predicted, Bodmin Moor was deserted. The red aircraft warning beacon on the Caradon Hill transmitter was the only light showing in the black, cloud-blanked sky. One or two lamps shone behind curtained windows in scattered farmhouses and cottages, but they encountered no traffic after leaving the B road at Upton Cross. They approached the shaft cautiously along the lane from Minions, pulled in beside it, turned off the engine and lights and waited until their eyes had adjusted to the darkness and they were certain there was no-one about.

They got out of the car and stood together, listening to the enveloping silence. Then they lifted the bundle out of the back, stumbled up the short slope and felt their way slowly round the fence enclosing the shaft until they reached the loosened stretch of wire. Pulling the wire up high enough for Andrew to crawl beneath it, dragging the bundle with him, seemed to make a lot of noise to Nick's ears. He could only hope it would not carry far on the fitful wind, especially since this was the moment when he had to switch on the torch and shine it at the mouth of the shaft.

'OK,' coming in a whisper from Andrew, was the first word spoken since they had left the car. He pushed the bundle through the undergrowth ahead of him, the tarpaulin snagging on thorns and stalks, until it was hanging over the edge of the shaft. Then he gave it a final shove and it tipped over. As it did so Nick switched off the torch. He heard the bundle strike the sides of the shaft several times until it finally thumped to rest far below.

Silence followed. Then Andrew said, 'Let's get out of here,' and began scrambling back beneath the fence.

A few moments later, they were on the road, the Land Rover's headlamps slicing through the darkness as they sped away. The deed was done.

Andrew became noticeably relaxed as they left the Moor. To him, though not to Nick, it seemed clear that their problem was solved; it was plain sailing from here on. The most obvious sign of this new lightness of heart was a sudden transition from tight-lipped terseness to what counted in Andrew as extreme loquaciousness.

'Tom's spending tonight with his mother. And he'll be stopping off with her for a few days on his way back. I should be glad, I suppose. At least it means she won't have an excuse to show up at the funeral. I'm picking the lad up from Bodmin Parkway tomorrow afternoon. I spoke to Irene earlier and we thought we could get together for tea at Trennor. Her and Laura, me and Tom. Plus you, of course. And Anna and Basil, if Irene can talk them into it. Anna might be feeling a bit left out, with Zack on the other side of the world. We'll have to try and cheer her up. All that OK with you?'

Nick was barely aware of what Andrew had said. In his mind's eye he could see a splintered hole in the skull of a long-dead stranger. And in his hands he could feel the weight and shape of the bone. And beyond that an unanswered question clogged his thoughts: why had Elspeth lied?

'Nick?'

'Sorry?'

'Is that OK with you?'

'What?'

'A family get-together at Trennor tomorrow afternoon.'

'Oh . . .' Nick struggled to summon a reaction. 'Yeah. Fine.'

Nick did not expect to sleep well that night. Strangely, though, he plunged into nine hours of dreamless oblivion, mind and body closing down to dramatic effect. It was mid-morning when he woke.

It was also the fourth Sunday of the month, which meant there was an 11.15 service at Landulph Church, according to the parish newsletter somebody had delivered earlier in the week. For reasons he did not care to analyse too closely, Nick decided to abandon the idea of a run and go to church instead. He tried Elspeth's mobile before leaving the house. It was still switched off.

The brass plaque commemorating Theodore Paleologus had been recently polished. Candlelight glimmered across its inscribed surface as the service unfolded. Nick's gaze wandered often to it as he sang the hymns and murmured the prayers with a true agnostic's lack both of practice and of confidence. Yet he was aware also of something chilling and soulful that the previous night's work had stirred in him. It amounted, he realized, to a desire for absolution. But before absolution came confession. And what he and Andrew had done they could never confess.

Theodore Paleologus had been convicted in Italy of attempted murder. He had come to Cornwall as a fugitive and an exile. His ancestor, Michael Paleologus, had ascended to the throne of Byzantium in 1259 after murdering the Regent of the baby Emperor, John IV. Within a couple of years of his accession as co-Emperor, the founder of the Paleologus dynasty had had the infant John blinded and imprisoned for life. His successors had exhibited equal ferocity in clinging to power, until dispossessed by the Turks two hundred years later. If there was a Paleologus gene, it did not tend to squeamishness, as the clear evidence of another Michael Paleologus's ruthlessness seemed to confirm. They were a violent lot when they needed to be.

But genetics was not an all-encompassing process. Stepping out of the church at the end of the service into a meek and mild splash of Cornish sunshine, Nick recognized in himself none of that ancestral ruthlessness. He did not understand it. He certainly did not believe himself capable of it.

Which might merely mean, he reluctantly acknowledged as he walked back along the lane towards Trennor, that for him the need had simply not arisen. Yet.

Irene and Laura were first to arrive for tea that afternoon, bringing to a halt Nick's unavailing half-hourly calls to Elspeth. He had last seen his niece at his father's eightieth birthday party. Since then, she had grown from a slight and diffident eleven-year-old with braced teeth and a ponytail into a tall and self-possessed fifteen-year-old looking more like eighteen and already displaying much of her mother's poise and elegance.

Nick had never taken his role as uncle any more seriously than Laura had. He had moreover never been sure how much Laura knew about his troubled past, an uncertainty which he had usually dealt with by saying as little to the girl as possible. Accordingly, Laura could not be blamed for finding him dull. As they conversed less than sparklingly about her exam schedule and the train journey from Harrogate, Nick had no doubt that she was silently summing him up in one word, or perhaps three: boring, boring, boring. Which was ironic, since had she known what he and her uncle Andrew had been up to the previous night, boring was unlikely to be the way she would describe it.

'Mum's told me about Mr Tantris,' said Laura at some point. 'Who is he, exactly?'

'A very wealthy man,' put in Irene.

'Yeah, but you must know more about him than that.'

'We don't really need to.'

'That's a matter of opinion,' said Nick.

'Great,' said Laura. 'A family row.'

'There's nothing of the kind, young lady,' Irene responded snappishly. 'Mr Tantris will pay more than he strictly needs to for this house and we'll all benefit from that, you included, so, if the poor man wants his privacy—'

'But he isn't poor, is he?'

'You know what I meant.'

'What do you think, Nick?'

'I think there's a difference between privacy and secrecy.' He smiled appeasingly. 'But I also think your mother probably knows best.'

The arrival of Anna and Basil relieved the pressure on Nick to contribute conversationally. Laura's three negligent uncles were compensated for by an attentive aunt. Anna, indeed, seemed not in the least depressed by Zack's absence, flourishing a printout of an e-mail from the boy, in which he expressed his sorrow at missing his grandfather's funeral. She possessed a sharper instinct for the passions and pre-occupations of a teenage girl than Irene and homed in on them effortlessly.

After some time had slipped vapidly by, Nick and Basil

136

conspired to drift into the garden, leaving the girls to chatter in the drawing room. Outside, among the wintry borders, Basil volunteered quite neutrally that Nick was not looking his best.

'Careworn is how I'd put it, Nick. Distinctly careworn. Not on account of this discrepancy in Miss Hartley's summary of the Bawden letter, I hope.'

'Andrew told you about that, did he?'

'Telephone call this morning. Irene was treated to one as well, I believe. Apparently, we all think you're worrying unnecessarily.'

'What do you mean by "apparently"?'

'Well, my opinion's irrelevant, isn't it?'

'Not to me.'

'Really? How pleasantly surprising.'

'Spit it out, for God's sake.'

'Very well. Miss Hartley claimed the letter referred to the Doom Window quite explicitly, whereas in reality it's altogether more . . . *im*plicit.'

'You could say that, yeah.'

'Quite. Now, should that worry us?'

Only when it became apparent that Basil did not intend to answer his own question did Nick turn to him and say, 'Well? Should it?'

At which Basil grinned unhelpfully. 'I really . . . don't know.'

Nick's last encounter with Tom would have been, as with Laura, at his father's eightieth birthday party, but for a more recent crossing of paths in London. One dismally wet afternoon the previous October, they had met by chance outside the British Library, Nick *en route* for Euston station, Tom for King's Cross. A ten-minute chat over cardboard-cupped *cappuccinos* in the Library's street-front coffee-shop had followed. What they had discussed Nick had no memory of, although that almost counted as a memory in itself. Both had been evasive, he recalled, paying mutual lip service to the uncle–nephew relationship. Tom, of course, had postgraduate unemployment to draw a veil over, while Nick had his own reasons to be reticent. Tom had looked well – soft blond floppy hair, big brown puppy-dog eyes, square jaw emphasized by several days' growth of beard, gym-honed physique filling out fashionable clothes – but, as to how he felt, Nick would have been no worse informed if they had passed each other by without exchanging a word.

When Tom came in with Andrew, Nick noticed a change in him that he suspected the others were probably in no position to. He was certainly more communicative than on that rainy day in the Euston Road, but that was only to be expected, with aunts and uncles and a cousin to be faced in the company of an all but estranged father. The change that Nick detected was hard to define but clear to him nonetheless. Tom's gaze had become narrower, almost wary. And he had lost a little weight. Unemployment, Nick reckoned, had taken its toll.

Andrew was in over-compensatory mode, talking too much and too loudly. Tom, for his part, deflected questions about life in Edinburgh with charm and adroitness, before expressing his fondness for his late grandfather and his regret at not having seen more of him in recent years. He slotted into the family mood of restrained mourning with such ease that it came as a surprise to Nick that he had not been told about the Tantris offer.

This only became apparent when Laura, who had clearly decided her cousin had become something of a dish since she had last set eyes on him, said suddenly, 'What do you think we ought to spend the money on, Tom?'

'We haven't gone into that yet,' put in Andrew, with an exasperated glance at Irene.

'What's this all about?' Tom's look around the room was an understandable mix of curiosity and irritation.

'We've been made a generous offer for Trennor,' Andrew explained. 'Well, it was made to your grandfather, of course, but it falls to us now.' Clearly, he saw no need to mention what Tom's grandfather had thought of the offer. 'It seems there may be some historically important stained glass hidden—'

'*Stained glass*?' Tom sounded suitably incredulous.

'Believe it or not, yeah. It's all tied up with the Civil War. This historian thinks glass from an ancient window in St Neot Church was concealed here some time in the sixteen forties to protect it from Cromwell's troops and that it's almost certainly still here. She works for someone who's willing to pay handsomely for the chance to find out.'

'So how are they going to do that?'

'Well, they're going to do whatever it takes.'

'Pull the place apart, you mean?'

'Not quite.'

'But nearly,' observed Basil.

Tom gave an ironic whistle. 'Don't suppose Grandad went a bundle on the idea.'

'Not at first,' Andrew cautiously admitted.

'Who's the man with the money?'

'Does it matter?'

'Just asking.'

'His name's Tantris,' said Irene. 'That's about all we really—'

'*Tantris*?' Tom stared at his aunt in apparent stupefaction.

'Yes. As I—'

'You can't be serious.'

'Why not?' Anna said with a laugh. 'It's not as unusual a name as Paleologus.'

'Yeah, but—' Tom seemed to be having difficulty grasping something that was, on the face of it, very simple. 'He can't be called Tantris.'

'But he is,' said Irene.

'Come off it. This is a joke, right?'

'What's wrong, Tom?' Nick said suddenly. 'Why can't he be called Tantris?'

'Don't you know?'

'Self-evidently,' said Basil, 'we do not.'

Tom looked from one to the other of them, absorbing the reality of the situation. Then he said, 'I'm just going to get something from my bag, OK? Can you give me the key, Dad?'

With a puzzled frown, Andrew pulled the car key out of his pocket and handed it over. Tom hurried from the room, leaving the others to share their bemusement.

'Weird,' murmured Laura.

'You can say that again.' Anna shook her head. 'What's this about, Andrew?'

He shrugged. 'No idea.'

'Some bizarre misunderstanding,' offered Irene.

'Bizarrerie is a family speciality, after all,' Basil observed.

'Shut up, Basil,' snapped Anna.

'Weird,' Laura repeated.

'Don't worry.' Andrew smiled gamely. 'We'll soon sort it out.'

A few minutes later, Tom walked back into the room holding a slim paperback in his hand. He plonked himself down in his chair and held the book up for them to see. It was a Penguin Classic: *The Romance of Tristan*, by Beroul. 'Grandad sent this to me a couple of weeks ago with a note attached. "You should read this." That was all. Some joke of his, I reckoned, though what the joke was . . .' He shrugged.

'You never mentioned it to me,' Andrew complained.

'I didn't think it was any big deal. You didn't mention a much bigger one, did you?'

'I was going to.'

'What's the significance of the book, Tom?' Nick intervened.

'Oh yeah. Well, I guess we've all heard of Tristan and Yseult, the original star-crossed lovers.'

'Remind us,' said Irene.

'Right. OK. I flicked through the book on the train down, basically to see if I could work out why Grandad sent it to me. Beroul's the name of some twelfth-century storyteller. His version of the romance is the oldest surviving. The way he

140

tells it, Tristan was the nephew of King Mark of Cornwall, who—'

'Whose court was at Tintagel,' Basil interrupted.

'Yeah. Well, I thought that must be the point. You know, Grandad going down memory lane, reminding me of the legends linked to the place he helped excavate back in the Thirties.'

'But he was always scornful of the legends,' said Nick.

Irene sighed. 'Why don't you just come to the real point, Tom?'

'I'm trying to. The legends aren't it. I get that now. Yseult is the daughter of the King of Ireland. Tristan kills her uncle in fair combat, but is wounded in the process. The wound refuses to heal so Tristan casts off in a boat with neither sails nor oars, trusting to God to take him wherever he needs to go to be cured. He's washed up on the Irish coast, taken into the court posing as a minstrel in distress and has his wounds tended by Yseult, who turns out to have the magic touch. Tristan's cured and returns to Cornwall. He and Yseult only become lovers later, when Yseult is sent to Cornwall under Tristan's escort to marry King Mark. Her mother gives her a love potion to drink with the King on their wedding night, but it gets mistaken for wine on the voyage and she shares it with Tristan instead. The tragic love story unfolds from there. But earlier on, when he first meets Yseult, Tristan uses a pseudonym to avoid identifying himself as her uncle's killer. The pseudonym is actually an anagram of his own name. He calls himself—'

'Tantris,' said Basil softly.

'What?' Irene looked sharply across at her brother.

'Tantris,' Basil repeated. 'Yes, of course. The two syllables turned the other way round. I should have thought of that.'

'Yeah.' Tom nodded. 'Tristan called himself Tantris when he needed to conceal his true identity.'

'Wait a minute,' said Andrew. 'Are you saying—'

'There's no such person as Tantris.' It seemed to Nick as he spoke that he had known this for some time, but only now been forced to admit it. 'There never has been.'

141

Anna stared at him in obvious bafflement. 'Would someone mind telling me what the hell we're talking about?'

'There's no Tantris,' said Nick. 'It's as simple as that.'

'And no Tantris,' Basil began, 'means—'

'No money.' Andrew's words were muffled by the hand he had raised to his face. 'Oh God.'

# CHAPTER ELEVEN

At ten o'clock the following morning, with their father's funeral only two hours away, Andrew, Irene, Basil, Nick and Anna sat, black-suited and sombre-faced, in their solicitor's cluttered office in Plymouth. Maurice Baskcomb, also black-suited but somehow failing to look sombre despite a frown, kneaded his large, sausage-fingered hands together and leaned forward on his desk.

'I think it fair to say I've never experienced the like of this in my far from short legal career,' he said, forming the words slowly and deliberately. 'When you telephoned me last night—'

'We're sorry to have disturbed you at home, Mr Baskcomb,' said Irene.

'Think nothing of it, Mrs Viner. It was, I think we can agree, an emergency. In some ways, it still is. As you suggested, I contacted Mr Tan—' He paused, pursed his lips, then continued. 'I contacted the solicitor I've been dealing with on your behalf, Miss Palmer of Hopkins and Broadhurst, London. She could not tell me a great deal, bound as she is by rules of confidentiality.'

'I'll bet,' growled Andrew.

'Such rules exist for the protection of the client, Mr Paleologus, not the solicitor.'

'We understand that,' said Irene. 'What *could* Miss Palmer tell you?'

'Well, it appears she's never met Mr Tantris, which is hardly surprising, given the unusual circumstances. She's dealt only with his assistant, a Miss Elsmore. Now, I did give your description of Miss Hartley to her and, though she wouldn't commit herself, I had the distinct impression that the description could easily have fitted Miss Elsmore. I also contacted Bristol University's personnel department this morning. There is an Elspeth Hartley on their academic staff, but she's currently on sabbatical . . . in Boston.'

'Would that be Boston, Lincolnshire,' Basil enquired, 'or Massachusetts?'

'The latter, Mr Paleologus.'

'She set us up,' said Anna, whose tone was still fixed in the disbelief that had overtaken her the previous night.

'She's clearly been less than open with you,' Baskcomb went on. 'And with me. And indeed with her own solicitor.'

'What about the money?' asked Andrew, the undertow in his voice suggesting he already knew the answer to his question. 'What about the half a million quid Tantris was supposed to have deposited with Hopkins and Broadhurst?'

'Withdrawn late Friday afternoon,' Baskcomb gloomily replied. 'Miss Palmer was apparently about to telephone me to report that development when I telephoned her.'

'How was it withdrawn?' asked Irene.

'In the form, I imagine, of a Hopkins and Broadhurst cheque.'

'Payable to whom?'

'To Miss Elsmore, presumably. Or to whomsoever Miss Elsmore nominated as payee. Miss Palmer had no authority to give me that information.'

'But it's the only way to track down the bastard behind this swindle.' Andrew glanced round at his siblings for support. 'She has to tell.'

'There's been no swindle,' Baskcomb calmly responded. 'I'm afraid it amounts to nothing more than an elaborate practical joke.'

'A *joke*?'

'I don't see the funny side of it either, Mr Paleologus.'

'But you don't lose by it, Mr Baskcomb, do you? You haven't had the prospect of quitting a farm that grows debts thicker than thistles dangled in front of you, only for it to be snatched away. My God, when I think . . .' Andrew looked away towards the window.

Then his gaze slowly drifted back to Nick. Only they knew just how far they had gone to ensure Tantris's offer remained on the table. And now they knew it had never really been there in the first place. It *was* a joke, a horribly good one. But no-one was laughing. No-one in Baskcomb's office, anyway.

'Didn't you say, Mrs Viner,' Baskcomb resumed, 'that you had one further line of inquiry to follow where Miss Hartley is concerned?'

Irene looked at Nick for an answer. 'She mentioned a friend who works at the Museum,' he said. 'It'll be another ruse, I'm afraid. A name she picked up from a staff list or something of the kind and dropped into the conversation for the sake of . . . well . . .'

'Verisimilitude,' said Basil.

'Exactly. Her mobile phone was switched off over the weekend. Now the number's unobtainable. Draw your own conclusions.'

'Sadly, I'm afraid you'll have to,' said Baskcomb. 'I'm entirely at a loss.'

'Loss,' murmured Andrew. 'Yeah. There's plenty of that to go round.'

Andrew had not been making even an oblique reference to the ceremony they were about to take part in. It was a measure of the degree to which they had been made fools of by the Tantris deception that they could find no space for the sorrow they were supposed to display – and to feel. They emerged from Baskcomb's office into a damp, grey morning that had not even the decency to be appropriately cold, each churning with anger and humiliation. And loss, of course: the kind of loss Elspeth Hartley had decreed they should experience.

'The bitch,' hissed Anna. 'Who is she? Why did she do this?'

'It has to be some sort of con trick,' said Irene, her self-control still intact. 'But I don't understand. What did she gain from it?'

'I suspect Dad could have told us,' said Basil.

'What do you mean?'

'He saw through the pseudonym at once. He was meant to. As the book he sent to Tom demonstrates.'

'Why did he send it to Tom? Why didn't he warn us instead?'

'There again, he could have told us. Alas, it's too late to ask him now.'

'I'm not sure I can face this bloody pantomime,' said Andrew. 'You may have to get through it without me.'

'We'll get through it together, Andrew,' said Irene. 'It's time we all went back to Trennor and waited for the cortège. Let's hope Laura and Tom haven't strayed from the car park. I don't want us to run late.' She at least was determined to maintain a dignified front for the funeral. 'The last thing we need is Archie and Norma getting wind of what's happened.' Norma, their late mother's sister, and her husband Archie, retired lawn-mower entrepreneur, were pledged to attend, despite being given plenty of encouragement to excuse themselves on grounds of age and distance. 'I've told Laura to say nothing. Can we rely on Tom?'

'Of course,' Andrew edgily replied.

'Good. Then I suggest we get on. All this' – she glanced up at Baskcomb's office window – 'will have to wait.'

But one thing would not wait. Irene was taking Andrew, Laura and Tom in her car, leaving Nick to chauffeur Basil and Anna. There was time, Nick reckoned, to check if Elspeth's reference to Tilda Hewitt really was the ruse he thought. He dropped Anna off outside the Museum, then drove back and forth between Charles Cross and Drake Circus for as long as he judged she might need.

Anna was waiting to be picked up when he returned ten minutes later, with just the report he had expected. 'The Tilda creature deigned to speak to me and made it crystal clear she'd never heard of an Elspeth Hartley.'

'But which Elspeth Hartley is that?' pondered Basil as they headed up North Hill. 'The one currently on Bostonian sabbatical . . . or another?'

'Another,' said Nick ruefully. 'Or, rather, somebody else altogether.'

'And so the lady vanishes.'

'Yeah.'

'But with what accomplished?'

'Not sure.' But there had to be a logic to what had happened. Nick knew that. Maybe there never had been a hidden Doom Window. But the buried body was real enough. Except that now it was no longer buried. Could he and Andrew somehow have been manipulated into doing someone else's dirty work? Surely not. No-one could have predicted Michael Paleologus's death and the consequences that would flow from it. Could they?

'Do we know exactly who's showing up?' Anna asked as they joined the A38 and headed west, her mind turning only now to what was close at hand.

'Apart from locals, you mean?' Nick responded.

'I mean people we'll have to talk to afterwards over smoked-salmon sandwiches and sausages on sticks.'

'Ah. Right. Well, there'll be Archie and Norma, as you know. And I imagine we'll have to ask the Wellers back.' The Wellers were Michael Paleologus's closest neighbours, with whom the family maintained superficially amicable relations. 'Of the Oxford lot, only old Farnsworth is coming down.'

'Oh God,' Anna groaned. 'I'd hoped I'd never have to have my bum fondled by that lecher again.'

'He obviously felt the opportunity was too good to miss,' said Basil.

'Shut up, Basil.'

'He *was* just about Dad's closest colleague,' Nick pointed out. 'It's natural he'd want to pay his last respects.'

'Maybe,' said Anna. 'But I'll still be standing with my back against the wall if he starts circulating.'

'Don't worry,' said Nick. 'I'll keep him away from you.' It had suddenly occurred to him that engaging Farnsworth in conversation would be no bad idea. It was clear to Nick that they knew less about their father than they had supposed. Julian Farnsworth was a social magpie, a collector of the curious details of other people's lives. For once it was possible he might have something to say that Nick wanted to hear.

To Nick's surprise, the anxieties besetting him fell away as soon as he climbed into the car following the hearse and realized that his father's funeral had begun. His mind was so numbed by recent events and his part in them that an hour of immemorial ceremony offered a mental refuge where he could calm himself with trivial but poignant memories of his childhood, when life had seemed both simple and joyful. It could not last, of course. He had been perceptive enough as a child to realize that even then. But, while it had, it had been wonderful. And his father, for all his faults, had been part of the wonder.

The hymns were sung, the prayers were said. The rector offered up some kindly words and made passing mention of Michael Paleologus's celebrated lineage. Then they processed to the graveyard and watched the coffin being lowered into the earth, while the rector made the final pronouncements, to a chorus of rooks and a murmur of wind in the yew trees. Anna sobbed, Laura wept and Aunt Norma dabbed her eyes. Irene merely squeezed her gloved hands together and breathed deeply.

Andrew caught Nick's gaze and held it for a moment as he stepped forward to sprinkle his trowelful of earth on the coffin. Neither could help thinking of another burial, the truth of which their father had taken to the grave with him. That other body had no coffin, nor brass plate to give it name. Yet no doubt there were loved ones who would have liked the chance to bid him or her farewell.

The graveside party progressed slowly to the churchyard gate, where Nick stepped quietly to one side while Aunt Norma embarked on a round of hugs and endearments. Archie wobbled from foot to foot behind her. The Wellers hovered nearby. And Julian Farnsworth struck an extravagantly mournful attitude on the fringe of the group.

Nick's rough calculation put Farnsworth in his mid-seventies, though he looked younger, thanks to suspiciously dark hair and an erect bearing. He had creases at the edge of his mouth that made him seem permanently on the point of smiling and sparkling blue-grey eyes that compounded the effect. He had not run to fat, nor grown gaunt with age. He dressed more smartly than most academics and was presumably the owner of the preposterously Parisian old Citroën parked a little further up the lane. He was the best-manicured archaeologist Nick had ever met; according to Michael Paleologus this was because he never engaged in any actual archaeology. He had even been nicknamed 'the Commodore' because of the general belief that naval officers of that rank never went to sea.

But he had driven two hundred miles to see off an old friend and Nick hoped that signified something. 'Dr Farnsworth?' he ventured.

'Nicholas.' They shook hands. 'A pleasure to see you again, despite the occasion.'

'I'm impressed you remember me.'

'Put it down to the *Daily Telegraph* crossword puzzle.'

'I'm sorry?'

'It keeps the memory in training. Very important.'

'Of course.'

'A decently done service, I thought.'

'Good. I'm glad you could make it.'

'Retirement has a liberating effect on the diary, if not on the bank balance. Besides, I could hardly have stayed away in the circumstances.'

'The circumstances?' Nick felt sure he had caught something odd in Farnsworth's tone.

'Well, I'd spoken so recently to Michael . . .'

'You had?'

'Why, yes. He died on Sunday the twenty-first?'

'That's right. A week ago yesterday.'

'Then it can only have been a few days before.'

'Really?' Nick tried not to sound as curious as he was. 'Do you mind my asking what you spoke to him about?'

'Not at all. It's—'

''Scuse me,' put in a voice. 'Mr Paleologus?'

Nick turned to meet the squinting gaze of an old man in a threadbare overcoat and a black suit, white-shirted but tieless, the shirt buttoned to the neck. He was not much above five feet tall, loose-limbed and built like a whippet. In one hand he clutched a dark brown cap, in the other a crumpled copy of the order of service. His white hair was cut so short that it was no more than a light dusting on his head. His face was narrow and frowning, the eyes twinkling darkly through the compressed lids.

'I didn't think it fitting to come to the graveside, see, not being family and all. You likely didn't spy me at the back of the church. I just wanted to make myself known before I left. I'm Frederick Davey.'

Nick covered his discomposure with a smile and shook Davey's hand. 'I'm Nicholas Paleologus. This is Dr Julian Farnsworth, an old colleague of my father's. Pleased to meet you, Mr Davey. Do you live around here?'

'No, no. Tintagel. I'd not have known about this but for the notice in the paper.'

'You drove down?' Nick asked, partly because he could see no car parked in the lane that Davey was likely to have driven and partly because he did not dare stray beyond the blandest of topics.

'I got no car. Can't afford one.'

'How did you make the journey, then, Mr Davey?' Farnsworth enquired.

'The Plymouth bus dropped me at Paynter's Cross. 'Twas shanks's pony from there.'

'You walked from Paynter's Cross?' Nick was genuinely surprised.

'Had no choice. If I was to be here. As I thought I should, like.'

'How did you know Michael?' asked Farnsworth.

'Who?'

'My father, Mr Davey,' said Nick.

'Oh, sorry, I'm sure. Always thought of him as . . . Mr Paleologus. Well, young Mr Paleologus, when I first met him. He was helping his father on the dig up at the castle then.'

'The dig?' Farnsworth's archaeological senses were suddenly alert.

'Under Dr Radford.'

'You mean the Tintagel excavations of the nineteen thirties?'

'That'll be them.'

'My, my, that *is* interesting. What was your involvement, Mr Davey?'

'Well, I was took off quarrying to do the spadework. Me and a good few others. 'Tweren't so very scientific, now I look back.'

'Fascinating.' The expression on Farnsworth's face suggested that he was not being sarcastic.

'I think we should be starting back for the house, Nick,' said Irene as she suddenly appeared amongst them. 'You'll join us, Dr Farnsworth?'

'Gladly.'

'And, er . . .'

'This is Mr Davey, Irene.' Nick caught her eye. 'From Tintagel.'

'What time's your bus back, Mr Davey?' asked Farnsworth.

'Quarter to five. There's only one a day, see.'

'How very inconvenient. Still, I could give you a lift some of the way . . . if we were leaving at the same time.'

And so, courtesy of Julian Farnsworth, Fred Davey was added to the party that assembled for a late buffet lunch at Trennor. There were fifteen in all, rather more than Pru had catered for, though there was ample slack in her assessment of the quantities required, which was as well, given Davey's swiftly exhibited capacity to consume her sausage rolls.

His presence was a far greater complication in another sense. Once word about him had passed between Nick's siblings, a tension entered the atmosphere that only they were aware of. Davey had witnessed a will they had subsequently destroyed. It was hard for them to believe he had made the journey from Tintagel purely because he and Michael Paleologus had worked on the same dig more than sixty years before. A whispered settlement of tactics took place in the kitchen. Irene was to monopolize Baskcomb; he and Davey obviously had to be kept apart. Anna would keep Laura and Tom out of mischief. Basil would seek to shepherd Archie and Norma into conversation with the Wellers. Andrew would swap Cornish lore with Davey. Which left Nick to probe Farnsworth's recent contact with their father, a task all agreed he was best qualified to undertake.

He made an adroit start by luring Farnsworth into the study to admire Michael Paleologus's collection of archaeological books. Farnsworth had done no more than finger a few spines when Nick reminded him of what they had been discussing before Davey's arrival at the church gate.

'Ah yes. On that subject, I was half-expecting to see David Anderson here.'

'You were?'

'Well, when I spoke to Michael, he mentioned that he'd also been in touch with Anderson. The young man's done well for himself, given his pedestrian cast of mind. I'm sure he was the ideal choice for whatever Michael wanted of him.'

'Some archival research at Exeter Cathedral Library.'

'Ah. You were privy to Michael's enquiries, then.'

'In part. I spoke to David Anderson last week. He'd have liked to be here today, but his teaching commitments didn't permit.'

'How sad. What did Michael have him burrowing after in Exeter?'

'It had to do with a seventeenth-century occupant of this house, by the name of Mandrell.'

'Really?' Farnsworth's expression betrayed no reaction. 'He didn't . . . speak to you about Mandrell?'

'Not at all. Probably knew better. I'm no historian. Not much of an archaeologist either, in Michael's opinion. You have to dirty your hands to do it properly.'

'Why did Dad contact you, then?'

'Checking up on an old acquaintance. Very much my speciality. Though, as it turned out, I couldn't help him.'

'What old acquaintance was this?'

'Digby Braybourne. Heard of him?'

'I don't think so.'

'No reason why you should. A contemporary of Michael's. Also an archaeologist. Briefly a fellow at Brasenose. An entertaining character. I have one or two fond memories of him. Left Oxford under something of a cloud, I'm afraid.'

'What sort of cloud?'

'The sort that involves a spell in prison. Fraud, as I recall. Authenticating fake artefacts for one of the big auction houses, hence bringing the University into disrepute. You're not likely to need a college parking space after that. It would have been the bum's rush for Digby whatever the jury decided.'

'When was this?'

'Oh, it must be more than forty years ago now. Let me see. Yes. Michaelmas term of 'fifty-seven, I'd say.'

'And Braybourne went to prison?'

'I'm afraid so. I visited him a couple of times in Reading Gaol, which I thought kinder of me than he did. He asked me to stop going. So, I stopped. And that is the last I ever saw of him. He never returned to Oxford, gown *or* city.'

'What happened to him?'

'Haven't the foggiest. As I told Michael. But . . . I agreed to ask around. Still turned up nothing, though. A cold trail.'

'Why did Dad want to trace him after all these years?'

'For a reunion of old army pals, apparently. They served in the war together.'

'Did they?' Nick was puzzled. His father had never once, as far as he knew, participated in regimental reunions. His time in uniform was not something he had ever dwelt on. He had done his bit for king and country without running many personal risks, the way he had told it. Whiling away most of the war on Cyprus, conveniently bypassed by all hostilities. 'Would that have been on Cyprus, do you think?'

'Quite possibly. I remember they both spoke of being stationed in the Med. But was it Cyprus?'

'Dad always said so.'

'There you are, then. Of course, I imagine they may have . . . passed through other places.'

'They may have, yes.'

'Who can say?'

'Well, Digby Braybourne, I suppose.'

'Indeed. But where is Digby?' Farnsworth smiled. 'Just like the fellow, really. Never to be found when you want him.'

The party fizzled to a close without incident. Archie became drunk, as was not unexpected. Anna escaped molestation by Farnsworth. Mrs Weller turned out to be an old girl of Laura's school, which delighted her more than it did Laura. And Fred Davey never had a chance to talk last wills and testaments with Baskcomb. Though what Farnsworth meant to give him the chance to talk about *en route* to Tintagel was in its way an equally disturbing thought.

Even when the generally less than mournful mourners had left, Nick and his siblings were not free to review in all its ramifications the reversal of fortune that had overtaken them.

A team effort at clearing away and loading the dishwasher brought forward Pru's departure by a good hour, but they were still constrained by the fact that Laura and Tom knew nothing – and could be allowed to know nothing – about their grandfather's second will. Nick and Andrew harboured their own gruesome secret, of course, one that made the burning of the will seem the most trivial of acts. But they could not speak of it. Nor did Nick see how they could engineer an opportunity to do so before he went back to Milton Keynes.

'It's "now you see it, now you don't" where the money's concerned, then,' Tom carelessly remarked, when discussion of the funeral had run its course and he had followed up numerous glasses of wine with a bottle of Grölsch.

'This Hartley woman was just having you on?' asked Laura.

'Apparently so,' said Irene.

'What are you going to do about it?'

'There's nothing we *can* do.'

'You could try to track her down,' said Tom.

'To what purpose? She's duped us, but she hasn't actually defrauded us.'

'Nevertheless,' said Nick, 'I was planning to stop in Bristol on my way back tomorrow and see if there's any way to confirm the real Elspeth Hartley is in Boston.'

'You're leaving tomorrow?' Andrew looked shocked by the news.

'I'm expected back in the office on Wednesday.'

'Life goes on,' said Anna. 'And work too. Without an end in sight, now. Tantris has disappeared in a puff of smoke.'

'We can still sell the house,' said Irene.

'Yeah. But not as quickly. And not as lucratively.'

'What was the point of the deception?' asked Tom. 'Like you said, there was no real fraud involved. So, what was the object of the exercise?'

'We don't know,' Irene replied.

'But there has to have been one.'

'Presumably.'

155

'Stands to reason. Anyway, Grandad would have got the Tristan and Yseult reference straight off. He'd have known Tantris was a ringer, right?'

'Yes.'

'So, why didn't he blow the whistle?'

'He did, Tom,' said Basil. 'He blew it to you.'

'Yeah, but what good did that do? It was you guys who needed to know. Why didn't he tell you?'

It was a good question. And one to which nobody had an answer. Not an answer they could admit to, anyway, although a chilling possibility had taken root in Nick's thoughts. Michael Paleologus had rumbled Elspeth from the first, as he had been meant to. But he could not speak out, because of what he knew lay in that hole beneath the cellar. He could only send a message to Tom, knowing Tom was highly un-likely to come south in the near future, save in the event of a death in the family – such as his grandfather's. Michael Paleologus had been prepared to warn his children, but only when he was no longer there to suffer the consequences of doing so. Which surely meant he had foreseen his death. And a death foreseen is not much of an accident.

Irene and Laura left around dusk. It was business as usual for Irene at the Old Ferry that evening; and for many evenings to come now the goose that had promised to lay their golden egg had flown. Irene had clearly wanted to speak more freely than she could during the afternoon, but she was nothing if not self-controlled.

The same could hardly be said of Anna, who fumed and fretted mutely but very obviously. When Tom announced he was stepping out for a smoke and a breath of night air, nobody volunteered to go with him, though not because – as his father pointed out – the smoke was unlikely to be tobacco. In the circumstances, any chance of unfettered discussion was welcome.

'Did Davey ask you about cousin Demetrius, Andrew?' Anna blurted out as soon as Tom had gone.

'No. He'd have worried me less if he had. I mean, he has to know about him, doesn't he?'

'Not necessarily,' said Basil.

'He knows,' Andrew insisted. 'He asked me if all the family was present. Why would he do that unless he was in a position to be sure they weren't?'

'It could have been an innocent enquiry.'

'Innocent my arse.'

'He can't prove anything,' said Anna.

'Let's hope you're right. If he had another copy of the will, even the pittance we stand to salvage from this mess will slip through our fingers.'

'It's hardly a pittance,' said Nick.

'Easy for you to say.'

'Not so easy, actually, Andrew. I've put my neck on the line just like you.'

The two brothers stared at each other for a moment. Nick blamed Andrew for talking him out of doing what they should have done when they discovered the body in the cellar. If they had gone to the police then, they would not be left now wondering just how comprehensively they had been set up. He could not come out and say it, but the accusation was there in his gaze, as he meant it to be.

'We all put our necks on the line,' said Anna, deaf to the true meaning of Nick's words. 'Squabbling like schoolboys won't help.'

'You sound like Irene,' said Basil.

'Shut up, Basil. This is important. Did Farnsworth say anything that implied he'd ever heard Dad mention a Venetian cousin, Nick?'

'No.' For some reason, Nick did not feel inclined to expand on his answer.

'Right. And it's paranoid to think Davey might have a copy of the will. My bet is we destroyed the only copy.'

'What are the odds on this bet?' Andrew glumly enquired.

'The best we're going to get. I'm as pissed off about all this as you are, Andrew, but—'

157

'I doubt that.'

'All right. You can take first prize if you want. I don't care. I'd like to get hold of that Hartley bitch, but I don't think I'm going to get the chance. I don't know why she played such a cruel trick on us, but the only way—'

'There has to be a reason,' said Basil.

'Really?' Anna stared at him. 'And what is the reason?'

'I don't know.'

'Exactly. You don't know. I don't know. *We* don't know. And I can't imagine Elspeth Hartley's going to let us find out. So, I suggest we concentrate on making the best of it.'

'Ah. The philosophy of last resort.'

'Thanks to putting that piece of paper on the fire last week, we have this house and equal shares of what it's worth. That's all that matters now. Everything else is just a losing lottery ticket. We have to put it behind us. I'll speak to Irene once Laura's gone back, but I'm sure she'll agree. We must go on as if we'd never heard of Elspeth Hartley.'

'What about cousin Demetrius?' asked Andrew.

'Him too. In fact, especially him. We have to draw a line under this, boys.' Anna took a large swallow of gin and tonic. 'And move on.'


Moving on was precisely what Nick had in mind. He could only hope the humdrum routine of his everyday life in Milton Keynes would enable him to forget the events of the previous week. After the others had gone, he went into the study and stared at the photograph on the wall of his father and grandfather at Tintagel with Ralegh Radford in the summer of 1935. Michael Paleologus had been nineteen then, though he looked older, with his middle-aged tweeds and earnest expression. There were two blurred figures in the background Nick had never noticed before: a pair of workmen leaning on shovels and looking towards the camera, visible only from the waist up because of the ditch they were standing in. Could Fred Davey have been one of them? Nick peered long and hard, but knew he would never be certain. Not that it mattered. Davey *had* been there. And in some sense Nick could not begin to understand, that *did* matter.

The thing Nick's father had concealed in the cellar had seared itself into his mind's eye. Sleep lured him back down to see the slab being raised and to watch as the light fell across the unblinking stare of a fleshless skull. He jolted awake to escape it, not once, not twice, but three times, as the night passed, dark and silent hour by dark and silent hour.

Before dawn Nick was up and washed and packed. He wanted only to be on the road now, away and alone. He decided to leave a note for Pru rather than wait for her, as he had said he would. After a hasty breakfast and the late dawning of a grey and mizzly day, he went out to the car to check the tyres and top up the windscreen-washer for the journey.

The tyre gauge was in the glove compartment. As he opened the passenger door to fetch it, he saw an object on the driver's seat which had certainly not been there before. It was a large brown envelope, unsealed and evidently containing something bulky. On the face of the envelope, in felt-penned capitals, were the words D.C. WISE, CROWNHILL POLICE STATION, PLYMOUTH.

Nick stared at the envelope for a moment, wondering what it contained and how it had got there. None of the windows had been forced; the car was securely locked. Someone must have borrowed his key. It had been in his coat pocket, hanging in the hall, since he had driven back to Trennor from Plymouth the previous morning. Someone at the funeral party must have taken it, slipped out into the yard and then slipped back again. It would not have been difficult. It would have taken no more time than a visit to the loo. But who would do such a thing? Who – and why?

Nick picked the envelope up and slid the contents out on to the seat in front of him. It was a video cassette. Whoever had put it there wanted him to see something – before the police saw it.

A few minutes later, Nick was in the drawing room, staring at the television as the video began to play.

It had been shot at night, with an infra-red camera. Nick recognized the grainy, bleached look of it from TV News war-zone footage. But this was no war zone. This was the ghostly night-as-strange-day world of Bodmin Moor. The camera dwelt on the Caradon Hill transmitter and the more distant hump of Kit Hill long enough to fix the approximate location. Then it panned round to something closer at hand: a fenced-off patch of bush and bramble. Nick knew exactly what it was. And he already knew what he was going to see.

A vehicle, by its shape obviously a Land Rover, pulled up at the side of the road further down the slope. Its lights died. A few minutes passed, then two figures climbed out and looked around. Identification would not have been easy, though to Nick they were all too recognizable. They opened the back door of the Land Rover, lifted out a bundle about six feet long and carried it up the slope, until they were probably about twenty yards from the camera. They hoiked up the lower half of a stretch of fence and one of them crawled through, pulling the bundle after him. The other switched on a torch, its pool of light like a splash of acid on the film. The bundle was pushed forward. It vanished from sight. The torch was switched off. The man inside the fence crawled back out, then he and his companion retreated down the slope.

As they climbed into the Land Rover, the camera started moving, the picture joggling as its operator hurried down the slope after them. The vehicle performed a three-point turn and, by the time it had completed the second, reversing leg of the manoeuvre, the camera was only a few yards from the rear bumper, the lens focusing fast on the number plate. And there the number suddenly was, clearly legible for two or three seconds before the Land Rover moved forward and accelerated away down the lane, its lights coming on as it gathered speed, its occupants confident that they were leaving no trace of their visit behind them.

# CHAPTER TWELVE

'Carwether Farm.'

'It's me, Andrew.'

'Nick? You're up early.'

'Yeah. Look, er, when's Tom leaving?'

'His train's at eleven. Why?'

'Could I come over to see you after he's gone?'

'I suppose so. But there are things I need to get on with. I do have a farm to run, you know.'

'It's important. Very important.'

'I thought you were going home today.'

'There's something you have to see, Andrew. Believe me.'

'What is it?'

'I can't explain that on the phone. But you've got a video, haven't you?'

'Yeah. So?'

'So expect me around noon. And say nothing to Tom.'

Nick had plenty of time to consider their situation while he was waiting to set off. He replayed the video until every grainy image was printed on his mind. He tried in vain to deduce the motives of whoever had videoed them that night. Just as he tried in vain to decide what they should do about it.

He left shortly before Pru was due to turn up and took a circuitous route via Launceston to make sure there was no danger of reaching Carwether before Tom's departure. It was in fact just after noon when he drove into the yard. Andrew was in a disgruntled mood. Nick's phone call had made him anxious and hiding his state of mind from Tom had been a strain. But that, of course, was nothing compared with the condition watching the video plunged him into.

'Oh my God,' he murmured when it had finished playing. 'Oh my God.'

'Do you want to see it again?'

'What?'

'*Do you want to see it again?*'

'No.' Andrew rubbed his eyes, struggling to organize his thoughts. 'I *never* want to see it again.'

'It exists, whether we like it or not. And it would be naïve to imagine it's the only copy.'

'Show me the envelope.'

'There.' Nick handed it to him.

Andrew stared at the name and address for several seconds. 'What does it mean?'

'Not sure. Whoever put it in my car wants to tell us something. It's a message. They're going to send it to the police. They *might* send it. They've *already* sent it.'

'What would the police make of it?'

'Not much, as it stands. We could be going to ridiculous lengths to fly-tip a roll of carpet. But if a note goes with it, suggesting it's more than a roll of carpet . . .' Nick shrugged. 'I guess they'd have to investigate.'

'They could work out where the shaft is from the direction and distance of the Caradon Hill transmitter.'

'Yeah.'

'Then they'd find the body.'

'Yeah.'

'And then they'd come looking for me. My registration number's clear to see.'

'Yeah.'

'Shit.' Andrew dropped the envelope, stood up and walked to the window. He stared out into the wet and windswept yard for a moment. Then he moved away suddenly, striding across to the television set. He stabbed at a button on the video player, releasing the cassette, and pulled it out of the machine. 'Who did this, Nick?' he asked, almost rhetorically.

'It must have been put in my car by someone at the funeral party. My coat was hanging in the hall, with the keys in the pocket.'

'That narrows the field.'

'To two, I reckon. Obviously, the family, Pru, Baskcomb and the Wellers aren't in the frame. That leaves . . .'

'Farnsworth and Davey.'

'Yeah.'

'One or the other.'

'Or both. They left together, remember.'

'But they couldn't have shot this.' Andrew slapped the cassette against his palm. 'Neither of them is agile enough – or technologically wised up, at a guess.'

'I agree.'

'Then it has to be Elspeth Hartley.'

'Looks that way.'

'She knew the body was there all along, didn't she? That's what it was all about. She must have followed us when we went to Minions on Saturday morning and watched us poking around the shaft. That's how she knew where to lie in wait for us. And we didn't let her down, did we?'

'She certainly seems to have been one step ahead of us all the way.'

'Yeah. And she still is. What does she expect us to do about this video?'

'I'm not sure. Maybe she's giving us a chance to go to the police before she tips them off.'

'Why would she do that?'

'I don't know. But then . . .'

'What?'

163

'We don't know why she's done anything. We don't really know the first thing about her.'

'Except the people she's in with.' Andrew stared down at the cassette clutched in his hands. 'Sitting back, waiting to see which way we jump, laughing at us, having a ball at our expense.'

'I'm not sure abou—'

There was a loud crack as Andrew hooked his fingers under the plastic cover of the cassette and wrenched it off, dragging a loop of tape with it. Then he started pulling the rest of the tape out, breathing heavily as it bunched and tangled in his grasp, until finally it snapped off at the end of the spool. He threw the empty cassette on to the floor and headed for the kitchen, taking the jumble of tape with him.

'What are you doing?'

Getting no answer, Nick followed Andrew into the kitchen, where he saw him standing by the range, leaning against the rail as he dropped the tape into the fire. He replaced the lid with a thud and turned slowly round. 'You're going to tell me burning it's a waste of effort, aren't you?'

'We have to assume—'

'I know what we have to assume.' Andrew grabbed his coat and made for the door. 'The fucking worst.'

'Where are you going?'

Slamming the door behind him was Andrew's only response. Nick started after him, then stopped. What was the point? Whatever he said, Andrew would not listen. He heard a shout of 'Stay!' out in the yard, directed at the dog, followed by the noise of the Land Rover engine. Then a shadow roared past the window. Andrew was gone.

A few minutes later, Nick started back for Trennor, this time taking the direct route. He did not know what to do for the best. Go to the police? Or go home to Milton Keynes and wait to see what happened? Why had Elspeth given them the chance to choose? What did she want – or expect – them to do?

164

His mind was as full of questions as it was empty of answers. Strictly speaking, they did not know Elspeth was responsible for the video. Nor could they be certain either Farnsworth or Davey was involved in planting it in Nick's car, although how else it could have got there was hard to imagine. He would have to speak to Andrew again later, when he was calmer, and try to find a way forward. Meanwhile—

A thought burst suddenly upon him. Whoever had put the video in the car had necessarily had the run of the boot, where Nick had put the envelope holding the contents of the file his father had kept on his breakdown. Was it still there? He pressed his foot to the floor, desperate to reach the next lay-by.

Where all, it transpired, was well. The envelope did not look as if it had been tampered with. Nick stood by the open boot, the chill moorland air buffeting around him as he leafed through the documentary evidence of his loosened hold on reason. It was all there, every letter, every bill, and much more besides.

Including, chanced on by his questing fingers, the printed programme for the degree ceremony he had not been supposed to attend. He pulled it out and stared at it for a moment. *Visitors are asked to enter and leave the Senate House only during the interval between the presentation of the candidates from different Colleges*, the heading read. *Photography and smoking are not permitted.* There was the date: *Friday, 29 June 1979.* And there were the names, in orderly columns. He knew he would find his own, if he looked, listed as one of those proceeding to a degree *in absentia*. His father must have asked for the programme to be sent to him, a small and poignant memento of an occasion he had no doubt hoped to witness proudly and in person, whereas instead—

It was then that Nick remembered Elspeth's brother, the brother she had supposedly gone to see collect his own degree that day. That must have been a lie, of course, devised to account for her knowledge of Nick's breakdown. But why tell it at all? What had she gained by it?

165

Or was it, perhaps, the truth – the one thing she had told him that was not a lie? Nick closed the boot and got back into the car, the programme clutched in his hand. He began scanning the names, unsure what he was looking for. Not Hartley, obviously. But something, someone. King's College, Trinity, St John's, Peterhouse, Clare . . .

'My God,' he heard himself say. His finger trembled where it had stopped at the place in the Clare College list. *Braybourne, Jonathan Charles.*

Pru was on the point of leaving when Nick reached Trennor. He told her he would be staying at least for another day and saw her on her way. Then he got busy on the telephone, though to little effect. Clare College had no current address for Jonathan Braybourne and would not have volunteered it if they had, though they would have been willing to forward a letter. Bristol University cagily referred Nick to Boston University for current information on Elspeth Hartley. The switchboard there offered to leave a message for her. Their records did not extend to her residential status. Nick half-heartedly asked them to ask her to ring him and left it at that.

The breakthrough, such as it was, had led nowhere. That was the truth of it, a truth Nick bleakly confronted as he took himself off for a run round the lanes in the hope that physical exercise might clear his mind. It succeeded to an extent. Jonathan Braybourne and Elspeth Hartley, the *real* Elspeth Hartley, were red herrings, he suddenly understood. Pursuing them was a distraction, as perhaps it was meant to be. The only certainty was the money lodged with Hopkins & Broadhurst. Who had it been repaid to? The answer to that question was all that really mattered.

The telephone was ringing when Nick opened the front door back at Trennor and stepped breathlessly into the hall. He hurried to pick it up, wondering if it might be the genuine Elspeth Hartley, returning his call. But it was not.

'Nicholas? Thank goodness I've caught you. This is Julian Farnsworth.'

'Dr Farnsworth? What can I do for you?'

'I'm phoning from Tintagel.'

'What are you doing there?'

'I decided to spend a few days up here before returning to Oxford. But that isn't really the point. I'm phoning about your brother.'

'My brother?'

'Andrew.'

'Yes?'

'He's behaving very strangely. I met him at Mr Davey's house.'

'You were with Davey?'

'Yes. I wanted to ask him some more questions about the excavations. Then your brother arrived. To say that he was overwrought is to put it mildly. He accused us of . . . well, some kind of conspiracy against him – and you. None of it made the slightest sense. He was ranting. Raving, I think it fair to say. We had to threaten to call the police before he would leave. I was genuinely fearful that he might become violent. I still am, as a matter of fact.'

'I don't understand.' The lie was a reflex. Nick understood all too well that discovering Farnsworth and Davey together must have seemed to Andrew like confirmation of their darkest suspicions about the pair. What he did not understand was how Andrew thought charging up to Tintagel to confront Davey – and Farnsworth, as it had turned out – would help. But maybe Andrew was beyond thinking. If so, Nick would have to think for both of them. 'Where's Andrew now?'

'I've really no idea. He stormed out of the house just as he had stormed into it. But he said he'd be back. Mr Davey took it as a threat and I can't say I blame him. Whether your brother knows where *I* am . . .'

'And where is that?'

'The Camelot Castle Hotel. On the headland.'

'Do you want me to come up?'

'I rather think I do. I suspect him of lurking somewhere in the neighbourhood, Nicholas. Biding his time. Waiting till dark. I could not forgive myself if some harm came to Mr Davey for lack of action on my part. I should hope you might feel the same.'

'I do, obviously, though—'

'I'll expect you within the hour.'

'Yes, but—'

There was no more to be said. The line was dead.

An hour was cutting it fine. Nick drove faster than usual, north through the clearing afternoon. The cloud thinned and tumbled away in scraps of grey as a keen wind blew across from Bodmin Moor, emptying the sky and scouring the land. The sun appeared, late and low, skimming blindingly over the hills.

Nick reckoned he had last been to Tintagel more than twenty years ago, though twenty years would not, he felt sure, have wrought many changes in such a place. The worn stump of the medieval castle would still be there, on its virtual island of storm-sieged rock, while inland the pubs and cafés and gift shops doubtless still lined the village street. Many of them would be closed at this time of year, of course. The car parks would be empty, the track down to the castle scarcely trodden. The place would be held in an out-of-season trance.

As Nick rounded a bend on the upland road in from the east, he suddenly saw the crumpled coastline below him, a blue-grey sea spilling whitely over black rocks. Barras Nose and Tintagel Island butted into the ocean and, between them, on a platform of land, looking far more like a castle than the nearby ruins, stood the Camelot Castle Hotel, a Victorian architectural folly intended to serve as the terminus hotel for a railway line from Camelford that had never been built.

As Nick descended the hill into the village of Bossiney, which tourist development had turned into an annexe of Tintagel, the coast ahead was lost to view, and the hotel with it. It was then that he remembered something his father had said to him more than once about Tintagel. 'It's a strange-looking place; and it's stranger than it looks.'

But its main street looked merely prosaically drab and predictably quiet as Nick drove along it. He had no reason to stop there *en route* to the hotel – until he saw Andrew's Land Rover, parked outside the Sword and Stone pub.

Nick pulled in on the other side of the road and got out. Andrew was nowhere in sight. But the Sword and Stone, though just about the least inviting of Tintagel's hostelries, with its stark frontage, peeling paintwork and BIGGEST PASTIES IN TOWN sign, appeared at any rate to be open. He crossed over and went in.

The bar was as dismal as he might have expected, sparsely decorated and cavernously chill, with a pool-table at the far end and a country-and-western tape playing through indiscreetly placed loudspeakers. Two middle-aged men with big bellies and blank faces, dressed in matching jogging kit, sat at one of the tables, drinking pints of lager. The only other customer, propped on a bar stool, was Andrew. The glass in front of him looked as if it contained whisky, though clearly not as much as Andrew had already consumed. He was so drunk he did not even seem surprised to see his brother walking towards him.

'Hey, Nick. Want a drink?'

'What's going on, Andrew?'

'Buggered if I know.'

'Farnsworth phoned me. Said you'd been making trouble at Davey's house.'

'They made all the trouble.'

'Going there wasn't a very bright idea, you know.'

'Wasn't it? I caught them together, though, didn't I?' Andrew's gaze narrowed. 'The pair of them. Scheming against us.'

'You can't prove that.'

'Don't need to. I know. And now they know I know.'

'You're not thinking of going back there, are you?'

'Maybe. Davey on his own could be an easier nut to crack.'

'That's crazy. Do you want the police involved?'

'Only a matter of time before they are anyway. Now, are

169

you drinking?' Andrew nodded at the bleary-eyed barman who had shuffled out from a back room.

'I'll have a Coke.'

'The real thing, hey? Very adventurous. You heard the man, squire. I'll have another Bell's. Make it a large one.'

The drinks were supplied and the money taken from a pile of change next to Andrew's elbow. The barman stared glumly into the empty ice-bucket for a moment, then wandered off with it into the rear.

'Do you believe in coincidence, Nick? I don't. Farnsworth wasn't round at Davey's place to see how retired quarrymen live. *Or* catch his reminiscences of digging up old pots out at the castle. His being there is all the proof I need. They're what we're up against. The bastards.'

'What do you propose to do about it?'

'I'm thinking about that. But more than you. That's for sure.'

'Look, I'll go and see Farnsworth. Smooth things over as best I can. Then I'll drive you home. How about that? You obviously can't drive yourself.'

Andrew cast him a woozy gaze. 'Smooth things over? You must be joking.'

'It's all we can do for the present. We need to . . . take stock.'

'Take stock? Bloody hell, Nick.' Andrew shook his head slowly in disappointment. 'What use are you, hey? What fucking use?' He slid off the stool and lumbered away towards a door beyond the pool-table marked GENTS, flapping a dismissive arm behind him. 'Go and lick Farnsworth's arse if you want to. I don't care. I'll deal with him and Davey – and that Hartley bitch – my way. I'll have to, won't I? No choice if you're chickening out. Should have known, I suppose. It's only what you've always done when the going got rough. It's only—'

Andrew's words were choked off by the slamming of the loo door behind him. The other two customers stared at Nick, their faces marginally less blank than before. Nick took an evasive swallow of Coke. Then he noticed Andrew's car key lying beside the pile of change on the bar.

He thought the matter over for no more than a few seconds. Then he picked up the key, drained his Coke and headed for the exit.

It was a short drive to the Camelot Castle, out at the northern end of the village. A ribbon of new executive-style dwellings had closed the gap between the jumble of bungalows Nick remembered and the hotel itself. The building was a stolid mass of castellated Victorian Gothic, cast in deep shadow by the sun, which was dazzling still as it sank over a cloudless horizon.

Nick parked next to Farnsworth's Citroën and climbed out. It was colder here, he noticed at once, his breath frosting. The air seemed to be chilling by the second. He glanced across at Tintagel Island, where the shadowed stumps of the medieval castle looked like a row of worn-down dragon's teeth, planted on the cliff. Then he hurried towards the hotel entrance.

Before he reached the door, however, Farnsworth stepped out into the porch to meet him. He was muffled up in overcoat, scarf, gloves and a deerstalker that might have looked charmingly eccentric on the streets of Oxford but here looked merely bizarre.

'Ah, Nicholas. I thought I'd take a breath of air before nightfall to calm my nerves.' He treated Nick to an entirely nerveless smile. 'I had begun to despair of seeing you, I must admit. You are somewhat later than we agreed.'

'It couldn't be helped. I bumped into my brother.'

'Rather you than me. Has he calmed down?'

'Yes. As far as he needed to. He was no clearer about your . . . disagreement . . . than you were.'

'I'm not surprised. He hardly seemed to know what he was alleging. Certainly I don't. Can you shed any light on the matter?'

'Not really, no.'

Farnsworth raised his eyebrows. 'You have no idea what prompted his . . . extraordinary behaviour?'

'Not if you haven't.'

A momentary silence fell. Then Farnsworth said quietly, 'That's a pity.'

'He was obviously surprised to find you at Davey's house.'

'Surprise I can understand, Nicholas. But not outrage. There was nothing sinister about it. Mr Davey participated in one of the most significant British digs of the twentieth century. I was interested to know what he remembered of it.'

'Nothing my father couldn't already have told you if you'd asked him, I imagine.'

'Another point of view is always illuminating. Alas, I gleaned little of value, thanks to your brother's intervention.'

'I'm sorry if Andrew upset you.' Nick exerted himself to sound genuine. The truth was that he felt as suspicious of the improbable pairing of Farnsworth and Davey as Andrew did. Someone had spirited the video into his car and this elderly aesthete gazing blandly at him through the Tintagel twilight was a prime candidate. But it was an accusation that had to go unlevelled. If Farnsworth really was threatening them, they could not afford to admit it. 'I'll take him home myself and make sure he causes you no further problems.'

'Where is he now, may I ask?'

'A pub in the village.'

'I suppose that will suffice, then. Will you call in on Mr Davey to set his mind at rest?'

'I think it's more important for me to take Andrew home, don't you?'

'Perhaps so. I'll telephone Mr Davey and let him know what's happened.'

'Good.'

'It was a most disconcerting experience, Nicholas. There was no occasion for your brother to behave as he did.'

'I'll phone you in the morning, Dr Farnsworth. OK?'

Farnsworth nodded thoughtfully. 'Very well.'

\*　　\*　　\*

172

Nick drove back round to the Sword and Stone in a turmoil of competing thoughts. Getting Andrew out of Tintagel was essential given his present condition. But what were they to do about the video? Andrew's tactic of direct confrontation had been disastrous. But no other tactic Nick could devise promised to be any less disastrous. They were dangling on a hook. But they could not say for sure who was twitching the line. And as to why . . .

The blank-faced pair were still nursing their lagers. The barman was leafing through *Exchange and Mart*. But of Andrew there was no sign. The slew of change on the bar in front of the stool he had been occupying had vanished.

'He's gone,' said the barman, anticipating Nick's question. 'Left right after you.'

'Did he say where he was going?'

'Nope. But it can't be far. He said as you'd half-inched his car keys. He was seriously pissed off about that. But maybe you were just being a good citizen, him being well over the limit, like.'

Where had Andrew gone? Only one answer came to Nick's mind. 'Do you know a bloke who lives round here called Fred Davey?'

'Nope.'

'His address is three, Butcher's Row.'

'Butcher's Row?' The barman gave a reasonable impression of thinking. 'Not sure I know it.' He thought some more. 'Hold on. The row of cottages out beyond Tregatta, off the Camelford road. Isn't that called Butcher's Row?' He looked at the blank-faced pair, who responded in their own good time with a slow, synchronized nod of confirmation. 'Yeah. That's it.'

Night had fallen by the time Nick drove clear of the village. The B road to Camelford was a busier route than the one he had arrived by, with the modest local version of the rush hour cranking itself up. Tregatta was a hamlet about half a mile south of Tintagel and according to the barman Butcher's Row was about another half-mile further on. But this was the only road to it. If Andrew was set on revisiting Davey, Nick should be able to overhaul him on the way. He was in no state to have covered a mile in the time that had passed since their parting.

But there was no sign of him. For that Nick was in one sense grateful, because beyond Tregatta there was no footpath and not much of a verge. The roadside was no place for a drunken pedestrian.

Butcher's Row was down a minor road just past the first bend after Tregatta. Nick slowed to a crawl, getting horned by the car behind. But he succeeded in spotting the lane in time and turned off along it. A terrace of four low-roofed slate cottages fronted directly on to the lane. Nick pulled over as far as he could opposite it under a straggling thorn hedge, jumped out and headed for the Daveys' door.

There was only the dimmest of lights visible through the front window, behind thin curtains tightly drawn. Nick gave the knocker several loud raps and heard a shuffling approach on the other side of the door.

'Who's that?' came a female voice.

'Nicholas Paleologus,' he shouted.

'Who?'

'Mrs Davey?'

'Yes.'

'I'm Nicholas Paleologus. Is my brother with you?'

The door was suddenly wrenched open, to reveal two figures standing in a narrow hallway. Fred Davey looked shorter than Nick remembered him from the funeral and his wife Margaret was shorter still. Their clothes were threadbare and there was no gust of warmth from the adjoining sitting room, only a faint, musty chill. But there was no hint of frailty in their expressions. The Daveys were a well-matched pair, worn by hard lives to stony old age.

'Your brother's been and gone, Mr Paleologus,' said Fred. 'A couple of hours since.'

'I thought he might have come back.'

174

'That he hasn't.'

'We're glad to say,' put in Margaret. 'I thought there'd be violence done, the bait he was in.'

'I'm sorry if he caused you any trouble.'

'So Dr Farnsworth said,' Fred responded. 'We've just had him on the blower, saying as you'd be taking your brother home out of harm's way.'

'So I will, once I find him.'

'Given you the slip, has he?'

'Something like that.'

'He wants to be careful, carrying on like he did. It'll get him into bother.'

'I can only apologize on his behalf, Mr Davey.'

'Maybe your father's going has sent him cranky.'

'Maybe.'

'Well . . .' Fred pushed out his bottom lip thoughtfully. 'See him home and we'll say no more about it.'

'I'll do my best.'

Nick reversed out awkwardly on to the main road and headed back towards Tintagel, reckoning Andrew must simply have gone to another pub after leaving the Sword and Stone. There were several to choose from. Perhaps getting roaring drunk was a sensible policy in the circumstances. Sober deliberation had certainly failed to net Nick any reward.

Then, as he accelerated away, he suddenly saw Andrew on the roadside ahead, blundering towards him, one arm raised to shield his eyes. Nick braked sharply to a halt, earning a horning and a flash of lights from behind. The offended driver sped past, nearly taking off the door as Nick edged it open.

'What the hell are you doing, Andrew?' Nick shouted, darting out and round to the front of the car. 'It's me. Nick.'

'Why should you care what I'm doing?' Andrew stopped and squinted at his brother through the glare of the headlamps, his face distorted by shadows into a Hallowe'en mask of rage.

'Because we've got to stick together.'

'You stole my car keys. Funny bloody way to—' The rest was lost in the roar of a passing lorry.

'You're in no state to drive.'

'Maybe not. But I'm in a good state to squeeze the truth out of Davey.'

'Don't be stupid. Get in.'

'Don't tell me I'm stupid.' Andrew stumbled forward and prodded Nick in the chest. 'I'm going there whether you like it or not. Now, get out of my way.'

'Listen to me, Andrew.' Nick grabbed his brother by the arm. 'We need to—'

'Let go of me.' Andrew was the stronger of the two by far. He pulled Nick off him and shoved him towards the car. Nick fell back across the bonnet, while Andrew, carried off balance by his effort, reeled against the offside wing.

What happened next was compressed into a second, though, to Nick, as he pulled himself upright, it seemed more like a minute or more of slow, unfolding chance. Andrew's already shaky sense of his own bearings deserted him. He took three staggering, stooping steps out into the middle of the road and was lit for an instant by a clash of headlamps from both directions. A horn blared. There was a squeal of skidding tyre on tarmac. Then the dark, barely glimpsed shape of a van closed on him.

There was a thump, a blur of tumbling shadows. The tyres squealed on. The horn jammed and the wheels bounced and juddered. Something was crushed, snapped, spattered, in the mangling darkness; something that had been, until that second, Nick's brother, but was now . . .

No more.

# INTERLUDE

# CHAPTER THIRTEEN

The video ended. Detective Inspector Penrose rose and removed it from the television, activating a brief flash of *Teletubbies* on the screen before he pressed the off switch. He slipped the video into a large manilla envelope and handed it to his colleague, Detective Constable Wise.

They made a contrasting pair. Penrose was fortyish and shambling, with the face and build of a rugby prop forward, his voice gravelly and Cornish-accented. Wise, on the other hand, was slim, smart and sharp, his thinning hair fashionably shaven, his eyes clear and bright. He darted a swift glance at each of the other three occupants of the room as he placed the envelope next to the coffee-cup on the table beside him.

Sunlight was filtering through the windows of the room, casting a pattern of shrub shadows on the opposite wall, but the sunlight brought no warmth with it. A fire would have been a help, but the grate was empty. Trennor was without a permanent resident and that lack too imparted its own particular chill to the occasion.

The audience for the video show comprised Irene Viner and Basil and Anna Paleologus, bunched somewhat awkwardly on the sofa so that all could have a good view of the television. A momentary silence elapsed, then Basil cleared his throat and a look passed between the two sisters.

179

'What should we make of this, Inspector?' asked Irene.

'I'd hoped you might be able to tell us that, madam,' Penrose replied, sitting down heavily. 'The registration number visible on the video corresponds with the registration number of your late brother's Land Rover.'

'It's the same vehicle,' said Wise.

'Indeed,' Penrose resumed. 'Now, a positive identification of the two figures is difficult, I know, but—'

'They could be anyone,' said Anna.

'We're assuming one of them is Andrew.'

'Just because it's his Land Rover.'

'It's a good reason,' said Wise.

'Granted,' said Irene. 'But where does that get us? How exactly did this video reach you?'

'It was mailed to me,' Wise replied. 'Posted in Plymouth on the thirty-first of January – the day after your brother's death.'

'You see a connection?'

'We see a coincidence. Sometimes they can be meaningful.'

'It might help if we knew what took Andrew to Tintagel that day,' said Penrose.

Irene frowned. 'I thought we'd established that.'

'To see this old fellow Davey, yes. But it seems . . . odd, it has to be said. The way Mr Davey tells it, Andrew wanted to ask him what he remembered of your father. But they'd met only the day before. Why couldn't he have asked him then? It's not as if Mr Davey knew your father well.'

'Grief can be . . . discombobulating,' remarked Basil.

'Indeed, sir.' Penrose sighed and shifted in his seat. 'Naturally, we've shown the video to your brother Nicholas and questioned him about all this, but, as you know, his memory of the period leading up to the accident is still very patchy.'

'Shock, according to the specialist,' said Irene. 'Seeing Andrew killed in front of him like that . . .' She shook her head.

'And I understand he does have a history of . . . psychiatric problems.'

'Yes,' said Irene briskly. 'But isn't that beside the point? Surely the sequence of events is clear enough. Dr Farnsworth telephoned Nick because he was concerned that Andrew was . . . overwrought. Nick drove up to Tintagel and found Andrew in a pub, drinking heavily. He took his car keys away, to stop him driving while under the influence. He visited Mr Davey and met Andrew on the road as he was driving back to Tintagel. Then . . . the accident happened.'

'But why was Andrew overwrought, madam? That's the question. Because of his father's death . . . or because of what we've seen on the video?'

'Nick's told us Andrew was too drunk to make any sense.'

'As he's told us. But it's possible, given his memory lapse, that there's something he's forgotten.'

'I'm sure he'll tell you if he remembers anything significant.'

'Until and unless he does,' said Wise, 'all we have to go on is this video, sent to us anonymously, apparently to alert us to the disposal of a body.'

'You don't know the . . . object . . . is a body,' said Irene, with a moue of distaste.

'Right size and shape. And a couple of people going to some lengths to get rid of it. We were bound to take it seriously.'

'Yet you found no body in the shaft,' remarked Basil.

'That's true, sir,' said Penrose. 'Which in one way makes it all the more puzzling.'

'Maybe it was just a hoax,' said Anna. 'You know, some mischief-maker giving you the run around.'

'Using your brother's Land Rover,' Wise pointed out. 'With – or without – his permission.'

'Why do you say the fact that you found nothing in the shaft makes it more puzzling?' asked Irene. 'Surely it solves your problem. There seems – literally – to be nothing for you to investigate.'

'My Chief Super will probably see it that way,' said Penrose. 'But the video shows a heavy cylindrical object being dumped in the shaft. The position relative to Caradon Hill pinpoints it as Hamilton's Shaft, north of Minions, one of the few round there not capped for safety reasons. We searched the shaft and found no body, as you say. In fact, no heavy cylindrical object at all. Why not, I wonder?'

'Because it was never there?' suggested Anna.

'Perhaps, madam.'

'Or perhaps because it was removed before the search,' added Wise.

'That seems an extraordinary notion,' said Irene.

'Indeed, madam,' said Penrose. 'It does, doesn't it?' He looked from one to the other of them. 'Can any of you recall anything your late brother said or did in the weeks before his death that suggested he might be mixed up in something like this?'

'Something like what exactly?' countered Irene.

'He was worried about the farm,' Anna put in. 'And about Dad.'

'We all were,' said Irene, with a fleeting frown at her sister. 'I doubt that's what the Inspector means, though.'

'It isn't, madam.'

'I'm afraid there's nothing else.' A glance from Irene induced nods of confirmation from Anna and Basil. 'Nothing at all.'

'What about your nephew, Tom? Do you think he might know something?'

'Tom's had very little contact with his father these past few years. It was something Andrew regretted, I know. His divorce from Tom's mother didn't help, but . . . there you are.'

'Was Andrew seeing anyone?'

'I'm sorry?'

'Did he have a girlfriend?'

'Not that I know of. In fact, no. Definitely not.'

'Once bitten, twice shy,' murmured Anna.

'Can you be certain?' asked Wise. 'I get the impression you didn't see that much of him yourselves.'

'I'd put a lot of money on it,' said Anna. 'And I don't have much to spare.'

'The sale of this house will be quite a windfall for you in that case.'

'Is that relevant?' Irene asked sharply.

'No, madam,' said Penrose with a forbearing smile. 'It isn't.'

'Do you have some particular reason for asking about girlfriends, Inspector?' Basil enquired. 'For the record, I don't have one myself.'

Penrose smiled, as if in sympathy. 'Tell them about the phone call, Dave.'

'Right.' Wise nodded to his superior. 'We searched the shaft four days after receiving the video, on Monday the fifth of February. As you know, we found nothing, aside from rocks and general rubbish. A local farmer said he'd seen some . . . activity . . . around the shaft at the end of the previous week. He couldn't be specific, but we think what he saw may have been someone else searching the shaft – and removing what the video shows being dumped into it. The day after our search had drawn a blank, a woman telephoned me at the station. She wouldn't give her name. Part of the conversation was taped. I'll play it for you.'

Wise took out a pocket recorder and pressed a button. A crackly female voice cut in. '. . . *at the shaft yesterday. What did you find?*'

'*Did you send me a video last week?*' came Wise's recorded reply.

'*What did you find?*'

'*Can I have your name please?*'

'*What have you done with it?*'

'*Done with what?*'

'*What you found in the shaft.*'

'*We found nothing.*'

'*I don't believe you.*'

'*It's true.*'

'*It can't be.*'

'*Did you send me the video?*'

'Nothing?'

'At least give me your first name. Then we can—'

'You're lying. It was there.'

'I'm afraid not.'

'It wasn't? It truly wasn't?'

'Like I say, we found nothing.'

'Then they must have . . . Oh God.'

'Who—'

The recording cut out. Wise switched off the machine.

'Do you recognize her voice?' Penrose prompted.

'No,' said Irene.

Anna shrugged. 'Nor me.'

'Sir?' Penrose looked at Basil.

Basil's eyes rolled. Then he grimaced and said, 'I don't think so.'

'Do you want to hear it again?'

'I, er . . .'

'You may as well, Dave.'

Wise played the recording again. When it had finished, Irene said, 'I definitely don't know her.'

'Same here,' said Anna.

There was a moment's pause before Basil added, 'That goes for me too.'

'Sure?'

Basil nodded. 'Absolutely.'

'I'm afraid we can't help you, Inspector,' said Irene. 'Much as we'd like to.'

'No. Well . . .' Penrose smiled ruefully. 'Thanks for trying.'


After seeing the two policemen out, the Paleologus siblings walked silently back into the drawing room. Irene lit a cigarette and Basil enquired mildly if they wanted more coffee. Anna expressed a marked preference for a very large gin and tonic. Irene concurred. And Basil went along with the majority.

'What a pair,' said Anna after her first sip of gin. 'Let's hope we've seen the last of them.'

'They've no reason to take this any further,' said Irene.

'Assuming they believed us,' Basil observed.

'Why shouldn't they? We answered their questions truthfully enough.'

'The woman on the tape was Elspeth Hartley. You know that.'

'I know no such thing.'

Basil shrugged. 'Have it your way.'

'What good would it have done to mention her anyway?'

'Oh, none, I admit. It's too late for honesty, even though it may well have been the best policy at the outset. What a tangled web we've woven for ourselves.'

'There's nothing tangled about it. If they really had found a body in the shaft, it might have been different. As it is . . .'

'Who did you think the two people on the video were, Irene?'

'I don't know.'

'Really?'

'*I don't know.*' Irene clunked her glass down on the mantelpiece. 'Whatever this is really all about has harmed us enough. Telling tales to the police now can only make matters worse. We need to draw a line under the whole dreadful business. You're not to discuss this with Nick. Is that understood? Let him recover in his own time. I don't know what he and Andrew did or didn't do. And I don't want to know.'

'Amnesia can be a very convenient thing. There seems to be a lot of it about.'

'What do you mean by that?'

'I mean we may not be allowed to draw a line under this. And that we should be prepared for such a contingency.'

'How, exactly?'

Basil made a face. 'I'm not sure.'

'I want you to promise you'll say nothing to Nick.' Irene stared meaningfully at her brother.

'Won't he assume they'll have shown us the video?'

'Maybe. But let him raise the subject – if he wants to.'

'And if he doesn't?'

'Then let it lie. It's only for a few days. He's going up to Edinburgh to see Tom. You know he was in no state to explain what happened when Tom was down for Andrew's funeral. Well, he reckons he's equal to it now and God knows they do need to talk. Maybe they can help each other come to terms with the situation.'

'Tom seemed totally withdrawn to me,' said Anna.

'Exactly. So, the visit could be good for both of them. But Nick's still very fragile. I don't want anything to upset him before he goes.'

'Message received and understood,' murmured Basil.

'Good.'

'But remember what the Inspector said. Finding nothing in the shaft is in a sense the most puzzling aspect of the whole affair.'

'You think too much, Basil,' said Anna. 'You really do.'

'Maybe you're right.'

'I am, believe me. Where you're concerned, I'm an expert.'

'Maybe I need a holiday.'

'Don't we all?'

'A complete break.' Basil nodded, as if in contemplation of a sun-soaked beach somewhere. 'A change of scene.'

'Not planning to don the habit again, I hope,' said Irene.

'No, no. Not that.' Basil clinked the ice thoughtfully in his glass. 'Something else altogether.'

# PART TWO

# CHAPTER FOURTEEN

Nicholas Paleologus stepped out of the door of the Old Ferry Inn into a chill, grey, salt-tanged morning. He heaved his bag on to his shoulder and gazed up at the twin spans of the Tamar Bridges. The road bridge was busy with workmen and traffic, headlamps and floodlights blurring in the murk, but the rail bridge was empty and silent. He breathed deeply, wondering if the palpitations would start again. But they stayed away. He was calm and in control.

Three weeks had passed since Andrew's death. For the first of those weeks Nick had no coherent memory to draw on at all. His recollections – of people and places and incidents – were a jumble, as detached from sequential reality as the weirdest of dreams. He knew it all now: what had happened and when in the cavalcade of consequences. He could even have given a reasonable account of his own collapse and slow recovery in the wake of that sickening, disabling moment when he had seen and heard his brother die. Yet still it lacked for him the actuality of first-hand experience. It was all at one remove from him and he from it, as if he had witnessed it from inside someone else's head.

The drugs were partly to blame for that, of course, or to thank, since the condition was both a curse and a blessing. It had certainly kept the police off Nick's back until he had been

189

able to assemble a version of events that did not involve admitting he had helped Andrew dump a body in Hamilton's Shaft. The irony was that he had pleaded memory loss for the period *prior* to the accident merely as a delaying tactic. There had been no danger of his forgetting the night he and Andrew had tipped a tarpaulined bundle into the black mouth of a disused mine shaft. Nick had assumed a moment of reckoning for it was bound to come in the end. But it never had, for the most astonishing of reasons: when the police had gone to look, the body had vanished.

Nick could share his astonishment with no-one. Nor could he point out to the police that the voice on the tape belonged to Elspeth Hartley. If he did, and if they found her, she might swear the two figures seen in the video were his brother and him. She would only be telling the truth, after all, which would be a first of sorts. But what would he say then? How would he explain what they had done?

He turned and headed up Albert Road towards the railway station. His car stood gathering grime and guano in the yard behind the Old Ferry. Its bumper was crumpled and one set of lights smashed as a result of being rear-ended in a minor adjunct of the major collision that had claimed Andrew's life. The vehicle was still driveable, but not by Nick. His nerves had been shredded far more drastically than his memory.

He very clearly remembered driving down to Saltash five weeks before, comfortable in the assumption that he would be staying only for a couple of days. Now, at last, he was leaving, at dawn, on foot, with much lost and nothing gained: his father and brother dead, a family sundered, a carefully composed life carelessly dismantled. As he had said goodbye to Irene over breakfast, he had sensed one of the bitterest of those losses: trust. Nick was sure the police must have shown her, and Anna and Basil, the video and played them the tape. But nothing had been said; not a word. They had obviously claimed not to know the voice, otherwise the police would have been back on to him. But all had been silence from that quarter. Nor had they said what they must have realized:

that he had assisted Andrew in covertly disposing of something which, if not a body, looked as if it might very well be one. There had only been solicitous enquiries about his health amidst a welter of reticence. Yes, there had been a lot of reticence: a whole conspiracy's worth of it.

There were a few people gathered at the station, waiting for the train to take them into Plymouth for the working day. Some were smoking or reading newspapers. These few moments on the platform at Saltash were part of their fixed routine. Nick did not know whether to envy or pity them, because for him routine was something he had as much difficulty recalling as envisaging. The doctor had signed him off work until the end of March. He was supposed to use the period to reduce his drug dosage and ease his way back to stability and normality. That was not exactly what he had in mind, though. He had already halved his pill intake without suffering a recurrence of the panic attacks and he planned to halve it again. What he needed was to be sure of himself, confident that his state of mind was his own, not some pharmacological ideal of moderation. It was time to reclaim his life.

The train came in and the passengers shuffled aboard. They trundled over Brunel's bridge and on by way of the commuter halts to Plymouth. Nick picked up a discarded *Western Morning News* and read it aimlessly through, noticing little until one small article seized his attention. Foot-and-mouth disease had been detected at an abattoir in Essex; there were fears it might be the tip of an iceberg. He suddenly imagined Andrew's anxious reaction to the news, forgetting, for one split-second, that Andrew was no longer around to react to anything. Tears welled in Nick's eyes. He dropped the paper and took several deep breaths to calm himself. The neighbouring farmer had taken over Carwether on a peppercorn rent, pending a decision from Tom about selling the place. But it was a foregone conclusion, of course. Now Andrew had gone, Carwether would go too. His struggle with the land was over.

They reached Plymouth with ten minutes to spare before the London train was due. Nick made his way slowly across to the platform and waited, staring vacantly into space. He wondered if he should drop into the bookstall and buy something to read on the journey, but he knew he would be unable to concentrate on whatever he chose. There was no refuge to be found in fiction. And he no longer craved refuge anyway. He was done with that.

'Good morning, Nick.' A familiar voice sliced through his thoughts. He turned to find Basil standing next to him, dressed as if for hiking, in cagoule and walking boots, with a bulging rucksack on his back. 'Surprised to see me?'

'You could say that, yes.'

'Irene told me which train you'd be catching.'

'Are you catching it too? You surely didn't pack a rucksack just to see me off.'

'I'm going on holiday. I thought we could travel to London together.'

'Holiday? This is the first I've heard of it.'

'Anna didn't take me seriously until I packed this morning. Couldn't believe her luck, I suppose.'

'Where are you going?'

Basil's reply was drowned out by the Tannoy announcement of their train. Nick thought he heard him name a destination, but could not quite believe he had heard correctly.

'What?' he shouted above the recital of West Country station stops.

Then the recital abruptly ceased. And he heard Basil's answer, clear as a bell.

'Why are you going to Venice?'

Nick managed with some difficulty to delay asking the question until they had settled in their seats and the train had pulled out of the station. Strictly speaking, the question was unnecessary. There was one very obvious reason for going to Venice. And a guided tour of the Doge's Palace was not it.

192

'Well?'

'I think we're in the quiet coach, Nick. Have you turned off your mobile?'

'What are you up to, Basil?'

'Nothing hole-in-the-corner, I do assure you. After all, I could easily have caught another train, couldn't I?'

'In that case, why not just come out with it?'

'Because Irene has told me to tread carefully where you're concerned. She didn't exactly say "Handle Nick like Dresden china", but it's what she meant. As for Venice, my interest in Byzantine history can never be slaked. I've been meaning for a long time to immerse myself in a study of the treasures the Venetians looted from Constantinople during the Fourth Crusade. This—'

'Demetrius Paleologus.' Nick's mention of their mysterious cousin was no more than a murmur, but it sufficed to halt Basil's peroration in its tracks.

'Ah.' Basil smiled. 'Memory not so very fallible after all, Nick?'

'What do you hope to achieve?'

'An understanding of the Venetian address system, to begin with. Houses are numbered by *sestiere*, providing no clue as to their precise location. San Polo three one five-o, to cite an example, could be anywhere within the *sestiere* of San Polo, one of the six the city comprises. Fortunately, there is a directory available, the *Indicatore Anagrafico*, which—'

'Why are you doing this?'

'To explain that, I need to tell you a story. But first, I think, I'd like *you* to tell *me* a story.'

'What about?'

'This trip of yours to Scotland. This . . . northern progress. What precisely is it in aid of?'

'You already know. I owe Tom a better explanation of what happened to Andrew than I was able to give him when he was down for the funeral.'

'And is a better explanation . . . a complete explanation?'

'As complete as I'm capable of.'

'Really? You don't happen to have brought any cards with you, do you?'

'No. Why?'

'I think it's time we put them on the table. You've seen the video, Nick. So have I. You've also heard the tape. Well, so have I. Irene and Anna are all for letting sleeping dogs lie. But I fear they're failing to guard against the day when the dog wakes and comes snapping at their heels. Sorry. Too many metaphors. But I trust the point is made.'

'I'm not sure it is.'

'Then let me be specific. I've been packing up some of Dad's possessions for disposal. Books, clothes, bric-à-brac, that kind of thing. Don't worry. Nothing's gone yet. Irene and Anna merely thought it prudent to separate the decent stuff from the obvious rubbish and delegated the task to me, as one with time on his hands. Naturally, they didn't like to bother you with the details and I'd be happy to spare you them myself, but for' – Basil lowered his voice – 'a discovery I made in the cellar.'

Nick said nothing. There was nothing he *could* say. He stared fixedly at the seat-back in front of him.

'I put everything back as I found it. If it was filled in with concrete and painted over – as it'll have to be before the house is sold – no-one would notice anything amiss. Of course, as one who's also seen the video, I have little doubt as to what was there when you and Andrew . . . came across it. I assume removal was Andrew's idea. He was always too headstrong for his own good. I quite understand why you co-operated. It must have seemed a simple solution to a complicated problem. You might tell me: approximately how long had it been there, do you think? You have the advantage of me. You know what condition it was in.'

Nick forced himself to turn and look at his brother. 'Ten years or more,' he whispered. 'At a guess.'

'Thus is Dad's reluctance to sell explained at a stroke.'

'Yeah.'

'Poor Nick. It must have been a harrowing business.'

'It was.'

'Had you and Andrew seen the video before he went up to Tintagel that day?'

Nick nodded. 'A copy was put in my car during the wake at Trennor.'

'You suspected Dr Farnsworth?'

'And/or Davey.'

'Plus Miss Hartley.'

'Yeah.'

'An unholy alliance formed in pursuit of . . . what exactly?'

'Haven't a clue.'

'I spoke to Dr Farnsworth the day after the accident. He told me about an old army buddy of Dad's: Digby Braybourne.'

'Did he, now?'

'Present whereabouts unknown.'

'Like one or two others.'

'I telephoned Dr Farnsworth a few days ago. After seeing the video, I was suddenly curious to learn more about the long-lost Mr Braybourne.'

'Get anywhere?'

'Don't tease, Nick. You had more or less the same conversation with his housekeeper as I did. She was hardly likely to have forgotten the name Paleologus. Why do you think Dr Farnsworth's gone to Edinburgh?'

'To visit an old friend, the housekeeper said.'

'I know what she said.'

'It could be true.'

'And the Pope could be infallible. But you don't believe it. Which is why you're going to Edinburgh. To find out what Dr Farnsworth is up to.'

'I'm worried about Tom.'

'With good reason, I'd say. Irene tells me you'll be seeing his mother before going up there. Is that right?'

'I'm staying with Kate and Terry tonight, yes.'

'Will you be mentioning any of this to them?'

'What do you think, Basil?'

'I think pretending the problem will go away is a fool's counsel. These people aren't going to give up until they've got what they want.'

'And what's that?'

'I've no more idea than you. But we have to find out. Which is why I'm going to Venice. And why you're going to Edinburgh. Isn't it?'

No more was said until the train left Exeter. Nick sifted his options slowly and carefully, while Basil, sensing he needed to be left to do so, leafed contentedly through a Michelin guide to Venice. Nick could not decide how much to tell his brother. Basil had been right about everything, of course. There was a time when Nick had been reckoned the most brilliant of Michael Paleologus's children, but now he realized that all along, brilliant or not, Basil had been the cleverest of them, happy though he had often seemed to be thought the most foolish.

'We could both be taking a big risk,' Nick said at last, as the train gathered pace through the flooded water meadows of the Exe. 'You do understand that, don't you?'

'Sometimes doing nothing is the riskier choice.'

'But only sometimes.'

'And this is one of those times.'

'What will you do when you reach Venice?'

'Locate our cousin's abode. Spy out the land. Consider how and whether to approach him. I think I will find a way. For one Paleologus not to call upon another could almost be considered impolite. If he is there, I believe I can create an opportunity to make his acquaintance.'

'And if he isn't?'

'I shall learn what I can. Certain it is that I shall learn nothing without trying.'

'Be careful.'

'I will be. And I trust you'll do likewise.'

'Do you have my mobile number?'

'Of course not.' Basil grinned and handed him his train

ticket. 'Write it on there.' Nick obliged. 'I'll call you tomorrow and let you know where I'm staying.'

'Do that.'

'Much of what's happened has been our own fault, Nick. I don't need to tell you that. If we hadn't destroyed Dad's will . . .' Basil shrugged. 'Who knows?'

'Clever of you to memorize Demetrius's address.'

'I thought I might have need of it.'

'Is he Tantris, do you suppose?'

'Possibly.'

'If he is, you'll be stepping into the lion's den.'

'There are a lot of lions in Venice. Bronze or marble, for the most part.'

'You will call tomorrow, won't you?'

'I said I would.'

'I might have some valuable information by then, you see.'

'So soon?'

'I'm meeting a guy I know in London.'

'From whom you may learn . . .'

'Quite possibly nothing.'

'But then again . . .'

'It's a stab in the dark. Let's leave it at that.'

'Very well.'

'I'd thought I might have to go to Venice myself, you know. After Edinburgh. Depending what happened.'

'You may still have to go.' Basil chuckled. 'There's just no telling what trouble I'll get into on my own.'

They parted at Paddington. As was only to be expected of a confirmed aviophobe, Basil was travelling the whole way to Venice by train. It would be Friday morning when he arrived. The next leg of his journey was the Eurostar to Paris. He ambled off down the steps leading to the Underground, pausing at the bottom for a farewell wave and toothy grin. As an eccentric middle-aged backpacker, he was entirely convincing. As a brother, he was the only one Nick had left. And Nick had never fully understood how fond of him he was until he saw him turn and lose himself in the Tube-bound crowd.

Nick left the station on foot and headed south towards Hyde Park, reckoning he had time to walk to his rendezvous with Marty Braxton. A former and fleeting colleague of Nick's at English Partnerships, Braxton was a fast-talking chancer with a barely veiled contempt for the observances of bureaucratic life. He had moved on and up since they had shared an office in Milton Keynes into the more fitting and remunerative domain of a West End advertising agency. To counter his many vices, he had some stubbornly endearing characteristics, notably a willingness to repay favours. As it happened, he was substantially in Nick's debt, on account of the blind eye Nick had turned to his use of the office telephone and computer systems for the operation of a customized numberplate mart. And the time had finally come to call in the debt.

They were to meet at the Windmill, halfway between Bond Street and Regent Street. Braxton had described it as a pub he knew but seldom used; he doubted he would bump into anyone he knew there. Nick hoped he was right. He also hoped, very much, that he would have something to report.

Braxton was already installed at the bar when Nick arrived. Judging by the inroads he had made into a steak and kidney pie and a pint of beer, he had been there for quite a while. He had put on weight since Nick had last seen him, but was carrying it well. There had always been something faintly phocine about Marty Braxton. Now he had acquired an extra layer of sleekness to go with the honking laugh and smug expression.

'Hi, Nick,' came the greeting through a mouthful of pie. 'You're looking well.'

'That's a minority view at present.'

'Really? Well, dare to be different is my motto, mate. Pint?'

'OK. Thanks.'

'I can recommend the snake and pygmy.'

'I'm not hungry.'

'Suit yourself.' Braxton signalled to the barmaid and a pint was pulled. 'Want to stay here – or slope into a corner?'

'Wherever you're comfortable.'

'In the circs, we'd better slope. Come on.' Braxton piloted Nick off to a table near the stairs and toasted happy days as soon as they had settled. 'My finely tuned emotional antennae tell me they aren't so happy for you, though, Nick. Is that right?'

'Family problems.'

'Can't help you there. My earliest memory's the underside of a gooseberry bush.'

'I was hoping you *could* help me, actually.'

'Ah. No time for foreplay, then?'

''Fraid not.'

'The direct approach wouldn't do you any good in the advertising game, I can tell you.'

'I'm not in the advertising game.'

'Nor ever likely to be, with that attitude.'

'Marty—'

'OK. No more arsing about. Was I able to work the magic on a certain solicitor's computer system? That's what you want to know, isn't it? Did I hack it, so to speak?' Braxton grinned. 'When did I ever not?'

'You mean . . .'

'It's more of a colander than a computer, mate. Not much of a challenge. Still illegal, mind.' With an effort, Braxton dropped his voice, the intended whisper emerging as more of a growl. 'The things I do for an old pen-pushing pal, hey?'

'I'm grateful, Marty. Really.'

'So you should be. Especially since I went the extra mile for you. Just to make it worthy of my attention.'

'What do you mean?'

'It shakes down like this. That cool half million paid out by Hopkins and Broadhurst on twenty-six January? The payee was a company called Develastic. Know them?'

'I don't think so.'

'Jersey-based. Probably just a shell. Info's thin on the ground.

But that goes with the territory. I managed to get the names of the directors, though. Just in case you were interested.'

'I might be very interested.'

'There you go, then.'

Braxton handed Nick a slip of paper, on which were written three names:

> MAWSON, Terence
> MAWSON, Catherine
> RAMIREZ-JONES, Clive

'Friends of yours?'

'Not exactly.'

'But not exactly strangers either, unless you've gone pale because that pint's off.'

Nick took a swig from his glass and looked Braxton in the eye. 'There's nothing wrong with the beer.'

'Thought not.'

'But something else' – Nick glanced back down at the slip of paper in his hand – '*is* wrong.'

Nick made dismal company for the rest of Braxton's lunch hour, as Braxton more than once complained. It was a relief in the end for both of them when they parted. Nick headed south, down through Green Park and St James's Park towards Westminster Bridge, his thoughts moving faster than his feet, but with a vastly inferior sense of direction. He had feared Braxton might have nothing for him. Or nothing of much use, while hoping with little confidence for a direct lead to Elspeth Hartley, or maybe to Demetrius Paleologus. But neither his fears nor his hopes had come to pass. Instead, enemies had appeared from the least expected quarter. His brother's ex-wife and her present husband were the source of the Tantris money. One or both of them had helped Elspeth Hartley pull off the deception. Or she had helped them. There was no way to tell who the prime mover was, nor what his or her motive might be.

Though not necessarily for long. Nick had warned Basil that, by going to Venice in search of their cousin Demetrius, he might be stepping straight into the lion's den. Ironically, Nick was now the one about to put himself in harm's way. Kate's invitation had suddenly acquired a sinister connotation. Was his visit an opportunity for her and Terry to decide whether he posed a threat to them? And what would their response be if they decided he did?

But he could not cancel the visit without arousing their suspicion. Nor could he deny to himself that an opportunity for them to take the measure of him was also an opportunity for *him* to take the measure of *them*.

He phoned Kate from the concourse at Waterloo to tell her which train he would be on.

'It leaves in a few minutes. Due into Sunningdale at a quarter past four.'

'I'll pick you up at the station.'

'I can get a taxi if it's easier for you.'

'Don't be silly. It's no problem. I'll be there.'

'OK. Thanks.'

'How are you?'

'Oh . . . All right.'

'We've been worried about you.'

'You have?'

'Naturally. We were glad to hear you were feeling better. You *are* feeling better, aren't you?'

'Yes. I am.'

'Good.'

'Well . . .'

'See you soon.'

'Yeah. 'Bye.' Nick rang off and glanced up at the departure board. His train was ready. There was no time to be lost. He started walking.

# CHAPTER FIFTEEN

Andrew and Kate had met on a diving course at Fort Bovisand. They had married while Nick was still at school and thrown themselves into making a success of Carwether Farm. Things had only begun to go wrong after Tom was born. By then things were going wrong for Nick as well. The final break-up of their marriage had passed him by. As far as he could recall, Terry Mawson had not been on the scene at the time, though he shortly after was. Kate had married him in the mid-Eighties, just as his Devon-based building business was transforming itself into a nationwide property company. He had made a medium-sized fortune before the boom turned to bust and timed his exit from the housing market to perfection. Since then he had invested here and there and God knows where to ever better effect, such that he and Kate now led a semi-retired life of leisure, divided between a big house in Surrey and a scarcely smaller villa in Spain, with a golf course on both doorsteps.

It was difficult to begrudge them their prosperity, though naturally Andrew had. The fact was that Terry had worked hard for what he enjoyed and freely admitted that what had looked like shrewdness had often been luck. He was a genially blunt-mannered bear of a man, fond of cigars, golf and fast cars. The stereotype did not extend to a roving eye, however.

He was a devoted if not uxorious husband, despite a lack of children which had reputedly led him to spend a lot of time and money on exotic fertility treatments – to no avail. Andrew's one consolation for losing Kate had been her failure to bear Terry a son to compete with Tom.

Kate's view of the matter was unrecorded. She had preserved the unsentimental, level-headed demeanour of the farmer's wife she no longer was. Not for her the gin bottle and the poolside lounger. She owned a riding school in Ascot and an interior design studio in Camberley. She was very much her own woman. But she was no longer as busy as she had formerly been. Her and Terry's concerns ticked by profitably without much day-to-day involvement on their part, freeing them to . . .

What exactly? Nick turned the question over in his mind as the train ambled down through Hounslow and Staines. He could not believe what it seemed he had to. A less likely pair of conspirators than Kate and Terry he could not imagine. They had everything they wanted, including each other. And the Paleologus family had done them no harm. More criticism had been levelled at Andrew over the divorce than at Kate. Friendly relations had always been maintained. Tom was held to be a credit to his mother and by implication to his step-father. There had been no feud.

But Marty Braxton's delvings left no room for doubt. Kate and Terry's fingerprints were on the Tantris money. And money was one thing they were not short of.

As promised, Kate was waiting for him at Sunningdale station, looking tanned and fit and smart-casually elegant in blue jeans, red sweater and black thigh-length coat. There were a few flecks of grey in her dark hair and laughter-lines around her eyes, but otherwise she was a walking advertisement for the benefits of middle-aged affluence. She appeared carefree and wholly unconspiratorial.

'Hi, Nick,' she said, hugging and kissing him. 'It's great to see you. And looking so well.'

'You're the second person who's said that today.'

'It must be true, then. There's been quite a change since . . .'

'Andrew's funeral? I know. I was pretty well out of it then. Blame the drugs they had me dosed up with. I'd still fail an Olympic dope test, but . . . I'm getting there.'

'Glad to hear it. And to see the evidence. Now, talking of getting there, let's go.'

Kate's Mercedes was parked outside. They climbed in and started away, Nick noticing already the anxious tightness in his stomach. He slowed his breathing and tried to relax his facial muscles.

'It's really good of you to be going up to see Tom. We're worried about him, but he wouldn't welcome me fussing around, so this visit of yours is a real blessing.'

'Is there any reason to worry about him? I mean, obviously, losing his father . . .'

'There's nothing specific. But, when he was down, he was so . . . tight-lipped. I wish he'd talk about it, that's all. Maybe he'll open up with you.'

'I can only tell him what happened and see where we go from there.'

'And what happened was just a crazy accident. I wonder if that doesn't make it worse.'

'How do you mean?'

'I wonder if Tom doesn't want there to be someone he can blame. Only no-one is to blame, are they?'

'No.' Nick looked straight ahead at the road. 'No-one at all.'

A few minutes later, they turned off onto the private road through the Wentworth estate. Kate slowed to a seemly 20 m.p.h. as they cruised past the security-gated properties. Triple garages and towering gables peeked at them from the distant ends of tree-lined driveways. A manicured, emerald green swathe of golf course intervened, then they entered a still more exclusive enclave of seven-figure des res and followed a curvaceous cul-de-sac to the house that Kate and Terry called home.

There was, Nick, felt sure, no place quite like it, but humble it was far from. Mariposa was quite possibly the biggest bungalow in Surrey, terracotta-roofed, picture-windowed and land-hungry to a fault.

Thanks to Kate, the interior was as tastefully furnished and decorated as the exuberantly extensive ground plan would permit. Mariposa was no more her natural habitat than Carwether had been, but she disguised the fact well. She was, Nick reflected, an expert at disguise, perhaps more of one than he had ever supposed.

After a brief excursion to the guest wing to dump his bag, he joined Kate for tea in the pastel vastness of the lounge. Terry, she explained, was entertaining a party of clients to an afternoon's racing at Sandown Park; he would be back in time for dinner.

'If it hadn't been arranged so long ago, I'd suspect him of deliberately engineering his absence.'

Nick smiled and glanced through the window into the lushly landscaped garden, where a soft rain had begun to fall among the snowdrops and early daffodils. 'Why would he want to do that?'

'Because he's more sensitive than people give him credit for. He knows I want to talk to you about Andrew.'

'What is there to say, Kate? I wish I'd done more to stop him, but—'

'I don't mean the accident. In one of the few conversations I managed to have with my son while he was here last month, before . . . well, before it happened . . . he told me about this weird Tantris business.'

'Ah.' Nick's senses suddenly sharpened. He could hear the rain now as well as see it, dampening the patio with a gentle, ophidian hiss. 'Did he?'

'Was it a secret?'

'Not really. Anyway . . .' Nick sipped his tea. 'I'm glad he told you. It's better to have things . . . out in the open.'

'Isn't it just? That was one of the reasons why Andrew and I broke up. He always kept so much to himself. Whereas with Terry . . . what you see is what you get.'

205

'Someone played a strange and rather cruel trick on us, Kate. The strangest part of it is that we don't know who – or why.'

'You've no idea who was behind it?'

Nick shook his head. 'If we understood their motive . . .'

'You'd be able to figure out who they are.'

'Probably.'

'Was Andrew particularly upset about it?'

'Well . . . Yes. Selling Trennor at a premium price would have been advantageous to all of us, obviously, but especially to Andrew. Farming's been a mug's game for quite a few years now.'

'That's what Terry says. That he must have seen the deal as a lifeline.'

'I suppose he did.'

'And then the lifeline was snatched away.'

'Yes. It was.'

'Which is why we're so worried about Tom.' Kate leaned forward in her chair. 'He figured out Tantris was a fraud, didn't he?'

'Yeah.'

'He exposed the trick for what it was.'

'Well . . .'

'We're worried he blames himself for his father's death, Nick. That's what it comes down to. He was so . . . withdrawn . . . at the funeral. He wouldn't talk to me. Not really *talk*, you know? He takes after Andrew that way. He just won't open up. I think, inside, he's decided he somehow tipped Andrew over the edge.'

'That's absurd. We'd have had to find out the truth sooner or later.'

'I know. But it was thanks to Tom that you found out when you did.'

'Even so . . .'

'I *know*. Of course it doesn't make sense. Grief and guilt don't tend to. But I'm worried – *really* worried – that he's convinced himself he's in some way responsible. Which is why

206

I'm so pleased you're going to see him. If anyone can make him understand, it's you.'

'I'll try.'

'Bless you, Nick.' Kate stretched across to clasp his hand. 'That's all I'm asking.' And looking into her eyes, he found it hard to doubt that she meant exactly what she'd said.

Lying in the bath before dinner, Nick stared up through the whorls of steam towards the sunflower-sized showerhead, focusing on the gradual formation of a droplet of water at its centre and wondering just how long it would take to drip free. Slowly, slowly, it glisteningly grew, and with it grew also his dread of the evening that stretched before him. He had almost convinced himself that Kate was being entirely honest and knew nothing about the source of the Tantris money. But, if so, then Terry had deceived her as well as the Paleologus family. And the consequences could only be worse as a result. Everything seemed normal and placid and restrained. But nothing remotely was.

Nick climbed out of the bath, suddenly impatient with his own anxiety. He towelled himself down vigorously and pushed open the window to clear the steam. Then he heard it: the low, thrumbling engine-note of Terry's Ferrari. It growled up the drive and came to a halt with an extravagant scrunch of rubber on gravel.

Nick wiped a clearance on the mirror in front of him and stared at the damp, drawn face he saw there. The fleeting impression struck him of a man seeking to avoid his gaze. Then he remembered: he was that man; it was his gaze.

'Terry's taking a shower,' Kate called to him from the kitchen as he passed the door a short while later. 'And I'm at the messy stage of a recipe. Make yourself comfortable in the lounge and one of us will join you in a mo.'

Nick tried to do as he was told, but comfort required more than soft furnishings. He poured himself a nerve-numbingly large gin and tonic and turned on the television news. A

207

reporter was talking sombrely about the foot-and-mouth out-break. Nick switched it off again. He walked to the patio door and parted the curtains. Outside, it was still raining. He could see the misty motion of it in the coppery glow of a floodlight countersunk in the lawn. A minute passed. Then several more.

'Nick,' came Terry's booming voice. 'Sorry we're neglecting you.'

'Don't worry about it.' Nick turned to meet the broad smile and merry, sparkling eyes he remembered better than any other feature of Terry Mawson's appearance. He sounded as big as he looked, balding and jowly, his cigars-and-whisky baritone rumbling inside a barrel-chested frame. His voguishly black shirt was cut generously enough to disguise a considerable paunch, and a glittering gold belt buckle was the only hint of the medallion-man fashion he had once favoured. Everyone liked him because it was so hard to dislike him. Kate had certainly refined his dress sense over the years, but his personality was still the raw force of nature it had always been. Or so, in normal circumstances, Nick would have con-fidently declared. 'Good to see you, Terry.'

'You too.' They shook hands and a meaty paw clapped Nick on the shoulder. 'What's that you're drinking?'

'G and T.'

'I'll join you.' Terry grabbed the bottle. 'Freshener?'

'No, thanks.'

'Very wise.' Ice rattled in a glass. Gin glugged over the cubes, followed by a fizz of tonic. 'Cheers.'

There was that impossibly broad smile again, accompanied by a wink as they touched glasses. Nick's mind reeled. Nothing made sense. Terry Mawson could not have dreamed up the Tantris scheme. Intrigue and secrecy were alien to him; medieval literature was *terra incognita*. Nick was missing some-thing, something as simple as it was obscure.

'When were you last down here, Nick?'

'Not sure. Tom's eighteenth birthday party, maybe.'

'A few years ago, then.'

208

'Must be.'

'In that case you won't have seen this.'

Terry moved towards the marble-hearthed fireplace and nodded at the painting above the mantelpiece. Nick had not noticed it earlier and could not have said whether he had ever seen it before or not. Big, clean-lined, and acrylically bright, it depicted a woman in a ballgown dancing on a beach with a non-existent partner. Something about it was faintly familiar.

'Vettriano. What do you think?'

'It's, er, very good.'

'You probably recognize the style from all the greetings cards they flog with his pics on.'

'Yeah. I think I do.' Thus was the familiarity explained. 'I didn't know you were into art, Terry.'

'I'm not really. But you've got to put something on the walls, haven't you? And I like this guy's stuff. I can understand it. At least, I think I can. Besides, my accountant tells me he's a good investment.'

'Is that so?'

'Red hot, apparently. Let's hope so, after what I forked out for this one.' Terry's roar of laughter filled the room so suddenly that Nick jumped. 'Are you OK? Didn't mean to startle you.'

'Sorry. I . . .' Nick shrugged. 'Nerves aren't too good, to be honest.'

'Not surprised, after what you've been through. Sure you don't want a splash more gin?'

'No. I'm fine, thanks.'

'Right you are. It's been rough, I know. Enough said, hey?'

'Yeah.'

'Kate talk to you about Tom?'

'She did.'

'Between you and me, she's worried sick. So, anything you can do . . . we'll be grateful. More than grateful.'

'I can only try.'

''Course. Understood. The way I see it, at times like this, people have to help one another. Know what I mean? Stick together. Pull together.'

'Right.'

'That's why I've been thinking about your . . . situation.'

'You have?'

'You bet.'

'And what . . . have you been thinking, Terry?'

'Well, it's just an idea. Something for you to consider.'

'Go on.'

'Are you planning to go back to English Partnerships when the quack signs you off?'

'Of course.'

'Because you've got to pay the bills, right?'

'Well . . . yeah.'

'It's not like you have a vocation for tarting up industrial wastelands.'

'No.'

'So, if a better proposition cropped up . . .'

'What are you getting at, Terry?'

'I might be able to offer you a job. Higher salary. Flexible hours. And lots of fringe benefits. What do you say?'

'I say it sounds good. But—'

'What's the work? Undemanding, Nick, that's what. I have all these business interests that basically look after themselves, but I still need to keep tabs on them, just in case some bastard out there tries to rip me off. What I need is someone I can trust – *really* trust – to do the monitoring for me. See what I mean? Someone to watch my back, financially. You're a systems man and clever with it. Plus you're family, more or less. I reckon you're just the guy I need. We'd be doing each other a favour.'

Nick could not seem to frame a response. Terry was grinning at him and his eyes were sending their own encouraging message: *Get on board and I'll see you all right.* Nick had no doubt that he would. But why? Why now? What exactly had led him into this? Generosity, for which he was undeniably noted? Or something he had less of a reputation for – a troubled conscience?

'Don't give me an answer right out, Nick. Think it over. I haven't discussed this with Kate, so keep *shtum* over dinner, OK? She'll go along with it, I can guarantee. She's always on at me to take more time off. But there's no sense me mentioning it until I know where you stand. You can see that, can't you?'

'Yes.' Nick shaped a hesitant smile. 'Obviously.'

'Great. Just let it gel.' Terry squeezed Nick's shoulder. 'This is one of my better ideas, believe me.'

For Nick, dinner was a blank. Kate was a good cook and the food doubtless delicious. Certainly the wine flowed and the conversation probably did likewise, considering he could not afterwards recall any awkward silences. But his mind could only cast back to his discussion with Terry beforehand and forward to the moment when their discussion would resume, accommodating nothing between. The job offer was real. That was clear. But so was the money Hopkins & Broadhurst had repaid to one of Terry's shell companies. *Everything* was real. But nothing was certain.

Kate went to bed shortly before midnight, leaving Terry and Nick to their whiskies by the dying fire. Terry tossed a last log on the embers and lit a cigar. Nick declined to join him. But he accepted a top-up of Scotch and felt grateful for the warming strength of it. He did not want to force the issue that was there, between them, hovering in the lamplight, but he also knew he had no choice but to do so. There had to be an end of doubting. It was time to know his enemy.

'Maybe I should have left it till now to float the job idea,' said Terry, savouring his cigar.

'Why?'

'You were a bit distracted over dinner, that's all. Not sure Kate noticed, but I did.'

'Distracted?'

211

'Seemed that way to me.'

'Well, you're right of course. You gave me a lot to think about. More than you may have realized, actually.'

'How d'you mean?'

'What it boils down to, Terry, is why?'

'Why the offer?'

'No.' Nick measured his moment. 'Why do you hate my family?'

'What?' Terry plucked the cigar from his mouth. 'What did you say?'

'Why do you hate my family?'

Terry stared at him uncomprehendingly. 'Have you gone mad? What the bloody hell are you talking about?'

'I'm talking about the half a million pounds you lodged with Hopkins and Broadhurst to back up the fictitious Mr Tantris's offer for Trennor. The money was routed through an offshore outfit called Develastic. But you *are* Develastic, Terry. So, it was and is your money. Which means it's all down to you. And that's what makes me ask: why – why did you do it?'

Nick had never seen such an expression on Terry's face as the one that now crossed it. The bombast and the bluster, the good cheer and the ready smile, had vanished. In their place was something crushed and guilty. Nick had expected a denial, probably a vehement one, at the very least defiance, leading to he knew not what. Instead, the shoulders were slumped, the eyes downcast. Terry ground out his cigar in the ashtray on the table next to his chair. 'Wait a minute,' he said thickly, rising to his feet. He crossed to the double doors, which stood half-open, and peered out into the hall, listening for a moment. Then he quietly closed them and moved slowly back to the fireside. 'Keep your voice down, can you?'

'I wasn't shouting.'

'Kate mustn't know. Not at any price. I don't like to think what it would do to her.'

'Nothing worse than it's already done to us, I imagine.'

'Yeah, but . . .' Terry sat down on the very edge of his chair

212

and leaned forward. Hesitantly, he met Nick's gaze. 'I never imagined . . . any harm would come of it. You have to believe me.'

'Do I?'

'How did you find out?'

'Hopkins and Broadhurst's computer system isn't as secure as it should be. And money leaves a trail. You should have thought of that.'

'Didn't know I'd have to.'

'What's it all about, Terry?'

The question was met with a shrug. 'Not sure. You aren't the only ones who were taken for a ride.'

'What's that supposed to mean?'

'I just put up the dosh. I didn't know what it was going to be used for. Property speculation. That's what he said. Something to get him started in the world. It sounded kosher to me. It's how I started, except no-one put up any capital. If they had, well, I'd have cracked it all the sooner. So, why not? That's the way I saw it. Give him a leg up, treat him like my own. It's what I've always tried to think of him as, anyway.'

'You mean—'

'Tom. Yeah. He landed me in this.'

'*Tom*?'

'As God's my witness, I hadn't a clue what he was planning to do with the money. He said he had his eye on some property in Plymouth, ripe for conversion into flats. He reckoned he needed to buy several houses at a time to turn a good profit. I let him have his head. The half mill was chicken-feed to me. I suppose I should have smelt a rat when he asked me not to tell Kate. It was to be our secret, he said. Well, I fell for it. Sentiment's always been my weakness. I knew Kate badly wanted him to make something of himself. I only found out what he was up to when he came to see us after your dad's funeral. I hadn't even realized then that the money was back with Develastic. And it hadn't crossed my mind there might be a connection with Michael's death. I was gob-smacked when he told me. Speechless. Too utterly bloody amazed even to get angry with him.'

'How did he explain himself?'

'He didn't. Not really. He told Kate and me about the Tantris escapade, but I never tied that in with the money I'd loaned him. He had to spell that out for me later. But he wouldn't spell out what was behind it. "That's between me and Grandad," he said. Arrogant little . . .' Terry's right hand tightened into a fist, then slowly relaxed again. 'He made it clear as bloody day that I was in nearly as much shit as he was if I blew the whistle on him. He said he'd put in the poison with Kate if I did; tell her I'd gone along with his scheme for the sake of shafting Andrew. Well, I could see he meant it. So, I agreed to keep my mouth shut. Didn't have much choice, really. You can imagine how it would have looked to Kate.'

'Bad.'

'And then some.' Terry sighed and took a gulp of whisky. 'I didn't figure out the worst of it until he'd gone, though.'

'The worst?'

'The story about Michael sending him the book that tipped him off. Cobblers, of course. He knew already, seeing as he'd dreamt up the story. He planned it all. Including when to break the bad news. Which means I wasn't just a convenient source of cash. Oh no. He wanted to tie me into it. He wanted to implicate me.'

'Why?'

'Search me. But that goes for you lot with knobs on. What was the whole bloody charade about? Proving his family is averagely greedy isn't such a big deal, is it?'

'It proved a bit more than that.'

'Yeah. Like too much for the old fellow. No question the argy-bargy must have been a factor in Michael's death. Not that Tom felt responsible for it. There wasn't a lot of remorse on show, take my word for it. Not where his grandad was concerned, anyway. His dad, mind, that was different. Andrew's death got through to him big time. I guess he saw it all running out of control. He's been different since. Kate's right to be worried about him. He was so full of himself when he was putting the squeeze on me. But that had changed when he came down for Andrew's funeral. He was suddenly . . . a frightened kid.'

'With good reason.' Nick was angry now, angry at the thought of how deeply and deviously Tom had plotted against them. 'He's going to have to answer for what he did.'

'He'll deny it. He'll try to put the blame on me.'

'That won't wash. You didn't come to Dad's funeral, did you?'

'So?'

'So Tom did. He was at Trennor during the wake.' Nick was thinking of the video and how it had got into his car. He and Andrew had ruled out the family as suspects. That was why they had settled on Farnsworth and Davey; there was no-one else. But there was now, someone as capable of shooting the video as he was of borrowing Nick's keys to plant it. 'I wondered why Dad chose him as the recipient for *Tristan and Yseult*. Now I understand. He didn't. It was all a lie. Forget Farnsworth and Davey. Tom and Elspeth Hartley cooked it up between them. My God, it's obvious.'

'He'll still deny it.'

'Let him.' Nick was suddenly looking forward to his nephew doing precisely that. 'Let him try.'

# CHAPTER SIXTEEN

'How late did you and Terry stay up?' Kate asked as she rustled together a breakfast for Nick in the sun-filled kitchen. 'I was too far gone to notice when he came to bed.'

'Not so very late,' said Nick, sipping his coffee.

'He didn't go on about the Ferrari, did he?'

'No.'

'He tends to, when I leave him and friend to it. Boys' talk, you know? Or should I say torque?' She giggled. 'I wondered if that was why he was so insistent about driving you to the station this morning.'

'Was he?'

'Yes. In fact, it was about the only coherent thing he said before stumbling into the bathroom. "I'll take Nick to the station." So, I'm hoping he hasn't promised to show you how the car handles at a hundred and ten on the way into Sunningdale.'

'I'd have remembered that, I'm sure.'

'Yeah.' Kate slid a plate of bacon, mushrooms, tomatoes and scrambled egg on to the table in front of Nick. 'There you go. A proper farmhouse breakfast.' A look passed between them. Each knew what the other was thinking.

'Thanks.'

'About Tom . . .'

'Don't worry.' The intimacy was gone as swiftly as it had come. Nick felt surprised by the ease with which he slipped at once into a reassuring lie. 'I'll go gently with him.'

Terry was sounding as gruff and unnaturally restrained as the Ferrari when he drove Nick out through the dozing acres of the Wentworth estate an hour or so later. He was not looking wonderful either, sporting spectacularly bleary eyes and a lot of stubble.

'Couldn't face the razor this morning,' he explained, rubbing his sandpapery jowls. 'Didn't get much kip, to be honest.'

'I can't make any promises, Terry. But I believe you. And I think Kate will, if it comes to the point.'

'You don't understand how a mother's mind works. Tom can twist her round his little finger.'

'Well, I hate to say it, but that's your problem.'

'Yeah. And not a new one, either, so I should be better at dealing with it than I am. But being a stepfather is trickier than the real thing, take it from me.'

'I wouldn't know.'

'Lucky you.'

'Do you really mean that?'

'Just now I do. The lad's got me dancing on needles. Kate's the best thing that ever happened to me. I don't want it to go wrong. I couldn't cope if it did.'

'Then I don't suppose it will. Whatever I find out in Edinburgh.'

'Whatever's a big word.'

'I can't argue with that. I didn't sleep so well myself last night. I couldn't stop turning a question over in my mind that I'm hoping to persuade Tom to answer.'

'What's that?'

'What in God's name is this all about?'

Nick went on asking himself that as he travelled up to Waterloo on a virtually empty train, proceeded to King's Cross by crowded Tube and boarded the busy noon express to

Edinburgh and points north. Kate had freely admitted her bafflement at the life Tom had been leading since graduation. No job, no steady girlfriend and no apparent purpose constituted cause for maternal concern. What Kate did not realize – and Nick was only just beginning to understand – was that Tom's life was very far from purposeless. He had entered into a conspiracy against his own family, a conspiracy which might not yet have run its intended course. He had declared a secret war. But the secret was out. And the war was about to become a reciprocal process.

It was probably inevitable after the restless night he had had that Nick fell asleep somewhere between Peterborough and York. His brain had reached the limit of pondering the unanswerable and simply cut out. How long it would have stayed that way Nick never learned, because the warble of his mobile roused him just as the train was approaching Durham.

'Hello?' The line was crackly.

'Basil here, Nick. Here as in Venice.'

'Good journey?'

'Better than my arrival. I'd failed to take the Carnival into consideration. It runs until Tuesday. Which means the city is full of masked revellers. A man dressed as a plague doctor is currently waiting to use this payphone.'

'Have you found somewhere to stay?'

'With difficulty. The Zampogna would be top of no-one's list of recommended accommodation. My room does not boast a telephone, so the plague doctor and I may be seeing more of each other.'

'Is the Carnival going to interfere with your plans?'

'I can only hope not.'

'Well, don't fight it. There's a lot to be said for you lying low until I've . . . looked into a few things.'

'Such as?'

'I can't go into it now, Basil. There's been a development and I think it's best if you let me follow it through before you take any action.'

218

'How long do you need?'

'Not sure. Phone me at my hotel around six – seven, your time – and I'll explain. I gave you the number, didn't I? It'll be cheaper for you to use that than the mobile.'

'Very well. I'll call you then. In the interests of eking out my Telecom Italia card, I suppose it would be wise to forget the idea of pressing you for details now and ring off.'

'Reckon so. Speak to you later. 'Bye.'

Nick sat with the phone in his hand for several minutes, gazing at the receding view of Durham Cathedral. Then he decided to wait no longer. He punched in Tom's number.

To his mild surprise, Tom answered straightaway. 'Yuh?'

'Hi, Tom.'

'Is that Nick?'

'Yeah. I said I'd let you know when I was on my way up and here I am, on the train.'

'You're coming to Edinburgh?'

'I said I would.'

'Yeah, but somehow I . . . Anyway, that's great. Really great.' Tom sounded as if he meant it. 'I could use a shoulder to lean on right now.' And this too he sounded as if he meant.

'Are you OK?'

'Not exactly.'

'What's wrong?'

'Best not to get into it on the phone. When are you arriving?'

'Four thirty.'

'And staying? I mean, you're welcome to slum it here, but—'

'I've booked a room at the Thistle.'

'Leith Street. I know it. OK, look, there's a place just round the corner from there. The Café Royal. It's a pub, despite the name. They'll direct you from the hotel. Six o'clock would be good for me.'

'Make it six thirty.'

'Six thirty it is. See you then.'

*     *     *

219

The train reached Edinburgh no more than a few minutes late. Blue sky and a tearing wind greeted Nick as he left Waverley station and walked the short distance to the Thistle Hotel. His room was blandly functional, though it did boast a partial vista of the Calton Hill monuments. Nick decided there was time for a walk up to the summit before Basil's promised six o'clock phone call. Feeling in need of some exercise after the hours he had spent on various trains, he headed out.

He returned, refreshed by the climb and contemplation of a purple-clouded sunset over the city. But a clear head did not mean he knew how to handle his encounter with Tom, whose eagerness to see him had added a new element of uncertainty. Logically, Tom should have been trying to avoid him. Instead, he had given the impression that Nick was doing him a favour, which was not an impression Nick expected to last.

He sat in his room as six o'clock came and went with no call from Basil. The silence was a puzzle, but not a worry, given his brother's perverse reliance on Italian payphones. At six twenty, Nick left, switching off his mobile on the way; an interruption from Basil during his meeting with Tom was definitely not what was needed.

The Café Royal was literally just round the corner from the Thistle, in an alley off Princes Street. After-work drinkers sat in semicircular banquettes round two of the walls, while others propped up the island bar. Nick bought a pint, installed himself in the only empty banquette and waited.

Tom arrived within five minutes. He looked pale, his skin the colour of the smoke curling from his cigarette. His leather jacket, T-shirt and jeans, all in various shades of black, only accentuated the effect. 'Hi, Nick,' he said with a nervous smile. 'Good to see you.' There again was the hint of gratitude, which Nick found at once disarming and unaccountable.

'Good to see you, Tom. Can I buy you a drink?'

'Stay where you are. It'll be quicker if I do it.' Tom's deftness at threading his way to the bar and getting served seemed to confirm this. He returned in short order with some kind of alcopop, swigging from the bottle before he had sat down. 'Never thought you'd come through with the visit,' he said, giving Nick a frown of scrutiny as he drew on his cigarette.

'A promise is a promise.'

'Yeah, but I wasn't sure you'd remember. You weren't exactly in regular orbit at the time.'

'Not sure I am now.'

'No? Well, you look it. A guy fully restored, I'd say.'

'Your mother said much the same.' Nick smiled. 'It's getting to be a conspiracy.'

'When did you see Mum?'

'I stopped overnight with Terry and her on the way up.'

Tom nodded slowly, apparently giving the modest revelation considerable thought. 'Right.'

'There are things I want to tell you, Tom, about your father and how—'

'No-one's blaming you, Nick.'

'Perhaps they should be.'

'Not the way I see it.'

'And how's that?'

'Something's going on. Something weird.' Tom dropped his voice to a husky whisper. 'It's tied in with the Tantris deal, but I can't figure out how. Where'd the money come from? Did you ask yourself that?'

'Well, I—'

'Let me tell you the story. See what you make of it.'

The last thing Nick had expected was for Tom to mention the Tantris money. Was he going to confess before he had even been accused? All Nick could do was guard his expression – and listen.

'When I went down for Dad's funeral, Mum and Terry picked me up at Reading and we drove the rest of the way together. You probably weren't up to speed with the practicalities. Well, we couldn't face staying at Carwether. The place was in a serious mess anyway. Dad had let things slide. And Mum didn't reckon we should stay at Trennor. You were back at the Old Ferry by then. Anyway, we booked into the Moat House in Plymouth, up on the Hoe. You know it?'

'Of course.' Yes, Nick knew. In its previous incarnation as the Holiday Inn it had hosted Andrew and Kate's wedding reception, though whether Kate had mentioned that to Tom was an open question.

'Right. Well . . .' Tom stubbed out his cigarette and lit another. 'Christ, I don't know whether I should really tell you this, but I've got to tell somebody or . . .' He shook his head. 'How was the . . . atmosphere . . . at Mariposa?'

'Fine.'

'Terry . . . OK, was he?'

'Seemed to be.'

'Nothing on his mind?'

'Well, he's . . . worried about you.'

Tom snorted. 'I'll bet.'

'It's true.'

'Yeah. But not worried like you mean.'

'You've lost me.'

'Suppose I must have.' Tom sighed. 'All right. I'd better lay it on the line. The morning after the funeral I was up early. Truth is, I hardly slept. Anyway, I went out at dawn. Walked down to the Barbican and mooched about a bit. Started back round the Citadel and followed the steps up on to the Hoe. Where I saw them.'

'Them?'

'Terry . . . and Farnsworth.'

'What?'

'Farnsworth. You know, that creepy old mate of Grandad's.'

'I know him.'

'What was he doing in Plymouth the day after a funeral he definitely hadn't been invited to, rendezvousing at dawn with my stepfather? Exactly. What *was* he doing? And what was Terry doing?'

222

'I don't . . . quite understand. You say they were together?'

'By the War Memorial. Standing and talking. *Close* together, like they didn't want to be overheard. And grim-faced. You know? Like it was serious, *dead* serious.'

'Perhaps they . . . met by chance.'

'Get real, Nick. It was no chance.'

'Then what?'

'I don't know. I just can't . . .' Tom shrugged. 'It beats me.'

It beat Nick too. If Terry Mawson was in cahoots with Julian Farnsworth, everything he had told Nick about the Tantris money was almost certainly a lie. It had sounded true. But Tom sounded as if he too was speaking the truth.

'I turned round when I saw them and went back down the steps, hoping they hadn't spotted me. I realized straight off something was wrong, of course. They're not even supposed to know each other. I couldn't work out what it meant, though. Still can't. But Dad went to Tintagel that day to see Farnsworth, didn't he?'

'Yes.'

'I reckon he'd rumbled them.'

'Farnsworth . . . and Terry?'

'Must have done. Lucky for them he didn't live to tell anyone about it. Unless . . .' Tom's eyes widened. 'You haven't remembered anything, have you – anything he said when you met him?'

'I've remembered everything. But it doesn't help.'

'I was afraid it wouldn't. Shit.' Tom rubbed his forehead. 'There's worse, you see.'

'Worse?'

'I was pretty confident they hadn't clocked me on the Hoe. But I couldn't be sure. Now, I reckon they must have. It's Farnsworth, you see. He's—'

'In Edinburgh.'

Tom started. 'You know?'

'He has a talkative housekeeper. Visiting an old friend up here, she said.'

223

'Vernon Drysdale.'

'That's him.'

'He was a professor at the University. Retired before my time. But I'd heard the name even before Farnsworth mentioned it.'

'You've spoken to Farnsworth?'

'Not much choice. He's stalking me, Nick.'

'What?'

'Everywhere I go, every which way I turn, he's there, grinning like the fucking Cheshire cat and saying' – Tom suddenly made a reasonable stab at imitating Farnsworth's voice – ' "What an extraordinary coincidence, young Thomas." Coincidence? Leave it out. He's on my case.'

'Because they know you saw them that morning on the Hoe?'

'Has to be.'

'But how could they, if they were deep in conversation and you were, what, fifty yards or more away?'

'Maybe someone was watching their backs for them. Maybe *they* spotted me.'

'That's a bit—'

'Paranoid? Too fucking right. Being stalked makes you paranoid.' Tom looked away. 'Sorry. My nerves are stretched that tight right now.' He sucked at his cigarette and looked back at Nick. 'I guess you know the feeling.'

'Not of being stalked. Are you sure about this?'

'He pops up wherever I go, Nick. What else am I supposed to think? He's old, right, and not exactly light on his pins. So, how does he do it? I reckon someone else – maybe that Elspeth Hartley I've heard so much about – is in on it. I reckon they think I know more than I really do. Well, I can't take much more of it. That's one thing I *do* know.' Tom frowned. 'You believe me, don't you?'

'Of course. But . . . it's . . . not possible, is it, that these . . . encounters . . . really are coincidental?'

Tom took a long swig from his bottle before answering. He spoke slowly, suppressing his voice with evident difficulty.

His tone was low and clotted. 'Tell you what. There's this coffee-shop halfway between my flat and Princes Street. I drop in there for a caffeine fix most mornings around half nine. Most mornings lately, guess who's been sipping an *espresso* and leafing through the *TLS* when I've gone in?'

'Farnsworth.'

'Too right. So, why don't you judge for yourself? Robusta, in Castle Street. I'll give it a miss tomorrow morning. But it's a good bet Farnsworth won't. See how he explains himself. Then see if you believe him. My guess is you won't. And then you'll have to ask yourself: what's he really up to; what are *they* up to?'

The evening had grown blurred at the edges by the time they left the Café Royal. Tom was rushing his drinks and Nick was finding it hard to calculate how many he had consumed himself. Over a pasta supper and a couple of carafes of Chianti in an Italian restaurant nearby, they swapped increasingly maudlin reminiscences of Andrew, the father and the brother they had lost. Somehow, after that, they made their way to Tom's flat.

It was the ground floor of an end-of-terrace house in Circus Gardens, plumb in the centre of the cobbled crescents and elegant edifices of the Georgian New Town, affordable for an unemployed Edinburgh graduate thanks only to the generosity of his mother and, of course, his stepfather.

'The lease is in Terry's name,' Tom explained as he hunted down the whisky. 'He can get me out any time he likes.'

'But he'd never try.'

'I guess that depends how much trouble I cause. Will I tell Mum about him and Farnsworth? Or have I already told her? I hope he's sweating about that.'

'Will you tell her?'

'No.'

'Why not?'

'Because she wouldn't believe me.' Tom grinned, but Nick

sensed that only intoxication enabled him to derive amusement from the thought. 'What do you reckon to the décor round here?'

'Very nice.' And so it was. The flat was so tastefully furnished and decorated in fact that it hardly seemed like Tom's natural home at all. Nick would have expected more clutter, more bachelor grunge. But there was none. Even the Oasis CD playing in the background sounded designer-sanitized. There was scarcely any domestic impression of Tom at all.

'Mum's idea of how I should live. And Terry's idea of where I should live. If I'd just let them find me a job – career, I should say – everything would be perfect. From their point of view.'

'We all have to find our own way, Tom.'

'Yeah. But what happens if we lose our way?'

'We hope to find it again.'

'Like you did?'

'I suppose so.'

'Depends, though, doesn't it?'

'What on?'

'How far you've strayed.' Tom took a deep swallow of whisky. 'Too far . . . and there's no way back.'

At some point Nick was tempted to tell Tom what Terry had said about him. Drunk as he was, though, he was not drunk enough to make that mistake. He had travelled to Edinburgh fully intending to accuse Tom of setting in motion the events that had led to the deaths of his father and grandfather. Now, it seemed, the accusation was misdirected. Terry was the culprit after all.

Or was he? Nick's head would have been swimming even without the alcohol he had taken on board. Some time after midnight, he stumbled back to the Thistle, buffeted by an icy wind, a new moon winking at him between scudding clouds. Truth had never felt more elusive, certainty never seemed further from his grasp. Even the things he had done

226

himself were questionable now. Even the few solid facts in his possession were beginning to dissolve.

The alarm roused him at eight the following morning. Only when he was standing under the shower did he remember that he had still not spoken to Basil. If Basil had phoned the hotel after Nick's departure for the Café Royal, he had evidently left no message. He might have tried Nick's mobile, of course, but that had been switched off all night. There turned out to be no message on that either. No matter; they would talk later.

Nick had known the wine was a bad idea after so much beer and the whisky to follow an even worse one. Now he knew why. Every movement of his head induced a painful throb behind his eyes. The morning was grey and cold, rain spitting in his face as he headed out along Princes Street. He needed to be at his best to outwit Julian Farnsworth, but he was a long way from that. He could not help hoping the good doctor would fail to show.

But Tom had read his man right. Robusta boasted few customers so early on a dismal winter Saturday, but Julian Farnsworth was one of them. He was at a table in the far corner, overcoat and scarf slung over a vacant chair, the preposterous deerstalker resting by his elbow, a half-finished double *espresso* in front of him. Only the reading matter did not chime. The *TLS* had given way to the weekend edition of the *Daily Telegraph*.

'Nicholas,' he said, looking up with apparently genuine surprise. 'What are you doing here?'

'Same as you, minus the paper.' Nick bought himself a large *Americano* from the sleepy-eyed assistant, declining the auto-pilot offer of a Danish. 'Mind if I join you?'

'Not at all.'

'I'm up here visiting my nephew.'

'Ah, young Thomas. Yes. I've seen him in here a couple of times.'

'Not surprising. He lives nearby.'

'So I gather.'

'But you don't.'

'I too am visiting. An old friend. He has a house just outside Edinburgh.'

'Vernon Drysdale.'

'The very same.'

'Odd you should decide to look him up so soon after meeting Tom at his grandfather's funeral.'

'Not unconnected, actually.' Farnsworth smiled his serpentine smile. 'Michael's death reminded me that time is running short. Who knows at my age when a meeting with a friend may prove to be a last meeting? Every greeting may also be a farewell.'

'How true.'

'They told me you were unwell, Nicholas. Distressed following your brother's tragic accident. I'm glad to find you . . . much as I recall.'

'I'm getting there.'

'Splendid. Please do accept my condolences. Andrew's death . . .' Farnsworth shook his head. 'A sad waste.'

'It was, yes.'

'You should not blame yourself.'

'I don't.'

'No-one is to blame for such . . . vagaries of fate.'

'Are you sure about that?'

'Of course. Fate is not manipulable by man. And God is above blame.'

'Professor Drysdale a late riser, is he?'

'Quite the reverse, since you ask. And why do you ask, might I enquire in return?'

'I simply wondered why you come into Edinburgh every morning to patronize this unremarkable establishment.'

'Oh, it's not unremarkable. The *espresso* is really rather good. And my sojourns in Italy have left me with an abiding love of *espresso*. Vernon is a man of the mind. The only coffee he keeps is instant – and powdered at that.'

'You visit Italy often?'

'Not as often as I should like.'

'What's your favourite part?'

Farnsworth pursed his lips and frowned thoughtfully. 'Venice,' he eventually announced.

'I thought you might say that.'

'How astute of you. Is it perhaps your favourite also?'

'I've never been there.'

'You should. It has many connections with your family. The Byzantine diaspora after the fall of Constantinople took numerous bearers of the Paleologus name to Venice. You probably have cousins there aplenty.'

'I don't think so.'

'Distant and/or unknown.' Farnsworth smiled insistently. 'I think you must.'

'How long are you staying with Professor Drysdale?'

'I'm not sure. Until he tires of my company, I suppose. Before he does, you should pay us a visit. Let me give you the address and telephone number.' Farnsworth plucked a card from his pocket and jotted the details on the back with his fountain pen. 'There.' Nick took the card and glanced down at it. *Roseburn Lodge, Manse Road, Roslin, near Edinburgh, (0131) 440 7749*, was inscribed in Farnsworth's copperplate hand in brown ink. 'Do call. I know Vernon would be delighted to meet you.'

'Really?'

'Why, yes. He's a medieval historian. I happen to have drawn his attention to your family's lineal descent from the last Emperor of Byzantium. He'd naturally be interested to meet any scion of the imperial dynasty.'

'You could have invited Tom.'

'What makes you think I haven't?'

'He didn't mention it.'

'There may be much he has not mentioned.'

A moment's silence intruded while Nick sipped his coffee. 'Besides,' he resumed, 'our lineal descent, as you call it, is unproven.'

'I understand differently.'

'If you don't mind my asking, Doctor Farnsworth—'

'Julian, please.'

'How would you know, then . . . Julian?'

'One picks things up, if one knows where to look.'

'Does one?'

'Oh yes, I do assure you.'

'As regards my family, would Terry Mawson be someone you've . . . picked things up from?'

'Who?'

'Terry Mawson. Tom's stepfather.'

'I'm unacquainted with the gentleman.'

'I understand differently.'

'*Touché.*' Farnsworth seemed genuinely impressed to have the phrase turned against him. 'I fear trust is the issue, is it not? You don't trust me, do you, Nicholas?'

Nick took another sip of coffee, delaying his reply. But they both knew what it had to be. 'No. I don't.'

'I quite understand. Blood is thicker than water. What has young Thomas told you? That I am harassing him – following him, perhaps? That I am in cahoots with his evil step-father? Some such *mélange*, no doubt. Desperation tactics, I fear. Ask yourself: is he entirely credible? Be honest now. Is he?'

'I'd be prepared to stand by him.'

'Naturally. But if he's lied to you, what then? If he's set out to deceive you and in the process done untold harm . . .' Farnsworth spread his palms. 'There's something I need to show you.'

'What?'

'I don't have it with me. Perhaps I could arrange for it to be delivered to you later. Are you staying with your nephew?'

'No. I'm in a hotel.'

'Excellent. I'll have it sent to you there. Which one?'

Nick hesitated, but could see no reason to conceal his whereabouts. 'The Thistle. In Leith Street.'

'Very well. Before the day is out, the proof will be in your hands.'

'Proof of what?'

'You'll see.' Farnsworth smiled. 'I promise.'

Farnsworth invited Nick to join him in a saunter round the National Gallery of Scotland, where he claimed to adjourn most mornings for a refreshing dose of fine art. 'I find ten minutes spent in the Impressionist room quite sets me up for the day.' Nick declined and was happy to let Farnsworth turn left outside Robusta while he turned right.

He headed north to Circus Gardens, having promised Tom an immediate report on the encounter. Tom answered the door unshaven and dressed only in a thin towelling bathrobe. He looked as if skipping his normal early visit to Robusta had been no hardship. He looked, in fact, as if Nick's departure the night before had not necessarily been his cue for lights out.

'It's well gone ten,' Tom said huskily, dragging back the sitting-room curtains to let in a flood of grey light. 'I guess you must have found our friend.'

'He was there.'

'Said he would be.' Tom slumped down in a chair and yawned. 'How'd he explain that?'

'Implausibly.'

'But slickly?'

'Very.'

'He didn't admit to dogging my footsteps, then?'

'No.'

'But you can see he is.'

'I'm sure of it.'

'Then they must know I'm on to them.'

'Guess so.'

'Yeah.' Tom rubbed his face. 'I could use a coffee. Want one?'

'No thanks. I just—'

'Had a decent cup at Robusta. 'Course you did. Well, see me to the kitchen. I might keel over on the way.'

Tom stood up, stretched and padded off to the kitchen, with

231

Nick tagging along. Once there, he filled the kettle, switched it on and spooned some coffee granules into a mug, then propped himself against the worktop and yawned again.

'What am I going to do, Nick?'

'About Farnsworth? I'm not sure. You can't stop the man hanging around Edinburgh. And you can't prove he and Terry are up to no good.'

'Them knowing each other proves that to me.'

'Setting up the Tantris fraud involved a lot of money. Half a million pounds in ready cash. Would Terry have that amount on tap?'

'Easily.' There was a spark of alertness in the glance Tom shot at Nick before the kettle boiled. He turned away to fill his mug. 'You think he bankrolled the operation?'

'Maybe.'

'It would fit, I suppose.' Tom topped up his coffee from the cold tap and took a wincing sip. 'I'd wondered myself, to be honest. If the money was his contribution, I mean. I also wondered if Farnsworth might have told Dad that when they met up at Tintagel.'

'In front of Davey? It seems unlikely.'

'We've only Farnsworth's word for it that they didn't continue their chat somewhere else.'

'Andrew said nothing about it to me.'

'He wouldn't, would he? The whole Terry, Mum and me situation would have been mixed up in his mind. He'd have worried that no-one would believe him, that they'd write it off as a pathetic attempt to get Mum back.'

'I suppose . . .' The layers of pretended knowledge and ignorance were becoming too much for Nick. He decided to cut through them. 'Farnsworth's sending me something later.'

'What?'

'Proof, he called it.'

'*Proof*?'

'Of why he's to be trusted, I think he meant.'

'But he isn't to be trusted.'

'No. So, it can't amount to much, can it?'

232

'The guy talks in fucking riddles.'

Tom thumped his mug down on the worktop and padded out into the hall, leaving Nick to contemplate a black crescent of spilt coffee at the base of the mug. From the hall came the sound of a lighter being flicked. A few seconds later Tom reappeared in the doorway, dragging on a cigarette.

'Can you remember the last thing Dad said to you, Nick?'

'Very clearly.'

'What was it?'

' "Let go of me." '

' "Let go of me." ' Tom repeated the words so softly and swiftly they almost sounded like an echo. 'And you did. We all did.'

'He didn't know they were going to be his last words, Tom. They don't signify anything.'

'I disagree. The fact that he didn't know makes them all the more significant.'

'You've lost me.'

'Yeah.' Tom gazed at Nick through a slowly spreading haze of cigarette smoke. 'Maybe I have.'

Nick left Tom to shower and breakfast and walked back into the city centre. He had no idea what to do next, except wait on Farnsworth's promise. The man was not to be trusted. Tom was right about that. But who *was* to be trusted? The only name that came to mind was Basil's.

And Basil, bless him, had telephoned at last. When Nick switched his mobile back on, he found a message waiting for him.

'I've tried your hotel twice to no avail. It's Saturday morning here, as I hope it still is there when you hear this. I have, as a matter of simple fact, nothing to report. Hardly surprising, since you've forbidden me to do anything until we've spoken, which I trust we'll soon be able to do. I'll try again later. *Arrivederci*!'

Basil's impatience was understandable. But what was Nick to tell him? That he was being played for a sucker by someone

233

but he did not know which of several candidates that someone was? It was true. But it was no help to either of them.

The rain was harder now and the wind was strengthening. His box of a room at the Thistle holding no appeal, Nick decided to take Farnsworth up on his recommendation of the National Gallery. It was busy but not unduly crowded. There was no sign of Farnsworth, even in the Impressionist room. Nick wandered round, gazing up at one picture after another, some of them beautiful, some brilliant, some neither, unable in his distracted state to appreciate the differences. After an aimless hour or so, he left.

A gale was raging by now. He struggled through it to the Café Royal and saw off his hangover with rather more than the hair of the dog. It was mid-afternoon when he returned to the Thistle. By then he had drunk enough to have stopped caring about the uncertainties gnawing away at him. He lay down on the bed in his room and fell instantly into deep, dreamless sleep.

It was dark when he woke. Night had fallen. He could hear the rain still beating against the window. He peered at the luminous dial of his alarm clock: it was nearly half past eight. He switched on the bedside lamp, waited until his eyes had adjusted to the glare, then sat up.

He saw it at once: a square white envelope, lying on the floor near the door. It had been slipped beneath the door while he was sleeping. There came a sudden, fluttering rush of palpitations. He took several long, slow breaths, waiting for the attack to pass. Then he rose, crossed the room and picked up the envelope.

It was blank, the flap unsealed. Nick carried it back to the bed and sat down again. He lifted the flap of the envelope, reached inside and pulled out an A5-sized black-and-white photograph.

The photograph had been taken through a café window. There were reflections of passers-by in the glass and, beyond the window, a couple of tables in, a man and a woman were sitting opposite each other. The woman appeared to be talking and was gesturing with her hand, while the man was listening impassively, staring at her apparently in rapt attention. They were in Robusta, Nick realized. The photographer was some distance away, judging by assorted blurs in the foreground. The pair were clearly unaware that they were being filmed. And no wonder, since the man was Tom Paleologus and he was sharing a table with Elspeth Hartley.

# CHAPTER SEVENTEEN

The ground-floor flat at 8 Circus Gardens was in darkness, the curtains open. As far as Nick could tell as he craned over the basement railings, there was no-one at home. He rang Tom's bell several times, more in hope than expectation. There was no response.

It was close to nine thirty on a cold, wet night. But it was Saturday, so Tom's absence was hardly suspicious. Nick *was* suspicious, though. Tom was the conspirator, not Terry. The photograph proved that. The rendezvous between Terry and Julian Farnsworth on Plymouth Hoe could well have been an invention. But Tom's rendezvous with Elspeth Hartley was real and undeniable.

Nick retreated to the Café Royal and sipped a pint till closing time. He was tempted to phone Farnsworth, but something held him back. The photographic evidence suggested he owed Tom nothing, but still he felt he owed him a chance to explain.

How could he explain, though? Tom had known of Farnsworth's promise to supply Nick with what he had called proof. And he must have realized Nick would want to discuss it with him, whatever it turned out to be. Was that why he had gone missing? If so, it was a futile evasion. He would have to return eventually. And Nick would be waiting when he did.

But midnight came and went in Circus Gardens with no sign of Tom. It had stopped raining by then, but the temperature was plummeting. None of the windows at number 8 was lit. In the end, Nick had no choice but to give up – until the morning.

Nothing had changed when Nick returned, early on a chill New Town sabbath. The curtains of Tom's flat did not look to have been drawn overnight. Nick could see straight into the room where they had sat drinking whisky in the small hours of Saturday morning. And the room was empty. He took a few pointless stabs at Tom's bell. Silence was the only answer.

Then, just as he turned away, a bustling figure rounded the corner from the next street and started up the steps leading to the door, only to stop abruptly at the sight of Nick, who found himself looking down at a short, plump, middle-aged woman with a beehive hairstyle that added at least six inches to her height. She was wearing a beltless fur-trimmed white raincoat, sheepskin mittens, black leggings and thick-soled cherry-red boots, with a pair of sunglasses perched somewhere in the auburn beehive. Under one arm she held a thick wodge of Sunday newsprint.

'Looking for me, dear?' she enquired with a quizzical smile.

'No, er . . . Tom Paleologus.'

'It's a mite early for young Tom. He's probably sleeping off last night.'

'You know what he was doing?'

'No. But he's young and it was Saturday. Tell me' – she frowned at Nick – 'are you and he related?'

'I'm his uncle.'

'Yes, there's a resemblance. So you'd be . . .'

'Nick Paleologus.'

'Pleased to meet you, Nick. I'm Una Strawn. I live in the first-floor flat.'

'I'm anxious to contact Tom . . . Una. I'm worried about him. His father died recently.'

'So I heard. Terrible, quite terrible. But Tom seemed fine

237

when I last saw him. Friday, it would have been. I don't think you need to be worried.'

'Even so . . .'

'Tell you what. Come in with me and see if you can raise him.'

Una shook a key out of one of her mittens and led the way into the communal entrance hall. Nick went straight to Tom's door and gave it several loud knocks. 'Tom?' he called, following that up with some still louder knocks. But there was no sound from within.

'Do you want a coffee, Nick?' asked Una as she went on up the stairs. 'I set some to perk before stepping out for the papers.'

'Well . . . thanks.' Nick started after her. 'Very kind of you.'

'Not at all. I may have misled you about Tom. He could have gone away for the weekend for all I know.'

'I saw him yesterday morning. He didn't say he was going away.'

'Maybe not, but the impulsiveness of youth . . .' Una opened the door to her own flat and Nick followed her in.

The layout was identical to Tom's flat, but that was hard to remember when faced with Una's enthusiasm for purple walls, shag-pile rugs and bead-fringed throws. The kitchen seemed to contain more books and magazines than pots and pans by about fifty to one, but the percolator had done its work in her absence. She filled a couple of chunky breakfast cups with the aromatic brew and invited Nick to sit down at the *Tatler*-littered table. Then she took off her raincoat to reveal a voluminous pink mohair jumper that reached almost to her knees and sat down opposite him.

'Have you come far, Nick?'

'From Cornwall.'

'Where Tom's father lived?'

'That's right.' Nick sipped some coffee. 'I *am* worried about him, Una.'

'So I can tell. And it's true . . .'

'What is?'

'He's not been himself this past month or more. Not since the turn of the year, in fact.'

'We can't put that down to his father's death.'

'No more we can.'

'What, then?'

'He did break up with his girlfriend. Such a pity. They made a lovely couple.'

'Do you know what went wrong?'

'There was someone else, I think.'

'In Tom's life, you mean?'

'Yes, though she doesn't seem to have made him very happy. I've never seen her, mind, and Tom's said not a word. But Sasha—'

'Who?'

'Sasha Lovell, the girlfriend I mentioned. I bumped into her recently and she was still raw about the whole thing, but quite clear that Tom had ditched her because of . . . well, someone she called . . . Harriet.'

'Harriet . . . Elsmore?'

'Just Harriet.'

'Take a look at this.' Nick pulled out the photograph and showed it to her. 'Recognize the woman with Tom?'

Una peered closely. 'Where did you get this picture from? It looks like it was taken at the Robusta.'

'It's a long story. Do you recognize the woman?'

'I don't think so. Who is she?'

'She could be Harriet.'

'Well, as to that . . .' Una gave a mohaired shrug. 'I couldn't say.'

'Maybe Sasha could.'

'Maybe.'

'How would I contact her?'

'She's a student at the university. She was a year behind Tom. They'd have an address for her, I dare say, though getting hold of it on a Sunday . . .'

'You don't know where she lives?'

'No. That is . . .' A thought seemed to strike Una. 'When I

met her I was coming out of the Odeon in Clerk Street. My friend Queenie and I often go there of an afternoon. It's cheap rate before five o'clock, you know. Anyway, Sasha was walking past as we came out, on her way home from the University. "I live just over there," I remember she said, pointing across the road. We chatted for a few minutes while Queenie went to wait for our bus. That's when Sasha mentioned this Harriet creature. "She's no good for him," she said, "but he just doesn't see it." Then our bus came along and I had to dash.' Seeing Nick's frown, she added, 'It's the best I can do, I'm afraid.'

'Sorry. I don't mean to seem ungrateful.'

'I'm sure there's no serious cause for concern. Tom's grieving for his father and maybe wondering if throwing Sasha over was such a good idea. That'll be all there is to it.'

'You're probably right,' Nick lied, thinking as he did so: if only.


It was a long shot, but the only one Nick could take. Clerk Street was a stretch of the main road leading south from the city centre. Nick's taxi dropped him opposite a closed Odeon cinema in a neighbourhood of burger bars, kebab joints and betting shops, with bedsits above most of them. It was, he supposed, the sort of area where students lacking a wealthy stepfather ended up.

But Sasha Lovell's name did not appear next to any of the bell-pushes in nearby doorways. Most bells lacked a name altogether, so Nick's search was beginning to look as if it was over before it had begun. 'Just over there' from the Odeon, as Una had quoted Sasha as saying, could have included the adjacent side-street, however. Nick decided to check it out.

Rankeillor Street was lined with Georgian terraced houses in varying states of disrepair. The Salisbury Crags loomed dull red in the middle distance, skewing Nick's sense of perspective. He trudged from door to door, along the northern side of the street, the conviction growing on him that he was wasting his time, although what better use he could make of it was a moot point.

And mooter still when, at the far end, he found himself staring somewhat disbelievingly at the name SASHA printed in faded capitals on a small laminated card. He pressed the bell next to it. Ten seconds slowly and silently elapsed. He pressed it again.

There was a squeal of swollen wood somewhere above him, a rattle of window and sash. He stepped back from the door and looked up to see a round-faced young woman with orange, spiky hair staring down at him from two floors above.

'What can I do you for?' she called.

'Sasha Lovell?'

'That's me.'

'I'm Nick Paleologus, Tom's uncle.'

'Are you now?'

'Could we have a word?'

'What about?'

'Tom. I'm worried about him.'

'Well, maybe I'm not.'

'I really would be grateful for a few minutes of your time, Sasha. It's important.'

Sasha looked undecided. She glanced behind her, then back down at Nick.

'Can I come up?'

'No. Stay where you are. I'll come down.'

She appeared a few minutes later, clad in black from her Doc Martens to her beret, fleeced collar pulled up against the wind. For all the shabby-*chic* clothes, nostril-stud and chewing gum, there was a mature practicality in the glance of scrutiny she gave him.

'There's a place round the corner where we can talk,' she said, leading the way. 'Are you the monk or the bureaucrat?'

'Tom told you about Basil and me, did he?'

'Sort of. Two aunts and two uncles were mentioned. Basil would be the monk, then?'

241

'Former monk.'

'Does that make you a former bureaucrat?'

'Could be. I've not been at my desk in quite a while.'

'Why's that?'

'Family troubles.'

'Are they why you're worried about Tom?'

'Yeah.'

'Here we are.'

Sasha turned in at the door of a muddily decorated café where one or two people were leafing through Sunday papers over steaming mugs to a soundtrack of subdued jazz. Sasha knew the girl behind the counter, merely nodding in answer to the question, 'Usual?' Nick ordered a coffee and they sat down near the window.

'I can't stay long. Rick's a bit . . . you know.'

'Rick?'

'You don't want to get me started on him. Tell me about these family troubles of yours.'

'Tom's father and grandfather have both died recently.'

'Shit.' Sasha winced. 'That's rough.'

'Very.'

'How—' She broke off as Nick's coffee and her herbal tea arrived. 'Thanks, Meg.'

'I gather you and Tom broke up a while back.'

'Who told you that?'

'Una Strawn.'

Sasha smiled and sipped her tea. 'If you've spoken to Una, you probably know it all.'

'She mentioned . . . a woman called Harriet.'

'Harriet. That's right. The one I couldn't compete with.'

'This her?' Nick showed Sasha the photograph.

'Yeah. That *is* her. Where'd this come from?'

'It was sent anonymously . . . to Tom's mother. I think someone was trying to warn her that Harriet could be a bad influence on Tom. He's been behaving strangely. Even before the two deaths in the family.'

'How did they happen? The deaths, I mean.'

'A fall, in my father's case. Not unexpected, given his age and frailty. As for Tom's father, my brother Andrew, he died in a road accident.'

'Farmer, wasn't he?'

'He was.'

'Well, it's tough, but, look, Tom finished with me back in January. I don't—'

'Finished because of Harriet?'

'Not according to Tom. But when I saw him with her soon after, it was obvious.'

'Do you know her surname?'

'Elsmore, I think. Yeah. Harriet Elsmore.'

'What else do you know about her?'

'Nothing. It was just the one encounter. And not what you'd call a warm one. He was . . . under her thumb, somehow. Cowed. Not the Tom I knew. That's not just jealousy talking either. I'm over it now. I'm seeing it like it is. When I came back after the Christmas vac, he was different. Cold. Almost a stranger.'

'Thanks to Harriet?'

'Who else? She's got her claws into him somehow. And you're worried about how deep, right?'

'That's more or less the size of it.'

'Well, I don't know. She's a weird one, for sure. And not Tom's type, I'd have said. 'Course, I thought *I* was his type. He told me he was staying on in Edinburgh so we could be together until I graduated this summer. He even wanted me to move in with him. He was keen, right? Then Harriet comes on the scene and he's suddenly . . . ice. I mean, who is she? How does she make a living? She must be . . . what, thirty-five? It doesn't stack up.'

'Did you ask Tom about her?'

'I asked. He didn't answer.'

'Does she live in Edinburgh?'

'Not sure. But I don't think so.'

'He's done a bunk since I got here. I wondered if he could be with her.'

'More than likely. But where would that be . . .' Sasha

shook her head expressively. 'That photograph was sent to Tom's mother, right?'

'Yes.' Nick wondered if he was going to regret the lie he had instinctively told.

'Any idea who by?'

'None.'

'Only . . .'

'What?'

'You're not the first to ask me about Harriet Elsmore.'

'Who *was* first?'

'Some old guy, about ten days ago. Well-spoken, well-dressed, a bit camp.'

'Give a name?'

'Harmsworth. Something like that.'

'What did he want to know?'

'Anything I could tell him about her. Which, like I've told you, isn't much. He buttonholed me as I was leaving a lecture. Said he was anxious to contact her and understood I might be able to help. Managed to make "understood" sound really sinister. Called me "my dear", which didn't win him any favours. I asked him if he knew Tom and he said yes, he was an old friend of the family. That true?'

'More acquaintance than friend. His name's Julian Farnsworth. He's a former colleague of my father.'

'An archaeologist, you mean?'

'Yeah.'

'He didn't look like one.'

'What do they look like?'

'Not like him.'

'No, well, sinister is right. He's up here staying with a friend you may have heard of. Professor Vernon Drysdale.'

'Professor of Medieval History as was. Yeah, I've heard of him. Retired years ago, but still slinks around the Uni.'

'I'm thinking of paying him and Farnsworth a visit. Happen to know where this is?' Nick showed her the card on which Farnsworth had written Drysdale's address and telephone number.

'He lives at Roslin, does he?' Sasha nodded. 'That figures.'

'What do you mean?'

'Ever heard of Rosslyn Chapel?'

'No.'

'Spelt differently, but it's the same place. Roslin's a village a few miles south of here, just outside the city. Rosslyn Chapel's its main claim to fame. Dates from the fifteenth century. Incredibly ornate stone-carving and a whole heap of legends. Tom took me there once. It's something else, that's for sure. Gave me the creeps. Crops up in a lot of those books about the Knights Templar and the Ark of the Covenant. You know, the Holy Blood and the Holy Whatsit – that kind of crap.'

'They seem to have slipped past me.'

'Yeah? Well, I bet it won't stay that way if you drop in on the Prof. He wrote one, you see. *Shades of Grail*. Some sort of academic overview. Sold more than all his other stuff put together, so they say.'

'Read it?'

'No.'

'What about Tom?'

Sasha thought for a moment. 'I'm pretty sure I've seen a copy at the flat. Can't remember him talking about it, though. He might have bought it after we visited the chapel. I don't know.' She thought some more. 'This Farnsworth. Could he have sent Tom's mother the photograph?'

'It's possible, given that he's here, where the photograph was taken.'

'And sniffing after Harriet.'

'Exactly.'

'What's Tom got himself mixed up in, Nick?'

'Not sure.'

'Something bad?'

'Could be.'

'Shit.' Sasha stared into her tea. 'Just when you think you're over someone . . . you have to start worrying about them.'

*       *       *

245

They left the café shortly afterwards. Sasha made straight for the newsagent-cum-grocer a few doors down and Nick started to take his leave of her, but she insisted he tag along. 'There's something at the flat I want to give you,' she explained as she grabbed a pint of milk and a *Sunday Times*. 'When are you thinking of going to Roslin?'

'No time like the present.'

'Guess not.'

'What's the best way to get there?'

'Oh, just follow the Penicuik road until you see the turn for Roslin.' Sasha paid and they stepped out on to the pavement.

'Actually, I'm on foot.'

'Then it'll have to be the bus. The thirty-seven, from opposite the Odeon. There's one every half-hour.'

'Thanks.' They turned the corner into Rankeillor Street. 'What are you giving me, Sasha?'

'I should return them to Tom, anyway. If you see him, say I asked you to pass them on. If you don't see him . . . if he stays away . . . it's up to you what you do.'

'What are we talking about?'

'Wait out here.'

Sasha went ahead of him into number 56, closing the door behind her. Nick did as he had been told, with rapidly mounting puzzlement. Then he heard the second-floor window squeak open. He looked up and Sasha met his gaze. She tossed some small object down to him. In the instant before he caught it, he realized it was a bunch of keys.

There were three keys, tied together with string: a mortise and two Yales. Nick stared at them, nestled in his palm. Then he heard the window close.

Standing at the bus stop in Clerk Street, fingering the keys in his pocket, Nick promised himself he would not use them unless he had to. But the promise only begged a question: when might he have to?

The chirrup of his mobile came as a welcome distraction. And the sound of Basil's voice when he answered was also

246

welcome, even though how much to tell Basil was a scarcely less delicate issue.

'Good morning, Nick. How do I find you?'

'Confused.'

'About what?'

'Tom.'

'Why so?'

'He's behaving oddly.'

'Bereavement can have that effect.'

'Well, let's hope that's all there is to it.'

'And what of the "development" you reported when last we spoke?'

'It's kind of connected.'

'With Tom?'

'Yes.'

'Telecom Italia's international tariff is not set with elliptical communication in mind, Nick. Would you care to be specific?'

'I can't be. As soon as that changes, I'll let you know.'

'Until then you'd prefer me to twiddle my thumbs?'

'Yeah. Sorry.'

'No need to apologize. As it happens, I disregarded your preference in the matter and called at cousin Demetrius's residence yesterday.'

'You did what?'

'I presented my compliments at the Palazzo Falcetto, a residence sufficiently grand to suggest its owner is unlikely to be greatly bothered about the inheritance of a modest house in Cornwall.'

'For God's sake, Basil, I asked you to—'

'You need not worry. Apparently Demetrius regularly flees Venice during the Carnival. He is expected back on Wednesday and will be informed of my visit. It hardly amounts to a great deal.'

'Maybe not, but—'

'Seen anything of Dr Farnsworth?'

'Well, yes, we've met.'

'With what outcome?'

'None really. He insists he's here to see an old friend.'

'You are telling me everything, aren't you, Nick?'

'I'm telling you as much as I can be sure of. I just need a little more time . . . to pin things down.'

'Then Demetrius has done you a favour. You have until Wednesday. Meanwhile, the display on this telephone indicates that my credit is draining away like sand. Goodbye, Nick.'

'Listen, Basil—' But it was too late. The line was dead.

The 37 bus did not divert to Roslin on a Sunday. Nick had to walk the last half a mile into the village from the main road. It felt colder now he was outside the city. A chill wind was blowing down from the Pentland Hills to the west. There was a dusting of snow on their whale-backed summits, making the grey clouds massed beyond them look bruised and threatening.

Roslin herself seemed an unremarkable place: a mix of old and new housing centred on a few shops and a couple of pubs. A man walking his dog directed Nick to Roseburn Lodge. On his way there, Nick passed a sign for Rosslyn Chapel and glimpsed a structure of some kind in the middle distance, screened by trees. But the chapel could wait. He had more pressing concerns than old buildings and ancient legends.

Roseburn Lodge was a plain-fronted greystone Georgian house, draped in ivy and half-hidden from the road by a straggling excess of blackthorn hedge. A battered old estate car was parked on the short gravel drive, but there was no sign of Farnsworth's Citroën.

Nick tugged at the bell and, just when he was about to give it another tug, the door was opened by a woman possessed of a pair of the darkest eyes he could ever recall seeing. She wore an apron over a threadbare dress and had her hair scraped back severely in a bun. 'Aye?' she said, looking down her sharp-boned nose at him.

'I'm looking for Dr Julian Farnsworth.' Nick ventured a smile, but it did not prove contagious.

'He's no here.'

'Are you expecting him back soon?'

'I wouldn't know.'

'What about Professor Drysdale? Is he at home?'

'Aye, he is.'

'Could you ask him if he'll spare me a few moments? Dr Farnsworth may have mentioned me to him. My name's Paleologus. Nicholas Paleologus.'

'Paleologus, you say?'

'That's right.'

'Wait here.'

She stumped off, half-closing the door behind her. Nick was left to listen to the rooks cawing in the trees either side of the house. Inside, he could hear a clock ticking ponderously and, somewhere farther off, a mumble of conversation. Then the woman reappeared.

'Come away in.'

'Thanks.'

She led the way down a shadowy hall past the clock Nick had heard to an open doorway near the end, where she stood back to let him proceed.

The room Nick stepped into was obviously the professor's study. The windows looked out on to an overgrown garden, while a vast leather-topped desk strewn with books and papers filled the principal bay. Two walls were lined with crammed bookshelves, but their capacity was clearly insufficient in view of the piles of books on the floor. Some were even stacked on the seat of one of the armchairs flanking the fireplace, where no fire burned despite the prevailing chill.

From the other armchair an elderly man rose stiffly to his feet and smiled in greeting. Nick recognized the type from long filial experience. The superannuated academic, here encountered in his bookbound lair. Vernon Drysdale shared Michael Paleologus's taste for corduroy and lambswool, though physically he was a contrasting specimen of the breed: stout, pigeon-chested, ruddy-faced and bald as an egg, the lack of hair on the top of his head offset by white sideburns that met in a grey moustache and made him look more like a Victorian master of foxhounds than a twentieth-century historian.

'Mr Paleologus.' Drysdale shook Nick's hand firmly. 'It's an honour.' The Scottish burr in his voice was subdued, almost superficial.

'Good of you to see me, Professor Drysdale. I don't know about an honour.'

'A living, breathing Paleologus. It's a wonder as well as an honour. I met your father a few times, of course. Please accept my condolences.'

'Thank you.'

'Julian tells me your elder brother also died recently. A terrible coincidence.'

'Not really a coincidence.'

'No?'

'Actually, it's Julian – Dr Farnsworth – I'm hoping to see.'

'You're out of luck, I'm afraid. He's been called away.'

'Back to Oxford?'

'I'm not sure. Julian plays his cards close to his chest, as you may be aware. He left yesterday afternoon, in something of a hurry.'

'I saw him yesterday morning. He said nothing about going away.'

'There was a phone call, then he was off, barely finding time to mention you might pop in.' Drysdale smiled. 'For that at any rate I'm glad. And Julian's absence means he can't monopolize your attention. So, won't you sit down?' He waved airily at the other armchair. 'Dump those books any-where.'

'All right. Thanks.' Nick made a clearance and sat down, trying not to voice the irritation he felt. The fact that Drysdale was – or had been – Farnsworth's host did not mean he was necessarily his accomplice in whatever game Farnsworth was playing. It was possible, though. Very possible.

'Will you be wanting any tea?' the old woman put in.

'It's nearly noon,' Drysdale replied. 'I'll be taking something stronger. A drop of Scotch for you, Paleologus?'

'Thanks. Don't mind if I do.' Nick noted how swiftly Drysdale had lapsed into addressing him by his surname.

'Then you can leave us, Mrs Logan.' Mrs Logan tossed her head and wandered off. Drysdale moved to a section of the bookcase where a bottle of Jura malt and some tumblers were stored in front of a run of historical journals. He poured generous measures for each of them, handed Nick his glass and lowered himself stiffly into his chair. '*Slàinte.*'

'Cheers.'

'I'm sorry about Julian.'

'Not your fault.'

'One feels a measure of responsibility for one's friends, even when one shouldn't.'

'How long have you known him?'

'We were at Oxford together. A little after your father's time. You and I have met before, as a matter of fact. A garden party at your family's home in Oxford. Summer of 'seventy-five. Julian took me along. Your father introduced you to me as the prodigy of his progeny, if I recall the phrase correctly.'

Nick winced. He too recalled the phrase. 'I'm afraid I don't remember the occasion.'

'Why should you? It was more memorable for me than you. Julian tells me . . . well, that your life hasn't been easy . . . since then.'

'Whose has?'

'Julian's, for one. And mine, if I'm to be honest.'

'Does Julian visit you often?'

'Not at all. This is the first time in years.' Drysdale grinned. 'I've no doubt he had a more compelling motive for his visit than the pleasure of my company. As evidence I cite the frequency of his absence.'

'What's been occupying him?'

'I don't know. He's been reticent on the point. By nature he's garrulous yet unrevealing, as you may have found yourself.'

'It's true.'

'Has he intimated anything to you?'

'No. But he seems to have been paying close attention to my nephew.'

'Ah. The last of the Paleologoi.'

'I'm sorry?'

'As the only known descendants of the Imperial family—'

'*Supposed* descendants, Professor. The lineage was a triumph of wishful thinking on the part of my grandfather.'

'Really? That's not my understanding.'

'Julian said you're something of an expert on Byzantine history.'

'That too could be described as wishful thinking. A scholar, Paleologus, no more. But who can be more than a scholar? There's no higher calling.' Drysdale frowned. 'Though in the opinion of some I've forfeited the right to call myself one.' He fell silent.

'How?'

'Oh, by writing on a vulgarly populist theme. A hanging offence in certain circles.'

'Are you talking about *Shades of Grail*?'

'You've read it?'

'No, no. But . . . Julian mentioned it.'

'Did he? How very . . . obliging of him. Well, I have no regrets. The book sells. Why should I apologize?'

'I don't suppose you should. What's it about?'

'Have you visited Rosslyn Chapel, Paleologus? We're just across the way from one of the Lothians' premier tourist attractions.'

'I've not been there.'

'Well, you should go. And if you do you'll no doubt be impressed by the vast stock of esoteric literature they carry in the chapel shop. There'll be some copies of *Shades of Grail* there. It's my humble contribution to the debate.'

'What debate is that?'

'Such an active one I sometimes assume everyone's a participant on some level. Hubris, indeed. But I'd wager you're aware of the subject, even if you don't realize it. Heard of the Knights Templar?'

'Well, I know they were a medieval order of knights, founded during the Crusades. I, er . . .'

'What?'

'I have the impression there's a mystery about them.'

'Indeed. And it's a mystery that's fed a modern obsession. People want to believe in something, Paleologus. To believe in nothing, isn't that what Conrad really meant by those words he put into the dying Kurtz's mouth at the end of *Heart of Darkness*? "The horror, the horror." This is an agnostic generation. Scepticism is universal. And so people doubt what they are told to believe and believe what they are told to doubt. UFOs, crop circles, big cats . . . and the Holy Grail. They're all part of a continuum. They feed our need for myths. And they feed also our stubborn, guilt-ridden conviction that those myths conceal irrational truths. Books aren't the half of it. The Internet is aswarm with such notions. The academic establishment looks down its disapproving nose at those who peddle them. But there they err. Every debate must be joined, else it will be lost by default. That was my reason for writing *Shades of Grail*.' Drysdale's eyes twinkled as he grinned. 'Aside from the royalties, of course.'

'Where do the Templars come into this?'

'I'll distil it for you as best and briefly as I can. For a fuller version I must refer you to my book, a bargain at six ninety-nine. But here goes. The Holy Grail is a constant in Western literature. What is it? The cup from which Christ drank on the Cross. Some at least accept it as such. Others look for symbolic or hidden meaning. Is it to be found in the Old French word *Sangréal* – the royal blood? Proponents of this school of thought believe Christ had children by Mary Magdalene, the Grail being no more and no less than the Divine bloodline. Mary Magdalene and Christ's hypothetical children fled to Provence after the Crucifixion and their descendants supposedly founded the Merovingian dynasty of French royalty. So far, so diverting. There's no evidence for it,

253

of course, not a shred, although the belief may have under-pinned the hazy theology of the Cathar heretics, who were certainly active in Provence and were brutally put down by Pope Innocent the Third early in the thirteenth century. An authenticated bloodline of Christ would have been an unanswerable challenge to Papal authority, so his ruthless suppression of the Cathars is held to prove the theory.

'What does this have to do with the Templars? Nothing directly. We must turn to another school of thought to learn their role in alternative history. Its proponents equate the Grail with the Ark of the Covenant, the greatest treasure of the Jewish people. They believe the Ark was buried deep beneath King Solomon's Temple in Jerusalem to prevent it falling into Roman hands when the city fell to the legions of Titus in seventy AD – or CE, as I'm now required to call it. They also believe the Ark contains a wondrous secret. And they further believe the Knights Templar were formed after the capture of Jerusalem by the Crusaders in ten ninety-nine specifically to search for the Ark. I apologize for overtones of Indiana Jones, by the way. The knights supposedly spent many years excavating beneath the Temple and eventually found what they were looking for. If not the Ark itself, then what it had all along merely stood as symbol for: the secret of secrets; the truth; the gnosis of man's relationship with God.'

'And what's that?'

'A good question, Paleologus. A divine question, you might say. It's as unknown as it's unknowable. It's as broad as it's wide. These myths thrive because they are all things to all men. When Jerusalem was recaptured by Saladin in eleven eighty-seven, the Templars moved their headquarters to the fortress of Acre, along presumably with any treasure they held. When Acre fell in its turn, in twelve ninety-one, they moved again, to Cyprus. And there they remained until sup-pressed by fiat of Pope Clement the Fifth in thirteen hundred and seven on grounds of heresy, sodomy and blasphemy, though his motives were more likely envy of the order's wealth and influence compounded by subservience to King

Philip the Fourth of France, who happened to be massively in their debt. The last Templar Grand Master was burned at the stake in thirteen fourteen. Fetching names these medieval popes chose for themselves, don't you think? Innocent and Clement. They seem to have been neither.'

'What became of the Templar treasure?'

'If it existed, you mean? Ah, well, that's what so many books have been written about. Where did it go – this secret; this great and awful thing? Many have convinced themselves that the Templars got wind of the moves being prepared against them and sent their most precious possession away for safekeeping. Robert the Bruce having been excommunicated, the Templar properties in Scotland at the time were immune to the Pope's proscription of the order. The theory therefore goes that it was sent here and lies here still, somewhere beneath Rosslyn Chapel.'

'You're not serious.'

'I'm serious when I say that many believe it. Construction of the chapel did not begin until fourteen forty-six, more than a hundred years after the suppression of the Templars. To my mind that constitutes a serious objection to the idea, but the true believers finesse their way round it easily enough, arguing that the chapel was a permanent solution to what had originally been envisaged as a temporary problem. And there we have it, shorn of its many elaborations. I'll spare you Freemasonry, Rosicrucianism, the Priory of Sion and the mystery of Rennes-le-Château. They all have their place. But the long and short of the Templar myth is: did they find something – the Ark, the Grail, what you will – beneath the Temple? That's the question I tried to answer in *Shades of Grail*.'

'And what *is* the answer?'

'No-one knows. No-one *can* know. For certain, that is. There's no evidence. There's most certainly no proof. There's only . . .' Drysdale shrugged. 'Rumour and legend.'

'But what do you think?'

'As a historian, I think rumour and legend darken as much

as they illumine. Gnosis is a concept, not an object. It's not susceptible to excavation. Surely that stands to reason. Such treasure is by definition . . . intangible.'

'So there's nothing hidden under the chapel?'

'The bones of a few dead knights. That's all.' Drysdale gazed into the blackness of the empty fireplace. 'That's all people ever find when they dig for gold.' He looked up at Nick with the ghost of a smile hiding beneath his whiskers. 'The secret is that there is no secret.' Then he chuckled. 'Not my published conclusion, I must confess. *Shades of Grail* paints a more tantalizingly ambiguous picture. Such is the commercial imperative. But with someone of your distinguished ancestry I'll not dissemble. After all, you rather prove the point yourself.'

'I do?'

'Bloodlines lead nowhere. The past is neither curse nor salvation. We are what we are. That is the knowledge we have to learn to live with – and to die with.'

Nick left Roseburn Lodge unsure whether Drysdale had intended to preach a sermon about his siblings' cupidity or not. The myth of the Doom Window and the lure of Tantris's money had yielded precisely the discovery the professor could have claimed to predict. Worse, they had ravelled themselves into circumstances leading to the death of Nick's father and brother. The old man's warnings recurred to Nick's mind as he walked down the lane towards the chapel. If they had heeded them, if they had just listened to him . . . *'Trust nothing except primary sources in this game.'* At the time, Nick had taken this as a narrowly academic precept. Now he was beginning to suspect that his father had meant exactly what he had said. *'Nothing except primary sources.'* It was a fine principle. But where were such sources to be found?

The photograph on the front of the guidebook Nick bought at the entrance showed Rosslyn Chapel to be an oddly disproportionate structure, with oversized buttresses and a west

256

wall extended to either side as if part of some larger building that had never been completed, though he could see little of this for himself because of a huge steel cover positioned over the chapel to facilitate roof repairs.

Inside, it was apparent that the stone carving was as remarkable as Sasha had said. Imps, angels, knights and dragons adorned every beam and pillar. Archways teemed with imagery. Figures and symbols were waiting to be discovered wherever he glanced. The masons had worked the stone miraculously, as if it had been clay for them to squeeze and shape. The guidebook drew his attention to the many Templar associations, notably the tomb of William St Clair, great-grandfather of the founder of the chapel. A proclaimed Knight Templar, he had died heroically in Spain in 1330, while trying to transport the heart of Robert the Bruce to the Holy Land. His tombstone was decorated with the likeness of a rose within a chalice, or grail. The hint was hard not to take.

There were connections with the original Temple as well. According to the guidebook, the most gorgeously decorated pillar in the chapel was supposed to have been carved by a mere apprentice, in the master mason's absence. Enraged upon his return to discover this demonstration of his pupil's superiority, the master mason had slain the apprentice, by striking him on the head with his mallet. The guidebook suggested the apprentice's pillar was modelled on one that had supported the inner porchway of King Solomon's Temple and that the apprentice's murder was a reference to the slaying of Hiram Abif, architect of the Temple, also by a blow to the head.

Nick was thinking of another death now and another blow to the head. He had heard the story of Hiram Abif before, though he could not remember how. It had been a form of sacrifice, he had understood, a ritual murder. But who was master and who was apprentice in the reworkings of the myth? Did secrets always die with their holder?

Nick abandoned the tour and blundered out into the open air. It had actually felt colder inside the chapel, he realized,

257

cold as a tomb and silent as an unquiet grave. Some other visitors looked at him oddly as they passed him to go in. When he put his hand to his brow, it was damp with sweat.

He walked back up the lane to the village and went into the bar of the hotel on the corner of Manse Road. He sat with his beer by the window, isolated from the Sunday lunchers near the fire, drinking slowly, waiting for his thoughts to assemble themselves. Long before they had, his mobile rang.

'Nick?' It was Terry, already sounding anxious. 'This is the first chance I've had to phone you.'

'Is there something wrong, Terry?'

'Of course there's something bloody wrong. How have you got on with Tom?'

'Not very well. Before I could accuse him of anything, he did a moonlight flit.'

'He's run away?'

'That's what it looks like.'

'Oh Christ. Kate'll go spare. I was hoping . . . well, no news might be good news.'

'Not in this case.'

'Bloody hell. Kate's phoned him a few times and got no answer. Now I know why.'

''Fraid so.'

'Where's he gone?'

'Haven't a clue. Any suggestions?'

'I haven't a clue either. He's a closed book to me. For Christ's sake, Nick, can't you . . . do something?'

'What did you have in mind?'

'I don't know. Just . . . something to get us out of this mess.'

'Well . . .' Nick fingered the keys in his pocket. 'I'll see what I can come up with.'

Nick's patience – with Tom, with Terry, with the situation he had been placed in – was fading rapidly. Before leaving Roslin, he returned to the chapel shop. As Drysdale had said, its bookshelves were crammed with Rosslyn-related esoterica. Nick bought a copy of *Shades of Grail* and started back for the hotel, where the taxi he had ordered would soon arrive. He did no more than glance at any of the other titles. But a glance was enough. They held no answers.

In the taxi, bowling north through the Edinburgh suburbs, he settled his strategy. He would give Tom until nightfall. Then, if there was still no-one at home, he would enter the flat using Sasha's keys and see what he could find. That might be nothing, of course. But there was nothing else he could do.

He sat in his hotel room as the afternoon slowly uncoiled, reading Drysdale's book. The professor had already told him the gist of it and the full version added only details to the central theme. But those details were many and colourful, wreathed around one another like the carved serpents in Rosslyn Chapel. As promised, the Freemasons and the Rosicrucians had walk-on parts as possible inheritors of Templar secrets and beliefs, while a French secret society, the Priory of Sion, lurked in the shadows of the Templars' origins. Rosslyn was evidently only one candidate for the repository of their treasure. The old Cathar stronghold of Languedoc was another. Portugal was also in the frame, along, incredibly, with Nova Scotia. Many seemingly unrelated topics – from the Turin Shroud to Pre-Columban voyages of discovery – got in on the act. Drysdale summarized the various writings on the subject with no more than a hint of satire. He was content to let the evidence speak for itself. And where *was* the evidence? '*The secret is that there is no secret.*' Nowhere did the phrase appear, but it echoed in Nick's brain as he read.

Night fell. Nick ate a meal in the hotel diner and set out, stopping at the Café Royal on the way. There was no hurry, he kept telling himself. The longer he delayed, the greater the chance that Tom would return of his own volition.

But he had not returned. That was evident to Nick as he gazed at the black, uncurtained windows on the ground floor of 8 Circus Gardens. It was nearly nine o'clock. Delay was at an end.

The first of the Yale keys he tried opened the front door. Nick hesitated in the hall, listening for sounds on the stairs. There were none, though he thought he could hear music, drifting down from Una Strawn's flat. He opened Tom's door and stepped inside, shutting the door smartly behind him.

The kitchen, bathroom and bedroom were to his right, consumed in darkness. To his left, an amber, rain-dappled wash of lamplight stretched across the drawing-room carpet. He headed through the open doorway to the windows on the far side of the room, where he tugged the curtains closed before moving back to the light switch.

For a second, he was dazzled. Then he saw, in front of him, lying on the coffee-table, a white envelope, torn jaggedly open, and, half-hidden beneath, another copy of the photograph of Tom with Elspeth Hartley at Robusta.

Nick picked the photograph up and stared at it. It was the same, it was exactly the same, as the one that had been slipped under his door at the Thistle. This envelope too was blank. There was no accompanying note. But maybe there had not needed to be. Maybe Tom had got the message loud and clear.

Where should he look for clues to Tom's whereabouts? The drawing room was a sterile space. If there were secrets stashed anywhere, it was not here. The bedroom was a better bet. Nick dropped the photograph, turned and headed back along the passage.

The bedroom was at the rear of the house, overlooking the garden, so Nick felt less need to be cautious. He switched on the light as he stepped through the open doorway.

His heart jolted and he stopped in his tracks. For a shard of a crazy second he thought Tom was simply lying on the bed, watching him. But he was too still, too utterly motionless. And he was not watching anything. His eyes were staring blindly at the ceiling. His mouth was open, vomit crusted round his lips and chin. He was naked, his skin pale as marble. There were several empty pill foils and a toppled glass on the floor, close to the bed. And a drained syringe was crooked in his left arm, the needle still buried in a vein.

Tom had not run away after all.

# CHAPTER EIGHTEEN

Once again Nick found himself observing events – and his part in them – as if they were somehow distant from him. It was not an emotional reaction, he had come to understand, so much as a self-defence mechanism his mind had developed to hold off the demons who had once overwhelmed him. There were physical symptoms of shock as he retreated from the bedroom – palpitations, tremor, sweating – but he knew they would abate. There was horror, there was the numb quest for meaning. But there was also an unexpected confidence. He would come through this. He would survive.

He dialled 999 on the telephone in the drawing room, asked for the police and told them what he had found. They said they would be with him shortly. Then he put the telephone down and listened to the silence that death left in its wake. He could not stay in the flat. He certainly could not start the search for clues he had meant to carry out. That was too much to attempt. By the extremity of his act Tom had somehow forbidden him to continue with the pursuit. Besides, Nick felt strangely certain that there would be no clues to uncover. The only evidence of Tom's involvement with Elspeth Hartley was the photograph lying on the coffee-table. Nick picked it up, slid it into his coat pocket and walked out.

\*　　\*　　\*

Una Strawn seemed at first unable to believe what Nick had to tell her. 'He's too young,' she said in dismay. 'He wouldn't do such a thing.' By the time they heard the police car draw up outside, however, she had realized that incomprehension could not alter reality. 'This will be dreadful for his mother,' she mused. And so it would be, Nick acknowledged to himself; more dreadful than Una could possibly imagine.

'I'd better go down,' he said, starting for the door.

'Nick—'

'Yes?' He stopped and looked back.

'Do you know why he did it?'

Nick hesitated for an instant before answering in a murmur. 'Sort of.'

The front doorbell rang. 'Will you tell them?'

He hesitated once more, but in the end said nothing, merely shaking his head before turning to go.

The police were efficient and perfunctorily sympathetic. They did not challenge Nick's edited version of events. Why should they? An unemployed ex-student with a drugs habit under emotional stress was hardly a rarity in their suicide statistics. They nodded in weary familiarity as Nick explained how Tom's mother had become worried about him following his father's death. They made notes. They called for the pathologist and photographer. They did what had to be done.

Nick agreed to visit the police station next morning and make a formal statement. No more was required of him that night. He went back up to Una's flat and gratefully accepted her offer of whisky. Then he somewhat less gratefully accepted her offer of the use of her telephone. She left him alone to make the call no-one could make for him.

He remembered little afterwards of his conversation with Terry, apart from the relief he felt that he did not have to break the news to Kate directly. He said nothing about the syringe or the photograph and Terry asked no leading questions. There was an unspoken sub-text to their exchanges.

Both knew there was more to be said. Both also knew now was not the time to say it.

An hour or so later, Terry phoned back. (The police and the morticians were still going about their business downstairs, quietly and methodically; Tom's body had not yet been removed.) Kate could not bear to stay at home any longer, Terry explained. They would be setting off as soon as possible. The motorway would be at its emptiest and they should reach Edinburgh by dawn. They had booked a room at the Balmoral and would contact Nick when they arrived.

Another hour passed. The photographer left, then the pathologist. The men in gloves and overalls loaded Tom into an unmarked van and carried him away to the mortuary. One of the policemen who had been first on the scene told Nick they were done. The last car drove off into the night. 8 Circus Gardens lapsed into nocturnal stillness.

Nick had no wish to go back to the pitiless sterility of his hotel room and Una was not about to throw him out. Sleep was not an option for either of them. They drank a little more whisky and spoke of Tom.

'This isn't what one would have predicted for a boy like him, is it, Nick? He used to have a certain glow about him. An aura. I bet you did too, at his age.'

'Maybe.'

'You said you "sort of" knew why he'd done it. I wondered if you were . . . drawing on experience.'

'My experience doesn't stretch to what's been going on in Tom's life.'

'Do you want to tell me what that means?'

'I don't think I can. Too many other people are involved.'

'But it has to do with the girl in the photograph you showed me – Harriet?'

'It has everything to do with her.'

'Sasha was right, then. She was no good for him.'

'That's an understatement.'

'Someone will have to tell Sasha what's happened.'

'I'll see her tomorrow.'

'And what will you do about Harriet?'

Nick stared into his whisky for several silent moments, contemplating the question. With Tom dead, Elspeth Hartley's tracks were covered more effectively than ever. She would not know that, of course. Not yet, at any rate. 'I'll find her,' he mumbled in eventual answer. 'Sooner or later.'

When Nick finally left, he stopped in the communal hall and stared at the strip of blue and white police tape sealing the entrance to Tom's flat. It sealed also the mystery of his relationship with Elspeth Hartley. If Tom had been trying to protect her, he could not have done a better job. 'I will find you,' Nick murmured under his breath. But he was well aware that it was easier to say than to do.

He reached his room at the Thistle and lay down on the bed with little expectation of sleep. But sleep he must have done, because the next thing he knew was the ringing of the telephone. It was 7.38 by his watch and there was a grey hint of daylight seeping round the curtains. He grabbed the receiver.

'Mr Paleologus?'

'Yeah.'

'I have a Mr Mawson on the line for you.'

'Put him through.'

'Nick?'

'Terry. Where are you?'

'At the Balmoral.'

'Can you give me ten minutes?'

'Sure. I'll walk over to the Thistle and meet you in the lobby.'

'*I'll* walk over.' Nick noted the singular. Terry wanted a word, man to man, before Nick met Kate. Sure enough, he was waiting alone when Nick stepped out of the lift.

He looked like the husk of his normal self, a hunched and crumpled figure with bloodshot eyes and a heavy five o'clock shadow. He clapped a weary arm round Nick's shoulders and piloted him away to some chairs and a table on the far side of the lobby.

'This is the worst day of my life, Nick,' he said, his voice as rough as sandpaper. 'Kate's that broke up I . . .' He gave a despairing shrug. 'I don't know what to say or do.'

'I'm sorry, Terry. It's . . . beyond words.'

'Tell me what happened. Tell me what led up to it.'

So Nick told him everything that had occurred since his arrival in Edinburgh – Tom's attempt to cast suspicion on Terry; Farnsworth's sinister comings and goings; the photograph of Tom with Elspeth, aka Harriet; the gruesome scene at 8 Circus Gardens. There was no point holding anything back.

'You've got both photographs?'

'Yes.' Nick laid them on the table.

'Thank God for that.' Terry stared down at them. 'What a bloody awful business. Why did he do it? I mean, it was bad, OK. But it didn't have to be this bad.'

'I only wish it wasn't.'

'Me too.' Terry staunched some tears. 'Sorry. It's just when I think . . .' He shook his head. 'What's Farnsworth up to?'

'I don't know.'

'We've got to find out.'

'That won't be easy.'

'Maybe this mate of his – Drysdale – could point us in the right direction.'

'I doubt it.' Nick leaned across the table. 'Look, Terry, there's a more immediate problem. What do you want me to say to Kate? She doesn't know about any of this, does she?'

'No.'

'Well, don't you think she's going to have to?'

'Yeah, but . . .' Terry sighed heavily. 'I'll tell her. Now's too soon, though. She's still in shock. In a couple of days . . . she'll be better able to cope with it.'

'And until then?'

'Can't you just stonewall her, Nick? Say you met Tom, noticed how depresed he was, got worried, contacted his girlfriend and . . . found him? Can't you just . . . leave out the rest? I'll explain I asked you to when I tell her the whole story. I'll make sure you're in the clear.'

In the clear? Nick doubted he would ever be that. He also doubted Terry was thinking only of Kate in proposing this delay. There was the small matter of putting the best possible gloss on his own role in events to be taken into account. But there was an advantage for Nick as well. He would not have to explain to Kate why and how he had contributed to the pressure Tom had buckled under. Terry would do it for him, at a time of his choosing. 'All right,' he said at last. 'It's your call.'

'Thanks, Nick.' Terry looked mightily relieved. 'This is the best way, believe me.' He glanced at his watch. 'Kate was really stressed out after the journey. I persuaded her to take a couple of sleeping pills. She looked good for a few hours when I left.' He massaged the back of his neck. 'God, I'm tired.'

'Maybe you should try and get some sleep yourself.'

'Why did he do it? I keep coming back to that. *Why*? Whatever he'd done, whatever he'd got himself into, we could have worked it out.'

'That depends, doesn't it?'

'What do you mean?'

'I mean it depends on what it was he'd got himself into. We don't know, Terry. We *still* don't know.'

'No. But Farnsworth does.'

'I think he may, yes.'

'Let's go and have a word with Drysdale. Catch him cold. See what rattles out of his pockets if we give him a shake.'

'I'm not sure that's a good idea.'

But Terry was already on his feet, the decision taken. And Nick was sure it was a very bad idea to let him go alone. He had no choice but to follow.

The Ferrari drew many a glance as it roared and sputtered south through the Edinburgh rush hour. Nick soon abandoned his attempt to talk Terry out of the visit. Terry wanted answers. And he was not a man accustomed to being denied what he wanted.

Professor Vernon Drysdale, on the other hand, was not a man used to being interrogated. He was having breakfast when they arrived and clearly did not welcome the intrusion. There was no sign of Mrs Logan. Perhaps she did not show up until later. There was no sign of Farnsworth either.

'I explained to Paleologus yesterday that Julian's gone away. I don't know where and I don't know for how long.' Drysdale glared at Terry. 'Who did you say you are?'

'He's my nephew's stepfather,' put in Nick. 'There's something you ought to know, Professor.'

'About your nephew?'

'He's dead.'

'What?'

'He killed himself over the weekend. I found him last night.'

'Dear God.' Drysdale looked genuinely affected. 'That's dreadful news.'

'I'll lay it on the line for you, Prof.' Terry grabbed the arms of Drysdale's chair and leaned foward until their faces were no more than a few inches apart. 'Farnsworth's one of those who drove Tom to take his own life. The longer I have to wait to speak to him, the worse temper I'll be in when I do. And you're seeing me now on my best behaviour. So, stuff the academic freemasonry. Where is he?'

'I don't know, Mr . . .'

'Mawson. Terry Mawson.'

'I have no idea.'

'Pull the other one.'

'It happens to be true. After Paleologus here came to see me yesterday, I telephoned Julian on his Oxford number and got only his answering machine. He could be there, I suppose. Equally, he could be anywhere.'

'He's your friend, I hear. Maybe more than a friend. Had a few gay old times over the years, have you?'

268

'This is absurd.' Terry's attempts to intimidate Drysdale seemed to Nick to be making no impression whatsoever. 'I'm no more his keeper than you were your stepson's.'

'What the bloody hell do you mean by that?'

'I sympathize in your loss, Mr Mawson. If Julian is in any way responsible for it, then he should answer for what he's done. I'm not shielding him, I do assure you.'

'You'd better not be.'

'I think the time has come for you to leave, I really do. Paleologus?'

'Come on.' Nick laid a cautious hand on Terry's shoulder. 'We're getting nowhere.'

'All right.' Terry pushed himself upright. 'All right.' He sounded suddenly calmer. Nick wondered if his show of aggression had been just that: a show. If so, it had failed to impress its audience. 'When you hear from your friend, tell him he'll be meeting me whether he wants to or not.'

Drysdale nodded. 'I'll be sure to.'

'I suppose you think that achieved nothing,' said Terry as they started back for Edinburgh.

'I'm just not—'

'You're wrong, Nick. It made me feel better. And it sent a message. I want them to know I'm on their case. I want them to know Tom's death isn't going to go unavenged.'

'It was suicide. Are you sure there's anyone to blame but Tom himself?'

To which Terry's answer was more revealing, it seemed to Nick, than he probably intended. 'There's got to be.'

Nick asked Terry to drop him at the main police station so he could make his statement. Terry came in with him to find out if the post-mortem result was available yet. He was referred to the Procurator Fiscal's office for all information and left Nick to it with a whispered parting in the reception area, the gist of which was a plea for Nick to say as little as possible.

It was a plea easily complied with. The police had clearly

pigeonholed Tom's death as a drugs-related suicide. The post-mortem was a formality. So, in that sense, was Nick's statement. The version of events he signed his name to was the same as the one Terry wanted him to present to Kate. And it was accurate. As far as it went.

When he left the police station, he realized to his surprise that he was very close to Rankeillor Street. He had assured Una he would break the news to Sasha without thinking through the how and the when of it. Now the opportunity had presented itself to him he could hardly pass it up. She might well have left for classes at the University, though. He walked along to number 56 with no great confidence that he would find her in.

But the front door opened as he approached and Sasha smiled out wanly at him in greeting. Her eyes were moist and full, her jaw clenched. She knew.

'I saw you coming from the window. I must have been sitting up there for an hour or more staring out, just thinking about Tom.' She shook her head. 'The stupid bastard.'

'How did you hear?'

'I phoned Una. I was worried about him.'

'Did you sense something?'

'No. It's simpler than that. And worse. If only I *had* sensed something. You'd better come up.'


Sasha's flat was standard-issue student digs, complete with broken-backed furniture, Blu-tacked posters, unwashed crockery and an atmosphere scented with joss sticks and cannabis.

'I got this in the post this morning.' Sasha passed Nick a letter written in a jagged hand. 'It's from Tom.'

'He wrote to you?'

'Yeah. The first letter he's ever sent me. He even went to the bother of finding a box with a Sunday collection. Didn't want me to hear at second-hand, I suppose. But he didn't want me to hear soon enough to make a difference either.'

'It's a suicide note?'

270

'More or less. See for yourself. There's a message for you in it.'

Nick sat down in the nearest armchair and looked at the letter. It was a solid jumble of words, with a lot of crossings out. But the writing was legible enough.

Hi Sash. You won't understand why I'm doing this. You'll think it's a waste. As if. Truth is, there's no other way out. Everything's fucked. I didn't know it would go down like this. I promise you that. Maybe Harriet did. Maybe she planned the whole thing this way. Total wipeout. Could be. I've seen that side of her. But it's too late. For me, anyway. I can't deal with what I've done. It's too much. They'll be coming for me. But there'll be no-one at home. If you see my uncle Nick, tell him to let it go. I've sent him something. He should take it as a warning. There have been too many victims. But there won't be any victors. This is a no-win scenario. I'm getting out the only way I can. I'm sorry for hurting you. But this will be the last time. That's one promise I'll keep. I love you. Sash. If you want to do me a favour, get over me fast. Remember the laughs we had. No-one can take those away. Have fun. You're better at it than me. I've got to go now. This is it. All my love, Tom.

Nick's fingers were trembling when he handed the letter back to Sasha. He tried to speak, but had to clear his throat first. 'I didn't realize he was so unhappy. If I had I'd have . . . gone easier on him.'

'What did Harriet drag him into, Nick?'

'Old family secrets. So secret I don't know what they are.'

'Dangerous secrets?'

'Apparently.'

'Will you let it go?'

'I don't think I can.'

'But you haven't seen what he's sent you yet, have you?'

'No.' Nick stood up. 'I'd better get back to the hotel. It could be waiting for me there. Whatever it is.'

'A warning, he said.'

'Yeah. Somehow, though . . . I doubt I'll heed it.'

'This arrived for you earlier, sir,' said the receptionist at the Thistle half an hour later. She handed Nick a letter along with his key and he recognized Tom's writing at once.

He waited until he was upstairs, in the privacy of his room, before opening the envelope. There was no note inside, just a blown-up photocopy of a newspaper article. Maybe a photocopy of a photocopy, to judge by the degradation.

Nick sat down on the bed and looked at the pageful of print. In the top left corner was the title of the newspaper and a date: *Birmingham Post, Thursday October 5, 2000*. Beneath that was a double-column headline: ESTATE AGENT'S MYSTERIOUS HOLIDAY DROWNING. Nick read on.

An inquest at Sutton Coldfield Magistrates' Court returned a verdict of accidental death yesterday in the case of Birmingham estate agent Jonathan Braybourne, who died while on holiday in Venice earlier this year. The coroner dismissed a suggestion by Mr Braybourne's sister that he may have been murdered as groundless.

Mr Braybourne, 43, a partner in the long-established city-centre firm Oldcorn & Co., drowned in one of the Venetian canals on May 30. The Italian police failed to establish how Mr Braybourne came to fall in. There was no evidence that he was intoxicated or that he had been a victim of crime. Bruising on his left temple suggested he may have struck his head as he fell, perhaps causing him to lose consciousness. The incident occurred at night in a poorly lit district and Mr Braybourne's body was not discovered until the following morning.

Emily Braybourne, the deceased's sister, said in evidence that she believed the Italian police had not investigated all the circumstances of her brother's death. She said he had gone to Venice to visit an acquaintance who lived in the city and that this acquaintance had not been properly questioned. She believed him to be implicated in her brother's murder.

The coroner, in his summing-up, said the British Consul in Venice had written assuring him that the police investigation had been diligently carried out. There were no grounds for suspecting the person named by Miss Braybourne. He suggested that Miss Braybourne was allowing her natural feelings of grief to cloud her judgement and urged her to accept that her brother's death was nothing more than a tragic accident.

As Nick reread the article, its implications piled up in his mind. He reckoned he knew who Emily Braybourne was. Also the 'acquaintance' of her brother's, coyly left unnamed by the *Birmingham Post*. And this, he supposed, was Tom's warning. Go on digging and Nick could end up like Jonathan Braybourne and the man in the cellar, like Andrew and his father, like Tom himself. The list of the dead was growing. The accidents were becoming too numerous. The threat was not imaginary.

If that was true, Nick's position was nothing like as perilous as Basil's. He had alerted Demetrius Paleologus to his presence in Venice. He was suddenly a sitting duck. Panic seized Nick. He jabbed at his mobile, but there was no message from Basil. He rang international directory enquiries and gleaned with difficulty a telephone number for the Hotel Zampogna in Venice. He dialled it.

'*Pronto*?' The voice was female, the tone abrupt.

'Hotel Zampogna?'

'*Si.*'

'I need to speak to one of your—'

'*Pronto*?' came the bellowed interruption.

'Mr Paleologus. Can I—'

'*Chi parla*?'

273

'Listen. It's very important. *Molto importante*. I'm Mr Paleologus's brother. I need to—'

'*Il telefono non è per i clienti.*'

'But—'

But nothing. The line was dead.

What was he to do? He devoted several seconds to cursing Basil's aversion to modern technology, but that took him nowhere. Basil might be sipping an *espresso* in a café in St Mark's Square. Or he might be at the bottom of a canal. There was no way to tell.

Nick tried to calm himself with long, slow breaths, like the therapist had taught him. It helped, but not much. Basil might call him later and ask what all the fuss was about. Or he might not. If Nick simply waited, he might be doing the best thing. Or he might be frittering away the short time he had to save his brother.

He dialled another number. It was a call he was due to make anyway, though he no longer felt confident of managing it as sensitively as he had planned.

'Old Ferry Inn.'

'Irene, this is Nick.'

'Hi. Good to hear from you. How's it going in Edinburgh? You *are* in Edinburgh, aren't you?'

'Listen to me, Irene. I'm sorry to have to tell you this. Tom's dead.'

'*What?*'

'It looks like he killed himself. A drugs overdose. Kate and Terry are up here. I'm sorry I didn't tell you sooner, but—'

'When was this?'

'Over the weekend. But never mind that.'

'*Never mind?*'

'Have you heard from Basil?'

'Basil? No. What are you—'

'Is Anna at work this morning?'

'I think so, yes. Look, stop talking about Basil and Anna, Nick, will you? Tom *killed himself?*'

'You can contact Kate and Terry at the Balmoral Hotel.

274

Find out from Anna if she's heard from Basil. Will you do that for me? It's very important. I'll call you later. I have to go now.'

'Hold on, I—'

'Sorry, Irene. I *will* call later. 'Bye.'

He put the phone down and started to pack hurriedly. Suddenly, what he had to do was clear to him. Weighing risks and waiting on events was a hopeless course to follow. The only way to be sure Basil had not walked into a trap was to follow him to where the trap might be set.

He wrestled the GNER pocket timetable out of his coat and checked for the next southbound service. A glance at his watch told him he would never make the noon train, but he did not propose to miss the one o'clock. Yet he still had to explain his abrupt departure to Kate and Terry and he owed Kate an account of her son's death. What was he supposed to do? He could not cover every debt. He would have to go via Milton Keynes to pick up his passport. He phoned British Airways and they told him there were three flights daily to Venice from Gatwick, the last of them at 19.20. The scantiest of calculations told him there was no chance of his being on it. He tried to book a seat on the first flight the following morning, but it was full. Frustrated, he settled for the 13.15, due in at 16.25. Move as fast as he liked, it was still going to take him thirty hours or so to reach Venice. And a lot could happen in thirty hours. He only had to think about the last thirty to appreciate that.

The telephone rang. He picked it up, hoping it was not Irene and praying it might be Basil. It was neither.

'Ah, Paleologus. Vernon Drysdale here.'

'Professor Drysdale, I—'

'I wanted to say how very sorry I was to hear about your nephew. I may not have been able to convey my sentiments adequately thanks to Mr Mawson's belligerent manner, which I'm happy to attribute to the shock of his bereavement, but this is a historical as well as a personal tragedy. I can only imagine how you're feeling.'

275

Nick strongly doubted if Drysdale had the remotest clue how he was feeling. 'I can't talk right now, Professor. I'm going to have to ring off.'

'Don't do that. You see, I've reappraised matters in the light of this latest loss to your family and I'm forced to conclude that there may be some contemporary significance in events which I chose to make nothing of in my most widely read publication on the subject for fear that they'd be wrenched from their proper context by less scrupulous scholars than me and given an unwarranted and frankly unwelcome prominence. Where I did explore them in a more soberly academic treatment, there was no explicit cross-reference, you must understand, so unless—'

'I'm sorry, Professor, but I just don't have the time for this. I have to go, all right? Goodbye.'

'But—'

Nick put the telephone down, stuffed the last of his belongings into his bag and made for the door.

'You're leaving?'

Kate stared at Nick across the sitting room of her and Terry's suite at the Balmoral. She looked to have aged several years since Nick had last seen her. Her face was drawn, the skin stretched around her jaw and cheekbones, her eyes bloodshot and swollen-lidded. Wrapped in an oversized Balmoral bathrobe, she seemed to have become slighter and frailer overnight. Tom's death had killed part of her too.

'When are you leaving?'

'Now. Right away.'

'Can't you wait until Terry gets back? He won't be long.'

'No. I'm sorry. I have to go.'

'Why?'

'I can't explain. It's too complicated.'

'But there's so much I wanted to ask you . . . about Tom.'

'I told Terry everything.'

'I wanted you to tell *me*. The way it was. Anything that could—'

276

'I'm sorry, Kate. I can't do this now. Believe me. I've got no choice.'

'How can I believe you if I don't understand?'

Nick gazed helplessly at her for a second or two, then said all he could. 'I don't know.' And then he turned away.

Thanks to its departing ten minutes late, the one o'clock train left with Nick on board. Before it had cleared the outskirts of Edinburgh, Terry rang him on his mobile.

'What the bloody hell's going on, Nick?'

'I can't get into it, Terry. I'm doing what I have to do to make sure this doesn't get any worse than it already is.'

'What could be worse than Tom killing himself?'

'Go see Sasha Lovell, his ex-girlfriend. Fifty-six Rankeillor Street. He sent her a note. That tells you about as much as I know. Before you do, though, you'd better tell Kate the truth.'

'I can't do that. Not yet.'

'We're out of time. You and me both. Face her with it. That's my advice.'

'Some advice.'

'It's all I can offer. Goodbye, Terry.'

Nick was sorely tempted to turn his mobile off, but he had to keep it on in case Basil called. Basil did not call. Nor, following their terse exchange, did Terry. When a call next came, as the train glided out of York station, it was from Irene.

'I've spoken to Kate, Nick. She's devastated. And your behaviour isn't helping. Where are you going?'

'Has Anna heard from Basil?'

'No. But Basil can look after himself.'

'Do you know where he is?'

'Greece. Or on his way there. Why?'

'He's in Venice.'

'You're mistaken. He told Anna—'

'He was covering his tracks, Irene. He's gone to Venice to confront cousin Demetrius.'

'He can't have done.'

'But he has. And something I learned from Tom makes me think he could well be in danger.'

'You're going after him, aren't you?'

'Yes.'

'Well, you mustn't. It's as simple as that. For goodness' sake, Nick, this is no time for misguided heroics. If Basil's in some kind of trouble we don't want you getting mixed up in it as well.'

'You don't understand, Irene. I'm already mixed up in it. As a matter of fact, we all are.'

The train reached King's Cross just before six o'clock. Night had fallen in London. A chill, damp rush hour was under way. Nick hurried west towards Euston station, the route he had been following when he and Tom had met by chance the previous October. Nick thought of how carefree Tom had seemed then, of how stressless his life had apparently been. In the space of four months, everything in it had been turned upside down. And then it had ended. Tom was part of the past now. He was over. He was gone. But the things he had done and the reasons he had done them were not over. They had not gone. They had still to be faced.

Milton Keynes's rush hour had passed by the time Nick walked out of the station and got into a taxi. The journey along thinly trafficked dual carriageways felt nothing like the homecoming it technically was. The town somehow defied familiarity. Nick had lived there for eight years without losing a sense of transience. Nothing he had done there had greater durability than a footprint on a beach.

Home was a bigger house than he needed in a prim cul-de-sac in the Walnut Tree district. It did not look neglected to Nick as he walked up the drive after paying off the taxi driver. It wore his absence as lightly as it always had his presence. There was not even a great deal of post to obstruct the opening of the front door. The silent, empty house seemed not to have missed him.

He dumped his bag and the accumulated mail in the kitchen, then went round closing curtains and switching on lights. In a bedroom drawer he found the one thing he had come for: his passport. He put it in his pocket and went back down to the kitchen. There was no sense unpacking. But there was time to put some clothes through the wash. They would dry by morning. He set the machine going, then made some tea and drank it in the dining room that doubled as an office, listening to his answerphone messages, most of which he erased.

Next he sorted through the post, with similar results. His bills were paid by direct debit. His life operated by a set of interconnected administrative arrangements. Personal intervention was not required. Everything was orderly and predictable. At all events, it was here.

He had opened the freezer in search of a microwaveable supper, when the doorbell rang. He stood quite still, frowning in puzzlement at his own reflection in the glazed front of the oven next to the fridge. A neighbour, perhaps, concerned by the sudden blaze of lights? It was hard to think who else it could be, uncharacteristic of the residents of Damson Close though this was.

He looked out into the hall and saw the blurred shape of his unexpected visitor through the frosted-glass panel in the door. He had failed to switch on the porch light, so the shape was altogether too dark and indistinct for him to recognize, even supposing he knew the person. It occurred to him that it might be a canvasser or a charity collector or, worse still, a Jehovah's Witness. He drew back in the hope that they would go away.

But they did not go away. The fuzzy shape of an arm was raised. The doorbell rang, lengthily, insistently. Perhaps it was a neighbour after all. Perhaps they had something important to tell him, something they thought important at any rate. A lost tile, a wrongly delivered parcel. It could be anything. But it would have to be dealt with. Nick marched to the door and opened it.

The light from the hall flooded out onto Elspeth Hartley's face. 'Hello, Nick,' she said.

# CHAPTER NINETEEN

'Will you come for a drive with me?'

Elspeth Hartley was not as Nick remembered. Her hair was shorter and straighter. She no longer wore glasses. She was dressed in a different style as well – black leather jacket and trousers and a black roll-neck sweater; her true style, perhaps. She looked thinner in the face and had her hands buried tensely in her pockets. But, tense or not, she seemed able to brush aside a host of tragedies and deceptions with a breathtakingly insouciant invitation, to which Nick was barely able to frame a response.

'Well, will you? We can't talk indoors.'

'Have you . . . any idea . . . of the damage you've done to my family?'

'Yes.'

'Yet you come here like this and . . . calmly ask me to go for a drive?'

'Who said I was calm?'

'I just . . . don't believe it.'

'I know about Tom. I had a letter too.' She pulled a crumpled envelope from her pocket. 'He told me what he was going to do. I didn't really need the police to confirm it. He always did what he said he would. He also said he was going to tell you about Jonty.'

'Was Jonathan Braybourne your brother?'

'Yes.'

'Which makes you Emily Braybourne.'

'Yes.'

'How did you know I'd be here?'

'Tom wanted to warn you off. But after everything that's happened, I reckoned you couldn't be warned off. You've come back for your passport, haven't you?'

'You're very clever.'

'Not really. Just a good reader of people. I've been waiting for you since this afternoon. I don't think anyone followed you and I'm pretty sure no-one beat me to it. But I'll feel safer in the car. Are you coming?'

'Why should I?'

'Because you want to know the truth. And with Tom gone, I have to tell it to someone. You're the only one I can trust.'

'You trust *me*?'

'Yes. And when you've heard what I've got to say . . . we'll trust each other.'


'Where are we going?' Nick asked, after they had climbed into the Peugeot and started away. He was still gripped by disbelief at the turn of events. He had looked for her, but he had not found her. *She* had found *him*.

'We're not going anywhere. I'll just drive round the ring road.'

'While you tell me why you set out to destroy my family. Is that right?'

'No. It's not right. I didn't set out to destroy anyone.'

'You could have fooled me.'

'This is the deal, Nick. I talk. You listen. Are you comfortable with that? Because if not . . .'

'You promised me the truth.'

'And I'll deliver it. On my terms. OK?'

'OK.'

'Good.' She concentrated for a moment on joining the dual

carriageway that ran round the perimeter of the town, then resumed. 'How much do you know about my father?'

'Very little. According to Julian Farnsworth, my father and your father met during the War, when they were both stationed in Cyprus. But Dad never mentioned a Digby Braybourne to me. All three of them were archaeologists at Oxford. Your father got involved in an auction-house fraud and wound up in prison. That was in nineteen fifty-seven. And that's it.'

'Right. Then this is the rest. My mother worked in the kitchens at Brasenose College. She was a real looker in her youth. My father took a fancy to her and led her on with a promise of marriage. A lie, of course. It would have been unthinkable for a fellow to marry a servant. She got pregnant. Jonty was born just around the time Dad went to prison. When he came out, everything had changed. Now he was more than willing to marry Mum. He had no-one else to turn to. So, they got hitched. I was born in nineteen sixty-six. We lived out at Cowley. A long way from the university, metaphorically as well as literally. Mum pulled some strings to get Dad a clerical job with Morris Motors. But he couldn't stick office work. He started drinking and gambling. When he was drunk, or out of luck with the horses, he used to knock Mum about. He got the sack. Then he left us. And then he came back. And then he left us again. I didn't see much of him when I was growing up, but it was more than I wanted to see of him. It was different for Jonty. Dad could do no wrong in his eyes. He adored him. To do Dad justice, I think the feeling was mutual. He very much wanted to be a father Jonty could be proud of. But he didn't have it in him. In the end, Mum divorced him. By then, Jonty was at Cambridge and he told me later that Dad often went up from London, where he was living, to see him. Mum forbade him to go to the graduation ceremony. But he heard about it later, of course.'

'You mean he heard about me?'

'Yeah. The Paleologus prodigy. According to Jonty, your fall from grace gave Dad an idea. He was over sixty and none

283

too well. He wanted to do something for Jonty – and for me – before it was too late. He wanted to provide for us. For Mum too. To prove he wasn't a washout. His idea involved your father. In fact, it couldn't work *without* your father.'

'What was the idea?'

'I don't know. I still don't. I think Jonty knew, though. I think Dad confided in him. But I also think Jonty wrote it off as an old man's fantasy. Anyway, nothing came of it. Whether your father turned him down or he bottled out of approaching him we never found out, because, pretty soon, we stopped hearing from him. We had no address for him. He used to move from one squalid bedsit to another. At some point in the autumn of nineteen eighty, he dropped out of our lives altogether. Mum reckoned he was dead. That's the way I saw it as well. An unidentified body, pulled out of the Thames, or found in a doorway. Something like that. Little by little, we forgot about him. Jonty established himself as an estate agent, got married and had children. That's right. He left a family of his own behind when he drowned in Venice. I went to Cambridge as well, stayed on for my doctorate and started an academic career.'

'You really are an art historian, then?'

'Yeah. On sabbatical from the University of Wisconsin.'

'Do they know what you're doing with your sabbatical?'

'We had a deal, Nick. All you have to do is listen. Mum died in July 'ninety-nine. When we went through her affairs afterwards, we found she had a lot more money in the bank than we'd expected. There'd been regular quarterly payments into her account from a bank in Cyprus. It explained how Mum had been able to live a little better as the years had passed. It was like an extra pension. But who was paying it? The bank wouldn't say. But Jonty was determined to find out. He took Audrey and the kids to Cyprus for a holiday that autumn. While he was there, he hired a local private detective to do some digging. This guy established that the account Mum had been paid from was in the name of Demetrius Paleologus. Know him?'

'In a sense. I've never met him. He's some sort of cousin. Dad knew him. But he doesn't live in Cyprus.'

'No. Cyprus was his wartime bolthole. He still owns several Cypriot hotels, but he lives in Venice. When our fathers were serving together in Cyprus, though, Demetrius Paleologus was there too. That's when they all met. It has to be. And out of that, Jonty reckoned, came the money-making scheme Dad hatched years later. Jonty never believed Dad had willingly lost touch with us. He believed he'd been stopped.'

'What do you mean by "stopped"?'

'Jonty meant murdered. And since we both know what you and your brother found under the cellar floor at Trennor, murder is what I mean too. It was a body, wasn't it, Nick? Don't deny it. In fact, don't say a word. Just listen. Jonty looked up some old acquaintances of Dad's at Oxford, Julian Farnsworth among them. He also went to see your father, who basically told him to get lost. For Jonty, it all added up. The payments to Mum were conscience money. And Dad's murder was what troubled those consciences. Your father and his cousin Demetrius were in the frame. Jonty may have turned up some real evidence against them for all I know. I last saw him during the Easter holiday last year and by then he was a man obsessed. Audrey was worried about him. With good reason, as it turned out. He went to Venice a few weeks later, alone. He never came back.

'I knew the moment I heard he was dead I'd have to take up where he'd left off. First Dad, then Jonty. I couldn't let it lie. I tried. But I was never going to be able to. That outburst at the inquest was stupid, really. No-one cared. No-one was listening. But it was my vow, if you like. I was going to make people listen. Wisconsin had let me bring my sabbatical forward on compassionate grounds, so I had the time. It was a research project to beat any other. Jonty had accumulated a whole stack of books in the months before his death. I sifted through them. Medieval history for the most part – Venice, Byzantium, the Crusades. Plus a lot of esoteric stuff about Templarism and Freemasonry. I couldn't make out what it amounted to. But the name Paleologus cropped up a lot, as it would. Jonty also had a heap of literature about the archaeology and mythology of Tintagel and just about everything printed on the subject of the St Neot glass, which put me onto the Doom Window mystery, which connected in turn with Trennor, where who should live but Michael Paleologus, Dad's old Army pal.'

'Did it really connect? I know you lied to me about the Bawden letter.'

'It was a small misrepresentation. The "great and particular treasure of the parish" had to be the Doom Window. I'm fairly sure Mandrell, the man named by Bawden as custodian of the treasure, lived at Trennor.'

'Fairly sure isn't certain.'

'All right. I'll tell you what I *am* certain of. I needed to get inside your family. I needed an ally. I chose Tom because he was the next generation on and therefore less likely to be a party to whatever had happened. I sized him up carefully. I think he was flattered by my attentions, to be honest, then genuinely attracted to me, then, well, infatuated. It was one-sided, I admit. I did whatever I needed to do to make him willing to help me and keep him that way. Even so, that was only part of the reason why he went along with it. Your family's a mess, Nick. You must know that. It wasn't so very difficult to turn you in on yourselves. Tom had seriously fraught relationships with his father and grandfather. He felt disapproved of. He felt scorned. And that doesn't encourage loyalty.

'Besides, he remembered something from his childhood. His grandparents had been looking after him at Trennor while his parents had a weekend away. This would have been when he was nine or ten. Nineteen eighty-six or eighty-seven. Around that time. He'd been woken up one night by the sound of them arguing. He'd gone downstairs and listened to them shouting at each other, apparently, *down in the cellar*. He recalled feeling frightened by the intensity of the dispute between two people he'd thought of until then as soft old

Granny and Grandpa. He crept back to bed and never breathed a word about hearing them. But he never forgot. And one phrase of his grandmother's stuck in his mind. "I want that thing removed." Repeated several times. "I want that thing removed."

'It seemed to me – and to him – that the time had come to find out what she'd been referring to. I knew what Jonty would have thought. I was beginning to think it myself. My father's body was what she wanted removed. So, we devised a test. If Michael Palcologus really had murdered my father and buried him under the floor at Trennor, he wouldn't agree to sell the house at any price. He'd have to cling on to it, even if his children were pleading with him to sell, even if he could present no decent argument *not* to sell. And we wanted him to know, of course. We wanted him to realize what it was all about.

'I borrowed the name Elspeth Hartley from an art historian at Bristol I'd worked with occasionally who I knew to be on sabbatical herself. Harriet Elsmore was a straightforward alias. Tantris was more complicated. Tom devised it as a tease *and* an additional test. He also came up with the capital we needed to give the Tantris deal wings. By then he was enjoying himself, which worried me. He was beginning to take pleasure in tormenting his grandfather – and, by extension, the rest of you. That wasn't what it was supposed to be about. Not for me. I just wanted the truth. I still do.'

'You and me both.'

'Yeah. OK. Point taken. It gets rough from here on in. I want you to know that I wouldn't have allowed it to continue if I'd foreseen the consequences of our little plot. I even tried to call a halt after your father's death. But Tom wouldn't let me. He was determined to go on to the end. "We can't stop now," he said. "We can't stop until it's all out in the open." I suspect he was at Trennor the night your father died, though he denied it. You all thought he was in Edinburgh, of course. But he was much closer. He left that condolences card on your brother Andrew's Land Rover. He followed the pair of you to Minions, guessed what you were up to and was ready and waiting when you dumped the body there the following night. He got on the train from Edinburgh at Plymouth the next day and got off at Bodmin Parkway, where Andrew was waiting to pick him up, believing he'd been on it all the way. He led you on with that story of being sent a copy of *The Romance of Tristan* by his grandfather. During the funeral party, he planted the video in your car. Then he sat back to see which way you'd jump.

'And that's when he started to lose control. Andrew's death was an accident, but Tom was substantially responsible for it. Only then did he realize, I think, that it wasn't a game. Or, if it was, that it was a game with rules he didn't understand. There were other players, too, more powerful than either of us. They made sure there was nothing for the police to find in the shaft. And then they came after us. Farnsworth's one of them. But there are others. There must be. Who removed the body from the shaft? Who photographed Tom and me at Robusta? Who – and why? That's what I've been trying to figure out. I urged Tom to leave Edinburgh. He was too much of a target there. But he wouldn't. It was as if he wanted to be punished for what he'd done. He changed so much after Andrew's death. So much and so fast. In the end, I suppose he saw suicide as the only choice left to him.'

'And where were you, while his choices were being whittled away?'

'I was hiding. And thinking.'

'I've done a lot of thinking myself.'

'Is that why you're going to Venice?'

'I'm going to Venice because that's where Basil's gone and I fear for his safety.'

'Can't you just tell him to come home?'

'He's out of touch.'

'You mean he's missing?'

'Maybe.'

'Then I suppose you must go. You should be careful, though. Very careful.'

288

'Do you think I might end up at the bottom of a canal?'

'Yes. I'm afraid I do.'

'You'd better hope not. If I can't settle this, they'll still be on your trail, whoever they are.'

'I'd hope not in any case. I believe your father was complicit in my father's murder and by association in my brother's murder. But I don't hold you responsible. You should have gone to the police when you found the body, but you've had to face the consequences of that mistake. I'd like my father to be given a proper burial, but that's not going to happen. I dearly wish I'd done something to save Tom from himself, but it's too late. There's nothing I can do now. Except save myself – and hopefully a few others.'

'How do you propose to do that?'

'I'm going back to Milwaukee. I hope they'll leave me alone there. I hope they'll understand I'm giving up and let it go at that. I have to think of others as well as myself. I can't risk them targeting Jonty's children. I've told you the truth, Nick. I hope it helps. It's the only help I can offer.'

'It's not enough.'

'I never said it would be.'

'What can you tell me about Demetrius Paleologus?'

'Nothing. I read the report on him from the private detective Jonty hired in Cyprus, but there was nothing in it beyond what you already know. An elderly absentee hotelier, resident in Venice. In possession of a valuable secret, I assume. But what that secret is . . .' She sighed. 'There is one connection, tenuous in the extreme and impossible to interpret. It ties the Paleologuses in with St Neot and Tintagel. It links their histories. But it may be pure happenstance. You shouldn't—'

'What is it?'

'OK. I'll tell you. One of the books in Jonty's collection was a biography of Richard, Earl of Cornwall, the man responsible for the construction of Tintagel Castle. *The Left Hand of the King*, it's called. Years out of print. God knows where Jonty got hold of a copy. You may have heard of the author. Vernon Drysdale.'

'A friend of Farnsworth's. I met him in Edinburgh.'

'Mention his book, did he?'

'Not that one.'

'Jonty had another by him. *Shades of Grail*. Bit of a pot-boiler. Not worth wasting your time on.'

'Too late.' Nick remembered the telephone call he had taken from Drysdale just before leaving Edinburgh. The professor had been trying to draw his attention to something else he had written. But Nick had not been listening. He was now. 'Fill me in on the other one.'

'All right. The title – *The Left Hand of the King* – refers to Richard's close lifelong relationship with his elder brother, King Henry the Third. They were born just fifteen months apart and died within a few months of each other as well. Most historians dwell on their supposed rivalry, but Drysdale sees it differently. He thinks they were the loyalest of allies, who often found it convenient to pretend not to be. Their father, King John, died in twelve sixteen, when they were children. His widow married into the Lusignan family, rulers of Jerusalem before its reconquest by the Saracens. So, through his mother, Richard had Crusader associations from his earliest days. He was created Earl of Cornwall when he was sixteen and bought the manor of Bossiney some years later specifically in order to build a castle at Tintagel.

'It was a crazy project in its way, hugely complicated in engineering terms and therefore vastly expensive, with no conceivable strategic value. The castle was also deliberately old-fashioned. It had no military function. It was a wealthy young man's whim, we're told, a stage-set for some Arthurian play-acting. Drysdale has his doubts. He thinks King Henry put his brother up to it, or at least wholeheartedly approved. Why, Drysdale doesn't know, but he suspects a hidden agenda. By twelve forty, the castle was complete.

'In June of that year, Richard embarked for the Holy Land, exact intentions unclear. He arrived in October and stayed till May of twelve forty-one, during which period he seemed in some strange way to be accepted as overlord of the Crusader states, representing them in discussions with a delegate from the Byzantine Emperor John Vatatzes. That delegate was Andronicus Paleologus. He was accompanied by his son Michael – the future Emperor Michael the Eighth, founder of the Paleologan Imperial line. And one of the knights in Richard's retinue was Ralph Valletort, who owned the manor of Lewarne, in the parish of St Neot. Drysdale makes nothing of that, of course. He merely mentions the name in passing. But Valletort's important. His coat of arms appears in one of the St Neot windows, yet his family died out in the fourteenth century, more than a hundred years before the glazing scheme got under way.'

'What's all that supposed to prove?'

'It doesn't prove anything. But it means *something*. I'm sure of it. And there's one more thing you should know about Richard of Cornwall: his choice of wife. When he was twenty-one, he married a daughter of William the Marshal, Earl of Pembroke. Pembroke served as Regent during Henry the Third's minority. He was the strong man of the kingdom. He was also a Knight Templar. You can see his tomb in the Temple Church in London. Like I said, it could all be happenstance. But I don't think so. I doubt you truly think so either. The Crusades, the Templars, Tintagel, St Neot, Trennor and your family. They're connected. And my father and my brother died because of that connection.'

'So did mine, in case you'd forgotten.'

'I hadn't. But what do we gain by swapping reproaches, Nick? What's done is done. We can't repair the past. Only the future matters. Our futures. And those of our loved ones. That's why I'm giving up. It's why you should give up too.'

'Maybe I will. Once I know Basil's safe.'

'When did you last hear from him?'

'Yesterday morning.'

'And when did you last *expect* to hear from him?'

'Long before now.'

Elspeth Hartley – or Emily Braybourne, as Nick was trying to force himself to think of her – fell silent at that. The car bore them on through the amber-leeched night for several wordless minutes.

Then Nick said, 'What are you thinking?'

'I'm thinking you'll go after him whatever I say.'

'But you reckon it's too late, don't you?'

'I reckon it's not too late for you, Nick. I reckon you still have a chance.'

'I'm going anyway.'

'I know.'

'So, perhaps you should take me home.'

Nothing more was said as they completed their circuit of the ring road and headed back to Damson Close. Nick was physically tired and mentally overwhelmed. Every time he tried to piece it together – the stained glass of centuries past, the excavation at Tintagel seventy years ago, the secret supposedly shared by three men ten years later in Cyprus – it fell apart in his mind. He did not even have the comfort now of blaming it all on the elusive Elspeth Hartley. She was elusive – and Elspeth – no longer. She was Emily Braybourne, with her own claim to victimhood.

There had been little traffic on the ring road and there was none at all in the residential byways of Walnut Tree. Just as they approached Damson Close, however, a dark-coloured Transit van, driving without lights, surged out from the cul-de-sac and swept past them. Emily braked violently and blasted her horn, but the van sped on and away, its lights finally flicking on as it rounded the next bend and vanished from sight.

'Christ,' said Emily. 'What a way to . . .' Then she looked at Nick. 'I don't suppose they *do* drive like that round here, do they?'

'No.'

'I was going to drop you here. But perhaps I'd better take you to your door after all.'

She turned into Damson Close and drove slowly along to

his house. Nothing looked amiss. The lights that were on were the ones he had left on. She stopped and he got out. 'Wait here,' he called, starting up the drive. He saw her nod to him through the windscreen, her face sallow in the lamplight.

As he reached the front door, he noticed it was ajar. The lock had been damaged in some way. The snib no longer engaged. He stepped inside and, glancing through to the kitchen, saw the contents of his bag strewn across the floor. He instinctively patted his pocket, reminding himself that he had his passport on him. His chequebook had been left lying amongst his scattered clothing – a strange oversight for a burglar. But his visitor had not been a burglar, of course.

Nick looked into the dining room. The drawers of the desk and cabinet had been pulled open. And his computer disks were missing.

He hurried back out and down the drive. Emily was talking on her mobile, he was surprised to see. She rang off as he approached and lowered her window. 'What gives?'

'Somebody's broken in and had a look around.'

'Funny, isn't it? All this time you've been away, nothing happens. Now, straight after your return, you get turned over.'

'What do you make of that?'

'I imagine they were only interested in what you might have brought with you.'

'Then they'll have been disappointed.'

'You shouldn't stay here after this.'

'It's only until morning. I've nowhere else to go, anyway.'

'I could take you somewhere.'

'I thought you were getting out while the going was good.'

'I still am.'

'Who were you just speaking to?'

'Don't you trust me, Nick?'

'More than I did.'

'But not completely. I get the message. Since you ask, I was on the phone to a hotel at Heathrow I'm booked into.

There's safety in anonymity. I was checking they had plenty of vacancies.'

'And they do?'

'One more would be no problem.'

Nick considered his options. The break-in was something he could not ignore. They were onto him, whoever *they* were. And he was easy to find in his suburban isolation.

'Take it or leave it, Nick. I'd like to get moving.'

He hesitated for no more than a few seconds. 'I'll take it.'

Emily Braybourne was right about the hotel. It was one of a clutch of bland low-rise establishments lining the A4 on the northern side of Heathrow Airport. As a temporary refuge, it could hardly be bettered.

Emily went straight to her room, leaving Nick to down several slow Scotches in the bar. They comprehensively failed to relax him. While the pianist played and the cocktail waiter did his stuff, questions swirled frenziedly in his mind, but answers came there none. He knew he was too tired to think straight, but he could not stop. 'The secret is that there is no secret,' Drysdale had said. At times, Nick had almost believed that. But not any more. There *was* a secret. There was a pattern to events. And it was a pattern of the truth. But as to what that truth was, or might be, or could be . . . Maybe what Drysdale should have said was, 'The secret is that the secret can never be known.'

Just as Nick was nearing the last sip of what he had promised himself would be his last Scotch, a shadow deeper than the several other shadows in his subfuscous corner of the bar fell across him. He looked up, to be met by Emily Braybourne's nervous self-mocking smile.

'I wondered if I'd find you here.'

'Must be those people-reading skills of yours.'

'I couldn't sleep.'

'I haven't tried.'

'Mind if I join you?'

'Feel free.'

She sat down. The waiter glided promptly alongside. Emily ordered the same malt as Nick was drinking. And Nick ordered the same again.

'What time's your flight in the morning?'

'Eleven fifteen.'

'How long will it take?'

'About twelve hours including the stopover in Chicago.'

'So, this time tomorrow . . .'

'I'll be out of harm's way. In theory.'

'And in practice?'

'Probably that too. But . . .'

'But what?'

'But everything.'

The waiter hove to with their drinks. Neither spoke while the fellow arranged the glasses on coasters to his satisfaction and replenished the assorted nuts. The silence seemed tangible to Nick. Emily held his gaze, her face a mask. The waiter withdrew.

'How does it stack up? The damage your family has inflicted on mine – and vice versa?'

'It stacks up as too much. Far too much.'

'Time it ended, then.'

'I agree.'

'But how does it end? Tell me that.'

'I don't know.'

'Tom said . . .' She looked away and took a deep breath. Then she looked back again. The fragile smile fleetingly returned. 'Sorry.'

'What for?'

'You're not too good with emotions, are you, Nick? They disturb you. You must be one of the most self-controlled people I've ever met, yet at one point in your past you lost it totally. Is this . . . repression . . . your way of ensuring that never happens again?'

'What did Tom say?'

'He said . . .' She took another deep breath. 'He said the best way to learn the truth was to start telling it.'

'I've told you the truth, Emily.'

'Not the whole truth. I should know. I haven't told it either.'

'Haven't you?'

'We're both frightened and lonely. But we don't have to be quite as frightened and lonely as we are. And I don't want to be. Not tonight, anyway.' Her gaze was direct, as challenging as it was somehow yielding. 'How about you?'

# CHAPTER TWENTY

There was no farewell. That was the deal they had struck. Nick walked past her room when he left. The chambermaid was at work inside, grateful no doubt for the occupant's early departure. Nick knew Emily had gone before he got there, of course, because she had said she would be. He glanced at his watch and calculated that, while he was standing there, she was probably in the process of checking-in at Terminal 4. The parting of their ways was about to become irrevocable. He started walking towards the lift.

Aboard the courtesy bus to Victoria, the realization struck him that he was already beginning to doubt his memories of the night. What they had done seemed even less credible after the event than before. It should not have been possible. It should not have felt so right. He was half in love with her before he ought to have finished hating her. 'Tomorrow we'll wonder if this ever really happened,' she had said. Only now did he believe her. 'There's no afterwards for us. You understand that, don't you?' Only now was he beginning to. 'I'll call you when it's over,' he had said. But she had shaken her head. 'You won't.' And only now did the contradiction he had uttered ring as hollow to him as it must have done to her.

\*     \*     \*

It did not have to be like that, of course. Prophecy was not certainty, he told himself as the Gatwick Express sped south through Surrey. He could make his future better than his past. Maybe hers too. Some things were less likely than others. But all things were possible. Even happiness. For both of them.

Besides, as he reminded himself when the train reached Gatwick, looking further ahead than the next couple of days was futile. He had no idea what was waiting for him in Venice. And less than none of what might be waiting for him when – and if – he came back.

As if to prove the point, bad news of a totally unexpected kind greeted him at the North Terminal check-in. Marco Polo Airport was fogbound. All flights to Venice had been cancelled.

Nick was suddenly one of many travellers trying to reroute and rearrange. The obvious alternative – fly to Verona and take the train on to Venice – was already oversubscribed. The only choice open to him was an evening flight to Milan, with no clue on anyone's part about when he might reach Venice. He took it.

Several times during the long afternoon, he debated whether he should phone Irene. Or Kate and Terry. Or all of them. Once he even got as far as dialling the Old Ferry's number. But then he cancelled it. He paced up and down the departure lounge. He watched landings and take-offs. He steeled his nerves. He waited.

The 18.45 flight to Milan left on schedule. Twelve hours later, after a short and restless night in the closest hotel to Milano Centrale station, Nick boarded the first train of the day to Venice. By now he was beginning to doubt he would ever get where he was going.

But every journey has an end. For Nick it came when the train crossed the Venetian lagoon just before nine o'clock that morning. He was asleep at the time.

\*    \*    \*

Nick had told Farnsworth he had never been to Venice. That was not actually true. He had spent two days there on his way back from a visit to Greece in the summer of 1978. There was a certain irony attached to the memory, since the trip to Greece had been prompted by concern for Basil, already then embarked on his monastic career. But the memory was also unhelpful. Nick retained nothing but the vaguest impression of the city – canals, gondolas and crowds in the Piazza San Marco. He could not even recall where he had stayed. To all intents and purposes, he was a complete newcomer.

Santa Lucia station was therefore the start for him of effectively unknown territory. He bought a map, then went into the accommodation bureau and asked for the address of the Hotel Zampogna. It was, he learned, not officially classified, even in the most basic category, the implication being that he should give it a wide berth. But, if he insisted, as he did . . . it was in the Cannaregio district, within walking distance.

There was no queue at that hour of the morning, so the assistant was happy to provide Nick with another location. A directory was consulted and an X marked on his map. The Palazzo Falcetto was on the last curve of the Grand Canal before it reached the lagoon. Unless Basil was waiting for him at the Zampogna – a cheering but remote possibility – the *palazzo* of his mysterious cousin would be Nick's second port of call.

The route to the Zampogna looked simple enough on the map. The reality was rather different. The morning was cold and grey and the further north and east of the station Nick went the quieter and emptier Venice became. The absence of cars struck him as eerie rather than peaceful. He progressed by a series of uncertain zigzags along narrow alleys or beside turbid back canals, varied occasionally by courtyards strung with limp washing in which a scurrying cat was likely to be the only movement.

Eventually, after several wrong turnings, he found the alley he was looking for: Calle delle Incudine. At the corner stood a dingy-looking bar and the next building down the *calle* was the Zampogna.

Many years previously the name had been painted on the mustard-hued wall, but most of the letters had peeled off along with the plaster beneath them and those that remained had faded into ghostly images of what might once have been intended as a genuine invitation to passing travellers. The entrance now was dark and discouraging, though the door was half-open. Nick ventured in.

The lobby was a narrow, dimly lit passage. A threadbare rug concealed some of the chipped and uneven tiles forming the floor. Stairs led off to one side, next to what looked like a ticket-window at a run-down railway station. The window was raised and, through it, Nick glimpsed a woman he knew instinctively to be the person he had spoken to on the telephone. She was clad in a shapeless brown dress and shawl. Her face was lined and pinched and nearly as brown as the dress, which made her manifestly unnatural mop of curly red hair all the more startling. She peered at him with no smile.

'*Si?*'

'I'm looking for Basil Paleologus. He's my brother. *Basil Paleologus*. He's been staying here.'

'*Che?*'

'*Parla inglese?*'

'*Inglese?*'

'Yes. *Si. Inglese*. Me and him. Basil Paleologus. Is he here?'

'*Paleologus?*'

'That's right. I—'

But the name, once she had grasped it, was enough. She was suddenly ranting at him, gabbling incomprehensibly as she waved her hands, her voice echoing in the passage and bouncing back at him from the walls. Nick had no idea what she was saying, but it was not an encomium of praise for Basil, that was certain. She was very angry about something. He tried to placate her with smiles and apologies and appeasing gestures, but it did no good. In the end, all he could do was retreat.

Her imprecations followed him out into the *calle*, then subsided away. With little expectation of assistance but nowhere else to go, Nick entered the bar next door. Despite the weather, its doors were wide open, revealing a counter angled across half the space, behind which stood a beer-bellied *barista* somewhere between middle and old age. Bald-headed though luxuriantly moustached, he exchanged a knowing look with his only other customer, a younger man dressed in dusty working clothes, who was propped against the counter, then grinned at Nick.

'*Buongiorno.*'

'*Buongiorno.*' Nick made an attempt at nonchalance. '*Doppio espresso, per favore.*'

'*Prego.*'

The *barista* turned away and set the *espresso* machine hissing into action. The young man drained his cup, crushed an empty cigarette pack and dropped it on the counter. '*Ciao, Luigi,*' he said, moving past Nick and out into the *calle*.

'*Ciao, Gianni,*' Luigi called over his shoulder. He kept his back to Nick as the machine slowly and noisily did its job. Then he delivered the result to the counter. '*Eccolo.*'

'Thanks.'

'You're welcome. A *doppio*'s what you need after a meeting with *la dragonessa.*' Luigi grinned. 'What was the problem? She sounded really pissed off with you.'

'I'm not sure. I'm looking for my brother. He's been staying at the Zampogna.'

'Signor Paleologus?'

'That's right. Did he come in here?'

'A couple of times, *si*. But I got the name from Carlotta – *la dragonessa.* He's your brother?'

'Yes. Basil Paleologus. I'm Nick Paleologus.'

'English Paleologi. I didn't know they got so far.'

'What can you tell me about my brother?'

'He did the bunk. Left the Zampogna without paying his bill. Carlotta went like Etna when she found out.'

'When was this?'

'Some time Monday. He was in here early that morning for his *tè verde*. Then . . . poof! No sign. Things still in his room, Carlotta says. But no *signore*. And no money. Gone.'

'What did Carlotta do about it?'

'Shout at me. What else?'

'Didn't she contact the police?'

'*La polizia?* You're joking. They'd probably close her down.'

'But Basil might be in trouble.'

'He will be if Carlotta catches up with him. So will you, if she finds out you are family.'

'Look, I'll pay her if that's the problem. I'm worried about my brother. I'm trying to find him. He's not the type to dodge settling a bill. Surely the fact that he left his stuff behind proves he meant to return. Something stopped him.'

Luigi shrugged. 'Maybe.'

'Is there any chance you could explain that to her? You'd be doing me a big favour.'

'And that's what I'm in business for, yes? To do my customers favours.' Luigi sighed theatrically. 'OK. We give it the whirl.' He picked up the telephone and dialled, then winked at Nick. 'This way, she can't throw anything at me. *Carlotta? Buongiorno. Sono Luigi. Si, si. Si calma, Carlotta, si calma.*'

The conversation proceeded for several minutes. Nick had no idea what was being said, but the tone of its saying slowly turned towards the reasonable, until, by the end, the *barista* and the *padrona* were almost billing and cooing to each other. Luigi eventually replaced the telephone in its cradle with a delicate flourish and treated Nick to a triumphant grin.

'I have a deal for you, Signor Paleologus. See what you think. You can take your brother's room until he returns, or until . . . whatever. One hundred thousand lire a night from last Saturday. Plus tonight up front. Me, I'd stay at the

Cipriani. But, hey, if you like a hard bed and a rough tongue you'll like the Zampogna. What do you say?'

Nick said yes, of course, and made a cautious return to the Zampogna. Carlotta was on her best behaviour this time, accepting the negotiated fistful of lire with something approximating to gracious thanks, then showing Nick up to what had been Basil's room and was now his.

The room was small, low-ceilinged and minimally furnished, with a bed, a wardrobe, a cabinet and a hard chair. There was a wash-hand basin in one corner, a framed bird's-eye view of Venice in 1500 by way of decoration and a tiny window commanding a congested vista of chimneypots and washing lines.

It was immediately apparent to Nick that Basil had left with every intention of being back in the near future. His alarm clock was still on the bedside cabinet, his toiletries still jumbled around the basin. And his rucksack, half-filled with clothes, was still where he had stowed it in the wardrobe. In quest of some clue as to where he had been since Monday, Nick ferreted through the rucksack, discovering precisely nothing, before turning his attention to the rest of the room. But there was nothing to be discovered there either. The shallow drawer of the bedside cabinet contained a crumpled copy of *Corriere della Sera*. That was all.

Nick sat on the edge of the bed and stared blankly into the grey morning beyond the window. Where had Basil gone? Where and why? There was only one trail to follow. The sooner he set off for the Palazzo Falcetto the better. He stood up.

Then he sat down again, as a thought suddenly crystallized in his mind. Basil's Italian was certainly better than his, but did it stretch to combing the columns of *Corriere della Sera*? Nick slid the drawer open and picked up the paper. It was a week-old edition, folded open at an inner page. Nick laid it out flat on the bed. Almost at once, he noticed a circle of red ballpoint round one medium-sized article. He could make little of it, of course, but there was a word in the headline – *omicidio* – which he felt sure meant murder.

For the price of another *espresso*, Luigi supplied Nick with a rough translation. The article concerned the progress – or lack of it – of police enquiries into the murder of Valerio Nardini, a 54-year-old dealer in antique maps, whose body had been found in a disused warehouse in the Arsenale district early in January; he had been shot through the head. There was speculation linking Nardini's murder to the sale at auction in Geneva two months previously of several medieval *portolani* which had allegedly been exported illegally from Italy. Luigi could not find an English word equivalent to *portolano*. 'A special kind of map for sailors' was the best he could do. He remembered the case only vaguely. The Italian word for auctioneer was *banditore* and might as well be *bandito*, he joked. They were not to be trusted. He doubted the police would be making an arrest any time soon.

Nick headed south through the gun-metal morning, the page he had torn from the newspaper stuffed in his pocket. He was aiming for the nearest *vaporetto* stop, Luigi having advised him how best to reach the Palazzo Falcetto. Why Basil should be interested in a murdered map dealer he had no idea, but he also had no doubt that the reason was in some way connected with the other deaths that had brought him to Venice. If he could only grasp what the connection was, everything else might fall into place. Technically, he could not be sure the newspaper had not been left in the room by a previous occupant. It was dated two days earlier than Basil's arrival in the city, after all. But he felt sure. He felt absolutely certain. It was only a pity he did not feel so certain about much else.

The number 1 *vaporetto* criss-crossed slowly from bank to bank down the Grand Canal. It was half-filled with a subdued assortment of tourists and residents. The Carnival seemed explicitly to be over, as a drift of rain across the decaying façades of the canalside *palazzi* somehow confirmed. The massed architecture of Venice's glorious past drifted dankly

304

past as Nick's mind dwelt on ancient maps of the oceans. They specialized in dire warnings against entering certain waters, he reflected. 'Here be Sea-serpents' – that kind of thing. If you ignored the warnings, well, then as now, he supposed, the consequences were on your own head.

Nick spotted the Palazzo Falcetto while the *vaporetto* was nudging in towards the landing-stage at the San Tomà stop, where Luigi had told him to get off. It might well have out-Gothicked its elegantly proportioned neighbour – all quatrefoiled arches and traceried balconies – but there was no way to tell, since its façade was swathed in scaffolding and thick-gauge plastic. Workmen were unloading cement sacks from a boat on to a pontoon in front of a scaffolded porch, through which a flagstoned terrace could be glimpsed. The contractor's sign proclaimed RICOSTRUZIONE and there was clearly a lot of it going on.

Once off the *vaporetto*, Nick followed a devious route he had traced on his map round to the landward entrance to the *palazzo*. High walls blocked his view all the way along the narrow Calle Falcetto. At the far end, through a massive wrought-iron gate, he could see an overgrown garden to one side and a soaring, unscaffolded flank of the building to the other. He yanked at the bell.

He had yanked a second time before a heavy-lidded, un-shaven young man in dusty overalls wandered into view. '*Buongiorno*,' the man mumbled through a mouthful of mid-morning snack, followed by some unintelligible remark as he edged open the gate.

'*Parla inglese?*'

'A little. What you want?'

'I'm looking for Signore Paleologus. He lives here, doesn't he?'

'*Il capo? Si, ma . . .*' The man shrugged. 'He is not living here now. *Non al momento.* Because of . . . *la ricostruzione.* Understand? He comes to see the work. Then he goes.'

'But he's due today, isn't he?'

'*Si*. Later.'

'What time?'

'What time? You think he make . . . *un appuntamento*? He comes when he wants.'

'It's vital I speak to him. Believe me. It's . . . *molto importante*. Have you any idea when he's likely to be here?'

The man shrugged. 'Three. Four. Who knows? He comes with . . . *il architetto*. After they eat good lunch. You know?'

'When would be the best time to try?' Nick took some money from his wallet and proffered a note. 'Do you think?'

The man thought. 'About three forty-five.' He took hold of the note and Nick let go. 'This is when I would try.'

'Thanks.'

'You want me tell him you're coming?'

Nick hesitated, then said, 'No.'

'OK.' The man grinned and pocketed the cash. 'Our secret.' Then he closed the gate, turned on his heel and vanished.

Nick had hoped to speak to cousin Demetrius before trying his luck at the British Consulate, but it would have to be the other way round now. The Consulate might just know something about Basil and Nick suspected that the morning was the best time to go calling. According to the knowledgeable Luigi, it was located right next to the Accademia Bridge, two *vaporetto* stops south of San Tomà. Nick went straight there.

The area was a massing-point for tourists, what with the views along the Grand Canal available from the bridge and the artistic treasures of the nearby Galleria dell'Accademia. On one side of the crowded *campo* in front of the gallery stood a pink-stuccoed *palazzo* with a Union flag hanging limply from the *piano nobile* balcony. Access for the public was via a side-gate, controlled by CCTV and entryphone. Nick was relieved to note that he was within the limited opening hours displayed on the sign – Monday to Friday, ten till one. He pressed the buzzer, asked to be admitted and, without ado, he was. He crossed a walled garden, entered the building and followed another sign up an imposing staircase past a couple of vast Grecian busts to a reception area. No-one else was making any call on the receptionist's time and she seemed genuinely sympathetic when he explained that he was in Venice trying to find his brother, who had vanished from his hotel. She would see if there was someone who could help.

There was: a bland-faced, sandy-haired fellow called Brooks, who occupied a small office on the other side of the *palazzo*, looking north. He was a young man with middle-aged airs, dressed for Whitehall and perhaps dreaming thereof. But he greeted Nick cordially enough.

'You have an exotic surname, Mr Paleologus. Do you boast Byzantine ancestry?'

'So quite a few members of my family like to believe.'

'Who can blame them?'

'I was wondering if you knew anything about my brother, Mr Brooks. Basil Paleologus. He's been in Venice since the end of last week.'

'I'm afraid not. And I *would* remember the name. He's gone missing, as I understand it.'

'Yes.' Nick set out the facts of Basil's disappearance as succinctly as he could, without of course revealing their true context. He let Brooks believe he was dealing with a case of a tourist in distress. He made no mention of cousin Demetrius. Reticence was hardly the best policy when seeking assistance, of course, but for the moment it was the only policy he could afford to adopt.

'When did you last speak to your brother, Mr Paleologus?' was Brooks's opening shot when Nick had finished.

'Sunday morning.'

'And he was last seen at his hotel?'

'Monday morning.'

'Well, it's only Wednesday today. It may be premature to raise the alarm.'

'I don't think so. He left all his stuff in his hotel room. He obviously intended to return there.'

'Venice can be a distracting place. Perhaps he's . . . found a friend.'

'He'd still need to brush his teeth and change his clothes.'

'Point taken. What does the hotelier think?'

'She suspected him of doing a bunk. But I've sorted that out.'

'Good. We wouldn't want the police after him, would we?'

'I wouldn't mind, if they could find him.'

'Well, you could report the matter to them, of course. I could even phone them on your behalf – the Questura is hardly a bastion of multilingualism. But I doubt they'd take a disappearance of such short duration very seriously. There's really nothing to suggest he's come to any harm. A middle-aged man, alone in Italy, gone walkabout. Is it possible that you're . . . overreacting?'

Nick stifled his irritation. From Brooks's viewpoint, it probably seemed very possible. 'I came to check if Basil had been in touch with anyone here or if you'd heard anything about him. The answer's no. So . . .' Nick stood up. 'Thanks for your time.'

'Give it a few days, Mr Paleologus. That's my advice.'

'Maybe I will.' Then again, maybe he would not. 'Oh, you don't happen to know what *portolani* are, do you?'

Brooks's eyebrows shot up. '*Portolani*? As a matter of fact, I do. What makes you ask?'

Suddenly, Nick felt reluctant to mention the newspaper article. He substituted a simple if hasty lie. 'The word was scribbled on a scrap of paper I found in Basil's hotel room. It looked like his writing.'

'Really? Does your brother speak Italian?'

'A little.'

'Is he interested in old maps?'

'Not particularly. Is that what *portolani* are?'

'In a sense. In English, we call them portolans.'

'I've never heard of them.'

'They're a little known byway of cartographic history. I take a modest interest in the subject.'

'So, what are they?'

'Linear maps designed for mariners, charting coastlines and the waters between for specific journeys: harbours, headlands, shallows, reefs, rocks and so forth. They're often more accurate, within their limits, than general maps of the same period. The earliest surviving example dates from about thirteen hundred. A lot of them were produced here in Venice. The Correr Museum has quite a good collection if you want to see what I'm talking about. It's in the Piazza San Marco.'

'I might take a look.'

'Do. You'll find them fascinating, I think. Would they have appealed to your brother?'

'I don't know.'

'Only, it's odd . . .' Brooks frowned. 'They, ah, hit the local news a few months ago.'

'Oh. How did they do that?'

'There were allegations that a set of very early Venetian portolans auctioned in Geneva last November had been smuggled out of Italy. The set fetched more than half a million Swiss francs, as I recall. That was before the allegations blew up, of course. There was something else strange about those particular portolans, which prompted another allegation – that they were forgeries. I can't remember exactly what the problem was and I'm not sure whether they were ever authenticated or not. Either way, however, forged or smuggled, they were undeniably . . . hot.' Brooks smiled weakly. 'A local map dealer implicated in the affair was murdered earlier this year. Draw your own conclusions.'

'I'm not sure I'm qualified to.'

'Who is, Mr Paleologus? Deep waters, though. That we *can* say. Best not to dip one's toe in.' Brooks's gaze narrowed. 'There's no possibility your brother might have' – he cleared his throat meaningfully – 'become involved?'

'None whatever.'

'No. Thought not. In which case . . .' Brooks spread his hands. 'I'm confident he'll turn up soon.'

Nick did not share Brooks's confidence. He knew too much to be able to.

He left the Consulate, crossed the bridge and followed the

signs and the loose knots of tourists towards San Marco. The piazza, when he reached it, was much as he recalled, the crowds thickest in the arcades either side and in front of the Basilica and the Doge's Palace.

The Correr Museum had fewer takers. It occupied the upper floors of the buildings on two sides of the piazza and Nick had to march through room after room of statues and coins and suits of armour before he came to the maps.

The portolans on display were clearly designed for professional sailors. Coastal features were depicted in minute detail. Inland was a blank. They were mariners' strip-maps, conveying essential information and nothing else. Frolicking sea-serpents did not get in on the act. None of them was earlier than sixteenth-century, though. What fourteenth- or even thirteenth-century portolans would look like was hard to judge. And Brooks had not said just how early the controversial portolans auctioned in Geneva were supposed to be.

Nick left the museum and trailed slowly across the piazza, wondering what he should do next. He had more than two hours to kill before there was any point returning to the Palazzo Falcetto. He should probably have lunch, but he seemed to possess no appetite. He decided to walk up to the Rialto, eat something there, then take a *vaporetto* back to San Tomà.

His route lay along the Calle dei Fabbri, north from San Marco. It was narrow and crowded going, past innumerable small shops. Nick paid them little attention and quite why, as he rounded a bend in front of one firmly shuttered establishment, he glanced up at the sign above the door, he could not have explained. But what he saw halted him in his tracks. *Valerio Nardini, Carte Antiche.*

It was a strangely disturbing coincidence. Nick went into a nearby bar and ordered a *grappa* and a beer. The past seemed closer in Venice than ever it had in England. He was wandering abroad in a museum-city where every exhibit might conceal a threat. Jonathan Braybourne had died here.

310

So had Valerio Nardini. Maybe Basil too. Nick swallowed the *grappa* in two gulps, but it could not burn away his fear. The palpitations were a different matter, though. They faded as the alcohol kicked in.

Nick took his mobile out of his pocket, intending to check for messages. But it had lost its charge, as he should have foreseen. Nor did he have the charger with him. Though that, he conceded, was probably immaterial, given the likely condition of the electrics at the Zampogna. He shoved the phone back into his pocket and started on the beer.

Later, after a second beer and a ham roll, Nick headed on north to the Rialto Bridge. He had decided to walk all the way to the Falcetto in order to fill the time until 3.45. The route he took was a circuitous one, even by the standards of a circuitous city, but he was able to stop at a bar near San Tomà for a *doppio corretto* before presenting himself at the *palazzo*. Alcohol and caffeine on an emptyish stomach were not what his doctor would have recommended, of course, but, for the moment, they kept Nick a degree removed from the scale of the risk one part of his brain knew he was taking. And that was where he needed to be.

Who was Demetrius Paleologus? What had he been to Michael Paleologus? Something beyond mere cousinhood tied them together. Them and Digby Braybourne too. Something that had started on Cyprus during the War, or maybe even at Tintagel in the 'thirties. Old men, with still older secrets. Portolans and stained glass and Knights Templar and the Holy Grail – and the cipher buried within them all; the zero point where every mystery converged and a single answer awaited. Towards it, down the Calle Falcetto, that seemed to narrow as he advanced, Nick walked. It was 3.52 p.m.

The sleepy young man answered the bell, his unshaven chin a few hours darker. A flash of his eyes deep in the peak-shade of his Nike baseball cap was the only sign of recognition.

'Is Signor Paleologus in?'

'*Si.*'

'Can I speak to him, please?'

'You have appointment?'

'No.'

'Your name?'

'Paleologus. Nicholas Paleologus.'

'Paleologus?' The man smiled, as if in recognition of a good joke. 'OK.' He held the gate open and Nick stepped through. 'Wait here.'

Nick watched the man walk away through a high, open doorway into a dust-fogged stairwell where two other men, older and more smartly dressed, one of them holding a clipboard, were deep in conversation. The conversation was interrupted. The young man gestured with his thumb. The other two glanced past him at Nick. Then one of them advanced.

He was a slim, good-looking fifty-something, clad in couture casuals beneath an Aquascutum raincoat slung loosely over his shoulders, blond highlights camouflaging the grey in his hair, tinted glasses the lines around his eyes. There was a glistening chunk of Rolex on his left wrist, a faint swagger to his walk, a trace of aftershave in the cement-scented air. Nick had no idea who he might be, but clearly he was not the person he was looking for.

'I am Paleologus,' the man nonetheless announced in barely accented English. 'Are we related?'

'I'm looking for Demetrius Paleologus.'

'You have found him.'

'I don't think so. There must be some mistake. He's an older man. Demetrius Andronicus Paleologus.'

'Ah. I understand. I am Demetrius Constantine. Demetrius Andronicus was my father.'

'*Was* your father?'

'Yes. I am afraid you cannot speak to him. He is close to a year dead.' Demetrius Constantine plucked off his glasses and gave Nick a concerned look. 'I am sorry. You are a long time too late.'

# CHAPTER TWENTY-ONE

'I am sorry,' said Demetrius Constantine Paleologus for the third or fourth time since Nick's arrival. 'This is not the condition in which I would wish a Paleologus to see the Palazzo Falcetto.'

They were standing at the top of the vast if dilapidated marble staircase leading to the *piano nobile*. To their right, through an open doorway, stretched a still vaster and yet more dilapidated ballroom. Below, drilling could be heard, growling beneath the workmen's banter and the tap of hammer on chisel.

'My father allowed the *palazzo* to moulder around him, especially after my mother's death. I am restoring it to its former glory. I plan to convert it into a luxury hotel. It has not been easy. And it is not proceeding as swiftly as I would like. But, when it is finished, it will be beautiful. It will be . . . magnificent.'

'How long has your family lived here?'

'For more than two hundred years. My great-great-great-grandfather, Manuel Paleologus, bought the *palazzo* from the heirs of the last of the Falcetti in seventeen eighty-seven. But we have lived in Venice ever since the fall of Byzantium in fourteen fifty-three. I must tell you that I have never heard of an English branch of the family. If we

313

are cousins, you and I, I could not say which ancestor we share.'

'I believe our fathers met in Cyprus during the War.'

'It is possible, though Papa never mentioned it. He moved there in the Thirties, when the Fascists started to make life difficult for him here. He was no friend of Mussolini. I was born in Cyprus. We returned here when I was a child, after the death of the man Papa had let it to.'

'Did your father say much about his wartime experiences?'

'No. I had the impression there was little to say. There was no fighting on Cyprus. As an Italian citizen living in a British colony, he must have been lucky to escape internment. If he was related to a British officer based there, it may have helped. But he never spoke of it to me. Ah . . .' Demetrius nodded at the hard-hatted, middle-aged workman climbing the stairs towards them. 'We have news, I think.'

Demetrius had explained earlier that no-one had yet mentioned Basil's visit to him. Work had been in progress over the weekend and it was not clear who Basil might have spoken to. The foreman had been instructed to look into the matter while Demetrius showed Nick round. The foreman's investigation now appeared to be complete.

There was a conversation in rapid-fire Italian, during which the foreman did a good deal of shrugging. Then he retreated, leaving Nick to a few more moments of suspense. It was evident that Demetrius did not propose to explain until they were alone again. This seemed odd, since the foreman presumably spoke no English. But such a minor oddity made no impact on Nick. He was assailed by many greater mysteries.

'Someone did call here on Saturday afternoon,' said Demetrius once the foreman had vanished from sight. 'He spoke to Bruno Stammati, my business partner. I did not know Bruno had come here, but this stuff your brother was told about me avoiding the Carnival makes sense now. Bruno is fond of jokes. Some of them are funny, some not. Anyhow, we will call Bruno and sort it out.' Demetrius plucked a spectacularly slim and elegant mobile from his pocket and pressed a single digit. A few seconds later, he frowned and spoke briefly in a message-leaving monotone, then rang off and grimaced apologetically. 'It seems Bruno is taking his weekend today. *Tipico*. No matter. I will catch him later. Whether that will help you find out where your brother is *now*' – he shrugged, tilting the epaulettes of his raincoat at 45 degrees – 'I cannot say.'

'I'm really worried about him,' said Nick. 'Anything you can do . . .'

'Of course, of course. It is much easier for me to make enquiries than for you. I know Venice. Who to ask. *How* to ask. So, why not leave it with me? Give me twenty-four hours. If there is information, I will get it.'

'That's very kind. I —'

'Not at all. We are Paleologoi. It is my duty to help.' Demetrius smiled. 'And my pleasure.'

Nick left the Palazzo Falcetto in a state of shock. A wholly unconsidered possibility was now revealed as the truth. And the truth mocked all that had gone before. Michael Paleologus had bequeathed Trennor to a dead man. His late and hastily drawn will would presumably have counted for nothing. If so, it had been as self-defeating as its destruction. But it had not been the only thing destroyed. Andrew and Tom and maybe Basil too had been dragged down in the wake of that single collusive act.

A chilling suspicion began to form in Nick's mind as he wandered aimlessly through the fading afternoon. Could his father have deliberately drawn up an invalid will? Had it been a last, sick joke at his family's expense – an elaborate dare designed to test how far they would go to counter a threat that did not really exist? It could not be so, Nick told himself. The old man had acted in haste, without pausing to confirm that his cousin was still alive. That was surely the truth. That *had* to be the truth.

\*     \*     \*

Even if it was, it did not help Nick find Basil. Demetrius's enquiries were likely to be more fruitful than his own. But the idea of doing nothing for twenty-four hours was quite simply appalling. He could not just sit on his hands. Night was falling by the time he arrived, somewhat to his surprise and by an unretraceable route, at the Rialto. He had Demetrius's business card and a Telecom Italia phonecard in his wallet, representing between them about the only practical steps he had so far succeeded in taking. He joined the commuter crowds aboard a northbound *vaporetto*, got off at the next stop and picked as direct a path as he could through the *calles* of Cannaregio to the Zampogna. It was a destination of sorts and, though that was about all that could be said for it, it was, in the circumstances, quite a lot. There existed, after all, the faint possibility that Basil had returned to the hotel in Nick's absence.

But Basil had not returned. There was nothing waiting for Nick at the Zampogna.

He sat in his room for twenty minutes that seemed like more than an hour, until it was close enough to opening time at the Old Ferry for him to be sure of speaking to Irene when he phoned. He could not have borne screwing up his nerves for an abortive attempt. He still did not know what he was going to say to her. But he knew he had to say something.

He headed out to make the call. He had spotted a card phone in Strada Nova, just after getting off the *vaporetto*, and planned to use that if he did not come across another on the way. But first he needed some Dutch courage.

'Signor Paleologus,' Luigi grinningly greeted him as he stepped into the bar. 'You must have known.'

'Known what?'

'I have a package for you.' From beneath the counter Luigi flourished a large, bulkily filled envelope, on which NICHOLAS PALEOLOGUS was written in felt-tip capitals.

'What's this?'

'I don't know. It came this afternoon. I was taking a piss,

while there was no-one in. When I came back, it was here.' Luigi tapped the counter for emphasis. 'Right here.'

'That doesn't make any sense.'

'It's what happened.'

Nick picked the package up, frowning in bemusement. Quite apart from what the envelope contained, the mystery of its arrival troubled him. How could anyone be sure he would ever receive it? It would have been safer to drop it off at the Zampogna. Or would it? He looked quizzically at Luigi. 'No-one knows I'm here.'

'Someone does. You want a drink? Something that kicks like a goalkeeper, maybe?'

'Sounds good.'

'I didn't say good. Only the kick I promise.' He poured some clear liquid from a dusty bottle into a small tumbler. 'Are you going to open that package or try to X-ray it, *dottore*?'

'OK, OK.' Nick ripped up the flap of the envelope and peered inside. 'It's a book,' he announced.

'I like a good book. Mickey Spillane. That kind of thing.'

Nick slid the book out on to the counter and flinched with surprise. It was a dog-eared copy of Drysdale's biography of Richard of Cornwall: *The Left Hand of the King*.

'Not Mickey Spillane,' said Luigi.

'Definitely not.' Nick took a sip of the goalkeeper fluid and flinched again. The kick was a punt deep into the other half. Then he picked up the book and opened it. As he did so, he noticed that something was marking a place about a third of the way through. He turned to the page and focused at once on the name Paleologus, adrift in one of the paragraphs.

Then his focus shifted to the place-marker itself. It was a business card. *Valerio Nardini, Carte Antiche*.

Nick was unsure whether Luigi had been able to read the card or not. He suspected, despite slamming the book shut the moment he himself saw the name and the disadvantage of his having to decipher the words upside down, that the *barista* had probably managed to. But it could not be helped. Whoever Nick needed to protect himself against, it was not Luigi.

Nick retreated to the bleak privacy of his room at the Zampogna and reopened the book at the marked page. He stared at Nardini's card, certain that a message was being conveyed to him. But he did not even know which was the message: the card or the page.

His eye fell on the place where he had seen the name Paleologus. He began to read.

. . . Richard's meeting with Andronicus Paleologus at the citadel of Limassol on Cyprus in March 1241 was a more extraordinary event than has ever since been acknowledged. Relations between the Byzantine Empire and the Crusader states had never been warm and, since the sack of Constantinople by the Fourth Crusaders in 1204 and the subsequent seizure of significant portions of Byzantine territory by their Venetian allies, they had been positively hostile. Yet at Limassol Richard, temporary viceroy of Outremer, sat down to negotiate with Emperor John Vatatzes' *megas domestikos*. Andronicus Paleologus was John's most trusted adviser and, for the purposes of this occasion, his plenipotentiary.

The most difficult question to answer is what they were negotiating. The Latin Empire established in the Balkans by the Crusaders in 1204 by now amounted to little more than Constantinople itself. It has been suggested that John Vatatzes sought from Richard – and was given – a free hand so far as his ambitions to reclaim the city were concerned. Those ambitions were not ultimately fulfilled until after John's death. The Emperor who eventually reconquered Constantinople in 1261 was none other than Michael Paleologus, who had accompanied his father, Andronicus, to Cyprus twenty years earlier.

The Crusader states were, in truth, ill-equipped to obstruct John Vatatzes' progressive moves against the Latin Empire. He hardly required their consent, tacit or otherwise, although he may have seen it as a useful guarantee of non-interference by their more powerful patrons in Western Europe. If so, it is strange that no record of such a policy has ever come to light. The negotiations in Limassol cannot, strictly speaking, even be proved to have taken place. We know the principals to have been present there at the same time. It would be absurd to suggest that this was for any other purpose than serious discussion. But those discussions were unusually and enduringly secretive. We can still only guess at their content today.

One of the strangest consequences was the souring of several alliances which, at the time, must have seemed firmly founded. John Vatatzes was later to charge Michael Paleologus with conspiracy. Although Michael succeeded in evading the charge on a technicality, the episode has never been properly explained. As for Richard himself, his brother-in-law Simon de Montfort, Earl of Leicester, who served as his deputy during his stay in the Holy Land and participated in the Limassol negotiations, was later to wage civil war in England against Richard and his brother, King Henry III.

Mistrust and misfortune of several kinds devolved upon those who conferred in such unexampled secrecy at Limassol. For Richard, March 1241 was perhaps the apogee of his reputation and his achievements. When he left the Holy Land for good two months later, his viceregal service had reached what seemed a triumphant conclusion. But the triumph did not last for long. The peace treaty he had negotiated with the Sultan of Egypt was to collapse within a year and the Templars and the Hospitallers were soon to be at one another's throats.

Of Richard's activities on a wider diplomatic front during the remainder of 1241 we shall have much to say, but let us look ahead first to his return to England in January 1242, since we are told (Matthew Paris, *Chronica Majora*) that he was sorely downcast to learn upon his arrival at Dover that a vessel he had despatched ahead of him from Acre the previous spring had been lost in a storm off the Scillies, its journey tantalizingly close to completion. The vessel had been under the command of Ralph Valletort, Richard's aide-de-camp in the Holy Land, who had, we can safely assume, been privy to the agreement reached at Limassol, though whether his ill-fated voyage was connected in any way with that agreement – whatever it may have been – can only be conjectured.

This disappointment still lay in the future when Richard reached Sicily in June 1241 and was drawn at once into Emperor Frederick II's attempts to . . .

Nick stopped reading and tracked back a few lines to the mention of Ralph Valletort. It was as Emily had said. There was a connection. There was a meaning. And for a split second, like the fugitive memory of a dream, something – some trace, some fragment – flitted across Nick's mind. Then it was gone.

His imagination was playing tricks on him, he reasoned. He had no insight into the truth. He had no means of decoding the secret. All he could hope to do was to halt the sequence of events his family had become caught up in. In looking for Basil, he was looking also for a way out, an escape route for those still able to take advantage of it.

It was gone eight o'clock – seven o'clock in England. He had to phone Irene. He could delay no longer. He stowed Drysdale's book in his bag in the wardrobe, then headed out.

The night was cold, still and moonless, with a dank mist rising from the canals. Venice – the part of it Nick was in anyway – was a dead city, a place of silence and shadow. He hurried along the deserted *calles*, pausing only to check his route on the map. A few more pedestrians appeared as he neared Strada Nova. After no more than a couple of wrong turnings, he reached the *campo* with the row of payphones he had passed earlier.

As he approached, card in hand, one of the phones began to ring. He stopped and stared at it, the noise magnified by the enclosing walls of the buildings around the *campo*. A couple walked by, glancing curiously first at the phone, then at him. The ringing went on.

Nick stepped forward and picked up the phone. 'Yes?' he said hoarsely.

'Walk east along Strada Nova,' responded a voice he did not recognize. 'Turn right into Calle Palmarana. Follow it to the canal. There'll be a water taxi waiting for you.'

'Hold on. Who—'

'You've got five minutes.'

The line went suddenly dead. Nick stared around him into the jumbled shadows of the *campo*. Nothing moved. A minute slowly passed as fear and curiosity wrestled within him. Then he put the phone back in its cradle and started walking – east along Strada Nova.

The water taxi was where Nick had been told it would be, moored at the end of the *calle*, its engine idling. The pilot looked up as Nick approached and pitched the remains of a cigarette into the Grand Canal.

'Signor Paleologus?'

'Yes.'

'*Prego.*' The man offered Nick a hand. For a moment, Nick hesitated. Was this really a good idea? No, the cautious part of his brain insisted. But what other idea did he have? He hopped aboard and stepped down into the cabin.

The pilot slipped the mooring and started away, back up the Grand Canal in the direction Nick had come from. A few minutes took them to the Ca' d'Oro *vaporetto* stop, where Nick had got off earlier. There was no *vaporetto* at the pontoon, but a figure stepped forward expectantly as they approached. The taxi slowed and manoeuvred alongside just long enough for him to jump aboard. They were actually

321

closer now to the rank of payphones Nick had left a short while ago than they had been at the point where he had boarded the taxi. If the person who had spoken to him on the payphone had been near by, watching him, he could have made his way to the *vaporetto* stop in ample time – and could now be stepping down into the cabin to join him.

'Hi,' the newcomer said, closing the cabin doors behind him as the taxi accelerated away and dropping a bulging carpet-bag on to the floor. He was a short, corpulent figure dressed in a thin raincoat and baggy linen suit, with what looked like a cricket sweater beneath. His unshaven chin merged with a roll of fat around his neck, straining the frayed collar of his shirt. His hair, damp with rain or sweat or both, was plastered to his head. His eyes were sea-grey and skittering, his moist lips parted in a smile that revealed an orthodontic disaster area. 'Nick Paleologus?'

'Yes.'

'I'm Fergy Balaskas.' He lowered himself awkwardly on to the cream leather bench opposite and held out a large, wavering hand that Nick somewhat reluctantly shook.

'Where are we going, Mr Balaskas?'

'The airport. Well, I'm going to the airport. You're just along for the ride. You're coming straight back in this, as a matter of fact. The round trip will cost you four hundred thousand lire, but what the hell? I'm not jetting off anywhere, by the way. It's just that from the airport I can take my pick of onward transport. Bus, taxi, *motoscafo*: enough options to keep you guessing. You *and* anyone else who might be interested.'

'Why should I care where you're going on to?'

'No reason. But what you don't know you can't tell. You're a dog with fleas, Nick. I don't want to catch any.'

'What are you talking about?'

'Precautions, old boy. You should try them yourself.'

'Was that pantomime with the telephone one of those precautions?'

'It was. Thanks to which, we're having this chinwag out of

sight and sound. I gather you got the book, incidentally. Real page-turner, isn't it?'

'Who *are* you?'

For answer, Balaskas pulled a business card from his pocket and passed it over. Nick held it up to read by the light of the cabin-lamp. *F. C. Balaskas, Private Enquiries and Debt Recovery, 217a Leoforos Archiepiskopou Leontiou, Limassol, Cyprus.*

'You're the man Jonathan Braybourne hired to investigate Demetrius Paleologus?'

'I am indeed.'

'You don't sound like a Cypriot.'

'That's because I'm not one. My father was, through and through. But he emigrated to England straight after the War and married a Londoner. I went out to Cyprus during a career slump about twenty years ago to see the relatives and soak up some sun, but I spotted an opening for confidential services to the ex-pat community and stayed on. They've been generating more than enough debt and divorce work for me ever since. I wish I'd stuck to it and told Braybourne to stuff his conspiracy theories, but nobody needs glasses in the hindsight game, do they? I bet you've been looking back and trying to work out where exactly you took the wrong turning yourself.'

'Did you leave the parcel for me at Luigi's bar?'

'Yep. He tipped me the wink you'd shown up and I dropped the book off so we'd have what you could call a frame of reference for our *conversazione*. You're here to find your brother? Well, maybe I can point you in the right direction. I met him a few days ago. Funny sort of a fellow. I showed him the book too. You can hang onto it, by the way. I shan't be wanting it back.'

'How did you come to meet Basil?'

'I was keeping a leery eye on the Palazzo Falcetto when he showed up there on Saturday. I trailed him back to the Zampogna, checked him out, then the following day . . . introduced myself. We, er, compared notes.'

'What about?'

323

'Lighten up, Nick. We're on the same team. Well, the same substitutes' bench. Jonathan Braybourne hired me to find out who'd been paying his late mother hush money from a Cypriot bank. Well, I found out: Demetrius Andronicus Paleologus, wartime resident of Cyprus, later absentee hotelier and Venetian recluse. Since I dug into his affairs, the old boy's died. But Demetrius Constantine Paleologus, his iffy businessman son, is very much alive and kicking. I've got the bruises to prove it. And Braybourne has the headstone in Sutton Coldfield Cemetery. When a client of mine gets stiffed, I get nervous. With good cause, in this case. Someone came after me in Limassol a while back. Several someones, as a matter of fact. I had to vamoose. Which came hard for a bloke at my time of life who isn't a naturally swift mover. Seems what I found out about Demetrius the elder was a lot more than his son wanted anyone to know. Braybourne found out more still, I assume, hence the header he took into the canal.'

'You think Demetrius the younger had Jonathan Braybourne killed?'

'I think you'd be well advised to work on that assumption. I'm working on it.'

'Did you tell Basil this?'

'Of course. He didn't seem as impressed as he should have been, if you want my opinion. He had his own agenda. It's yours too, I imagine, and I don't suppose you're any likelier to let on what it is than he was. But I'm not a bad guesser. *And* my Greek's fair to fluent. The name Paleologus is a combination of two Greek words. Palaios: ancient. Logos: word. So, maybe it shouldn't be a big surprise if the Paleologoi carry old secrets.'

'What secrets?'

'Don't be coy, Nick. The newspaper cutting about Nardini gave your brother pause for thought, but he didn't take the threat seriously enough. Don't make the same mistake. Your family's tied into all this. If you don't know how, I sure as hell don't. What I do know is that an eight-sheet Venetian portolan dated thirteen forty-one, sold at auction in Geneva last November, appears to show navigational details of the North American coast more than a hundred and fifty years before Columbus sailed the ocean blue. So, it's either a fake or an authentic record of a secret chunk of history. Legend has it that Antonio Zeno, a Venetian merchant, sailed to Nova Scotia some time in the thirteen nineties, accompanied by a Scottish nobleman, Henry St Clair, Earl of Orkney, so who knows if—'

'Did you say St Clair?'

'Name rings a few bells, does it?'

It rang more than a few, though scarcely in harmony. 'What are you getting at, Mr Balaskas?'

'The truth, my old cock. And you're right. I'm getting *at* it, but not *to* it. Drysdale signed off his foreword to *The Left Hand of the King* with his address: Roslin, Midlothian. And Rosslyn Castle is the ancestral home of the St Clairs. If one of the St Clairs sailed to Nova Scotia with Antonio Zeno six hundred years ago, they'd have found a portolan like the one we're talking about hellish useful. Nardini acted as middleman for the sale on behalf of an anonymous client and there's no chance now of him putting a name to that client. But here's the strangest thing. Six months before the portolan was sold, Jonathan Braybourne came to Venice with a copy of Drysdale's book in his luggage. He wound up dead as well. When his wife got his possessions back, they included the book, which she later passed on to me. Inside, marking the page – the same page I left it in for you – was Nardini's business card.'

'Hold on. Braybourne's *wife* gave you the book?' Doubt was beginning to refine itself in Nick's mind. Ever since discovering that Demetrius Andronicus Paleologus was dead, he had been puzzled by Emily's apparent unawareness that the Demetrius her brother had gone to see in Venice could not be the same Demetrius their father had supposedly met in wartime Cyprus. She had also referred to her discovery of *The Left Hand of the King* among Jonathan's possessions. *Her* discovery, not his wife's. Something was wrong. Something could not be reconciled. 'When was this?'

'Early January. Just after Nardini was killed. Which is when it got a lot too hot for me in Limassol. Coincidence? I think not. Someone had decided to take out some expensive insurance. Nardini and I were part of the premium. Like I told your brother—'

'What about Braybourne's sister?'

'His sister?'

'Yes. Emily Braybourne.'

Balaskas stared blankly at Nick for a moment, then frowned. 'I've never heard of her.'

# CHAPTER TWENTY-TWO

The water taxi cruised on across the flat darkness of the lagoon. Glancing through the cabin window, Nick could see lights ahead of them in the distance. The airport, he assumed. He took another sip of whisky from the flask, then handed it back to Balaskas.

'Thanks.'

'Don't mention it, old boy. You looked in need.'

'It's the bouncing up and down. Made me feel queasy, that's all.'

'Yeah? Well, it's good for shocks too. And I'd say you've just had quite a big'un. If Emily Braybourne made a fuss at the inquest like you tell me, then I can only assume she decided to drop her protest straight after and shove off back to the States, because her sister-in-law didn't breathe a word about her to me. Cut and run would have been a wise policy, of course. Just look at my recent experiences. Maybe this woman who introduced herself to you as Emily Braybourne is an impostor. Have you considered that possibility?'

'I'm considering it now.'

'We're in uncharted waters, Nick. The only way out is to take a deep breath and swim like hell. That's what I'm planning to do. I advise you to do the same.'

'I can't. I have to find Basil.'

'I wish you luck. And I reckon you'll need it. I warned him to lay off Demetrius. I don't think he heeded the warning, though.'

'When did you last see him?'

'Monday. When he returned Drysdale's book to me. We'd arranged to meet on the forty-two *vaporetto* – one of the circular routes. I told him as much about Demetrius as I dared. And that was as much as I knew.'

'You'd better tell me, then.'

'OK. Demetrius the elder was straight-as-a-die patrician stock. Demetrius the younger is out of a different mould. He's *persona non grata* in Cyprus because of suspected involvement in cross-border money laundering. The hotels he inherited from his father have been closed down until he answers the charges. All his Cypriot assets have been seized.'

'Oh God.'

'He's being squeezed financially, Nick. And not just by the Greek Cypriot government. The Turkish Cypriots aren't any happier with him. There are whispers tying him in with organized crime here in Italy as well. However you slice it, the guy is bad news. The suspect portolan wasn't the first cartographic gem Nardini marketed last year. It wasn't even the most valuable. I think Demetrius used Nardini to offload some or all of his father's archive of antique maps and atlases. He needed the money to keep his creditors at bay. And his creditors are the sort who take payment in kind if they can't get it in cash. He has a villa on the Lido guarded by the sort of goons you'd expect to see on duty outside the residence of an exiled Latin American dictator. He's in trouble and he *is* trouble. He's not the sort of man you can do business with. I explained that to your brother. Very clearly.'

'What did he say?'

'He thanked me for the information. He shook my hand. Then I got off the *vaporetto*. He stayed aboard. It was going on to San Michele – the cemetery island. He said he wanted to take a look at the elder Demetrius's grave. Well, that was it.

The parting of the ways. There's been neither sight nor sound of him since.'

'Demetrius couldn't have been more charming when I spoke to him. Or more helpful.'

'He's playing you along, Nick. Don't trust him.'

'What do you think's happened to Basil?'

'I think Demetrius could answer that question for you straight off if he wanted to. I can only make an educated guess.'

'Go on, then.'

'You don't really want me to.'

'Yes, I do.'

'No.' Balaskas stared insistently at Nick. 'Believe me. You don't.'

That was almost the last thing Balaskas said to Nick before he climbed up on to the landing-stage at Marco Polo airport and walked away towards the taxi ranks and bus stops in front of the terminal building. The weight of the carpet-bag was dragging down his left arm so that he appeared to be limping. He did not look back.

'He say you pay,' the pilot growled.

Nick handed over a wad of lire. 'Fondamente dell'Abbazia?'

The pilot scrutinized the wad, then nodded. 'OK.'

It did not inevitably follow from what Balaskas had said that Emily had lied to Nick. She was not necessarily an impostor. She might merely have asked her sister-in-law to make no mention of her to a third party. It was her failure to dispel the confusion about Demetrius Paleologus's identity that Nick could not reason away, however hard he tried. As the taxi pounded back across the lagoon, he stared at the jaundiced reflection of his face in the cabin window, aware that the tremor in his hands and the fluttering in his chest were not caused by the vibration of the hull. No-one could be trusted. Nothing could be relied upon. Behind every deception was another deception. The secret was that there was no secret.

And that itself was a lie. Nick sank his head in his hands and closed his eyes.

He did not phone Irene that night. In a bar close to the Zampogna – but not as close as Luigi's – he drank enough *grappa* to loosen the spiral of his thoughts. Fatigue of many kinds overtook him after that. He slept deeply in the narrow bed where his brother too had slept, recalling when he woke that he had dreamt of his father. But what the old man had said or done in his dream he could not retrieve. So much that was buried was also lost.

The morning was bright, almost spring-like. Nick walked east to Fondamente Nuove, where he had a breakfast of sorts in a bar and gazed out across the lagoon at Isola di San Michele – the cemetery island to which Basil had carried on after his and Balaskas's parting three days before. Beyond the terracotta boundary wall of the cemetery itself all Nick could see were the massed green ranks of cypresses. But there would be ranks of graves, too. One of them belonged to Demetrius Andronicus Paleologus. It was a simple fact of death.

Nick had decided what to do. He would go back to the Consulate and ask Brooks to contact the police on his behalf. They could do more for Basil than he could. They were his only hope. He would speak to Irene later, when he might actually have something to report. She would demand explanations for things he could not explain if he called her now. Besides, it was only just gone eight o'clock in England. She was probably still asleep. He smiled to himself, acknowledging that he could find excuses even when he could find nothing else.

But some excuses cut two ways. The Consulate was not yet open. Nick left the bar, walked across to the *vaporetto* stop and studied the timetables. There was a service to San Michele in just a few minutes. He bought a ticket and waited, glancing around at the other people on the landing-stage and wondering if any of them might be following him. Balaskas

330

would have him believe his every footstep was dogged. And maybe it was. But his helplessness at the thought was a kind of liberation. They would show themselves or not as they pleased. Until they did, there was nothing he could do. Except follow Basil on the last journey he was known to have taken.

The *vaporetto* was bound for the island of Murano. So, it transpired, were all of the passengers save Nick and an immaculately dressed old woman carrying a large bunch of flowers, wrapped in cellophane. At the Cimitero stop, they were the only two to get off.

Nick followed the old woman through an archway into the grounds of the cemetery. The graves stretched away into the walled distance, separated by straight avenues of raked gravel, beside which the cypresses stood at measured intervals, as if to attention. The old woman hurried on ahead, a receding figure between the headstones. She knew where she was going.

Nick had not thought till then how he would find Demetrius Paleologus's grave. Spotting a sign pointing to the cemetery office, he headed back into the cloisters flanking the church of San Michele. The office was just being opened. The attendant spoke decent English and, to Nick's surprise, recognized the name of Paleologus. He handed Nick a map showing the layout of the cemetery and prodded at a section labelled *Rec. Greco*.

'He was Orthodox, yes? You will find him there. The stone is quite recent.'

Orthodox? Yes, of course. Old Demetrius had kept the faith of his Byzantine forefathers. Glancing at the map as he went, Nick headed past the crematorium building towards two separately walled compounds. One was reserved for Protestants, the other for those who had deferred in life to the Patriarch of Constantinople and had been granted in death a small measure of exclusivity on that account.

331

Arrows on the map pointed to the last resting places of two Russian Orthodox celebrities: Diaghilev and Stravinsky. They were of no interest to Nick. He wandered between the graves, looking for the brightness of new stone. It was warm now, the high walls trapping the heat of the sun. A dove was cooing somewhere. The tranquillity of commemorated lives seemed suddenly absolute.

Then he saw the name, spelt in the Greek style. PALAIOLOGOS. A lizard scurried from the stone as Nick's shadow fell across it.

QUI RIPOSANO
DIMITRIOS ANDRONIKOS PALAIOLOGOS
NATO IL 2 FEBB 1908    MORTO IL 24 MAR 2000
E  LA  CONSORTE
GIULIA AGOSTINI PALAIOLOGOS
NATA IL 11 LUG 1914    MORTA IL 22 AGOS 1986

Nick had read the inscription before he noticed, carved above it, as on his grandparents' grave at Landulph, the double-headed eagle of Byzantium. No Paleologus, it seemed, was permitted to renounce his past.

Gazing at the painstakingly chiselled record of his cousin's birth and death, Nick was struck by a hopeful thought – at a moment and in a place where he had not expected to find hope of any kind. Reading Balaskas's report, which she must have come across amongst her brother's possessions, Emily would not have known its subject was already dead. Jonathan Braybourne had probably only learned as much shortly before his own death. It was possible – yes, damn it, it *was* possible – that Emily still did not realize there was a younger, more ruthless and potentially more dangerous Demetrius Paleologus to be borne in mind. She had not necessarily deceived Nick after all.

Then his shadow seemed suddenly to stretch, blotting the sunlight from the inscribed words and dates. He turned and started with surprise at the sight of the very man he had just been thinking of: Demetrius Constantine Paleologus.

Demetrius smiled. 'This is a big coincidence, cousin.'

'Yes. It is.'

'When we spoke yesterday, I remembered I had not been here for too long. What brought you?'

'Curiosity, I suppose.'

'Perhaps you needed to see with your own eyes in order to believe.'

'No, I just—'

'It is sometimes hard for me to believe he is really dead. He was old. He was ready for death. Yet still I sometimes expect to hear his voice again, to see his eyes fixed on me. At the *palazzo*, when the workmen have gone, as it grows dark . . .' Demetrius shrugged. 'You know?'

'Yes. I know.'

'I spoke with Bruno this morning. He remembers meeting your brother. But that is all. And that is no help to you, is it?'

'Not really.'

'My other enquiries will take longer. You will have to be patient.'

'I'll try.'

'Good.'

'I'd better be off now. You'll want to be alone.'

'There's no need to leave. You came by *vaporetto*?'

'Yes.'

'You can ride back with me on my launch. Just give me a few moments. Take a look at the family vault while you wait.' Demetrius pointed towards an ivy-hung greystone mausoleum near the rear wall of the compound. 'My mother did not want to be buried there. So, my father rests with her here. His father and many fathers before his father are in the Paleologus vault.'

Nick walked slowly away, leaving Demetrius to stand, head bowed, by his parents' grave. Nick was not sure now whether his unease had any rational basis. Demetrius was dangerous, according to Balaskas. But was he? Was he *really*?

Nick reached the vault. The name Paleologus was inscribed

in Greek capitals within the pediment above the padlocked steel door: ΠΑΛΑΙΟΛΟΓΟΣ. The bones of *'many fathers before his father'* were gathered within these walls. Nick had never felt so close to the departed ranks of his ancestors. The dust they had been brought to seemed to float in the falsely warm air around him.

'Where are you, Basil?' he murmured. 'What happened to you?'

The last conversation he had had with Basil, on Sunday morning, suddenly recurred to Nick's mind. Basil had already spoken to Bruno Stammati by then. What were the chances that he could have done so without it emerging that the owner of the Palazzo Falcetto was far too young to have known their father during the war?

Nick turned to see Demetrius walking towards him. The raincoat of the day before had been replaced with a light cashmere overcoat that enhanced the swagger in his strolling gait. He was smiling, though whether the smile reached his eyes the tint of his glasses made it hard to judge.

'If only the dead could speak, eh?' said Demetrius. 'What secrets would they tell us?'

'Maybe they'd tell us whether there's really a heaven and a hell.'

'And a God and a Devil to preside over them. Yes, that would be useful.'

'Or maybe they'd say the biggest secret is that there is no secret.'

'No secret?' Demetrius chuckled. 'That would be a major disappointment.'

'Life's full of disappointment. Why not death too?'

'Why not, as you say? Though, speaking for myself, I have not been disappointed very often.'

'Lucky you.'

'Indeed. But luck is not the same as chance. You must make one and take the other.' Demetrius's smile broadened, his teeth gleaming whiter than marble in the sunlight. 'Shall we go?'

They walked round to the main part of the cemetery and headed down the cypress-lined central avenue, away from the church and the *vaporetto* stop. At the far end of the avenue the boundary wall was broken by a high, ornamental gateway. Nick could see a man leaning against the bars of the gate. He was dressed in dark, casual clothes and seemed to be watching them.

'We Orthodox are fortunate,' said Demetrius, breaking a silence of several minutes. 'Because of limited space here on San Michele, the Catholic dead are exhumed after ten years and taken to the public ossuary. No such fate will overtake the Paleologoi. We will remain . . . for ever.'

'That's good to know.'

'I'm glad you think so, even though, of course, it is ultimately irrelevant what becomes of a body.'

'Is it?'

'Why, yes.' Demetrius cast Nick a sidelong glance. 'Did you visit the Protestant section before we met?'

'No.'

'The poet Ezra Pound is buried there. *Il miglior fabbro*, as Eliot called him. "What thou lovest well remains," he wrote, "The rest is dross." '

'You believe that?'

'I believe part of it.'

'Which part?'

'The dross, cousin. The dross.' Demetrius looked ahead and raised one hand, signalling with his index finger to the man in the gateway. The man pushed himself upright and swung one of the pair of gates open as they started up the steps towards him. 'I'm going to my villa on the Lido. Why don't you accompany me? Bruno is coming there straight from the airport later this morning. I thought maybe you would like to speak to him in person.'

They stepped through the gate and out onto a landing-stage. Demetrius's launch, a sleek-hulled lagoon limousine with burnished honey-toned decking and glistening chromework, stood ready for them, its idling engine purring like a panther. The pilot glanced up at them through reflective sunglasses. He was tanned and muscular, like his crewmate, and Nick wondered if they were representative of the 'goons' Balaskas had claimed Demetrius employed to guard his villa. He heard the gate clang shut behind him and realized that the invitation to visit the villa was both an opportunity too good to miss and a risk too grave to run. What had Demetrius said? '*You must make one and take the other.*' But whose, in this case, was the luck – and whose the chance?

'A handsome craft, no?'

'Very.'

'Then, please, step aboard. We will show you what she is capable of.'

Nick hesitated for a fraction of a second, then went ahead.

The pilot helped him aboard. Demetrius and the other man followed. The mooring was slipped, the engine gunned. And the launch sped away.

The trip to the Lido was a high-octane surge. The blast of chill air soon forced Nick down into the cabin with Demetrius, who flung his coat casually aside and gazed back proudly at the sparklingly chevroned wake. Then his mobile rang, inaudibly it seemed to Nick, and a heavily one-sided conversation followed, to which Demetrius contributed little beyond '*Si*' at irregular intervals, supplemented occasionally with '*Subito*' or '*Senz'altro.*'

By the time he rang off, they were closing on the long, low western shore of the Lido. The pilot throttled back and steered in towards the narrow mouth of a canal, to either side of which terracotta-roofed villas were spaced along the lagoon frontage behind high walls and sheltering greenery.

Demetrius ushered Nick out of the cabin and pointed to the villa standing on the left-hand corner of the canal. 'Mine,' he announced. It was larger and starker than most of its neighbours, a plain cream-stuccoed edifice of simple lines and little obvious pretension, with a colonnaded terrace hung with vine running along the side facing the lagoon. The chimneys were twentieth-century versions of the medieval *fumaioli* Nick had seen all over Venice. They were the only aspect of the villa's design that was specifically Venetian. It was otherwise a standard-issue riviera residence. And not one that its owner made intensive use of, to judge by the number of windows on which the shutters were firmly closed.

A short distance down the canal was a landing-stage. The pilot hove to and tied up. Nick and Demetrius disembarked, Demetrius leading the way through a wrought-iron gate and along a gravel path round a thin screen of trees on to the drive on the landward side of the house. A silver Lancia was parked in the wide turning area, beside a dark-red Transit van.

The main door of the villa opened as they approached. A fellow looking like a close relation of the pilot and his crewmate, though more smartly dressed, held it back for them, twitching his head in faint deference first to Demetrius, then to Nick. They entered a cool, empty hall and moved on into a large drawing room that gave via French windows on to the terrace. The sea glinted at them through the colonnade across a manicured lawn and covered swimming pool, beside which stood shrouded loungers, waiting for summer.

The drawing room was expensively furnished in Art Deco style, with lots of pale leather and extravagantly veneered wood, elegantly at odds with a state-of-the-art widescreen TV and vertically arrayed hi-fi. A grand piano occupied a slightly raised area at the far end of the room.

'Make yourself comfortable,' said Demetrius. 'Coffee, perhaps? Or something stronger?'

'Coffee would be fine.'

'I'll join you.' Demetrius stepped back into the hallway and spoke briefly to the man who had let them in, addressing him as Mario. When he returned to the drawing room, he sat down in one of the pastel leather armchairs and gestured for Nick to sit down opposite him.

'When are you expecting Bruno?'

'Soon, soon. We have much to discuss in the meantime.'

'We do?'

'Certainly. I must begin by thanking you, Nicholas. Most sincerely.'

'For what?'

'For coming here.'

'It was no problem.'

'Indeed it was not. But it might have been, you see. You might have made it so much more difficult. As it is . . .' Demetrius smiled. 'Here we are. Here *you* are.'

'Why should I have made it difficult?'

'It hardly matters, since you didn't.'

'Am I missing something here?'

'Perhaps.'

A silence fell as Mario entered, carrying a lacquer tray with two cups of black coffee, a small jug of cream and a sugar bowl on it. He set the tray down and left without a word. Demetrius leaned forward, spooned some sugar into his coffee and stirred it slowly.

'I have had you followed, Nicholas. You should under-stand that. Apart from a couple of hours last night when you gave my men the slip, your movements have been closely monitored since your arrival. We did not meet on San Michele this morning by chance.'

Demetrius had spoken in the same affable tone he had employed throughout their exchanges and, for a moment, Nick could not quite believe he had heard correctly. 'What?'

'I think you heard me. Who were you with last night, incidentally? I'd be interested to know.'

'You've . . . had me followed?'

'Yes.'

'Why?'

'To make sure you did not stray too far. It was obliging of you to return to the Zampogna after we lost you. Obliging and, if I may say so, rather stupid.'

'Now, look here—' Nick started up from his chair.

'Sit down, Nicholas. There's something I want to show you.' Demetrius plucked a remote control from the low table

338

between them, pointed it at the television away to his right and pressed a button. A picture flashed into view.

Nick stopped halfway to his feet and stared at the slightly blurred, black-and-white image on the screen. Basil was looking up at him, or at any rate up at the camera. He was sitting on a hard-backed chair in the middle of an apparently featureless room. His feet were tied to the legs of the chair and his arms were pinioned behind him in some way. He was wearing a pale T-shirt, jeans and espadrilles. There was a fuzz of stubble round his chin and over the crown of his head. His expression was blank, neither fearful nor defiant. Mercifully, there was no sign that he had been maltreated. But he was a prisoner. Of that there was no doubt. Nor did Nick doubt that the man responsible for Basil's imprisonment was lounging in the chair opposite him, smiling blandly.

'Be very careful, Nicholas. What you're watching is a closed-circuit link with the place where Basil's being held. The people holding him are professionals who will not hesitate to kill him if I give the word. Allow me to demonstrate the peril of his situation.' Demetrius took his mobile out of his pocket, pressed a button and conveyed some *sotto voce* instructions. A figure appeared on the screen, dressed in archetypal terrorist gear: trainers, jeans, sweatshirt and balaclava. He stepped into position beside Basil and pulled out a gun, holding it ostentatiously in front of Basil's face. Basil pulled his head back slightly, but otherwise did not react.

'You've made your point,' said Nick, forcing himself to speak in a measured tone.

'Good.' Demetrius murmured into the phone and Nick watched as balaclava man lowered the gun and walked away out of the picture. 'Now, do sit down.'

Nick lowered himself slowly back into his chair and swallowed hard. By rights he should have been experiencing a full-blown panic attack, but actually he felt calmer than he had any right to. It was a relative condition, of course. His mouth was dry, his palms damp, his brain a chaos of competing thoughts. Yet he was still in control. Not of the situation, obviously, but of himself. And he knew that for Basil's sake he had to stay that way. 'What do you want?'

'Your full co-operation.'

'And if I give you that?'

'Basil goes free.'

'Then you've got it.'

'You should hear what it involves first.'

'Tell me.'

'Very well.' Demetrius picked up his coffee-cup and took a sip. 'Don't let yours get cold.'

'Just tell me.'

'All right.' Demetrius replaced the cup soundlessly in its saucer. 'But I wish to avoid unnecessary repetition. My associate will be arriving shortly. All will be explained then.' He flicked the remote at the television. The screen blanked out. 'Meanwhile, you may as well drink your coffee.'

'No, thanks.'

'As you please.'

'Is it Bruno Stammati we're waiting for?'

'No.'

'Who, then?'

'You will not have to wait long to find out.' Demetrius looked round, as if he had heard something. 'Ah. A car on the drive, I think.' He glanced at his watch. 'Gratifyingly on schedule.'

Nick had heard nothing. But now the sound of a slamming car door reached him, followed by footsteps, growing suddenly louder as the front door of the villa opened. The footsteps clacked along the marbled hall towards them. Nick looked up, cursing his own foolishness for hoping even at this late and desperate stage that he would not see the face of the woman he had come to think of as Emily Braybourne.

Then he saw. And it was her.

'Hello, Nick,' she said.

# CHAPTER TWENTY-THREE

She met Nick's gaze directly. There was no hint of shame or regret in her expression. Her eyebrows were half-raised, her mouth placidly unsmiling, her jawline relaxed. She seemed utterly calm, almost detached. She would not apologize. She would not gloat. She was present, as ever, on her own terms.

'What should I call you now?' Nick asked, not troubling to conceal the bitterness in his voice.

'Call her Emily,' said Demetrius. 'Oh yes. She *is* Emily Braybourne.'

'Is that true?' Nick threw the question at her.

'Yes.' As she walked across to the coffee-table, Nick noticed that she was carrying a slim silver-grey briefcase. She laid it on the table, then stepped back and sat down facing him, one hip propped on the arm of Demetrius's chair. 'A lot else I told you was true too.'

'You never mentioned getting into bed with your brother's murderer.'

'An interesting choice of metaphor, Nicholas,' said Demetrius, idly running his hand along Emily's black-trousered thigh. 'You speak in the business sense, of course. Which is appropriate, since Emily has long learned to view the loss of her brother as a sad necessity of business. Isn't that so, *cara*?'

341

'Yes.' She did not flinch as she said the word.

'You may be wondering what's in the case,' Demetrius went on. 'We'll explain that later. *If* we need to.'

'We will,' said Emily.

'She has a theory, you see. An elegant and plausible theory that fits the facts. We shall soon find out if it's correct. Either way, I'll get what I want.'

'And what's that?'

'You promised your full co-operation, don't forget.'

'I'm not about to.'

'Good.' Demetrius glanced up at Emily. 'Tell him.'

'Jonty found out about the portolans Demetrius was smuggling through Switzerland,' she neutrally began. 'He tried to pressurize Demetrius into letting him in on the deal, hoping that would enable him to crack the secret. But the secret has nothing to do with the portolans. And pressurizing Demetrius was a fatal mistake. When I thought it through, I realized he could be a better ally than a foe. So, we joined forces. Revenge doesn't make you rich or happy, Nick. But maybe becoming rich and happy is a kind of revenge. It's the one I've opted for. Demetrius's father left a lot of valuable stuff behind. But there was something far more valuable he had a stake in. If we can lay hands on it, we'll be able to name our own price. Literally.'

'And it will be a very high price,' said Demetrius. 'Papa used to hint to me when I was growing up that there was some great secret he would reveal to me one day. *Il segreto favoloso*, he called it. But he never did reveal it. He said later I had shown myself to be unworthy. What he really meant was that I did not choose to live according to his rules. So, he kept the secret from me. It was safe with another, he said. I could not be trusted. When your father tried to contact him recently, I knew why, of course, so I made sure he did not learn of his old friend's death. Papa had died with the secret. But it had not died with him.'

'The knowledge has been passed down from generation to generation,' Emily resumed. 'Your ancestor, Theodore

Paleologus, did not settle in Landulph by chance. He went there in quest of something *his* ancestor, Emperor Michael the Eighth, had heard described and discussed at Limassol in the spring of twelve forty-one. A relic of some kind, an artefact preserving sacred information. It had been discovered in Jerusalem by the Knights Templar and could no longer be safely left in the Holy Land in view of the deteriorating situation there. A secure repository was required. That's why Richard of Cornwall built his castle at Tintagel. He'd been instructed to do so – commissioned to provide a hiding-place that would look like a wealthy prince's folly, drawing no-one's attention to its true purpose, far enough from the battle-grounds of Europe's dynastic rivals to ensure its safety *and* its survival.

'He travelled to the Holy Land in twelve forty to report that all was ready. He met a delegate from the Byzantine Emperor and informed him of what was intended, presumably to ensure that both branches of Christendom were party to the decision. Shortly afterwards, Ralph Valletort set sail from Acre, bound for Tintagel, carrying the artefact with him.

'Land routes couldn't be risked for fear his precious cargo might fall into the wrong hands. But the sea also has its risks. The ship foundered off the Scillies. The artefact was lost. But Valletort survived. I think the reason the nature and meaning of the artefact is so elusive is that even those who decided its fate did not actually see it. An inner cadre of the Knights Templar guarded its secret. Several such knights doubtless accompanied Valletort on the voyage. Perhaps they confided in him. Perhaps he inspected the artefact for himself. I'm certain he *knew* – and that he was responsible for incorporating a reference to the secret in the Doom Window at St Neot, his native parish. Or maybe that was down to his son, or his grandson.

'The point is that the Doom Window predates and transcends the fifteenth-century glazing scheme. That's why it was removed in sixteen forty-six. The churchwardens knew it had to be preserved at all costs. Hence its concealment at

343

Trennor. And hence, I believe, your grandfather's purchase of Trennor in nineteen twenty-one.'

'Hold on,' Nick interrupted. 'What would my grandfather have known about all this?'

'More than you think. Remember what I said. From generation to generation. When the excavations began at Tintagel in nineteen thirty-three, your grandfather and your father were on the scene. But were they there to help – or to hinder? Fred Davey worked with his father on that dig. And his grandfather had worked on the last lead-mining venture at Tintagel, in the eighteen seventies. There have always been rumours that something came to light back then – an underground chamber of some kind, revealed during tunnelling directly beneath the great hall of Tintagel Castle. Such a chamber could easily be a repository, for an article of great worth. The article had never arrived, of course. It had ended up on the sea bed eighty miles to the west. Even so, the discovery of the chamber would have raised a lot of questions. I suspect the Daveys, father and son, conspired with the Paleologuses, father and son, to ensure it remained undiscovered.

'Later, serving on Cyprus during the War, your father met a long-lost cousin who knew as much, if not more, about the nature and meaning of the artefact destined for but never delivered to Tintagel in twelve forty-one. They became friends and confidants. Your father also confided in an Army pal, who was left in no doubt that something hugely significant – and therefore hugely lucrative to those who uncovered it – was concealed at Trennor. It's possible they were more than just pals, of course. If so, it would better explain why your father trusted him with such information.'

'You can't prove any of this,' Nick objected.

'Oh, but we can,' said Demetrius. 'That's the beauty of it. Your father would not have let the knowledge perish from his branch of the family. He would have passed it on to the next generation – or the one after that. He would have told one of you.'

'It must be so,' said Emily. She looked straight at Nick, something like guilt or pity darkening her face for the first time. 'One of you knows.'

'But which one?' Demetrius smirked. 'That's the multi-million-dollar question.'

'It wasn't Andrew,' said Emily. 'He was too keen to sell to the mythical Mr Tantris. Your sisters are ruled out for the same reason. It certainly wasn't Tom. He'd never have gone along with my scheme if it had been. Your niece is too young. Besides, your father was a traditionalist. He believed in patrimony. The secret goes down the male line. Which leaves you and Basil as the only possible candidates. You were both lukewarm at best about the sale.'

'But if it was Basil,' said Demetrius, 'why would he come here in such evident innocence? Why would he take such a risk?'

'He wouldn't,' said Emily.

'Exactly.' Demetrius and Emily were feeding each other their lines now. They were rehearsing for Nick's benefit a debate they had already had several times over. 'Besides, I have held a gun to the man's head with every appearance of being willing to pull the trigger. And he has revealed nothing.'

'You bastard.' Nick stared at Demetrius, willing him to understand what he could not afford to say: that if he could ever contrive a way to strike back at him he would not hesitate.

'It's you, Nick,' Emily said quietly.

'What?'

'You're the one.'

Nick looked straight at her. 'You're wrong.'

'Won't you tell us *il segreto favoloso*, Nicholas?' Demetrius sarcastically enquired.

'I don't know it.'

'You promised your full co-operation.'

'And I'm telling you the truth.'

'Disclose the secret and Basil goes free.'

'I don't have it to disclose.'

345

'You have it.'

'Aren't you listening to me? *I don't know.*'

'We think you do.'

'For God's sake—'

'You've had your chance.' Demetrius took his mobile out of his pocket.

'*Stop!*' Nick was out of his chair, lunging towards Demetrius.

'It's all right.' Emily was suddenly between them, her hands clasping Nick's shoulders, her face close to his. 'It's OK, Nick. He isn't going to make the call.'

Nick looked past her at Demetrius, who fixed him with his gaze and ostentatiously tossed the phone into an empty chair to his right.

'No call,' said Demetrius softly.

'Sit down, Nick.' Emily's eyes pleaded with him to ignore the many reasons why he should not obey her. 'Please.'

He pushed her away and stood where he was for a moment, swaying slightly. His breathing slowed. His muscles slackened. The tension eased by a degree. He sat down.

Emily crossed to the chair where Demetrius had tossed the phone, put it on the table next to the briefcase and sat down herself. 'Listen to me very carefully, Nick. We believe you know. But we also believe you may not know you know.'

'What the hell's that supposed to mean?'

'I'm talking about your breakdown and what may have caused it. I think your father told you the secret. You were the prodigy, the budding genius – the obvious choice, really. But it was too much for you, or one of several things that were too much for you. You couldn't cope with the knowledge. You rejected it. You put it out of your mind. But the subconscious doesn't take orders. It's still there, locked away. All you have to do is turn the key.'

A key did turn in his memory at her words. He stared at her as he saw himself in his mind's eye clambering up the river-bank near Grantchester after his leap from the punt. Only he had not leapt. He had merely stepped. Into the water. Out of the world. Away, through the long grey evening, across the damp and dusky fields. 'Keep walking,' he had muttered to himself. 'Keep moving.' Part of him was still the fugitive he had become that day. And the same part of him still did not want to know what he was a fugitive from. Could it be true? Could she be right? Could he have known without knowing, all along?

'I need to hypnotize you, Nick. Don't worry. I know how it's done. With your co-operation, we can unlock the memory you've suppressed for so long. We can learn the truth.'

'They gave me hypnotherapy at the time. Nothing like what you want came out of it.'

'They didn't ask the right questions.'

'Maybe not. But they told me a few things. Like probing suppressed memories under hypnosis can be dangerous.'

'I'll be careful.'

'We all have to take the occasional risk,' Demetrius remarked.

Nick kept his eyes trained on Emily. He could not afford to get angry. Not now. Not yet. 'The patient also has to trust the hypnotist. Otherwise it doesn't work.'

'It'll work,' said Emily with quiet insistence. 'You just have to let me take control. This will help.' She released the catches on the briefcase and raised the lid, swivelling the case as she did so to block Nick's view of the contents. From inside she took a slim plastic holder, snapped it open and laid it on the table. Inside was a syringe and a small bottle of fluid. 'It's a simple tranquillizer. It'll take effect more quickly if I administer it intravenously. We need you to be relaxed – open to the experience.'

'Full co-operation was our agreement,' said Demetrius, drawing a glance from Emily that hinted at irritation. 'This is the only way you're going to see your brother again.'

'What guarantee do I have that I'll see him again if I do go through with this?'

'None. But killing Basil – and you, if you want to take your suspicions that far – would draw the police's attention to the name Paleologus. And since I plan to buy Trennor from your

347

family in order to exploit what's hidden there, I'd be foolish to make such a connection for them. So, give me what I want and you and Basil can have a happy reunion back at the Zampogna later today. Then, in due course, you and your sisters can decide how to spend the money I'll pay you for the house. There'll be more than enough for you all, I assure you.'

'What do you say, Nick?' Emily's eyes had not left him.

Nick sighed. 'Get on with it.'

'The patient has given his consent, Emily,' said Demetrius.

'Yes.' Emily took a deep breath. 'All right. Roll up your sleeve.'

As Nick did so, she loaded the syringe, then sat on the table and leaned forward to inject him. He looked away from the needle, his focus blurring slightly, aware of her perfume tingling in his nostrils.

'OK. You can relax now.'

He sat back, feeling certain that relaxation was, in the circumstances, impossible. 'What if you're wrong? What if I truly don't know?'

'I'm not wrong.'

'No-one's infallible.'

'This is the answer. I'm sure of it.'

'Even so . . .'

'Basil will be fine. I promise.'

Nick chuckled, somewhat to his own surprise. It was futile to point out how little Emily's promises were worth. The truth was that he had to hope this one was worth something. 'Those other players in the game you told me about. There aren't any, are there? You arranged with Demetrius here for your father's body to be removed from the shaft.'

'We can't have the police digging around at Trennor, Nicholas,' said Demetrius. 'There's no telling what they might find.'

'But you sent the video to the police. You put them onto it in the first place.'

'And I telephoned them after the search,' said Emily. 'I had

348

to keep Tom on-side. I had to make him believe we were serious.'

'What did you do with the body? How did you dispose of your father, Emily?'

'Cremation,' she murmured. 'It was decently done.'

'That's all right, then.'

'Try to relax. Try not to think.'

'I wish I couldn't.'

'I'm going to record what you say under hypnosis, OK? Your words might be slurred, your meaning unclear. We need to be able to go over it later.'

'Be my guest.'

Emily took a pocket recorder out of the case and set it up on the edge of the table closest to Nick. 'How are you feeling now?'

'Great.' Nick had intended to be sarcastic, but actually a strange and disquieting euphoria was beginning to creep over him. The tranquillizer was taking effect more quickly than he had anticipated. 'Where does Farnsworth come into all this, by the way? Is he working for you?'

'Forget Farnsworth.'

'You're getting ahead of yourself, Emily. It's only when the patient's in a trance that you can tell him what to forget and what to remember. It'll be all forgetting in this case, won't it?'

'I think we're ready. Could you close the curtains, Demetrius?'

Demetrius stood up and walked away towards the windows. Nick heard the curtains slide across on their tracks one by one. The light dimmed. Emily took a pen-torch out of the case, laid it on the table and switched it on, with the light shining towards her. Then she switched the tape recorder on as well.

'Look at the torch, Nick. And listen to me. The torch and me. Nothing else. Relax as much as you can, physically *and* mentally. Breathe slowly. Slow everything down. We have all the time in the world. Keep looking at the torch. Keep listening to me. Forget everything else. Let it fall away. Let it go.

As you do, start counting in your mind, backwards from one hundred.'

Nick started counting. And Emily's voice seemed to keep pace with him, slowing as he slowed, falling almost to a murmur as the numbers wound lethargically down in his head.

'Your arms are beginning to feel heavy. Your legs are beginning to feel heavy. Your eyelids are beginning to feel heavy. Relax. Give way to the drowsiness. Close your eyes. Let yourself drift away. Keep listening to me. I'm with you. Your eyes have closed now, but you're still counting. Slowly. Very slowly. Let yourself go. Let yourself go completely.'

Her voice was all he could hear. He realized, though it felt more as if he was remembering, that her voice was actually one of the things that had most attracted him to her, especially when, as now, she was almost whispering. There was a sibilance to it, a susurration, like a gentle breeze in long grass. It reminded him, though this too he had not consciously thought of before, of another voice from deep in his past. It had belonged to a guide in one of the rooms at Buckland Abbey, Sir Francis Drake's old home near Plymouth. Nick had gone there with his father during one of his summer vacations from Cambridge and been entranced, almost literally, by the woman's particular tone and timbre. He had stood listening to her telling visitors much the same thing about the history of the house several times over. He recalled wishing that he could go on listening to her for ever.

Something else had happened that day. There had been a painting on display – an idealized Victorian depiction of Drake's burial at sea off the Panamanian coast in 1596. Something about the name of the Spanish settlement the ship had been lying off, mentioned on the caption, had struck Nick as eerily reminiscent of a phrase firmly lodged in his mind at the time. Nombre de Dios. That was it. That was the place. And the phrase it echoed? His Spanish had been quite good back then. Nombre de Dios. The Name of God. It resembled the Spanish rendering of another English phrase. He had said it under his breath, his father standing beside him. If he let his mind dwell on the moment, far off though it was, he would retrieve the words. He felt sure of it. There. He nearly had them. So very nearly. All he had to do . . .

'Ten. You remember nothing except that you remember nothing. You haven't forgotten. It simply hasn't happened. Nine. You aren't so deeply asleep now. Your limbs are lighter. Eight. The world is returning to you and you to it. It's easy. It's what you want. Seven. You are beginning to sense your surroundings, to hear other things than my voice. Six. You're aware of yourself and where you are. Five. You feel comfortable. Refreshed. Happy. Four. You're beginning to wake up. Light is seeping through your eyelids. Three. You're nearly awake. You have only to open your eyes. Two. You are awake. One. You open your eyes.'

Nick blinked and looked around. He was alone. The room was empty. There was a click as the tape recorder switched itself off. He stared at the machine, wondering how long had passed since Emily had gone, leaving him to obey her recorded instructions. She had not told him this was her intention, though perhaps another deception was only to be expected. He looked at his watch, but, since he did not know when he had entered the trance, calculating precisely how long it had lasted was impossible. Half an hour or so was his best guess, though it felt to him as if only a few minutes had passed, as if she had asked him nothing, as if she had merely hypnotized him and then immediately reversed the effect. But he knew that was not true. He knew she must have asked him many questions and he must have answered them.

The briefcase had gone, along with the syringe and the pen-torch. Emily had gone too, along with Demetrius. The house was filled with silence. Nick could hear the sound of his own clothing sliding across his skin as he stood up. He felt slightly woozy, as if the tranquillizer was still affecting him. He looked down at the tape recorder. Emily had said she would record what he said under hypnosis. But they must have taken that tape with them. This was a different

351

tape, recorded beforehand. Everything had been planned meticulously. And everything, apparently, had gone according to plan.

What about Basil? The urgency of the question burst suddenly on Nick's mind. Had he given them what they wanted? Had he done enough to save his brother? He stumbled towards the door.

That was when he noticed the blood – irregularly spaced blotches of it across the pale carpet, bright red and recently shed, leading in a meandering arc from the table to the door. He stopped and stared for a moment, struggling to comprehend what he saw. Then he moved to the door and pulled it open. Light flooded into the room, momentarily dazzling him. Then, as his eyes adjusted, he saw a man lying on the floor about halfway along the hall, close to the wall. There was a pool of blood around him, wine-red against the polished white of the marble. A gun was cradled in the upturned palm of his right hand.

Nick took the few steps it needed for him to see the man's face. It was Mario. His dark shirtfront was wet with blood. There was a smear of blood on the wall above him too, as if his left hand, which was splayed across his chest, had touched the wall as he fell. His mouth was open. His eyes were staring. He looked as if surprise had been the last thing his brain had registered.

Nick looked to his left, through an open doorway, into a room kitted out as a study, with desk, bookcase, filing cabinet and computer. Something on the desk, of which he could only see one corner, caught his attention. He struggled for a few seconds to identify it. Then he realized he was looking at the fingers of a man's hand. There was a signet-ring on the little finger, a ring Nick felt sure he had seen before.

As he edged clear of the pool of blood and stepped cautiously into the room, recognition stirred. It was Demetrius's ring. Nick craned round the edge of the door and saw Demetrius Constantine Paleologus lying dead across the desk, his left hand stretched out as if he had been trying to reach something. The telephone perhaps. It was upended on the floor. But the jackplug had been pulled from the wall. The howler was silent.

Demetrius's head was turned towards Nick, his right cheek flattened against the desk. His face was slackly twisted. There was blood beneath and around him, a dark meniscus of it pooled across the pale-brown wood. As Nick stared at the scene, a drip of Demetrius's blood formed and fell from the rim of the desk, plopping softly on to the carpet to join another, smaller pool, just beyond the edge of which lay a knife, its narrow blade and much of the handle red with yet more blood.

Nick began to tremble. He licked away some sweat from his upper lip. How could so much have happened without his being aware of it? Was he still unconscious, perhaps? Was this a dream? The trance had weakened his hold on reality. And it weakened still further in the face of so much blood. Two men were dead. But where was Emily?

He moved back into the hall, averting his gaze from Mario's body, sprawled close by. There were drops of blood on the floor at intervals between him and the front door. He walked carefully between them, his nerves and senses straining. As he reached the door, his ears detected a sound from outside. A low, thrumbling note. He eased the handle down and edged the door open.

The sound was louder now and more distinct. It was a car engine, in idling mode. He could smell its exhaust fumes. He peered round the edge of the door.

A small white Fiat was parked in front of the Lancia, its bonnet pointing away from the villa, a haze of exhaust rising behind it. The driver's door was wide open. And Emily was sitting at the wheel.

Nick rushed out and down the steps. He rounded the car and met Emily's gaze as she looked up at him. Her face was grey, her hair streaked with sweat. Her left hand was on the steering wheel, her right clutched to her stomach. Blood was oozing through her fingers and dripping down from the seat to the door sill and the gravel below. The briefcase lay on the passenger seat, blood smeared round its handle. A gun was wedged between the case and the back of the seat. There was blood on that too.

'Hello, Nick,' Emily murmured. 'It's . . . strangely good to see you.'

'What happened?' He knelt beside her.

'Things didn't quite . . . work out.'

'I'll phone for an ambulance.'

'Don't.' She let go of the steering wheel and clasped his arm. 'Please don't.'

'We've got to get you to a hospital.'

'I don't think so.'

'For God's sake, Emily—'

'Listen to me. While you still can. Demetrius sent the launch to pick up Basil. He'll be free by now. I waited until I was sure of that . . . before I made my move. Demetrius never saw the double-cross coming. He thought I really had sold out to him.' She laughed, inducing a grimace of pain. 'He underestimated me. But I underestimated him too. He had a knife. And I simply wasn't quick enough. Nearly. But not quite. Clever. But not clever enough. Story of my life.' She smiled through gritted teeth. 'And my death.'

'You're not going to die.'

'Clean away or nothing: that's the deal. I'm not prepared to spend the next couple of decades in prison. Let me go, Nick.' She tried to smile again. 'You're better off without me. Everyone is.'

'Where's your phone?'

'Didn't bring one.'

Nick stretched across her to reach the case. Her rapid breaths fanned his cheek as he prised at the catches. They would not budge.

'It's combination-locked.'

He looked round at her. She shook her head. She would not tell.

'Better this way. Believe me.'

354

'I'll phone from the house.' He ducked as he moved back out of the car. Her grip on his arm tightened.

'It was some secret, Nick. Quite some secret.'

'What?'

'You told me. There was no tape. Except the one I . . . pre-recorded . . . to bring you out of the trance . . . after I'd gone. So, with Demetrius dead, I'm the only one who knows. I'm the only one who can tell you . . . what it is.' She winced. 'Don't you want to stay . . . and find out?'

'We can talk later.'

'There won't be a later.'

'Yes, there will.' He lifted her hand off his arm as gently as he could and laid it in her lap. She had no strength left. Except where it mattered. 'I'll be back in a few minutes.'

'OK.' She closed her eyes. 'Have it your way.'

He ran towards the villa, his feet crunching on the gravel. Two strides carried him to the top of the steps. He flung the door open and rushed into the hall.

And then he heard the shot.

# CHAPTER TWENTY-FOUR

The *vaporetto* was halfway across the lagoon on its run from the Lido to the Grand Canal when Nick saw the police launch heading fast in the opposite direction. He had dialled the emergency number on the first payphone he had come to after leaving the villa and repeated the same message through a jabber of questions. '*Tre morti. Villa Margherita. Via Cornaro, il Lido.*' It was all he could say and all he could risk saying, however good his Italian. Emily was dead. Nothing could alter that. And nothing could wipe from his mind's eye the sight of how she had died. '*Tre morti. Villa Margherita. Via Cornaro, il Lido.*'

Nick swallowed hard and gripped the rail tightly as he watched the bouncing shape of the launch diminish as it sped on towards the Lido. The police would make their own sense of what had happened. It would be a long way from the truth. Emily had shot Demetrius and Mario and then herself. Those were facts. But they were facts that explained nothing. Only Nick understood the cause and effect of them, dearly though he wished he did not. Tears filled his eyes as he stared after the launch. The *vaporetto* was rolling in its wake now. The discovery was not far off. Three deaths at the Villa Margherita were about to become public property.

\*      \*      \*

Emily had said Basil was safe. But Nick needed to see him to believe it. Until he did, he could not afford to let himself be overwhelmed by the images flashing up in his mind: Mario's blood on the marble tiles of the hall; Demetrius's dead, frozen scowl; and the splatter of brain and bone across the gravel, where Emily had half-fallen from the car.

Nick closed his eyes and rewound the sequence of events that had led to the moment of Emily's death. He could have acted differently at every stage. But still, he suspected, she would have engineered her own destruction. 'Have it your way,' her last words to him, sounded now like an ironical farewell. He could not have chosen to save her. She had already chosen not to be saved. He could only have chosen to stay and to listen and to learn at last the secret locked in his memory. Instead, he had turned away.

Part of him was glad of that. What did the secret matter, after all? What secret *could* matter in the face of so much death? He no longer cared what it might be, nor whether he would ever find out. Curiosity had been burned out of him. All he cared about now was Basil.

By the time the *vaporetto* reached Ca' d'Oro, more than an hour had passed since Nick's phone call to the emergency services. The police would have started their investigation by now. But it would take them several more hours at least to question the workmen at the Palazzo Falcetto and start looking for the Englishman who had visited Demetrius the day before. They might not even look at all, once they had established Emily's identity and probable motive. For the moment, Nick was in the clear, though he felt anything but.

From the Ca' d'Oro stop, he hurried north by a route he now knew quite well to the Zampogna, hoping and praying he would find Basil waiting for him there.

Carlotta greeted him from her cubby-hole with a leer that might have been intended as a smile and an incomprehensible announcement that Nick desperately wanted to believe meant Basil had turned up.

'Signor Paleologus? My brother? Is he here?'

'*C'è qualcuno qui per lei.*'

'What?'

'*Con Luigi.*'

'The last word he understood. He rushed straight out and into the bar next door.

'Signor Paleologus,' boomed Luigi. 'You have more relatives in Venice than me. Here is another.'

But the bulky figure propped at the counter was not technically any kind of relative. Nor did he seem pleased to see Nick. Satisfaction of a sort crossed Terry Mawson's face as he swivelled his neck, but of pleasure there was no sign.

'Terry?'

'Surprised to see me?'

'Yes. I mean . . . what . . .'

'We need to talk.' Terry's tone suggested that the talk he had in mind was in no sense optional.

'Have you seen Basil?' No sooner were the words out of his mouth than Nick regretted them.

'No. Should I have?' Terry stood upright and glared at Nick. 'I want to know what the bloody hell you're up to.' Luigi rolled his eyes and stated polishing a glass. 'You can start with telling me where I can find Harriet Elsmore.' The glare hardened. 'Well?'

With some difficulty, Nick persuaded Terry to put his questions on hold until they had reached the spartan privacy of Basil's old room in the Zampogna. Half of Nick's mind was focused on the need to find his brother. Most of the other half dwelt on memories of Emily – the bitter *and* the sweet. There was little left over for Terry.

'Is this dump the best you can do?' Terry asked as he recovered his breath from the short climb up Carlotta's steepling stairs.

'It's where Basil was staying.'

'Where is he now?'

'Never mind. Why are you here, Terry?'

'Why do you think?'

'I don't know.'

'Irene said you'd come here to find Basil. That creep at the Consulate gave me the same story. But I don't buy it. You're here because Harriet Elsmore's here. That's it, isn't it?'

'No. That isn't it.'

'Tell Kate the truth. That was your brilliant idea, wasn't it? That was your considered advice.'

'She has to know.'

'Yeah? Well, she does now. I told her. Like you suggested. And now she blames me for Tom's death. She won't speak to me. She won't listen to me. There's no communication. She's cut me off.'

'I'm sorry.'

'Not as sorry as I am. I figure the only way I can repair the damage I've done – yeah, I admit it, the damage *I've* done – is to get the people who pushed Tom over the top. I caught up with Farnsworth, no thanks to you. I applied some pressure. It didn't take much. Mentally, he can go the distance and then some. Physically, it's a different story.'

'You beat up an old man?'

'I threatened to. That's all it took. He told me every-thing.'

'I doubt that.' Nick was understating the case. He was in fact certain that Farnsworth had played a more central role in events than he was likely to have admitted. But Nick was also certain that he no longer cared.

'Your father and grandfather uncovered some secret at Tintagel in the Thirties. Digby Braybourne knew what it was, but Farnsworth only ever heard hints and whispers. It's to do with Trennor. Something valuable's hidden there. Farnsworth reckoned your father's death gave him the chance to find out what, so he started digging. He claims Harriet Elsmore is Braybourne's daughter, out for revenge *and* the secret. She sucked Tom into her plans and, as far as I'm concerned, she's responsible for what happened to him.'

'She probably is.'

'Right. So, where is she? You know, don't you, Nick? You know where she's hiding.'

'She isn't hiding.'

'Where is she?'

'It's too late, Terry. For her, for you, for me. For everyone.'

'I'm not leaving until I find out where she is.'

'No. I don't suppose you are.' Nick stepped across to the basin, ran some cold water on to his hands and wiped his face. 'Well, OK, then. Here's how it is. Earlier this morning, Harriet Elsmore, real name Emily Braybourne, murdered Demetrius Constantine Paleologus, the man she blamed – correctly – for her brother's death. She murdered one of his bodyguards too. Then she killed herself. With a bullet through the head. These stains on my sleeve are her blood. I saw her die. The police are cleaning up the mess even as we speak. Picking up the pieces. Searching for clues. Go looking for her now and all you'll do is implicate yourself – and me. Things are bad. But you can only make them worse by pressing on with this. Go home, Terry. Make your peace with Kate. You'll find a way. A lot sooner than you'll find anything here, except a heap of trouble. I'm sorry, I really am. But there's no revenge to be had. It's all been used up. There's nothing left.'

After Nick had said his piece, Terry's bluster was suddenly spent. He had been sustained by the belief that he could bludgeon his way to justice and a reconciliation with Kate. Now he knew better. He was out of his depth and far from home. He had been foolish to come. But he was not so foolish as to remain.

'If she's dead, that finishes it,' he mumbled, his eyes downcast. 'I'd better get back to Kate.'

'Good idea.'

'There's a flight at five fifteen.' Terry glanced at his watch. 'I could be on it.'

'I think it'd be best if you were.'

'I can't afford to get mixed up with the police.'

'Neither can I.'

'I've been through the wringer these past few days, Nick. I probably haven't been thinking straight. Maybe Kate hasn't been either. I won't get her back by staying away, will I?'

'No.'

'That settles it, then.'

'Yeah. I reckon it does.'

But Terry's hangdog departure settled nothing for Nick. He could only wait for Basil to show up at the Zampogna, telling himself all the while that he *would* show up. Soon. Or later. Or eventually.

An hour passed. Then two. Fears and fantasies began to swarm in Nick's head. Perhaps Demetrius had never meant to release Basil. Perhaps the CCTV pictures had been faked. Perhaps Basil was dead, his body lying undiscovered in a disused warehouse, like Nardini's, or somewhere else – or anywhere else.

Then the memories crowded in. The last moments of Emily Braybourne's life jostled with Nick's recollections of the night they had spent together in the hotel at Heathrow. The closeness and the distance; the longing and the losing: they became one in the end.

He had waited long enough. There was nothing else for it. He was done with evasion. All he could do for Basil was go to the police and tell them as much as he knew in the hope that it would be enough. And all he could do had to be done now, while he was still capable of it. He threw on some clean clothes and set out.

It was a half-hour ride on the *vaporetto* from Ca' d'Oro to San Zaccaria, the nearest stop to the Questura. The boat was crowded with the usual assortment of tourists, students and shoppers, though as far as Nick was concerned it might as well have been empty. He stood in the stern, alone with more fears and regrets than he could hold in his mind. He was numb now, his thoughts amounting to nothing beyond an incoherent dread. What was to follow could no more be altered by him than what had already happened. He was a prisoner as much of the future as of the past.

The *vaporetto* chugged past the Palazzo Falcetto, where *ricostruzione* was still in progress, and on round the curve of the Grand Canal, while a grey shroud stretched itself slowly across the sky and a moist breeze began to blow. The afternoon grew rapidly cold and dank.

As Nick gazed blankly ashore, the march past of mouldering *palazzi* gave way to the greenery of the Giardinetti Reali and the stately flank of the Doge's Palace. Between them, a view of the Piazzetta and the Basilica was briefly framed by the two columns of San Marco and San Teodoro. Glancing up at the winged lion atop the right-hand column, Nick suddenly remembered his attempt to warn Basil against coming to Venice in the first place. '*You'll be stepping into the lion's den.*' But Basil had brushed the warning aside. '*There are a lot of lions in Venice. Bronze or marble for the most part.*' Nick smiled, despite himself.

And then he saw, standing near the foot of the lion's column, a figure he took at first for a hallucination – a figment of his own wishful thinking. It could not be Basil, he told himself. It simply could not be. He blinked. But the figure did not vanish. He blinked again. And still it was there. And this time he knew for sure. It *was* Basil.

The next four or five minutes were an agony for Nick. The *vaporetto* slowed as it approached San Zaccaria, and slowed again. Basil was out of sight now and Nick could only hope he had not strayed far. He leapt off on to the landing-stage while the boatman was still pushing back the rail, ran down the ramp, then sprinted along the *riva* towards the bridge leading to the Piazzetta.

As he crested the hump of the bridge, the area around the columns came into view. There was no sign of Basil. His heart jolted. But he kept running.

Then, as he rounded the corner of the Doge's Palace and glanced to his right, he saw him. Basil was sitting on one of the flood platforms stowed in front of the Basilica, staring into space. He was wearing the cagoule Nick had last seen him in, though it looked even scruffier, and his walking boots, rather than the espadrilles Nick had glimpsed on Demetrius's television. He had surely lost some weight, which, combined with the white stubble round his head and chin, made him appear old and haggard, almost pitiful.

Nick slowed to a walk, daring himself to believe what he saw. The distance shrank between them. Then he called his brother's name. Basil looked round. And the smile that lit his face was anything but pitiful.

'Nick! Thank God.' Basil jumped up and threw a hug round Nick. 'I'd nearly given up waiting.' Two surprises were thus compressed into one. Basil had apparently been waiting for Nick, just as Nick had been waiting for him, though they had been doing it in different places. The other surprise was that Nick had never been hugged by his brother before in his life.

It was a fleeting innovation. Nick unwrapped himself and gazed into Basil's smiling face, slowly realizing that he too was smiling, just as broadly.

'I've been at the Zampogna. Expecting you at any moment. For about three hours.'

'They said they'd bring you here, Nick. Some time this afternoon. They said I was to stay here until you arrived and that it would be the worse for you if I didn't.'

'When did they let you go?'

'It must have been around noon. They've been holding me in a derelict house on some abandoned island out in the lagoon. I was brought here by launch and told very clearly that I'd only see you again if I obeyed their instructions to the letter. Our cousin Demetrius Constantine is not a fellow to be trifled with, as I'm sure you're aware, nor yet to be trusted. In this case, however, I had no choice but to trust him, or at any rate his messengers. I'm more delighted than I can say that my trust has been vindicated.'

'I'm not sure it has.' Nick was actually sure of the reverse. Dropping Basil off at San Marco and telling him to stay put

363

had to be part of some devious ploy. But the ploy was now irrelevant. 'One thing's certain. We don't have to worry about Demetrius any more.'

'We don't?'

'Listen, Basil. We need to get out of Venice. In a hurry.'

'I wouldn't argue with that. My visit's hardly been a happy one.'

'Have you got your passport? I couldn't find it in your room.'

'It's in my pocket.'

'Same here. So, what's stopping us?'

'I ought to settle my bill at the Zampogna.'

'Already done. All we need to do is grab our things from the room and scoot.'

'I have the impression there's something you're not telling me, Nick.'

'I'll tell you everything once we're on our way. That's a promise.' Not quite, Nick reflected. He would tell Basil *almost* everything. And leave him to guess the rest.

'You're not going to try to force me on to an aeroplane, are you?'

'Not if you can find us a train to catch p.d.q.'

'How about the overnight express to Paris? It leaves at seven forty-five. That's how I'd planned to depart, after all. Though not necessarily tonight.'

'But tonight it is. Let's go.'


They took a water taxi up to the Fondamenta dell'Abbazia, as close to the Zampogna as it could get. Installed in the cabin with the door firmly closed, Basil related how he had been set upon while walking back towards the Zampogna after his visit to San Michele on Monday morning. Heavies had shoved him, bound and gagged, into the covered hold of a builder's boat and taken him out into the lagoon, where he had been trans-ferred to a launch, blindfolded and borne away to a bare, plastered room in a crumbling old house on a deserted island. Demetrius had shown up later, demanding to be told the secret that his father and Basil's father had apparently shared. But Basil could not tell him.

'It is surprisingly easy to refuse to disclose what one genuinely does not know, Nick. And the threat of death only confirmed the equanimity with which I regard the prospect. Monasticism taught me that as well as a tolerance for physical hardship. My lost vocation stood me in remarkably good stead, in fact. I was not really frightened at all until I realized that you too were in Demetrius's clutches. Unless, of course, you're about to tell me that you never were.'

'No. I'm not about to tell you that.'

'Doubtless he had you abducted for the same reason.'

'Yes. The same.'

'Why have we been released, then? Because he came to understand that neither of us could help him? Or . . . because one of us could?'

But there Nick called a halt. He wanted to be out of Venice before he told Basil what had happened. He wanted to be sure they had made good their escape before he revealed what they were escaping from.

Basil's grasp of basic Italian got them in and out of the Zampogna within minutes, leaving Carlotta bemused but content, given that Nick had already paid her for the night's stay. Denying themselves a final visit to Luigi's bar, they headed west towards Santa Lucia. Night had fallen, but time was on their side.

It was still on their side after they had bought their tickets, so Basil proposed telephoning Irene to reassure her that they were both well. Nick could hardly object. But he could insist on being the first to speak to her.

'Old Ferry Inn.'

'Irene, this is Nick.'

'Nick? Where in God's name have you been?'

'I've found Basil. He's fine. So am I. We're at the railway station in Venice, waiting for a train out.'

'Where did you find him?'

'A monastery. He'd booked himself in for a retreat.' As cover stories went, Nick reckoned the one he and Basil had just cobbled together was far from implausible.

'*Without telling anyone*?'

'You know Basil.'

'Put him on.'

'I will in a minute. The thing is, Irene, I literally only caught up with him an hour ago. There hasn't been time . . . to go into everything.'

'Have you told him about Tom?'

'Not yet.'

'Do you want me to?'

'No. I'll do it later.'

'All right. But there's been a lot of anguish here in your absence, you know. I've had Terry on to me. He and Kate have had a pretty major row, apparently. And he seems to blame you.'

'I'm sure he does.'

'What's that supposed to mean?'

'We're all to blame, to greater or lesser degrees.'

'Are you feeling OK, Nick? You sound . . . odd.'

'I can't imagine why.'

'Have you contacted this cousin of ours – Demetrius?'

'Demetrius Andronicus Paleologus died a year ago, Irene. Dad's will meant nothing.'

'What?'

'I'll explain when we get back.'

'When's that going to be?'

'Oh . . .' Nick contemplated the wilderness of his short-term future for a moment. 'Soon enough.'

While Basil spoke to Irene, Nick cast his eye around the station concourse. Everything was calm and orderly. There was no sign of the police, nor of pursuit in any form. Their train was up on the departures board. They were going to make it. He thought suddenly of Emily and seemed to feel the

366

coldness of the mortuary slab against his skin, a coldness Emily could no longer feel. He shuddered, certain in that moment that he would never stop regretting his failure to save her from herself – and certain also that he would never want to.

The Rialto Express to Paris pulled out dead on time. They had paid for a sleeping compartment, but made no early move to occupy it. The restaurant car was busy, but there was a virtually empty seating carriage just beyond it. The train gathered speed across the night-blanked flatness of the Veneto Plain. Somewhere between Padua and Vicenza the whiskies Nick was drinking started to take effect. He began to talk.

# CHAPTER TWENTY-FIVE

Nick woke to the sway of the train and the snores of his brother on the bottom bunk. They had gone to bed in sombre spirits, for the truth in their situation was no comfort. Basil had taken the news of Tom's death as a judgement on the whole family's folly in pursuing the Tantris offer. 'We failed him,' he had said several times the previous night. And so they had, Nick supposed, although it was equally true to say that Tom had failed them. But Nick was done with apportioning blame. What should have broken him had somehow remade him. Lying there in the yawing dark, he sensed a change within himself. Where he should have felt cowed and overwhelmed by all that had happened, he felt instead released, in some strange way restored. He still flinched at the memory of how Emily had chosen to die, but he glimpsed now the essence of her act. She had controlled her destiny to the last, whereas Nick had never controlled his from the start. Or maybe, he thought, as he looked at the luminous dial of his watch and calculated that they would be in Paris in less than two hours, he had simply not started *yet*. To him beginning seemed more possible than continuing. And the time to begin had unquestionably arrived.

*     *     *

Three hours later, after a meagre breakfast and a walk beside the Seine, Nick and Basil were sitting on a bench in the square behind Notre-Dame as a Parisian morning of early spring coolness and clarity cast its spell over the city. From where they were sitting, the cathedral's flying buttresses looked like the legs of some giant stone spider, squatting above the trees. But it was a spider without a web. No thread twitched at Nick's sleeve, no reproach at his conscience. He had reached a decision. And he knew, with wholly unfamiliar certainty, that it was the right decision.

'I'm not coming back with you, Basil.'

'There's a surprise,' said Basil, flicking a croissant crumb from his knee towards the nearest sparrow.

'You don't sound surprised.'

'That's because I knew you weren't.'

'How?'

'The explanation can wait. Though not as long as the one you will eventually feel obliged to proffer to Irene and Anna. There's no reason, as far as I can see, why they should hear about this.' Basil held up a folded copy of *Corriere della Sera*, which he had bought at the Gare de Lyon. The lower front-page headline *Lido di Venezia: Strage Sanguinosa in una Villa di Lusso* – helpfully if loosely translated by Basil as *Murder Most Foul at Lido Villa* – was printed above an article that made absolutely no mention of an English cousin of the deceased Demetrius Paleologus being sought by the police, although it did imply a connection between Demetrius's murder and the supposedly accidental death nine months before of an Englishman by the name of Jonathan Braybourne. 'I hardly think the *Western Morning News* is likely to devote even the briefest of paragraphs to such an event. The *Birmingham Post* is quite another matter. But fortunately our sisters don't live in Birmingham. For the rest, what is there to say? You found me and all is well. Or, if not well, then not as bad as it might be.'

'I need to go away. To think. To put my life back together.'

'I quite understand. Although, if you'll take my advice,

369

you'll not think too much. Thinking is what makes people unhappy. I never do more than the bare minimum myself.'

'What's the minimum in this case?'

'The modest amount necessary to reveal that Irene and Anna cannot sell Trennor without our consent. We risk nothing by delaying our return.'

'*We*?'

'I'm not going back either. Which is how I could be so certain you weren't going back with me.' Basil smiled. 'I for one would welcome a travelling companion.'

'So would I.' Nick returned his brother's smile, appreciating as he did so just how welcome company would be on the road to wherever he was going.

'Do you remember our first visit to Paris, Nick?'

'Of course.'

In September 1976, a few weeks before going up to Cambridge, Nick had accompanied Basil on a long weekend trip to the French capital. He had gone home alone, however. At the top of the Eiffel Tower on their last afternoon, Basil had announced that he was proceeding to Greece in quest of what being a Paleologus ultimately meant. He had seen Nick off later at the Gare St-Lazare on the train to Cherbourg, without having managed in the interim to give his brother the meagrest of insights into the workings of his mind.

'I'm not likely to have forgotten.'

'Indeed not. My behaviour was inexcusable. I couldn't face Dad. That's the simple truth of it. I knew he would think I was running away from him. As, in a sense, I was. I knew he would regard my vocation as no more than a triumph of self-delusion. Which, in another sense, it also was. What I overlooked was that he would think me a wretch as well as a coward for sending my sixteen-year-old brother home alone.'

'I quite enjoyed the journey, actually.'

'Without your crackpot brother to embarrass you at every turn, you mean?'

Nick chuckled. 'Something like that.'

Basil pursed his lips. 'We must take care lest honesty become too fixed a habit.'

'It'd be good to leave Paris with you this time, Basil. Honestly.'

'Do you remember the Texan we shared that room with near the Sorbonne?'

'The Vietnam veteran from Laredo with the Edith Piaf fixation? You bet I remember. Gary . . . something. Son of a rancher.'

'Gary Longfellow.'

'That's it.'

'I expect *he's* the rancher now.'

'Probably.'

'The Lazy K, the place was called.'

'That's right.'

'He invited us over.'

'So he did.'

' "It'd be great if you guys swung by the spread one day," ' Basil drawled.

'You've got him to a tee.'

'It's a direct quote.'

'Is it?'

'So, why don't we take him up on it?'

'What?'

'Why don't we swing by Laredo?' Basil grinned. 'Via New Orleans, perhaps. Or Las Vegas.'

'You're joking.'

'No.'

'You must be.'

'I don't see why.'

'For one thing, we'd have to fly.'

'Not necessarily. I believe you can hitch passage on a container ship if you know how to go about it. Antwerp would be the place to try. Or Marseilles.'

'Now you *are* joking.'

'About the container ship, yes. But not about the trip. Demetrius succeeded in reminding me that I am perversely unafraid of death. So, flying really should be no problem. I may experience the odd panic attack while we're airborne, but the worst that can happen is that I embarrass my kid brother all over again.'

'I'm old enough to cope with a little embarrassment.'

'It could be a lot.'

'Even a lot.'

'You're game, then?'

'Yeah.' Nick nodded. 'I am.'

'Excellent.'

'When shall we go?'

'When can you be ready?'

'I *am* ready. But we'd have to organize tickets. And it'll be a morning flight. So . . .' Nick suddenly realized how much he was relishing the prospect. 'Tomorrow?'

'Tomorrow it is.'

'We'd better find a travel agent.'

Basil raised a thoughtful finger. 'Actually, there's something I need to show you first. And to tell you. It's not far. And it won't take long.'

'Can't it wait?'

'No.' Basil gazed up at the flying buttresses. 'Now is the time.'

The chapel of Sainte-Chapelle, in the Palais de Justice, near the other end of the Île de la Cité, was their far from distant destination. Its soaring spire and slender buttresses lacked the massive Gothic presence of Notre-Dame. The building was a contrasting study in delicacy and elegance, its high stained-glass windows filling the nave with what could easily be taken for heavenly light.

But, as Basil seemed anxious to point out, the chapel was only eighty years younger than Notre-Dame. 'It was built for Louis the Ninth in the twelve forties to house the holy relics he'd brought from the Latin Emperor of Constantinople,' he whispered as they moved slowly, necks craning, from window to window. 'The Crown of Thorns, plus fragments of the True

372

Cross and the skull of John the Baptist. He'd paid several times more for them than it cost to build this. A pious dupe, I fear. What would he not have paid, I wonder, for the artefact entrusted to Richard of Cornwall? He bought the relics in the same year as the conference at Limassol, twelve forty-one. It occurs to me that Richard may have met Andronicus Paleologus specifically in order to reassure the Byzantine Emperor that the artefact wasn't destined for a rich monarch's collection, like the relics the Latin Emperor was so enthusiastically selling off to the highest bidder. A nice and generous touch on Richard's part, especially if, unlike Louis's acquisitions, it was the genuine article. Which prompts the question: what *was* the article?'

'I'm not holding out on you, Basil. I don't know.'

'Ah, but you *did* know. That day at Buckland Abbey you told me about last night. You knew then.'

'Yes. I think I did.'

'We didn't come here in September seventy-six, did we?'

'No.'

'Had we done so, the comparison with Louis the Ninth and his expensive relics – transferred to Notre-Dame long since, by the way – might have lodged in your mind rather than the echo of that Spanish placename, Nombre de Dios.'

'What are you getting at, Basil?'

'The truth, Nick. I think I know the other phrase you can't call to mind.'

Nick stopped and stared at his brother. 'You do?'

'Yes. In fact, I'm sure of it.'

'What is it?'

'*Número de Dias*.' Basil's voice dropped still further. 'The Number of Days.'

Nick went on staring. He could not speak. For the moment, he could not even move. Basil was right. *Número de Dias* was the phrase.

'Dad took me to Buckland Abbey one day not long after I came back from Greece. I'd forgotten the visit until you mentioned your own trip there with him. He spent a long time studying that picture of Drake's burial at sea up in the gallery they have there. Then he used the same phrase it had put you in mind of. *Número de Dias*. He must have heard you say it all those years before. "*Número de Dias*." He was remembering what you no longer could. He turned to me and said, "Do you know the legend of the Number of Days, Basil?" As it happened, I did, prompting him to make some crack about my years as a monk not being entirely wasted. Then he said, "When I'm dead and gone, tell Nick the legend. Bring him here – right here – and tell him. Will you do that?" I said I would readily enough, but I'm afraid it was rather a vague undertaking on my part. At the time, I was more than a little *distrait*. I dare say it struck me as a whimsical request which I needn't treat seriously. The point of it escaped me, as it was bound to. Only now do I understand. There was one more thing he said, you see, as he took a last glance at the picture before we left the gallery. I barely caught the words. "He'll remember." That's what he said. "He'll remember." He meant you, of course. And he may well have been right. I'd have called our visit – and my promise – to mind eventually. I'm certain of that. So, sooner or later, you and I would have gone to Buckland Abbey together and looked at the picture. And then, at long last . . .'

'I'd have remembered.' Nick let his unfocused gaze drift across the river. They had left Sainte-Chapelle and walked to the Square du Vert-Galant, the tree-bowered western prow of the Île de la Cité. They were standing at the very point of the prow, apparently studying the mansarded roofscape of the Louvre on the northern bank. But though they were looking in that direction, Nick for one was conscious of very little beyond his brother's words. A *bateau-mouche* moved sedately past them, a child waving to them from within. They did not wave back. 'We're a long way from Buckland Abbey. You'll have to remember for me. What is the legend of the Number of Days?'

'I first heard about it from an old monk on his deathbed. It revolves around the Lord's brother, James, an ambivalent figure in the history of the Church, since to the Catholics the existence of siblings of Christ is literally inconceivable, by reason of Mary's perpetual virginity. No dispassionate reading of the Gospels can leave one in any real doubt, however, about James's blood relationship with Christ. They were brothers. Or half-brothers, strictly speaking. James was plainly a prominent disciple, if not an apostle. He succeeded Peter as head of the Church in Jerusalem. Paul deferred to him in matters of doctrine. Some scholars take Paul's account in his first letter to the Corinthians of Christ's appearances after the Crucifixion to imply that he appeared to James before any of the apostles. James believed Christianity and Judaism could be reconciled. He maintained close links with the Judaist community in general and the Pharisees in particular. He enjoyed what for a Christian was a unique level of access to the Temple. He went on working for a *rapprochement* between the two faiths until his death in the year sixty-two, when he was done down by intrigue in the Temple hierarchy, slain, so the story goes, by a blow to the head with a club. Ritualistic and strangely familiar, wouldn't you say?'

'Yes, I would.' Nick looked round at Basil. 'Tell me the legend.'

'Very well. You shall have it as it was given to me by old Brother Philemon. During the forty days between the Resurrection and the Ascension, the risen Christ was several times asked by the apostles when he would return in glory; when the Kingdom of God would be inaugurated on Earth. He replied only that it was not for men to know. But some believe he relented in the case of his blood brother. Some believe he told James how many years would elapse before he came again.'

'The Number of Days.'

'Exactly so.'

'You can't mean . . .'

'I think I do mean that, yes. If James made a record of the

divine intelligence entrusted to him and arranged with his Pharisee friends to have it secreted in some vault beneath the Temple prior to his death, it may have lain there, undiscovered, until the Knights Templar began their excavations in the twelfth century. What they found would have been, of course, no harmless relic, but the heresy of a revelation that could not be countenanced in Rome. We should envisage an inscribed tablet, I think. Papyrus would not have been durable enough. Besides, no-one in their senses would have sent a papyrus text to Cornwall. Far too damp. No, a stone tablet it has to be. The inscription would be in Greek, of course, rendering it unintelligible to the average medieval man. James's command of Greek was excellent, to judge by his New Testament epistle, which even Rome finds it hard to attribute to anyone else.

'The Greek numbering system used letters: alpha for one, beta for two, gamma for three and so on up to ten, except that the extinct letter digamma stood for six; then kappa for twenty, lamda for thirty and so on up to a hundred, except that another extinct letter, koppa, stood for ninety; then sigma for two hundred, tau for three hundred and so on up to a thousand, except that yet another extinct letter, sampi, stood for nine hundred. A thousand was alpha with an accent, as I recall, and started the sequence over again. The point to bear in mind is that a number – a date – would look like just another word to the uninitiated. And a Greek word depicted in a stained-glass window in medieval Cornwall would doubtless have eluded the subtlest of interpreters.'

'I remember the phrase – the Number of Days,' Nick said dreamily. 'But not the rest. Not any of it.'

'I dare say you will, in time.'

'And I don't believe it anyway. There is no Day of Judgement. No set date. No pre-ordained apocalypse.'

'For our purposes, Nick, the ultimate reality of Doomsday is neither here nor there. The discovery of an inscribed tablet beneath the Temple of Jerusalem seeming to confirm the legend of James's unique foreknowledge of the Second

Coming was a remarkable, astonishing, awe-inspiring event. It makes not a jot of difference what we think about it. The people who found it believed it. As many still would. Unless the time recorded has already passed, of course. That would be a crack of doom of an entirely different order.'

'You think the Doom Window of St Neot held the secret?'

'Yes. I do.'

'And you think the glass from the window – with the secret in it – is walled up at Trennor?'

'Yes. Don't you?'

Nick thought for several long moments before replying. But thinking changed nothing. In the end, he sighed and gave a nod of resignation. 'Yes. Of course I do.'

Nick felt confounded by his own certainty. Whether he believed the legend or not was irrelevant. Others *had* believed it – and acted accordingly. In that sense, the legend was bound to be true. The secret was that there was a double secret: one of finding; one of knowing. What the walls of Trennor held they could be made to give up. Nick and Basil could will it to be so. But they could also will it not to be so. The choice rested with them. And it was really no choice at all. Nick understood that with the sharp and sparkling clarity of finely cut glass. The secret was a secret they could never allow to be known.

A few minutes later, the brothers Paleologus could be seen crossing the Pont Neuf linking the Île de la Cité with the right bank of the Seine. They were walking fast and confidently, almost jauntily. They were walking, in fact, like two men who knew where they were going.

'ÁXMƆ

*It was a chill winter morning, chiller inside St Neot Church than out, with no sun to gild the low and meagre light trickling through the windows of the south aisle. Richard Bawden stamped his feet and blew on his hands, his breath clouding in the air. His wife had sought to dissuade him from coming and there had been moments since his arrival when he had regretted not heeding her. But he knew the cold could make a fleeting coward of any man. When he opened the tower door and gazed up at the west window, he was strengthened at once in his resolve. This was God's work and his conscience would not permit him to turn aside from it.*

*He had always found it hard to believe how very old the window was. The colours in the glass were bright as new, even without the sunlight shining through them. It appeared to his eye no older than the Noah and Creation Windows at the other end of the church, which had been there for nigh on a hundred and fifty years. But the Doom Window dated from much further back, according to local lore, which also ascribed to it an importance beyond estimation.*

*The window was made up of twelve panes, nine main lights arranged in three panels with three tracery lights above. The images within – of flood and fire, of the dead rising from their coffins and sinners being ravaged by demons, of the ladder leading from hell to heaven and the scales of judgement in which every soul was to be weighed – had been familiar to Bawden since childhood. Often he had stared at them in awe and wonder and sometimes in doubt. But the war had banished his doubt for ever. Those who would destroy such a work of art and faith could not be in the right. And its destruction could not be permitted. It had to be made safe, without further delay.*

*They had perhaps waited too long already. But the vicar, who had kept of late to his other living at St Austell, had only recently and reluctantly given his consent. As matters now stood, there was no time to be lost. Fairfax was already reported to have taken Launceston and the havoc his troops might wreak did not bear contemplation.*

*Still Bawden was aware that what they meant to do amounted to sacrilege, justified only by the need to prevent a much greater sacrilege. He closed his eyes and uttered a prayer, begging God's pardon for the offence. Soon, very soon, the sexton would arrive and they would set about dismantling the window, prising back the leads and lifting out the panes, wrapping them in several layers of sackcloth and carrying them to the cart, where they would be placed in a crate and swathed in straw for their journey to Landulph. Bawden's prayer became a plea for God's blessing as well as his pardon. 'Let the day go well, Lord,' he murmured.*

*Opening his eyes, he looked from one light to another, taking his private farewell of them in their appointed places. It was idle to suppose that he would live to see their restoration. He could hope, of course, but his hope was more fragile than the glass itself. He pondered then the abiding mystery of the window: the green-garlanded gold letters at the base of each light. What did they mean? What was their message? Some and by implication all of the letters were Greek, a language of which he knew no more than any other parishioner. It was generally believed that they stood as symbols for some matter of deep significancy, but, if so, the symbols were too abstruse for men of this century and Bawden's limited learning to comprehend. He had heard the vicar express the opinion that the letters and pictures together formed what he called a rebus – a visual riddle, which he confessed to find unfathomable. Something of the kind had surely to be the case, though the truth of it might never be known. Certain it was, however, that the mystery could only be solved if the glass was preserved. And Bawden was determined to do everything in his power to ensure that it was.*

*The rattle of the latch on the south door drew his thoughts back to the task at hand. He retreated into the nave as the door creaked open just far enough for the sexton to make a sidelong entrance. Their eyes met. 'Metten daa tha whye.' The sexton, even if he was old enough to have served in the militia at the time of the Spanish Armada, as he claimed, was not old enough to recall a still more*

remote time when Cornish had been the common language
of discourse in the parish. His use of it now was in part an
acknowledgement of the secret nature of their meeting. He
was carrying in his right hand a heavy leather bag, in which
he transported his tools. Pushing the door shut behind him, he
advanced into the church.

'Good morrow, Master Davey,' said Bawden.

Davey moved past him into the tower, lowered the bag to the
floor and glanced up at the Doom Window, then bowed his head.
'Agon Taze nye, eze en Neve,' he murmured. 'Benegas bo tha
Hanow.' Bawden recognized the words as the Cornish rendering
of the Lord's Prayer. He too bowed his head as Davey continued.

When he had finished Davey opened a cupboard next to the
gathered bell-ropes, lifted out a ladder and propped it against the
wall beneath the window. Then he turned to face Bawden and
stared at him in solemn scrutiny.

John Davey was a difficult man to know. He was not of
Bawden's generation, nor yet his cast of mind. He so seldom
disclosed his opinions that it was tempting to believe he had none.
Bawden knew the untruth of that, however. Since the matter of the
glass had grown so pressing, he had come to understand
the sexton. Though scarcely companionable, Davey was utterly
reliable. What he believed, he could not be shifted from. What he
undertook to do, he always did. Bawden knew he could have no
firmer ally in the business of the day. And he reflected that he
could have no more appropriate ally, either, in the putting beyond
danger of the Doom Window than a grave-digger.

'Have you heard from Mandrell?' Davey asked, reverting to
English.

'I have,' Bawden replied. 'He will ride out to meet us on the
road.'

'You trust him?'

'I would trust him with my life.'

'Reckon you're a-doing that.'

'I know.'

'And mine along of yours.'

'I know that also.'

'But there's nothing else for it.'

'Truly there is not.'

'Shall us begin, then?'

'Yes.' Bawden looked up at the window. 'Let us begin.'

# AUTHOR'S NOTE

This novel has its origins in real places and their equally real if enigmatic histories. Why Richard, Earl of Cornwall, decided in 1233 to build a castle of no conceivable military value on the headland at Tintagel remains a matter of speculation. Similarly, the absence of a Doom Window from the remarkably well-preserved medieval glazing scheme at St Neot Church has never been satisfactorily explained. Theodore Paleologus was certainly buried at Landulph Church in 1636, but his descent from the last Emperor of Byzantium, as proclaimed on his memorial plaque, has not been conclusively proved. Genealogists have traced his own descendants as far as a great-granddaughter, Godscall Paleologus, born in Stepney in 1693 . . . but as yet no further.